"It has been a constant pleasure to read these stories. They are beautifully told in exquisite prose, and they convey contagiously the universe of a little girl with many talents—and many obligations. Step by step, one gets the impression of a childhood rich in loving family and creative interests; of a tight female world of absent men and controlling women in school and at home; of family loss and insecurity; and consequently of perfectionist claims transferred to or adopted subconsciously by Meg, the narrator. It is told with the finest understatement, but in the middle of relative idyll, the reader is also getting a double impression of both safety and requirements, here and there verging on quiet claustrophobia. I'm most impressed by the subdued passion of mingled feelings."

— **Hans Hertel,**
Reviewer, *Politiken*
author of many works including *PH: A Biography*
Editor-in-Chief of *A History of World Literature*

BUILDING MOUNT EVEREST

A NOVEL

ZOE MASON KING

Bridgewater Press LLC
San Francisco, California

Copyright © 2015 Bridgewater Press LLC

All rights reserved. No part of this publication may be reproduced, distributed or transmitted in any form or by any means, including photocopying, recording, or other electronic or mechanical methods, without the prior written permission of the publisher, except in the case of brief quotations embodied in critical reviews and certain other noncommercial uses permitted by copyright law. For permission requests, write to the publisher at info@bridgewaterpress.com.

Bridgewater Press LLC
San Francisco, California
www.bridgewaterpress.com

Publisher's Note: This is a work of fiction. Names, characters, places, and incidents are a product of the author's imagination. Locales and public names are sometimes used for atmospheric purposes. Any resemblance to actual people, living or dead, or to businesses, companies, events, institutions, or locales is completely coincidental.

Special discounts are available on quantity purchases. For details, contact the publisher at info@bridgewaterpress.com.

Building Mount Everest/ Zoe Mason King -- 1st Ed.
ISBN-13: 978-0-9961427-1-7

For W
finest companion
finest critic

CONTENTS

My Grandmother's Head 9
The Haircut 15
The Mosaic 23
Glasses 47
Nasturtiums 56
Staying Overnight 62
The New House 68
The Jumper 87
Queenie 93
The Egg Shell 99
Red Corduroy 104
Morning Glory 109
Phar Lap's Heart 115
Del 126
Masefield 134
The Revival Meeting 154
Sleepy Lagoon 159
Nan's Photographs 175
The Letter 184
The Car Ride 198
The Story 204
The Moth 212
The Order of Things 220
Communion 233
Sleepwalker 239

The Boat	247
Black and White	256
Building Mount Everest	269
Chang	280
Flowers	287
The Fever	301
Knitting	308
The Ribbons	319
His Hands	325
Lavender	332
Driving Into Town	343
Fat Brides	353
Mamma, Mahler, and Mann	363
Treble Clef	387
The Doll	393
Piano Lessons	401
The Suit	409
Otter	429

ONE

MY GRANDMOTHER'S HEAD

I don't think I would have noticed something was really wrong with Nan if I hadn't been so nearsighted.

She was seated in one of the mushroom-colored armchairs in her living room. I was standing in front of her.

We had been living with Nan for a year. My mother said it was because my father was starting a new project. My father said it was because my grandfather had died and Nan needed help. My grandfather's will was tied up because of something called probate and because he had left money to his Russian family if they could be found, so the Red Cross was searching for them, all untraceable since the war.

I stood in front of Nan while she pinned me into the wedding dress she was making me for the first graders' fancy dress ball. I had already walked the mile home from school and had had the day's deleterious effects washed off me in the olive-green bathtub with its olive-green gargoyle. "We need to wash school off you," my mother had said when I waxed loud and obstreperous on my arrival home.

I was not impressed with school. After the first few days,

I had decided I would not go back and, if taken, I would not stay. The novelty had worn off.

The day I made this decision, I walked home early. My mother walked me back. I walked home again. Perhaps she hadn't understood. When she saw me, she called my father. The phone sat on an elegant, miniature rosewood table carved by someone named Mehler for my grandparents when they were first married. My mother handed me the heavy black receiver linked to the phone by a braided silk umbilical cord.

"Why won't you go to school, Meggie?" my father asked. I held the phone with both hands and stared at the table whose top was level with my eyes. Long streaks of light from the stained-glass bird in the window colored the wood.

"I don't want to."

"You know you have to, don't you?"

"Yes."

"And you know what has to happen if you don't go."

"Yes."

"What has to happen, Meggles?"

"You'll have to come home."

"And what will I have to do if I come home?"

"You'll have to spank me."

"Now will you go to school?"

"No."

When he came home, he had to chase me around the fishpond and through the date palms before he caught me. He carried me up the stairs, put me over his knee, spanked me dutifully, and then asked, "Now will you go to school?"

"Yes."

"Then why didn't you go without my having to come all the

way home from work and spank you?"

"I thought it might help."

It had been several weeks since the spanking. I had gone to school each day.

I squirmed in the white netting as Nan pinned it. She was skilled. Her mother had died early leaving a group of upstanding, Methodist, partly grown children to be raised by the eldest daughter while the father worked. She later moved to the city, where she lived with her now married older sister and, loving fabric and clothing, worked with a dress designer. She met her future husband at a picnic and they moved north. An educated, pragmatic, well-traveled Russian with a gift for languages, my grandfather adapted quickly to his new, narrow colonial culture and did well fast. After that, Nan sewed for pleasure or when she couldn't travel south to buy good clothes or have her dressmaker design and sew styles she wanted.

I looked down at my grandmother's head as she worked. I didn't know it then, but I saw most of the world as a blur. I could only see clearly things that were a few inches from my eyes—but those things I could see very, very clearly. So I saw that, under her hair, her head was made of cloth.

I stopped talking. I felt sick. My grandmother was not right.

I knew I should not say anything about this. It was possibly something that only I knew. Maybe even my grandmother didn't know something was wrong with her head. I felt horror in my five-year-old torso.

"You can take it off now," she said. I wriggled out of the netting, avoiding the expertly placed pins.

That night, as my mother was putting me to bed on the verandah in the slightly cooler evening air, I said, "Nan's head."

I was sitting on my small, white chair, which allowed my feet to touch the painted wooden floor on the enclosed, second floor verandah. My teeth were clean, pajamas fresh, and long hair brushed. My mother was untying the mosquito net over my bed so I couldn't see her face.

"What about it, darling?" she said in a tone I'd only heard her use around my father.

"It's cloth!" I said.

My mother glanced around to see if my father or grandmother were in earshot, and then shushed me.

"Her head's not cloth, sweetheart." She sighed and sat down on the edge of the bed, taking care not to crease the sheet or pull on the mosquito net. "It's a secret. She wears a wig. A wig is pretend hair. To be accurate, it's not, in fact, pretend hair. It's real hair tied to cloth. Nan's hair got thin years ago, so she wears a wig. Don't let on that you know. It's Nan's secret. I'm sure Daddy must realize but better not to mention it. Nan likes to think no one knows."

As I drifted off, I could hear Nan sewing on the Singer machine in her sewing room in the back of the house. Whirr. Snip. Whirr. Whirr. Snip. I went to sleep staring at the part of the mosquito net close to the pillow. The mosquito net looked just like the wedding dress Nan was making me.

I awoke to my father's low, strong voice in the kitchen. My mother was always telling him he didn't know how to whisper. "She spoils her," I heard my father say. "And not once does she ever greet me or let Meg get up and hug me when I get home from the office. She just holds her tightly on her lap and keeps on reading to her."

"It doesn't mean something bad, Michael. She just wants to

finish whatever story they're on before dinner."

"Nan can do no wrong in your eyes. You can't—won't—see what's in front of you: it does 'mean something.' She wants Meg for herself, the same way she still wants to keep you tied to her apron strings. She has to accept sometime that I'm Meg's father and warrant being treated as such!"

A few days later, my father got sick. He went to stay with his parents. He said that over there he could sleep in a room by himself so not make anyone else sick. He took a large, well-used leather suitcase with him. It had a sticker on it from a ship on which my parents had taken their second honeymoon. I didn't know what a honeymoon was but I knew a second one must be good because everyone had said "Isn't that lovely" or "They missed the real one when his leave was cut short." Everyone except my grandparents. I remember sitting on Aunt Sarah's shoulder and her telling me to wave at a big blur she said was the ship. When my parents returned, their suitcases had stickers on them.

The first week he was gone, my father was too sick to talk on the phone. After that, I talked to him every evening just before Nan served dinner. My mother would sit me at the telephone table and dial my grandparents' number. When the phone would start to ring, she would hand the receiver to me. My father didn't sound sick then, but he must have been because he said that he couldn't come home right now and that he missed me.

Once, at the end of our talk, my father asked to talk to my mother. She must not have heard my calling her—although she usually did, even if she was downstairs. Nan said to tell my father that my mother was in the bath. She wasn't in the bath; I could see there was no light in the bathroom. So I told him she must be downstairs because that's where she would have been if she weren't in the bath.

After lots of days of being sick, my father reappeared. He and my mother stood in the garden near the fishpond where they had told me he had asked her to marry him. They spoke with arms crossed.

After he left, Nan let me powder my face in her bedroom and try on the feathered hats designed for her by a milliner down south.

One day, as Nan was putting a hat away on the left-hand side of the big bottom drawer of her wardrobe, I spotted bodies in the right-hand side of the drawer. In the low afternoon light, I could see their heads lying crumpled together. Nan didn't know I was right behind her. She was already a little deaf. But from my five-year-old vantage point behind her navy silk skirt and pretty, heavily stockinged legs, I could see them.

Just then, the phone rang. Nan left to answer it. I walked closer to the wardrobe, pulled the dark, polished drawer further open with both hands, and peered in. The heads came into focus: wig after wig, each in its own net holder.

When I heard Nan call my mother saying that my father was on the phone, I pushed the drawer with my knees and arms back to just where Nan had left it. When she reappeared in the room, I was sitting on the tapestry stool in front of her dressing table, holding her silver-backed mirror up to my face.

That night, my father returned with his leather suitcase with the stickers and I went to the fancy dress ball as a bride.

TWO

THE HAIRCUT

I have never liked that O. Henry story about the girl and her hair and the boy and the comb.

My hair has always been how I best know myself.

The first time I remember feeling scissors on the nape of my neck, I was in Nan's kitchen. The kitchen was large and on the second storey. The windows, with their cream-colored frames, overlooked the neighbor's frangipani trees and their large dog. If I climbed onto the chair in front of the windows, I could watch the dog run back and forth.

The wall opposite the windows had built-in cupboards, which, looking back, must have been unusual when they were built for my grandparents in the 1930s. A servery opened between the kitchen and dining room during formal meals. It could be closed off with painted wooden doors on the kitchen side and with stained glass doors on the dining-room side.

The servery fascinated me. Anything could be hidden in there. I was too short to open its doors unless my father lifted me up. Knowing what fun it was for me, he would hold me up with his broad, steady hands and press my back against his chest while I opened and closed the doors again and again.

In the middle of the kitchen was a large wooden table where we often ate our meals. It was usually covered with an ironed tablecloth. The table had been there since my grandparents and mother had moved in. I would play hide and seek underneath it while I listened to "The Children's Hour" on the radio. Sometimes I would have to stand on the table while Nan pinned the hem of a dress she was making for me.

On this particular day, no one was in the kitchen except my father and me. It was after Sunday lunch. I was sitting in one of the four kitchen chairs. My father was standing behind me. I remember his voice but not his face.

Having turned five, I had decided that I wanted to choose how my thick, wavy, light-brown, waist-length hair was fixed. I still liked it long but my preferences no longer included wearing a ponytail. I already had a reputation for persistence and I had begun running away when my mother would start to brush my hair up in a way I knew meant she was going to put my hair into a ponytail. I thought this was funny because I always won. My mother didn't think it was funny; she couldn't get under the bed where I would hide and giggle.

That day, the house felt oddly silent. My father had said that my mother and grandmother were in the living room but I could not hear them. I thought they might be on the other side of the servery listening or perhaps they were covering their ears in Nan's sewing room.

"Are you going to wear a ponytail when Mamma is in a hurry and has to give you a ponytail, Meg?"

"No."

I had already won battles over liver, spinach, and beans. My body ejected them. All food I did not like I called "beans," a generalization I was just becoming old enough to laugh at, along with my parents and Nan. Other foods were coaxed down my throat only by prolonged times at the table or by guilt. I could sit for a long time. Guilt worked faster.

"Have one spoonful darling—for me," my mother would say. "Just for me.... Goooood. Now, how about one for Daddy? ... And how about one for Nan? ... Darling, do you love Nan enough to have just one spoonful for her? Now Gran? Granddad?"

I would reach my limit when my mother started in on extended family.

My hair was different. I was not being made to feel guilty and I was not being asked to do this for anyone else. I just was being given a choice.

My father had gathered up my hair with the broad fingers of his left hand so that my hair formed a ponytail in his left hand. In his right hand, he rested the length of the scissors carefully along my neck.

"If you won't let me put it in a ponytail, I'll have to cut it off because Mamma won't be able to take care of it all the time. So take your pick, Meg: do you want a ponytail or do you want me to cut it off? It's your decision."

I remember a long silence. Even the tall palms, which normally rustled outside the kitchen window, were quiet. The scissors felt cold on my neck.

If I decided to let him cut my hair, I couldn't have it the way I wanted. If I decided to let him put it in a ponytail, I couldn't have it the way I wanted. So I decided I might as well not have it done the way I wanted and keep it long.

For a calm moment that was new to me, I hated my father.

"Yes."

"Yes what?"

"Yes, Daddy."

"'Yes, Daddy' what?"

"Yes, Daddy, I'll have it."

"Have what?"

"The ponytail."

"You mean you would like to have a ponytail. Is that what you mean?"

"Yes, Daddy."

"Then tell me properly, Meggie, and don't forget to say please. What you would like?"

"I would like to have a ponytail, please, Daddy."

"Good girl, Meg."

The coldness of the scissors left my neck and my father stopped holding my hair. I could feel it flow over my elbows again.

"Now tell me how sorry you are for forcing me go to these lengths and for upsetting Mamma."

"I'm sorry."

" 'Sorry' what?"

"Daddy."

He gave me a hug and called out to my mother.

She must have been just on the other side of the servery because she came too quickly to have been in the living room.

I apologized to her. She hugged me and then tied my hair back in a loose ponytail with just an old ribbon with shredded ends instead of using one of the rubber bands with the plastic clip. I hated them even though my mother was always careful not to pull my hair when she used them.

A minute later, Nan came in. She walked straight to the stove alcove. She didn't look at any of us as she struck a match and lit the blue flame under the old kettle. I remember thinking that it was early for her to have an afternoon cup of tea.

For the rest of that year, my mother would wash my hair and dry it in the sun by having me sit on the front steps—just where, she said, she had dried her hair when she was growing up. She once told me she didn't like the rag curls that Nan used to tie when she was little (I couldn't imagine my mother little) but she made me promise never to tell Nan in case it hurt her feelings.

In my second year of school, my mother said that I was looking thin and tired and that she felt as if my long hair was dragging me down. So she made up a story about Sweet Pea. Sweet Pea was a fairy with long, heavy hair that made her fly more slowly than other fairies. Her hair was so heavy that she could not keep up with the others. She fell behind and ended up flopping down in the garden—so tired, so tired—watching the other fairies fly away. A grasshopper came along and asked her what was wrong. When she explained her dilemma to him, he offered to cut off her hair with his legs. She agreed. He did an awful job but she could fly again.

In the end, I didn't object when my mother took me to her hairdresser. I had grown bored with my long hair. The hairdresser cut off my two plaits and gave them to my mother who wrapped them in tissue paper and put them in a box when we got home.

The only dolls that interested me were ones with long hair—hair I could brush with my Mason Pearson brush. The brush, which Nan had given me, was just like my mother's.

When I was twelve, I decided that hairdressing would be a good profession for me. My parents had higher aspirations—as did my hairdresser, I discovered. One day, on my regular visit to the hairdresser, I asked her to cut my hair off to just above my collar. The girls' school I attended didn't allow hair to fall below the collar without its being tied back on either one or two low ponytails. I still didn't like ponytails. My hairdresser said no one with hair like mine should chop it off and she refused to cut it. She also said I couldn't be a hairdresser because I was going to a private school and would go to university. She handed my coins back. I was so surprised that for once I was short of words and did not argue.

Ten years later, as I was traveling through Europe, I dropped my Mason Pearson hairbrush, which Nan had given me as a farewell present, in a communal shower at a youth hostel in Italy. The building was huge and ugly. Someone told us Mussolini had built it. I watched the brush float in a counter-clockwise spiral toward the hair-filled hole at the center of the shower. When I could not overcome my revulsion in order to rescue the brush, I realized that my long hair was a nuisance on this trip. So when we got back to London, I made an appointment at Vidal Sassoon's salon. This was just before I was to go to classes and work in Paris for a few weeks and just after I had received a hurtful you-left-me-to-travel-so-I'm-leaving-you letter from my fiancé who was studying, still, in Australia. With money I didn't have to spare, I asked for my hair to be cut in the latest geometric style.

I took the Tube back to the flat where I was staying for a couple of weeks. One of my three flat mates opened the front door, turned around without greeting me, walked back to the depressing kitchen where she had been having tea, and resumed reading the *Times* classifieds. I followed her down the long, dim hall to the kitchen and put on the kettle.

"Do you notice anything?" I asked with my back to her.

Being a friend of a friend, she didn't know me well enough to tell me the truth but she told it anyway. "I can't believe you did something so awful," she said without looking up.

I left the next day for Paris. When I arrived, Parisian women that autumn were all wearing turtleneck sweaters, Black Watch tartan skirts—and long, flowing hair.

I only cut my hair short one more time. As I walked out of the salon on that occasion, I knew it hadn't been worth cutting it over the end of a tender, doomed affair.

So I surprised myself last night when, without a mirror, I watched as I cut off my waist-length hair yet again. It was an impulsive, rash thing to do. Most of my hair came to just below my ears but I missed cutting one long strand. I found nail scissors and finished the job—badly.

My daughter, Olivia, walked in and told me she hated it. I tried to fix it but the more I tried, the worse it became so Olivia told me to see her hairdresser who, she thought, might be able to redeem it. I knew more would need to come off. Worse, I knew that when it was washed, it would curl and look even shorter—and horrible.

It has returned every few years, this dream of my somehow ending up with short hair and being horrified. But last night's dream was the first in which I did the cutting.

My mother kept my plaits for years in that long, cream-colored box lined with tissue. Occasionally, when she was tidying a drawer, she would bring out the box when I was visiting. She would handle the plaits gingerly. They still looked the same: before her hairdresser originally cut off the plaits, she secured the top with rubber bands and the bottom with some of those blue plastic clips with the rubber bands. If my father happened to walk by when my mother and I were looking at them, he would tell me the story of how I nearly made him cut off my hair—how he never would have done it, of course—and how I had been a persistent little devil, almost forcing him to do it.

The plaits were smaller than I remember. My mother was sentimental about them. She would let me hold them but never let me take them home with me.

THREE

THE MOSAIC

Nan was a bowerbird. She liked small things, pretty things, and shiny things. Except she didn't steal the way bowerbirds stole for their nests. She just collected things and never threw them out. So the secrets of her living room held endless fascination and power for me.

Few houses in subtropical Australia had fireplaces. Nan's and Grandpapa's did. My Russian grandfather had included a fireplace in the architectural plans for the house they had had built. Had they still lived in the south where the climate was colder, he would have had a real fireplace. But they built north, so Grandpapa substituted a special electric fireplace. It had finely wrought, surprisingly realistic, red and black logs that flickered. I turned the switch on and off, on and off, especially during winter and the rainy season.

Dark beams crisscrossed the living room ceiling, making square patterns on the white plaster. On nights when my parents were going to balls or dinner parties and I was staying with Nan, not Gran and Granddad, my father would pull together of Nan's big armchairs to make a special little bed for me. I could have slept in my mother's old bed but it was more fun to fall asleep in the living room with Nan playing the piano. I would lie on my back in my two-chair bed and count the ceiling squares as I fell asleep. If the fireplace were already turned on, its light would dance across the ceiling, making shadowy shapes.

The room also had a built-in window seat beneath stained glass, art deco windows that opened onto the wide front garden. If I heaved the long cushions off the seat so that they leaned up against the wall, I could, with effort, lift up the window seat. Inside were magazines, newspapers, news clippings—my Russian grandfather's things, many of them yellowing and really old. It also held scrapbooks Nan had made from early articles my mother had written as well as clippings about my mother from before I was born. Nan's photograph albums were in there, too. There was some order but not a lot, so I was able to take things out and put them back without bothering anyone. Nan was not organized like my mother. The only things Nan kept in order, particularly later in life, were her clothes, her sewing things, her paints, and a few leather-bound albums with black pages holding tiny photographs, each identified underneath in white ink with Nan's careful, pretty, Victorian script.

An excellent piano sat in the corner. My mother told me she had practiced on it daily for hours when she was a child, and then again when she moved back in with her parents after she was married and staying with them during the years my father was away at war. My grandfather's mandolin and balalaika leaned against the piano.

Handmade, light-boned furniture that my grandfather had commissioned from Mehler decorated the room: the wooden case for the grandfather clock he had ordered from Germany in 1930, the fragile hall stand, the delicate telephone table and chair, and the nest of tiny quarter-circle side tables that slipped under a larger table with slim legs. All were made of rosewood.

"Does the wood come from roses?" I asked my mother.

"No, darling, it's a special kind of wood that Mother and Daddy—Nan and Grandpapa—liked."

A built-in cabinet sat along one wall, the fine fretwork of its French doors allowing indistinct glimpses of what was inside. I was shown how to open the cabinet with a small key but a grownup had to be with me if I wanted to hold anything inside. The cabinet held treasures from faraway places, further than we had ever driven, further even than when I stood on the beach and peer, with my fuzzy vision, at where the ocean stopped. Nan grouped objects in the cabinet according to no order other than how they looked. That order made sense to me. Things were just where they were supposed to be.

When we went to live with Nan for two years after Grandpapa died and I began school from there. Nan and the solicitor were handling probate and attempting unsuccessfully to find Grandpapa's Russian relatives mentioned in his will. Nan was also learning how to write checks for the first time.

That year, I was just tall enough to reach the middle shelf of the cabinet where Nan kept a small box covered with faded, red-flowered paper. The box had six miniature drawers. I don't remember what was in every drawer, but I remember some things. Shells were nestled in several drawers; Nan liked shells. In the bottom left drawer, lying in silent and transparent state on cotton wool, was the fine-boned skeleton of a tiny, curved creature. I was sometimes allowed to hold the things in the drawers if Nan or my mother were there.

"Hold it in your open hand, duckie," said Nan. "It's delicate. It's a sea horse."

Having no glasses yet because no one had realized I needed them, I held the sea horse close to my eyes to see each articulated bone. I loved the curve of its head and opposite curve of its tail. It was the tiniest horse I had ever seen. It was a great and wonderful mystery to me, not to be spoken aloud, that such a tiny horse could swim. Not just swim, but swim upright. Not just swim upright, but underwater without breathing. Nan never said where the skeleton came from and I didn't really believe there were other little horses in the sea that could do these things, so I assumed Nan and the sea horse shared, if not a history, a secret. I never had the courage to ask.

In the bottom right drawer of the little box was a piece of dark blue, sequined netting. My mother and I were looking in the drawers together one day. "That's the P S de re ziss tonts," my mother said with a little laugh. At least, that's how I saw the name in my six-year-old mind's eye.

"That's French, darling," my mother explained. "I'm making a little joke."

Nan looked in to see what we were doing. When she saw what we were holding, she said the sequined netting was a relic.

"What's a relic?" I asked.

"Something old and valuable and still around—like me." Nan laughed her short, Cornish laugh.

"What's it relicked from?"

"It's not 'relic'ed from,'" darling," my mother said. "An easy way to ask that would be: 'Why is it a relic?'" My mother corrected my wording with as much dedication, frequency, and calm as she did her typing in her articles or her practicing of scales or big pieces on the piano. She couldn't continue until the correction was made.

"It's a relic," she explained, "because it's what remains from one of the lovely costumes Nan made for me and the other girls when I was studying ballet."

"Took two months to get that stuff from Paris," Nan added from the glass French doors that separated the living room from the dining room. "Then a month to make it."

Years ago, before I came along and before my parents got married, Nan had focused her sewing skills, endless patience, and frustrated artistry on any art form she could get her hands on: oil painting, murals, making costumes and clothing for my mother. She said my mother was really good at ballet. My mother, however, told me she couldn't arch her foot enough to consider being a professional and she was terrified of piano performance in public in case she made a mistake. So she started writing things; she was good at noticing the tiniest things that performers did or did not do. She submitted these for fun at first; to her surprise, they were published, then requested by other publications. She developed a "following." She liked being able to undo, reword, and retype what she wrote before sending things off. Ballet and piano were undoable.

"I think Grandpapa respected my piano work most," my mother added as Nan walked off to the kitchen. "He respected self-discipline. I practiced for hours and passed the Trinity College exams. The articles seemed less ... serious to him, I think. I wasn't trained in writing. Nobody was. One didn't "study writing." Literature, yes, but not how to write. I did send to America for a course once but it wasn't very good.

"Grandpapa enjoyed dance and music—but only if it was good.

Really good. He and Nan even entertained the Russian ballet here for evenings when one company was touring Australia. They all signed my autograph book with protestations of undying Russian love and it was lots of fun. They smoked and drank and sang. Grandpapa would ask me to accompany them. I didn't mind playing; no one could hear if I made a mistake. Nan used to play by ear. Grandpapa taught her Russian songs he remembered and ones he learned to play when he was in the Czar's Balalaika Orchestra."

"Zar?"

"A Czar was like a King. Nan used to accompany Grandpapa when he played the balalaika or mandolin. But when we had visitors, Nan wouldn't play. She and Grandpapa wanted me to play."

Nan would sometimes give me one of my mother's old dance costumes for my dress-up box. One of my favorites was The Flame. Long pieces of red crepe flowed in diagonals from my young hips and dragged on the ground. I would swirl until I was dizzy and flop to the grass under the overgrown date palms, which my grandfather was no longer there to tame. Then I would climb the frangipani tree to lie, I thought gracefully, with my sun-blonded hair and flames flowing down from the branch. Nan would take photographs of me, which she would color and "touch up" to her aesthetic content.

But long before I grew big enough to drape The Flame over my small body and lie in the frangipani tree, the blue-sequined costume had disappeared. All that remained was this relic. I had to imagine the rest. Each sequin shone like a moon and then went dark as I moved it in my hand.

"It was a beautiful costume," my mother said, as she gently picked up the square of sequined netting and put it back in the little drawer. "The whole thing was midnight blue." I knew my mother loved midnight blue. She wore perfume that came in a midnight blue bottle. I had filled my nose with its fragrance, my imagination with its name—"Evening in Paris"—and my eyes with the intensity of the tiny blue bottle, which was especially wonderful when I held it up to the light. My mother's engagement ring was the same blue. The color and my mother were inseparable in my child's mind.

Nan walked back in with one of her many cups of tea and biscuits. She put the teacup down on a side table. I could tell her feet were hurting her. She had to wear expensive shoes that were handmade for her down south. She said that, in Her Day, girls would buy boots one size too small so their feet would look prettier. Now, when her shoes and heavy stockings were off, her toes lay one on top of another like pegs that had fallen off the clothesline. Nan sat down with relief in one of the mushroom-colored armchairs between the cabinet and the French doors.

I stepped around my mother and opened the middle drawer on the right side of the box. Something else deep blue was in it, sitting on white cotton.

"What's this, Nan?"

"That's from a temple." My grandmother took a bite of her sweet biscuit and stirred the two heaping teaspoons of sugar she always put in her tea. She was using the blue and brown kitchen china today and a discolored silver teaspoon. My mother picked up the newspapers that Nan had pushed off the footstool when she had put her stockinged feet up. She lined up the edges of the pages, folded them in half, and laid the paper neatly on the worn Persian rug just by the footstool.

"Grandpapa brought it with him all the way to Australia."

"What's a tem pull?"

"T-E-M-P-L-E," my mother said automatically, sensing from how I'd pronounced the new word that my spelling would be inventive. "A temple is a place where people pray and sing—to a god or gods. Rather like the church where Daddy takes you."

"What's 'a summer can'?"

"Samarkand, Meg," my grandmother answered and had a sip of tea. "She's forgotten the cottage," Nan said to my mother who had just re-entered with her own cup of tea and a sweet biscuit.

I didn't understand what Nan meant.

Nan turned toward me. "Samarkand is a city a long way away from here. Grandpapa worked on repairing a famous temple there to earn money. He was well educated but wanted to do more than he thought he could in Russia. He also could do anything with his hands. So he worked his way from Russia to the Black Sea and bought a ticket to Australia. One of the things he did was to help repair that temple. Luce, get the map and the article out of the window seat, would you."

My mother sighed gently and set aside her tea. She went over to the window seat, picked up the cushions, which had turned multicolored in the late afternoon light that shone through the stained glass, and stacked them neatly on an armchair. She lifted the lid and pulled out, from among a raft of the papers in Russian, a faded map and a yellow newspaper article. Both were glued onto thin board. I sat on Nan's silk lap with my bare legs dangling on either side of her. My mother brought them over to us and laid the map over our legs. A red-ink line wandered across various colored shapes on the map.

"The red line shows where Grandpapa traveled and worked his way through all these towns to Odessa. Here's Samarkand. See how it's spelled, darling? It's easy to remember if you break it up: 'Sam.' That's Dr. Ruben's first name. 'Ark.' Remember learning at Sunday School about Noah and the animals? Then there's just 'and' at the end."

I didn't like the idea of a black sea, so I tried not to think about it other than to decide that my grandfather must have been brave to sail on a black sea. Then I thought about Samarkand. I looked at the picture of the temple in the yellowing article. I pictured my grandfather standing beside the temple with a hammer in his hand, putting it all back together.

"Go to the top right drawer, Meg."

I slipped off Nan's lap and went back to the cabinet.

"You can take it out," Nan said between sips. Carefully, I took out the little drawer, holding it with both hands.

"It's mosaic," she said.

Another word. No matter how many Roman and Greek floors I would later see, whenever I heard the word "mosaic," I would always picture this small piece of deep-blue porcelain.

"Grandpapa picked it up from the scrap heap at the temple at Samarkand. He brought it all the way to Australia. Later, after we moved up here and your mother was growing up, we bought land down at the beach and built a cottage. Grandpapa wanted to call it 'Samarkand.' You used to go there all the time. Do you remember it?"

"I think so."

"You remember Grandpapa, don't you?" Nan adjusted her silk skirt so it wasn't pulling on her stockings and looked over at my mother.

I thought about her question. I knew what the answer should be but I wasn't sure about it. I thought for a second. I could see my grandfather's smile. I could feel strong legs supporting me as I sat on his lap. I could feel a firm, flat belly laughing. I could see a Band-Aid on his forehead when I was standing on a chair in the dining room opposite him, ready to jump into his lap. I'd asked him why he had a Band-Aid. He said he had bumped his head while cutting fronds off one of the palms. I could remember a big storm one night when my parents were out and I was staying with Nan and him. Grandpapa held me up so I could see out the windows in the dining room. I saw blurs of light Grandpapa said were lightning and we heard thunder. Then he slid me down to the floor, took my hand gently in his callused one, and led me past the big dining table to the windows. He held aside the heavy, floor-length gold curtains and showed me a black box affixed to the wall. He told me that the box put the lightning where it couldn't hurt us. I never went near that box. I could remember pulling silk tassels on his camel's hair dressing gown when we went to see him in the hospital. I kept undoing the knot and he kept doing it up so I could undo it again. He got better and he was supposed to come home but something went wrong and he didn't.

"Yes, especially his dressing gown," I answered. Something in the room felt different. Nan patted my arm.

I put the tiny drawer on the arm of Nan's chair and carefully picked up the piece of mosaic with three fingers from each hand. I didn't want to drop it.

"When can we go? To the cottage? 'To 'Sam-Ark-And'?"

"We can't go in anymore but we can drive by. Grandpapa sold it a few months before he went into the hospital. He thought we weren't using it enough." Nan picked one of my long hairs off the arm of her chair and wound it around her slim forefinger.

I sat on Nan's lap again, holding the piece of mosaic in one hand and putting my other hand over it, peeking at it through my stubby fingers.

My mother took a sip of her tea and added, "Grandpapa used to say, 'I can't believe I own a bit of Australia.' He owned quite a lot really—commercial buildings—but this house and 'Samarkand' meant the most. He built them with the best materials. He always preferred the best quality. We used to go to 'Samarkand' often. Daddy and I even lived there for a while when I was expecting you."

I thought she must have been expecting me the way she expected me home from school. I couldn't think where I would have been. Probably with my grandparents.

"Let me up, Meg," Nan said. I gave her the mosaic, hopped off her lap, and tried to jump exactly on the line of little circles on the Persian carpet. Like hopscotch. Nan put the mosaic back in the little drawer from the box and set it on the side table. She went to the window seat, rummaged around, and eventually pulled out one of the many photograph albums. She sat down and leafed through it carefully until she found the page for which she was looking. She beckoned me away from the dots on the carpet and bade me sit on the arm of her chair.

"See?" Her slim hand pointed at a page of black-and-white photographs with deckle edges.

The small photos were of a sturdy child with a big smile, wearing a straw hat, with a long, thick tumble of brown hair falling over her overalls. She was playing with a hose in the front yard. A handsome man with laughing eyes and thick curly hair was sitting on a wicker chair behind the child. The ocean was just beyond, behind a low fence.

"Who're they?" I asked. Nan took her last sip of tea. The biscuit had long gone.

"You and Grandpapa. At 'Samarkand.'"

"Nan! That's not me! She's got hair to here but I've got long plaits to here! And Grandpapa wore a Band-Aid."

Nan put her empty teacup back on the side table, rose with difficulty, indicated to my mother to put the album, map, and article back in the window seat, and took the drawer with the mosaic back to the cabinet.

I followed her over to the cabinet, reached up with my nail-bitten fingers, and carefully opened the top right drawer. In it was a matchbox with an odd cross on it.

"That's a swastika. I kept a matchbox from the train Nan and Grandpapa and I were traveling on through Germany in 1938," my mother explained, looking over at me from where she was lining up the window seat cushions. "You can take it out, but be careful with it, darling. It's probably worth something now. The people who made it did bad things. Many people never saw their families again because of the ones who wore that sign. When we were traveling through Germany, we saw bad messages they wrote in windows too. They were written by the people who made the matchbox. I was only eighteen. I didn't understand. I thought they had lovely uniforms, especially the girls and boys who sang while they were marching and hiking. But Grandpapa knew. Nana gave me his travel diaries from that trip to reread recently. They're in English. My trip diary is mostly about what ballets and theater we attended—rather shallow really. Grandpapa's are detailed, better written. He didn't like what he saw in Germany at all. He didn't say much at the time. I think he didn't want us to worry."

Nan got up and moved over to the piano. My grandfather's mandolin and balalaika lay, unused, against the piano. On the top shelf, there were two long, hand-colored photographs. She reached up and took down both of them. They had always been there. They were the longest pictures I'd ever seen—about the length of my whole arm. She let me hold one end of the first picture while she held the other. It was a picture of a city with mountains in the back. It was hand-colored.

"We bought this when your mother and Grandpapa and I were in Lucerne," Nan said, running her finger along the top of the dusty frame and wiping it clean with her lace handkerchief. "Your mother and I were going to stay by the lake for two weeks while Grandpapa went to see his family in Russia. He'd been trying to get permission to visit Russia since before we left Australia. They never did let him in, so he stayed with us in Switzerland.

"He didn't see his family again. He did get a letter after the war saying they were alive. But he never heard anything more after that. This second picture is from the top of Mount Pilatus. It shows the names of the mountains."

That night, I had my bath in the olive green bathtub with the gargoyle—another amazing feature of my grandparents' house—and then my mother put me to bed. I was using her childhood room.

I lay there for a while until I heard my parents talking in low voices in their bedroom. They sounded upset. Since we had come to live here, I often heard them talking like that when they thought Nan and I were sleeping. Nan's and my bedrooms were in the other wing from theirs. But their room had big windows that overlooked the large back garden with its great palms and fern grotto. My windows also opened onto the back garden, so sometimes, on hot nights when all the windows were open, I could hear them from my bedroom.

I slid out of bed and tiptoed past Nan's bedroom. She had fallen asleep over an American magazine. Nan was already a little deaf, so I wasn't worried about her hearing me. I passed through the dining room (being careful not to look in the direction of the curtain hiding the black box), and crept into the living room. The moon was shining through the stained glass window, making patterns on the dark rug. Standing on Nan's footstool, I grabbed the key to the cabinet. I quietly unlocked it and pulled out the middle drawer on the right.

The mosaic lay there glinting in the moonlight.

I thought about Grandpapa with the bump on his forehead and the Band-Aid. I thought about visiting him in the hospital. I had to look up at him but I was tall enough to pull the tassel on his robe. I remembered his smiling down at me and laughing. He made me feel warm inside when he smiled and he had a laugh that made me giggle. It was only for me, my mother said.

I thought about the photographs Nan said were of Grandpapa and me.

Then I thought about the matchbox with the swass-ticket on it and the black box that my grandfather had told me meant no one could get hurt. Now there were two things I could never go near: the big black box and the little red box. If you didn't have a black box, you might die or never see your family again. And the red box somehow meant someone would die or you might never see your family again.

Making sure my fingers didn't touch the top drawer in which the red box lay, I managed to take out the piece of mosaic from the drawer below. It was bluer in the moonlight. Midnight blue. I put it down on the side table. I carefully locked the cabinet door, replaced the key, picked up the piece in both hands, tiptoed back to bed, and put the piece under my pillow.

The next morning when I was getting ready for school, dawdling as usual, I wrapped the mosaic in one of my handkerchiefs, then stole a safety pin from Nan's sewing drawer. I pinned the handkerchief into the pocket of the well-ironed blue blouse of my school uniform. The tunic I wore over the blouse hid the pocket.

I always sat in the back of the classroom where the clever or well-behaved students were told to sit. All through Writing and Sums and other boring things, I kept feeling my pocket. I pretended to feel sick at lunch so I didn't have to run around on the gravel playground with everyone. I loved playing hopscotch and knuckles with my friends but I was afraid I might lose the mosaic. Because I was one of the well-behaved students, my teacher believed I really did feel sick. I managed to pretend that I was just unwell enough to stay in the classroom but not so unwell that she considered further action.

At the end of the day, I packed my scruffy exercise books and the remains of my lunch into my heavy, brown horror of a school bag. I stuck my school hat on my head and walked to the front gates. I felt my pocket again, happy to be alone again with my secret.

There was nothing there except for the safety pin, which was undone.

I felt sick all the way to my socks.

I ran back to the classroom. The teacher was sitting at her desk supervising two boys who were having to do Lines for detention. She looked annoyed but beckoned me in. I asked her in a whisper if I could please look under my seat because I had lost my hanky.

"Quickly or I'll keep you in, for a change."

I looked under my desk. No matter how hard I stared at the

black iron curves of the desk legs, no handkerchief appeared. I opened my desk. There were my crayons, the pencil with the end broken, a dead fly, some of my marbles—my favorite ones with the swirls—and my slate board and pencil. But no handkerchief. I stuck the marbles in my pocket so they wouldn't get confiscated or stolen and left. I went out on the verandah and looked all over, including the spot where I kept my school bag. Nothing.

Tears spurted from my eyes. I grabbed a bit of newspaper to wipe them. The toilets were too far away to tear off a bit of their brown, non-absorbent, government-issue paper.

Ned was sitting below the verandah. I hated Ned. He was three years older, redheaded, big for his age, and mean. His father, a steamroller driver, had disappeared last year. Then his mother ran off, leaving Ned and his younger brother Johno, who was in my class, with their uncle. Some people said the father fell under a steamroller. Others said his mother ran his father over with the steamroller and was put in jail. Someone else said the brothers' parents were struck by lightning. Someone else said the father had another family out in the bush and his mother ran away with another steamroller driver. Someone in fifth grade said Ned must have been named after Ned Kelly, the bushranger, but someone else who was in Ned's class said he was named after a donkey. Ned hit the boy who said Ned was named after a donkey. Anyway, Ned had been even meaner since his parents had disappeared.

"Have you seen a hanky?" I asked him, knowing it was a terrible mistake to even speak to him. Once he'd cornered two of us in the girls' toilet and held up a big cockroach in front of us. Its legs were still moving a little but it had whitish stuff oozing out of it. Ned was horrible.

"Nup," he said, and spat on the ground.

"Please?"

"Say 'Please, sir' the way we do to Dopey Dodd."

"Please—sir."

"Nup."

"You have! You're fibbing. You're just pretending you haven't."

"Big words, big words. PreTENDing! Think you're clever, don'tcha?"

"It's my mother's hanky."

"How much will you give me if I seen it?"

I thought quickly. I had no money. "I have a really big marble you could have." He looked interested.

"Lemme see."

I dug one of the marbles out of my deep pocket and showed it to him. He took it with his filthy fingers and turned it around in the sun in front of my eyes. I could see his fingerprints all over it. He reached into his back pocket, pulled something out and let it drop to the ground just behind where he was sitting. I ran over so I could see what it was. It was the handkerchief. It had fallen onto a piece of white bread from someone's lunch. I went to pick it up but Ned pushed me out of the way and snatched it.

"Please."

"Please, sir."

"Please, sir."

He threw the handkerchief at me.

I reached low to grab it because I knew it would fall heavily with the mosaic wrapped inside and, if the mosaic broke, I might as well be dead. Instead, the handkerchief floated in the breeze.

"I didn't want it anyway. Johno just gave it to me to tie up cockies and let them out in the lav."

"Where's the—thing—that was in it?"
"What thing?"
"The colored thing. The blue thing."
"Dunno."
"Where'd you find the hanky?"
"I want another marble."
"I've only got three. Tell me where you got it. I already gave you one."
"Aren't we clever! We can count!"
"Where?"
"If you give me another one, I might tell you. Won't promise."

I handed over another marble. He didn't even look at it. He just put it in the dirty, grey pocket of his school pants.

"Where?"
"Didn't promise."
"Where?"
"Maybe. Just maybe under the verandah."
"Where under the verandah?"

He said nothing.

I raced down the stairs, nearly slipping on the remains of someone's jam roll and making sure to keep my bag with me because Ned had been known to take stuff out of people's bags or to put horrible stuff in. I started feeling around in the dirt. My fingertips encountered gritty things—half-eaten boiled eggs with gravel on them, old pitted crayons, a smelly grey sock with a hole. No mosaic.

"Ned. You've got to tell. Did you see a bit of blue stuff where you found the hanky?"

"Don't answer questions unless I'm paid. 'Specially questions from cockroaches. You're a cockroach. A cocky. A wooden peg.

Meg the Peg. You're just a second grader."

"Here." I handed over my last marble. It was my favorite: blue and white swirls, and the biggest of the three. They were my father's when he was growing up. He had given them to me when I started school. I loved them.

"Nup."

"I gave you my marble!"

"I said I'd answer your question. I answered your question, Cocky Pegleg."

I sat down in the dust and sobbed. Now I had lost not only the mosaic but also three of my father's marbles. Ned continued to sit there looking out over the playing field and throwing stones at the birds. He was a good shot. He even hit a crow. It flew off, squawking angrily. I finally got up, blew my nose on the dusty hanky, brushed myself off with tear-soaked hands thereby spreading the grime I had accumulated, picked up my school bag, and walked slowly towards the gate.

I had walked a few yards when I felt a sting on my leg. It really hurt. I thought I must have been stung by a bee but I only saw a scratch on my muddy leg. A little blood was oozing. I would need a Band-Aid when I got home—if I ever went home. I knew Ned must have thrown a stone at me. He had hit his mark. I hated him. I heard him laugh. I was so mad I was about to go back and swing my school bag at him when I heard him say in a singsong voice, "Pegleg Meg is dir-ty! Just a cock-a-roach!"

I put my bag down and grabbed a handful of gravel to throw in his general direction. But when I did, I felt something larger in the dirt. I picked it up. Despite the dirt covering it, I saw it was the mosaic. There was a spot of blood on the corner where it had hit me. I dropped the rest of the gravel and started to cry again.

Ned yelled bad words at me as I walked out the school gate.

My mother was shocked when she opened the door. I was a mess. "What happened, darling?"

"Ned—Johno's brother—said bad things to me and made me cry."

"He's a cruel boy and a bully. I'm so sorry. Let's get you into the bath and wash the school off you right now. I'll run the bath."

While she was making the green gargoyle spurt hot water into the tub, I ran to my room. I unwrapped the mosaic from the handkerchief and slid it under the sheets at the foot of my bed. I pulled off my grubby uniform and socks, dropped them on the polished floor, threw my hat on the dressing table, and walked in to the bathroom in my white underpants.

"Sweetheart, you have a little cut."

"He threw—something—at me."

"He should be reported."

"NO!"

"Why? He should be reported to Mr. Dodds. Bad words are wrong. I heard his family's had trouble, so perhaps that's why he's a meanie but throwing things is dangerous." She took a green washcloth off the rail. My towel lived next to Nan's, where Grandpapa's used to be, my mother said.

"Please, Mamma. Don't tell Mr. Dodds. It was my fault, sort of. I shouldn't have talked to Ned. If you tell Mr. Dodds, Ned'll tell a big fib about me. Johno'll tell fibs. They always fib. Then Mr. Dodds will believe them and feel sorry for them because of their parents and I'll get detention."

I had a bath. As I sat there, I talked too much to my mother out of fear and relief. My mother listened endlessly, treating all my stories as important. This usually pleased me but in this case I knew that I was not telling her the most important story, so I began to feel lonely and even sadder. Finally, as she was washing my back with the green washcloth, I started to cry again.

"Sweetheart, what is it?"

"Nothing."

"Yes, it is!"

I thought quickly. "Ned really scared me and I got my uniform dirty but when I was walking home, I thought about him never seeing his parents again and—." I got no further.

Dinner was subdued. I wore my Band-Aid with pride. It secretly made me feel like Grandpapa. I asked my mother if she could put one going the other way, too. Nan, who had heard the story from my mother, sat silent through most of dinner, angry with Ned. I could do no wrong in her eyes.

That night I didn't know how I was going to stay awake. I pretended to be asleep when my father tiptoed in, kissed my forehead, and touched the soft down that grew near my temples. He sighed and tiptoed out. I fell asleep before I heard my parents stop talking.

A clap of thunder woke me. Soon it started to rain heavily. I was glad Grandpapa had installed the black box. I used my toes to retrieve the piece of mosaic, which was between the sheets at the bottom of the bed. I took it in my hands. It was so dirty. I spat on it and wiped it with the hanky. I couldn't see much in the dark except when the lightning flashed. After I wiped it for a long time, I decided it had to be clean.

Under cover of the sounds from the summer storm, I tiptoed into the living room. I climbed the footstool, felt for the key, climbed down, unlocked the cabinet, put the mosaic back, locked the cabinet, climbed up again, returned the key to the exact position it had been in when I'd retrieved it, and climbed down again. My heart was pounding.

Once back in my bed, I lay awake. I was terrified: I couldn't remember if the pointed side of the mosaic faced right or left. I hoped I had got the bit of blood off. I felt slightly sick with fear; someone might notice. Then I fell dead asleep.

My mother asked me why I seemed so listless the next day. I told her the storm had kept me awake.

No one noticed that the mosaic had gone walkabout and returned. My father eventually did notice, with a little sadness, that I had lost three of the marbles his father had given him and which he had managed to keep for thirty years.

One day, when my mother was at the clothesline and my grandmother was sewing, I checked to make sure the mosaic was there. It was. On the unglazed side, there was a tiny pink smudge. My blood.

In later years, when we went for holidays at rental houses and motels by the beach, we would drive by 'Samarkand' at least once during our stay. Each time we would drive slowly past the cottage where I had been conceived and had grown inside my mother.

My grandfather had chosen a piece of land with a wide, long sweep of powdery white sand in front. Only a long stand of Norfolk pines and a quiet access road lay between the cottage and the beach and the Pacific Ocean.

The second owners had changed the name of the cottage to "Summastand" and had put up a new tile nameplate to the left of the front door instead of the right.

"The name doesn't make sense," my mother would comment sadly. "If they wanted to change it, why didn't they at least have it make sense—for example, 'Summersand'?"

My father would say to me, "Your mother's father was a good man. He was stern. He didn't put up with fools but he was honest and fair. After he did well, he gave a lot of men a start in businesses," he would tell me. "We didn't know until his funeral at St. Andrew's. A lot of established businessmen we didn't know came to pay their respects and told us what he'd done. It's a pity you didn't know him well. He wasn't too sure about me at first but he loved you from the day we brought you home. I never saw him laugh the way he did with you. He'd let you do anything."

We would stop at the corner just before the house so we could look at it discreetly.

"He built it with the best materials but he wanted it to be simple and modest. Jarra wood from Western Australia. The whole house. It's only used for furniture now. He insisted on copper pipes, too. He knew anything else would erode in the salt air. 'Do it well the first time and you don't have to do it twice,' he'd say. He was right about that. Pity he sold but he thought it wasn't used often enough."

We would drive on in silence.

'Samarkand' survived the years well. My grandfather had not left his family of intellectuals and worked his way from Russia to the Black Sea through all the red points on that map in the window seat without knowing what endured and what did not.

Once, after Nan died, my mother wrote a letter to the owner of 'Samarkand.' She told him we'd like to buy it back, if he ever sold. He wrote back and promised to tell us. Last time I drove by alone, the cottage had been replaced by a forty-storey high-rise.

The view my grandfather had chosen, however, was unchangeable: an uninterrupted view of the Pacific. On a cloudless day, the ocean's horizon is midnight blue.

My mother later transferred the long pictures from above the piano, the mosaic with the smudge on the side, the matchbox, the blue sequins, one "Midnight in Paris" bottle, and the sea horse to a silk-lined Swiss chocolate box she and my father kept from a later trip. She kept lots of other things, too.

The long pictures, mosaic, matchbox, and sequins, bottle, and sea horse are mine now. I don't let people touch them.

FOUR

GLASSES

"eg darling, I shan't be able to let you walk to school by yourself if you don't pay attention. Remember, 'look left, look right, look left again.'"

"I did."

"But there was a car coming."

"Not when I looked."

"You can't have been looking very carefully, darling."

"I was." I took her hand.

"Didn't you hear it?" she asked gently.

I thought about her question. There had been no car. Then there was. It hadn't been there a second before. So I learned to listen for a noise. I worked out that the louder the noise, the closer the car. Then a woolly thing would suddenly appear, turn into a car and whiz by, and recede as wool again. This was easy: I was supposed to listen for a car and then look at it. That was how ears and eyes worked. This solution sufficed for the first year of school and I walked the considerable distance from Nan's house, where we were living, to school and back daily. It was the same school my mother had started at.

During that first year, I learned to read and write and do arithmetic and whatever else we did. But I have few memories from that time and those I do have are not of reading, writing, and arithmetic. Nor do my memories include my first day of school. I base my conviction that I went that day on the movie my parents made. In the movie, I am standing on the top step at Nan's, dressed neatly in hat, white socks, and uniform, with a vague if determinedly cheerful expression, and a gap between my front teeth, which would later be corrected at considerable expense to my father.

My first memory from that period is, in fact, my deciding not to go to school. I'd tried it and it was not of interest. Looking back, I can think of another reason why I mightn't have been enthusiastic or remembered the year: I couldn't see anything clearly beyond my hand.

My second memory is of standing on the top step of the school landing, eye to eye with my father. To help me go to school, my father sometimes dropped me off on his way to work. When we arrived in the blue and white Holden, we would pretend he was a major in the army again and I was his "too I see." At least, that's how I thought it was spelled until he explained it was short for second-in-command. I would climb the steps in my ugly brown uniform and hat with its school ribbon. On the top step, I was the same height as my father. Serious, he would look me straight in my blue eyes with his deep brown ones and salute me. Tears would run down my cheeks as I slowly would bring my hand to my hat brim in a salute.

"Be a brave little soldier, now, Meggie," my father would say gently, but firmly. Then, as he would watch, I would turn around and walk down the long wooden verandah without looking back. I don't know who hurt more.

My third memory is of the big bass drum. The government school to which I had been sent was chosen to help toughen me up because I was an Only, and also to teach me how to get on with children from Different Backgrounds. Like every other government-run school, it had a drum and fife band.

One morning at parade, which included all grades one through eight, the Headmaster asked if anyone knew how to play the big bass drum. I didn't know life without music, so I was surprised no one put up a hand. I mean, how hard could it be to bang that thing in time to the music? Being taught to be honest, I raised my hand. I remember amusement in the headmaster's voice as he bade me come forward, which I did. I banged the drum. No one else in the band played while I was banging, so I banged out a march beat my mother had taught me: one heavy and three light beats. But without music to go with the beat, I couldn't see the point. They didn't make me the drummer.

Then there was the sugar disaster. The school was holding a fête and each parent was asked to contribute something. My mother, more adept at writing her articles for the paper than at cooking, contributed a big bag of sugar. On the day I brought the sugar, my father drove me to school. I stood on the top wooden step and saluted. Before I turned around to march down the verandah, he handed me the sugar. I took it carefully, holding it tightly against my damp chest.

Somehow I lost my grip. The bag dropped and ruptured, spilling white all over the shiny grey, wooden steps. Tears sprang from my eyes and dripped into the sugar, making it wet as well as spilled. My life was over. No matter what my father said in my ear or how tightly he held me, I was a blob of shame.

And then there was the gnat. Because I was deemed to be ahead of most of my class, I had been put in the back row where Brains and Goody-Two-Shoes sat. Because I already knew the stuff my teacher was teaching, I didn't realize that my classmates could see what was happening at the front of the classroom.

So there I was in the back row, in my red-and-white-checked dress the day a gnat began buzzing around my face. I swiped the air in my best Australian fashion—and the sound went away. Soon it was back. Suddenly, I felt The Thing crawl into my right ear. I swiped furiously at my ear. After that there was no sound—but I felt a crawly sensation in my ear: The Thing had got inside my head. It was flying around in there and it would never be able to find its way out. There was nothing anyone could do. I felt sick. I knew that forever and ever, I would have something flying around in the big, dark, empty space that was my head and that I could never tell a soul because they'd think I was weird.

The last thing I remember is Miss Horne and something that happened with her one day. She was the source of all knowledge outside of my parents and grandparents. Miss Horne was large, had black-and-white hair, and wore no makeup. She favored big black shoes and black dresses with long sleeves, even in summer. She had a great, black leather bag in which she carried heavy things back and forth to school.

One day when my father drove me past a small cottage in the inner city, he told me that the cottage was where Miss Horne lived. I was shocked to know she lived anywhere. She was the only person I could recognize from a distance.

Miss Horne had a reputation for being a gifted teacher but I remember nothing of her classes other than, toward the end of the school year, which coincided with the long summer Christmas vacation, Billy, who was sitting in the front row, asked for permission to go to the toilet, returned, and put up his hand again.

"Yes, William?"

Billy stood up and squirmed in his grey school shorts. He pushed at his greasy hair, then said, after a big sigh, "Please, Miss, Bluey says there's no Santa Claus. I told him he was a dunce. He said I was a double dunce."

Everybody laughed.

Miss Horne waited until the class quieted down, then said, "Robert is right, William. There is no Santa Claus. So you'd better apologize to Robert after school. I won't give you Lines today but if you call him a double dunce again, you'll get Lines. You'll stay after school, learn how to spell every word you said, and write it out ten times."

Then she turned to us. "Now, children," she said, "William has raised an interesting topic. You should know that there is no Santa Claus. He's a pretend person, like a fairy."

Later that afternoon, while my mother was giving me a bath, I thought I should teach her what I had learned. "Miss Horne says there's no Santa Claus," I said. "She says Bluey wasn't a dunce for saying there wasn't a Santa Claus and she said she'd keep Billy in and give him Lines the next time he called Bluey a double dunce, but when we were waiting to be dismiss-ded, he poked his tongue out at Bluey instead of saying sorry."

"Dismissed, darling. Not dismiss-ded."

My mother didn't seem happy that I was giving her this important piece of knowledge on the topic of Santa Claus and Billy. She told my grandmother over a cup of tea that Miss Horne shouldn't have said that. It was a parental decision, she said.

That was first grade.

The next year, we had Mrs. Barstow, whom we called, of course, Beasto. She wasn't half as nice as Miss Horne. She was cranky. That made me try harder. I wanted to do well and she was teaching stuff I didn't know in all three subjects.

In English: "Excuse me Mrs. Beas—Barstow, could I please go to the blackboard to copy the words you just wrote?"

"Yes, Meg."

In Arithmetic: "Mrs. Barstow, could I look at the sum on the board? The sun's shining on it."

"Very well."

In Social Studies: "Mrs. Barstow, could I please copy the list of crops from the blackboard. I can't remember what you said they were when you were writing them."

"For heaven's sake, Meg, you must need glasses. Hurry up."

In the green bath that afternoon, I regaled my mother as always about the day's transgressions—others', not mine. Then I told my mother what Mrs. Barstow had said about glasses, using the same tone of exasperation she had used with me. I couldn't see what I'd done wrong. My mother had a strong sense of justice. Things were fair or they weren't—and this was not fair. She was indignant. I was pleased by her reaction, promptly forgot about the incident, and moved on to a new story about Ned.

At dinner that night, as I was balancing mashed potatoes on my fork, my mother deftly summarized for my father the injustice done to me. Then she said, "I wonder if we should get her eyes tested. What do you think?"

"By all means," he replied.

A few days later, I found myself in the office of Nan's ophthalmologist. He held little circles of magic glass in front of my eyes and I could suddenly see things far away just the way I could see things up close. It was fun and I felt important.

"She's extremely myopic, I'm afraid. And she has bad astigmatism."

Why was he saying I was bad when I had read everything he had put in front of me through those bits of glass? However, he didn't seem cross like Mrs. Barstow and my mother just seemed worried.

"She needs glasses. Try these on, Meg, so your mother can look at them," he said, as he slipped springy wires over my small ears. "These are the only frames made for girls her age."

Two weeks later, we took the tram back into town. I loved sitting next to my mother and feeling the cabin rock.

At the ophthalmology office, the man put little round glasses with pink frames on my face and gave me a piece of paper to read. I read it out loud but it didn't make sense. All I could make out were individual letters and a few words. Why was he testing those?

He then asked me to look at a chart on the wall and read more letters and words and they didn't make sense either. This time he said, "That was very good." So why was it bad last time? It wasn't fair. However, he seemed pleased. My mother seemed both sad and relieved.

Before I got the glasses, people would say "Look at the stars, Meg," or "Look at the moon," and I knew they were pretending because no one could see the stars or moon in real life—only in books, and then only if you held those books close to your eyes. After I put on the glasses, my world exploded with detail. On the trip home, I described for my mother all the things that we passed on the side of the road, and I talked too loudly about people sitting in the upper cabin.

When we were home at Nan's, I stood close to the long mirror I had in my bedroom—my mother's old room—so I could see what I looked like with glasses on. Then I stepped back and was shocked: I could still see myself! I had never seen my whole body all at once before—arms and legs and face and hair and everything. All at once!

I stepped away from the mirror and looked down the hall. I could see Nan in the sewing room! I looked out my upstairs window and saw my mother underneath the palms in the back garden pinning clothes on the clothesline. I could even see the spiky things on the palms! I ran to the window seat and knelt on it, looking out. I could see freesias in the front garden. I could see a bird on the birdbath. I could see trees across the street. I could see people at the end of the road. I could see our car turning into the driveway and my father walking up the stairs—before he saw me!

"They look pretty, Meggie. You look quite grown up," my father said over dinner. After we had finished dessert, he asked me to sit on his lap. He gave me a big hug and I hugged him back. I could see beyond him to the dirty dishes piling up in the sink.

I sat on his lap and beamed. I had a loose tooth. Between that and the glasses, this was a good day.

"She didn't get it from my side," my father said to my mother while Nan was on the phone.

"Mother didn't wear glasses until she was older," my mother replied, "and Daddy never wore them. I only wear them for reading or typing. That's not very fair, Michael."

I didn't know about sides. All I cared about was whether my classmates at school would know who I was. After all, I didn't know who they were except by their voices, or if they were close. So I assumed that they must not know who I was either, if I wasn't talking or close by.

Now I could watch the faces of people even when they were far away.

When I walked to school the next day, I could see the cars at the same time as I heard them.

I broke ranks after parade and ran up to Miss Horne. I knew it was Miss Horne because I could see her face clearly from a distance.

"Miss Horne?"

"Yes, dear."

"Do you know who I am?"

"Of course I do, dear. You're Meg." She looked down and put her big hand with its chalky fingernails lightly on my uniformed shoulder. "How could I forget you?"

I was very disappointed.

FIVE

NASTURTIUMS

My mother tried to get me interested in growing nasturtiums when I was six.

Nan had a fernery with latticed shading. It also had flowerbeds, which Mr. McPherson, the Scots gardener, tended. Mr. McPherson called me "a silly wee teapot."

My mother bought seeds and proposed that we protect and water the seeds until they flowered. It would be fun, she said. I had as much interest in seeds as I did in cooking or dolls, which was not much. I preferred painting with Nan or my mother, pretending to write an article or play the piano like my mother, watching the goldfish in Nan's pond while I walked across its little stone bridge, sliding on the slime in the gutter after it rained, making mud drinks in the back garden and dipping my tongue in them, and playing doctor with the boy next door in the small garage my grandfather had built to house my trim little metal pedal car.

However, because my mother seemed to be happy about the future nasturtiums, I knelt beside her in one of the flowerbeds—that bit was fun—and dutifully dug down the requisite depth, placing the seeds in the dark holes. My mother showed me how to wrap a piece of cardboard around each seed to protect it while it was growing. I did this for some of the seeds but abandoned the rest to the mercies of the season because I was tired of making little cardboard rolls. It was supposed to be interesting to wait a really long time for plants to come up but I couldn't see what was interesting about it. I showed polite interest for my mother, who obviously saw more in this endeavor than I did. It was one of the only times I could not effortlessly join her in a passion.

By the time the seeds had sprouted, my parents had found a house to rent, one into which we could move while our new house was being built. I found out about the move in the laundry room, which was on the open-latticed first floor of Nan's home, where we were living.

"Darling, I have something to tell you," my mother said as she and my grandmother and I were about to ascend the white wooden stairs. "We aren't going to live with Nan anymore."

"Good!" I said happily.

"Darling, don't say that! You'll hurt Nan's feelings!" my mother remonstrated, shocked I would say such a thing in front of my grandmother, whose sensibilities my mother assumed to be like her own.

"I didn't mean that," I explained patiently. "I meant 'good' because you and Daddy won't fight so much."

My mother walked up the stairs behind my grandmother, trying to explain her way out of my honesty.

I stayed downstairs and wandered into the storage room. The rooms on this floor were the equivalent of above-ground basement rooms typical of a certain style of colonial house designed for hot climates. The rooms were dark and cool: the storage room; my grandfather's neat tool room, unused since his death; the laundry room; the in-ground fishpond with my grandmother's half-finished, lyrical painting of nymphs outlined in green on the wall behind it; the garage, where my father's car now lived; and a toilet. Having a second toilet in any house was a luxury and we had one in a compact, cream and dark green room with a louvered window that opened onto the side garden. My mother used to disappear into this room at regular intervals.

I went into the storage room and pulled down one of my old dolls. The doll did not have a porcelain head as later ones did but a synthetic one—pink rubber or latex. The head was detachable from its soft body, which was permanently damp from the humid summers. The baby clothes that Nan had made for it were strained at the seams from my handling. I untwisted the head as I had done many times before so that I could hear its sturdy rim make its usual satisfying pop.

Something jumped out. A large cockroach. When I say large, I mean large by antipodean standards: the kind that flies, the kind that flies at you even when you're not trying to kill it, the kind that is the length of your father's thumb, the kind that will not die even when your father stands on it with his polished brogues. The cockroach that sprang from inside my doll was this kind— and it was shiny, crackly, big, brown, and fast.

I dropped the doll and stood still. I felt sick. I decided not to pick up the doll from the concrete floor in case there were other cockies lurking where the first had been—a reasonable assumption in that humid atmosphere.

Nan and my mother were waiting for me upstairs. There was something so awful about a cockroach being inside my doll that I couldn't even mention it to my mother or grandmother. I had seen a disgusting thing and somehow I felt disgusting by association. I didn't know why but I knew it was true. So I said not a word. We had afternoon tea as usual. I sat under the kitchen table and listened to "The Children's Hour" on the radio while Nan and my mother fixed dinner.

When we moved into the rental house, my mother planted nasturtiums in the clay soil surrounding the house. We also returned to Nan's to see how the ones we had planted there were faring. They were chaotically colorful. The ones that had been sheltered from the sun were happier than those I had left to the elements.

I did not go into Nan's storage room again. I knew the cockroach was there, probably with friends and relatives.

Two years later, we moved into our own, newly built house. My mother planted nasturtiums again. She didn't ask me to plant them with her this time; I was off at my new school. She waged war against the clay soil to make things grow as lusciously as they eventually did and we all waged war against the cockroaches that flew through the windows at night. No one had screens. I regularly decided I would not think about the doll's head any more.

The nasturtiums were my mother's first success in the garden and she made little arrangements of them in brass bowls from India. I liked nasturtiums. I would lie in the garden with my ear to the ground and my glasses off so that I could see the flowers moving on their transparent, fragile stems, still shining from the previous night's storm. Backlit in the morning light, the stems were in perfect focus if I got them within an inch of my eye. I even tried doing a watercolor painting of them. Their unpredictable curves challenged my emerging sense of perspective.

I showed my painting to my grandmother over afternoon tea in our brand new cream-and-green kitchen with its nasturtium-printed curtains. Nan usually came for tea when my father was not home. She thought the painting very good and asked if she could borrow it. Next time she came for tea, she had two parcels. The first was for my mother. Nan had had my nasturtium painting framed in a little gold frame. My mother had trouble deciding where to put it; she said she couldn't find a place where it quite belonged. Out of loyalty—whether to Nan or to me or to her own relenting aesthetic—she hung it in the laundry room. The other parcel was for me: an early birthday present, Nan said. It was an expensive, French, bisque-headed ballerina doll with a pale-blue net outfit, real leather ballet pumps, and real hair. She came with a name, which was Celeste. Nan showed me all the ways her arms and legs moved.

I hugged Nan, thanked her very much, and then said, "Her head doesn't come off, does it?"

"Why would you want the head to come off?" Nan asked, glancing at my mother. Mamma looked back at Nan apologetically and then turned her eyes toward me with a slight raise of her eyebrows: a warning.

I remembered the lesson I'd learned on Nan's backstairs—the one about the dangers of being truthful.

"I just wanted to make sure I didn't hurt her," I lied. "She's beautiful and I can even comb her hair with my good brush like Mamma's."

Nan smiled, my mother smiled, I smiled, and then we had tea and biscuits with Celeste. Just before my father arrived from work, Nan took a taxi home.

Mamma suggested I put Celeste in my closet before my father walked in the door so he wouldn't think I liked Nan's doll better than ones I'd been given by my other grandmother. Celeste led a sheltered life from then on—except when Nan was around. Celeste's hair, however, eventually fell out from my brushing it so often.

SIX

STAYING OVERNIGHT

After she cooked me crisp bacon, eggs fried in butter with the yellow broken the way I liked best, and hot buttered toast—serving it all to me in bed—my father's mother helped me with my bath and then told me to come with her to her bedroom. She had not done this before. I was staying two nights in my father's old room. It was between what used to be the main bedroom, now my grandmother's bedroom, and my aunt's old room, now my grandfather's.

My grandfather slept in that bedroom because he was a light sleeper due to slowly worsening illnesses from the Great War. It was originally a verandah. His large desk, with pencils and papers neatly lined up, was below the window. He would let me sit there and draw while he silently came in and out, sharpening HB pencil after HB pencil for me.

I followed the firm march of Gran's high heels on the wooden floor past the pianola, which was pressed against the living room wall, and into her dimmed bedroom. The curtains were always drawn against impossible visual intrusion by a passerby a storey below. The furniture was dark and solid—inlaid, colonial furniture that smelled of mothballs, lavender, and polish.

Gran led me to a cabinet by the right side of the bed. Nailed to the wall above the cabinet was a two-foot-tall, oval-framed, sepia photograph of my grandfather in his Australian Flying Corps uniform. He stood trim and elegant, wearing leather leggings, hands behind his back.

I was being raised Presbyterian, so this photograph was the closest thing to an icon I had seen and it affected me the same way an icon might. When my grandmother was downstairs washing clothes in the copper basin, I would sneak into her bedroom and stare up at the young spirit of my grandfather, knowing that he understood things I could never understand.

Everything in my grandmother's bedroom held a slight sense of the regal to me, really. Things sacred were suspect to Presbyterians, so I thought of most of her possessions as more regal than sacred—the polished dressing table; the shining crystal boxes holding her good jewelry, which was all too big for me except for the brooches; ironed, starched, linen gifts from Home, which is what she always called Edinburgh; and mementos from her overseas holidays, including engraved silver spoons bearing crests of cities and towns. These spoons would sit in her saucer, ready to stir yet another cup of tea she would have made for herself.

The cabinet itself was around four feet tall, so it was taller than I. With her groomed, arthritic hands, my grandmother opened the cabinet. She pulled out a drawer that housed a neat arrangement of odd things—letters, papers, handkerchiefs. Her corseted torso was so close that I could see the shadows of the corset's vertical bones move slightly as she retrieved a large envelope.

On the previous morning, she'd come into my dim room and sat down on my single bed. Then, lying back, she'd shown me how one should pour one's white flesh into the back of a corset and, taking advantage of gravity, tightly lace the pink hooks in front. She'd said she was teaching me this now so I would know how to do it later.

    I'd thanked her and, once she'd stood up and adjusted her silk dress in the tall mirror on the front of the closet, explained to her that girls didn't wear corsets any more. She was indignant and said we would be hussies if we didn't. I dropped the subject. I never knew when her view of the world and mine would slip out of gear. In fact, our worlds were rarely in gear, only occasionally meeting in the kitchen or later, over the quality of clothing. The last time I had felt at ease with Gran was when I was still small enough to slide from her knees down her well-shaped, heavily stockinged legs and land on her plump feet in their high heels. She never wore anything but high heels, and good ones at that, because, she'd said, she had never worn anything else for thirty years, even when she was a General's secretary in Edinburgh during the Great War, and she declared that it was too late now to wear anything else.

    Gran sifted through the envelopes and flat things in the cabinet and then handed me a photograph in an embossed grey folder. I opened it reverently. It was a large, dark sepia studio portrait of a pretty baby lying on a velvet pillow. The baby wore a beautifully embroidered robe that fell away from its covered toes. Because the photograph was sepia, the white robe appeared to be the color of weak tea. The baby looked serious as it lay with a small hand curled toward its face. Its large, dark eyes peered solemnly into mine. I knew I was being shown something sacred, like the nearby portrait of my grandfather.

    I could hear Granddad walking slowly down the back stairs. I knew he would be going to the chicken coop, where he would collect eggs and strawberries. I wished I were out in the early morning spring light with him and Chang, his shih tzu, whose thick coat I brushed religiously every day and whose back I adorned regularly with all the ribbons he and Granddad had won. I wanted to be sitting with Granddad and Chang under the mango tree in silence while he peeled me transparent green grape after green grape. But I knew I was supposed to want to be with my grandmother. I had already been in trouble this visit because, when she asked me whom I would like to give me my bath, I had answered, "Granddad."

I looked long and hard at the photograph of the baby. I knew I was supposed to say something but I didn't know what. I thought hard. If I said the baby was pretty and it turned out to be a boy, I would sound rude. If I said the dress was lovely, Gran might be upset because I was saying something about the dress and not about the baby. Why was she acting as though I were the only one in the world to see this photo? What would my mother tell me to say? She was on the other side of town waiting for my father to pick me up. He had said he'd pick me up this evening after the officer's reunion. He would be wearing his dress uniform: white jacket, cummerbund, long set of miniature medals. Of all the things he wore—his lab jacket, his church suits, his navy sports jacket, his formal dinner suit that he wore to balls with my mother—this was my favorite.

My grandmother's voice dropped heavily and proudly on my head. "That's your father. On his christening day in Edinburgh."

So it was a boy. Knowing this made things easier. I could say something about this beautiful, serious baby wearing a long dress and supposed to be my father. The name of the studio was embossed on the deep sepia of the image. "He looks like a little Aboriginal baby," I said brightly, trying to be as polite and observant as I could. I thought little Aboriginal babies were very nice looking and I wanted to say something really appreciative and original because it was my father.

My grandmother snatched the photograph from my small hands and snapped, "Don't ever say that again. You don't deserve your father."

"I said he *looked* like, Gran. Not that he *was*." Long practice in getting out of trouble I'd not expected had honed my skills.

"Just because *one* of your grandfather's people turned out to be not from Home doesn't mean your grandfather and father weren't as good as anyone else." Gran's Scots accent made the word "people" unfamiliar and part of a world I knew I must not enter. "Granddad was fighting in France. My cousin used to bring him up to Scotland on leave. We were married at our family church and had a little holiday on Mull. A year later, your father was born. Your grandfather got leave for the christening.

"My father would have given him work but Granddad wanted us to live in Australia. I didn't know about his mother until I arrived. It was a shock, I can tell you. I never told my family she was Greek. No need to upset them. And at least she wasn't Roman Catholic. She was a good person even if she wasn't from Home— and she spoke the King's English perfectly. She and I got on. She knew what it was like to be new to a country, to have to raise children here. I told your father and aunt that even though they had one grandparent who wasn't British, they were just as good as everyone else." She said this with an injured flourish and placed the portrait indignantly in the drawer, underneath a stiffly ironed, linen handkerchief sachet embroidered with heather.

She walked me firmly out of her room, saying she had to start the washing before putting on the roast. She and my grandfather often prepared food together. They were each off doing different things a lot but when they were together, they laughed a lot even though they didn't talk about anything in particular.

I knew I would not see that photograph again and so I tried to fix it in my mind. I knew it would become one of my first dark secrets, and precious.

I heard Granddad coming up the stairs. I didn't want to go down with Gran to do the washing but I knew I'd better not upset her further by going into the kitchen with Granddad while he washed the eggs and strawberries, so I went to the pianola in the living room. I put in the one pianola roll that still lived in the piano stool, stood at the keyboard, and held on with both hands to the wooden piano frame. I pedaled and the broken yellow keys moved up and down by themselves while the burnished metal turned slowly, playing a waltz.

SEVEN

....

THE NEW HOUSE

We'd been building it for two years—the new house, I mean. It was on a steep hillside overlooking the town. We had been renting a house on a nearby hill but it wasn't ours. This new house was ours. I say "ours." Of course, I didn't have anything to do with it other than moving into it.

Our house was on the East Side, which was close to Nan, which was not close to Gran and Granddad. This was a source of ongoing tension. The river that ran through the town also divided the family camps. To build on the East Side was to risk being perceived as having chosen my mother's family over my father's, even though my father talked with his parents daily and we went there weekly.

If we went to Gran and Granddad's for Sunday lunch, we would drive over the Blamey Bridge, up another hill, and turn right. The house was halfway up yet another the hill. The whole town was hilly.

Gran, my father's mother, would cook a roast for us, although sometimes we'd just go to Gran and Granddad's for tea mid-afternoon if Nan had come to our place for lunch. If we went to Gran and Granddad's for lunch, Granddad would start the roast and potatoes while Gran was at church and Gran would do the rest of the trappings when she got home. My father and I went to a different church from Gran. Granddad didn't go. Mamma didn't go. Nan didn't go. When he was alive, Grandpapa, my Russian one, didn't go either.

If we went to Gran's for Sunday lunch, it meant we wouldn't see Nan on Sunday. As we'd cross the bridge, the tension would rise. My mother would gaze out the window in silence. I'd sit in the back and watch the grey struts on the bridge fly by in the depressing midday light.

Sometimes we took our shih tzu, Little Chang, to visit with Granddad's shih tzu, Big Chang. Sometimes we didn't take him. The days we took him were the best. He would sit in the back seat with me. Chang was the only sibling I had and he was a pretty good one. He didn't talk back and he'd settle his shih tzu fluff down the length of my leg. Being only eight, I was not yet allowed to shave and my legs had lots of blonde hair. In summer, Chang would lie beside me, alternating between panting and licking the sweat off my legs. We would drive with all the windows down, and Chang and I would both put our faces out the window eventually to get cool. In winter, Chang would lie right on my lap and keep me warm. The car was neither air-conditioned nor well heated. It was too early for those luxuries.

When we arrived, we would park in front and climb up the front stairs. Gran would be standing at the top step with the left side of the latticed double-door open. She was always in one of her well-made dresses or suits, a corset (I could feel it through the material), stockings (attached to the corset) and high heels.

She wore navy in winter, turquoise in summer, and her hair was always set. Later in life, it turned pale blue every time she went to the hairdresser. It didn't move an inch, unless after lunch she would let me brush the hairspray out and play with her natural curls while I sat on her ample, firm lap.

Regardless of whether the temperature was chilly or boiling, lunch was always a baked dinner: a leg of lamb; potatoes baked with the lamb until they were crisp, crackly, and brown; gravy, and peas. I could have done without the peas and neither Gran nor Granddad, who usually did the carving and remembered lots of things I liked, ever remembered that I hated, I mean, really hated fat. It made me dry-retch the same way the squiggly part of the egg did. Even seeing fat made my throat go funny. I would cast my mother a look across the table because I knew that she knew how I was feeling.

I knew my mother didn't want to be there. She liked Granddad but didn't like Gran really. Gran was a dutiful mother-in-law. She did all the right things: she gave my mother gifts on birthdays and Christmas and would ask after Nan, whom she would always refer to as "your mother." But the personal didn't extend beyond this.

My parents had lived with Gran and Granddad for a few months ages ago before I was born. They told me they had been looking for a better cottage to rent before I arrived. My mother did not share my Scots grandmother's love for and strict order of home care—one day for washing, one for ironing, one for cleaning, and so on throughout the week. She must have said as much in a private letter to her personal physician. Personal physicians were the closest thing our town had to psychiatrists then. I don't have my mother's letter but she kept the doctor's reply in its long envelope in the back of one of her bottom drawers until she died. The doctor had replied to my mother in elegant handwriting saying that my mother was a free spirit and nothing could extinguish that.

Gran and Granddad had a piano that didn't stay in tune, which also probably bothered my mother. I never found any articles or reviews she wrote for the paper or magazines during the time she was living with them so I'm guessing that keeping up with Gran's housekeeping schedule was not exactly inspiring for her and her beloved typewriter. I'm also guessing she wasn't too keen on living temporarily farther from her parents. A few rental houses later and after Grandpapa died, my parents and I moved in with Nan for two years.

We had appointed seats for meals at Gran and Granddad's oval dining table, which was always laid with a freshly starched, spotless, damask tablecloth. The clock on the mantelpiece ran around itself like a golden bird in a glass dome. Clockwise, counterclockwise, clockwise, counterclockwise. I learned years later that it was called an anniversary clock. Possibly Granddad bought it for Gran on a wedding anniversary. He really loved her. I couldn't quite see why. She really loved him, too. I could easily see why.

My grandparents seated me opposite the dining room windows. The windows overlooked the back garden and their lower panes were of colored, mottled glass. In summer, the windows were left wide open even when there was no breeze. Behind me, the living room, which opened into the dining room, was kept dim in summer. Its French doors opened onto a shuttered verandah on two sides, but Gran, being a Scot, shut the French doors and pulled dark green velvet curtains against the heat. From my seat at the dining table, I could see a bit of the great mango tree that shaded the garden and under which Granddad often sat on a wooden stool. Not talking or doing anything. Just sitting. He was a still man, even during his increasingly frequent illnesses.

When he had first become ill, Granddad had moved to my aunt's old bedroom. When my aunt had married and moved to Adelaide years ago, my grandparents had left the room empty other than when an overseas relative was visiting or when more than one grandchild was staying. Whenever Granddad was ill, he moved into the room. It opened onto the dining room so we could see him in his ironed, striped pajamas, lying on starched sheets and pillowcases. Granddad was never hungry. He would lie quietly and look out the window at the mango tree and down the back garden to his chicken coop and the sweet pea trellis he had constructed. If he were well, he would sit at the end of the dining table closest to the bedroom. Gran sat at the other end.

Gran would always ask my father to say grace because it was Sunday. Sometimes my father would then ask me. It was not really a question; it was an honor, whose refusal would have broken the clock's glass dome. I didn't like saying grace. It sounded soppy. I had to make my voice sound as though I meant it when I didn't. It wasn't that I was ungrateful to God or didn't—at that stage anyway—believe in God. And I did feel grateful. I just would have preferred to thank Gran and Granddad for the meal. After all, they were the ones who'd gone to all the trouble—and we usually did thank them too, of course, later. It was just that I felt odd thanking God on cue and I knew I needed to keep this feeling secret from Gran. This got complex: in some vague way, I suppose I felt grateful to God; yet I didn't want to show my true feelings of gratitude to God in front of Gran so I had to shut down my real gratitude but make my words sound like real gratitude.

Sunday lunch, being formal, always included dessert—something with homemade custard or a freshly baked, still warm apple tart. My grandmother was a fine traditional cook. After lunch, I would be allowed to either wash dishes in the single sink in the kitchen or dry them and put them on the kitchen table. Later, Granddad would put them away in the kitchen china cabinet if we'd used the kitchen china or the cabinet under the clock if we'd used better china. After all the work was done, Granddad would either lie down or go downstairs where I could follow and watch him.

If it was sweet pea season, Gran would ask Granddad to cut masses of sweet peas for us to take home. I would hold them as Granddad cut them. We could hear the children next door playing and the family on the other side putting away their Sunday dishes.

When it came time to leave, Gran would kiss us each and say, "Take care of yourself." This presented another tricky situation. My grandmother liked to kiss on the lips, even when she or we had colds. "I don't worry about such things," she would say with a slight Scottish burr of dismissal. Even when no one had a cold, my mother, being sure she would Catch Something, never kissed anyone on the lips, even my father. My father, although well aware of germ theory, allowed feeling to override health precautions in the kissing department and expected both my mother and me to accept my grandmother's quick, slightly-wet-at-the-corners kiss on the mouth.

"I wish Gran wouldn't kiss on the mouth," my mother would whisper later to me and I would agree. I didn't like the spit bit and I would follow my mother's example by secretly wiping my mouth as we walked down the stairs behind my father. It didn't do any good but it somehow felt as though it did. My mother was a great one for undoing things, particularly imperfections and wrongs. She specialized in her own, my father's, and mine. These errors were equaled only by the great number of things she thought actually needed doing. Her sense of Right and Justice was unbending and fiercely logical. My Scottish grandmother was rarely logical but was always convinced she was right. The two were not well matched.

As we left, we would wave out the car window until we turned the corner. Afterwards, my father would often get quiet. This was dangerous. On the many drives we took over the bridge from the East to the West Side, I had observed that there were only a few reasons he would get quiet. I would run through them all: he was feeling unwell, having eaten more than he wanted in an effort to please his mother, who always said, "Have some more, Michael"; he had glimpsed either my mother or me wiping our mouths and was hurt on his mother's behalf; he was worried about my grandfather's increasing periods of ill health; he was worried about something at the lab; he was upset about some offense my mother had unwittingly committed (she did go to considerable lengths to be Good but sometimes Logic got the better of her); he was upset about something I had done (brushing the dogs with Granddad instead of talking more with Gran); or—and this was most often the case—he was, without really knowing it, sad because we were driving to the East Side—to where he was living in the enemy camp, to where my mother's family had won, to where he was now committed to live forever because our new house on the East side was almost finished. None of these reasons made for a great Sunday afternoon. The unspoken hung in the air, like a cloud of Granddad's cigarette smoke, on the ride home. It even hung afterwards, when we walked up the gritty driveway and through the dark front door of that last rental house. My father's jaw would look dark and heavy. It looked like tiredness to me but he would bridle if my mother suggested he might be tired. In his estimation, he was never tired; if he bridled, my mother's already slightly rounded shoulders would sag, because she was sure "it"—whatever "it" was—was her fault.

I would go to my room. Its twin beds had headboards with a stubbly paint finish, which I both liked and disliked. Most of the furniture came with the rental.

If my father had a nap, the pall might lift a little. Sometimes late in the afternoon, he would wake on the couch in the sunroom and wearily offer to pick up Nan, should my mother wish to invite her to come for a quick supper. My mother would brighten and ring Nan.

Then my father and I would get in the car and drive the six minutes it took to get to Nan's house. The new house we were building would only be four minutes from Nan's. My father predicted Nan would be "in our pockets" day and night. My mother would get hurt when he said that and say it wasn't Fair. She would consult her diary or one of her many neat lists and read out loud who had visited whom when. But these were times when my father's unexpressed logic strongly resembled his mother's, so my mother's wounded tone and attempts at using facts to make his mood disappear were lost on him.

I often thought my mother had a rather good point but it was not in my best interest to say this. I would wait to say it until after my father had left the next morning for work and I was racing to get my school uniform on so I could catch the bus. When we moved into the new house, I would have further to walk home for a couple of years. Then I was to attend the same private school my mother had attended.

One evening, after my father got home from the lab, we went to a furniture maker. He had drawings of the furniture we were having made for our new house. His drawings were almost as good as Nan's. He asked me what sort of dressing table I would like. I knew exactly what I would like: a long mirror in the middle and two sets of three drawers on each side. My idea didn't resemble Gran's dark dressing table (with its crystal always clean and shining in her dark bedroom); nor did it look like Nan's dark dressing table (on which scattered face powder was often noticeable in the late afternoon sun).

With a special light hanging over his head, the furniture maker drew exactly what I wanted. I loved watching him make my words come to life on the thin paper. I felt important and special. That night my parents approved the drawings of the furniture for their bedroom, my bedroom, the guest bedroom, living room, dining room, and kitchen, including standing lamps and kitchen chairs. Everything.

"It's not every girl who gets to have her furniture made, you know, Meggers."

"I know, Daddy," I replied. I didn't know until he said it but knowing made me feel even more special.

"I don't think they're quite as good as Mehler," my mother commented idly on the way home.

"They're the best around," my father countered, taken aback at her not fully sharing his excitement. "Mehler was in his prime when your parents used him. But Mehler passed his expertise on to this lot before he sold out."

"I didn't mean to sound unappreciative. You *are* giving us the best available. I do appreciate that, Michael. The furniture will be lovely. Oh dear. I'm in trouble again. I was simply saying they don't have *quite* Mehler's touch. I looked around at some finished pieces and they're ... heavier. I wasn't implying I didn't like what we're getting or that I'm not appreciative of all you are doing, Michael. I was just thinking aloud really ... about proportion and things. You know what a stickler I am for proportion. Even the grandfather clock at Mother's—the case Mehler built for Daddy—somehow has delicate lines and good proportions." She sighed. "I never seem to say the right thing. I'm always getting into hot water."

"You are not in hot water. I just want to please you and give you and Meg the best. Even your father said, 'Do it well, do it once.' The furniture is taking a substantial bite out of the building account."

While they talked back and forth in the front seat on the way back to our rental house, I closed my eyes and imagined what my room would look like. I had already been allowed to choose the ice blue wallpaper and dusty blue carpet that eventually would cover the polished wooden floors.

When the time came, we packed up our belongings from the rental house in preparation for the move. The house didn't look very different after we packed from how it looked when we moved in, except the nasturtiums that my mother had planted in front and back were blooming wildly and the red-and-white checkered half-curtains she had made to cheer up the kitchen still hung from their rods.

I wasn't sorry to leave that house. The best things about it had been building Mount Everest out of clay in the back garden with my mother and listening to "The Children's Hour" on the large, varnished radio that stood in a dark corner of the living room.

In the new house, the boxes were piled as high as I was tall. I thought it was fun to wander through the passages between them. My parents didn't find the boxes as much fun as I did. All the stuff in them had to find a home in the house's modern, built-in closets or in the new furniture. Unfortunately, the architect had not consulted my parents about how many drawers were needed in the closets, forgotten that I was still a small child, and forgotten that my mother was short. What didn't fit in the closets went in the garage.

Two weeks before we moved in, the furniture arrived. It was beautiful. Seats and backs were covered in tapestry; solid wood arms gleamed with new stain and the sides of the arms were woven with cane. A few days after we moved in, my mother unearthed her typewriter from one of the piles of boxes; she had an article due. A month later, her piano finally emerged, triumphant, from behind another wall of boxes. Eager to practice, she resumed playing scales and her classical repertoire in earnest. The piano sounded different in the new house. The walls were plaster, so I couldn't hear her as well when I was falling asleep in my new, wide bed under my new blue and white Onkaparinga blankets in my new room far down the hall.

I loved my room with its view of the hills. Every bit of it was mine. My room at Nan's had been my mother's and a bit tired looking; my room at the rental house had been spacious but ugly. My new room was my design, from the carpet to the wallpaper to the furniture. I would lie on my new feather pillow and hold up a mirror as I spread my long hair across the white pillowcase my mother had pressed on her ironing machine—a circular thing she fed weekly with sheets, pillowcases, tea towels, handkerchiefs, and tablecloths. I'd also spend a lot of time looking at myself in my new full-length mirror, lining the drawers on each side of the mirror with blue and white paper, and arranging and rearranging the drawers.

Once we had fully moved in, my parents thought we should have all three grandparents over for a baked dinner. At least, that's what my father must have suggested; cooking never brought my mother the pleasure it brought her mother-in-law.

The piano Nan had given my mother and the television Gran and Granddad had bought us with an unexpected legacy were both arranged in the living room together with the new Mehler furniture and floor lamps. The kitchen, with its ivy and nasturtium theme, was organized in preparation for our first baked dinner.

But as the big day arrived, we were still arranging and rearranging the dining room. The architect had forgotten that people actually walk around in houses; the dining room, being only three-sided, couldn't help but function as a throughway from the verandah to the kitchen so the furniture was constantly being arranged to provide for dining and moving around. My mother, able to prepare dinner parties only in private, didn't feel protected enough with nothing more than a frosted-glass sliding door between kitchen and dining room to mask her silently panicked preparations, devoted but bored cooking, and frequent cigarette breaks away from the public eye.

While my mother cooked, my father lugged the last boxes, now stacked neatly in the garage, up onto the verandah. Being on a hill also meant a lot of up and down. Each box was marked "DINING/LIVING ROOM." He carefully unpacked them.

Out came the two chiming mantelpiece clocks. They were almost identical. Each had been a wedding present from a set of parents. My father valued the clock his parents had given him because it had cost them more than he thought they could reasonably afford. Although my grandfather had kept his government post throughout the Great Depression, my father remembered both their necessary and self-imposed privations during those years. I remember noticing that jewelry belonging to my father's parents—jewelry in their early photographs—was no longer around.

My mother's family had not been seriously affected by the Depression. In fact, her father's business interests had paid handsomely. My mother cleaved to the clock her parents had given her not because her father had sacrificed for it or even for aesthetic reasons, but out of fear that Nan would see her as disloyal, in thought if not in deed, if she did not cherish it.

In the rental house, this war had been avoided by placing one clock on the sideboard in the dining room and the other on the sideboard in the living room. Both had a place. Because Nan and my father's parents never visited at the same time, we avoided all faux pas by switching clocks between the two rooms depending on who was coming for dinner, ensuring the right clock sat in the place of higher honor in the dining room.

The dining room of our new house featured a china cabinet made by Mehler's successors. It had a mirror, a secret drawer to hide things, and a special space on top for a mantelpiece clock. There was no sideboard or appropriate space for a clock in the living room. After my father unpacked the two clocks, he placed them on a table on the veranda. There they sat forlorn and silent, waiting for someone to begin the battle.

"You need to decide about the clocks, Lucy," my father said to my mother. "You're the woman of the house."

"Whichever I choose will hurt someone's feelings. I'm trying to get the timing for the different parts of the meal just right. You'll have to decide."

"Why don't the clocks take turns, the way they did in the old house?" I suggested. I was taking a big risk by chiming in but my parents seemed to be missing the obvious.

"Not a bad idea, Meg," my father said brightly. It was one of the few times he ever gave me credit for a good idea.

"Which goes first and which goes second?" my mother asked.

"Lucy, at least you could decide this! Decorating the house is your department, not mine!" my father expostulated.

"If you insist on my making the decision," she replied, "it should be strictly objective. We could toss a coin. I could, however, take my life in my hands and point out that when they arrive today, your mother will arrive with your father; Mother will arrive alone. Logically, it seems fair that the clock she and Daddy gave us has first turn." My mother, now afraid to look at my father, turned away and went back to the kitchen, sliding the frosted glass door half closed behind her and saying, "My back is hurting. I have to sit down." She lit a cigarette and started a crossword.

Silence.

"Do you agree?" my mother called out to my father who was still on the verandah.

"I heard." My father crumpled up the newspapers that had been wrapped lovingly around the orphan clocks.

"Do you agree?"

"Whatever you want, Lucy. Whatever you want."

"You're cross."

"I'm not cross."

"You are."

I decided I would go and shine the mirror on my new dressing table. I slipped out of my parents' view, found an old pair of my cotton underpants, and started to clean the mirror carefully.

"Luce," my father said tiredly, "we're living near your mother. My work is near your mother. Your mother's been here every other day since we moved in. I don't think she's exactly getting the short end of the stick."

I peeked my head out the door of my bedroom. The new house afforded spying points different from those in the rental house. Looking one way, I could see half of the kitchen; looking the other way, I could see through the dining room to the verandah. My mother was stubbing out her cigarette early. I could tell she was about to consult her library of diaries on the bottom shelf of the linen closet to count how often Nan had visited since we had moved in.

My father must have sensed this because he said, "I don't have time for diaries now. I just know I've worked day and night to build this house for you and Meg and to give you the things your parents—and I—wanted you to have."

"Put your parents' clock up," my mother replied from the innards of the linen closet.

"I've put the other up."

"I said, put your parents' up," my mother countered.

"The matter's closed. I'm taking the boxes downstairs. Meg, help your mother finish up. Everyone will be here soon."

I went into the kitchen. My mother was sitting looking crestfallen at the kitchen table with the white laminate top that the lesser Mehlers had made. It was two inches too high for her. The chairs were also too high, so she used a footstool.

"What did I do wrong?" She looked at me, empty, despairing. "I was just trying to be fair and objective."

"Nothing, Mamma," I lied.

My mother got the cut linen out of the linen closet. Even at eight, I was a good ironer, so I ironed the back of each mat to make its grey embroidery stand out against the heavy linen. I laid the silver on the table, just as I had been taught.

My father went to pick up Nan, who didn't drive. In the meantime, Granddad and Gran arrived. I went to the door to greet them. My mother was still "powdering her nose," as Nan called it.

"Close the toilet door!" my mother called out to me when the doorbell rang. (The architect had put the toilet at the end of the long hall, so when the door was inadvertently left open, the view from the living room was of a distant white toilet.) I ran down the hall, slammed the toilet door, and ran to the front door. Gran was wearing a turquoise and green dress and white shoes. Her hair had been freshly set at the hairdresser. Granddad was in a sports coat and tie and his perennial, crisp, grey pants.

Gran handed me a large box that held a newly minted sponge cake. She bent down and gave me a kiss on the lips. It left a slight, wet spot. She had a little crack on one side of her mouth, which my father said had something to do with vitamins. I resisted the urge to wipe my mouth. I thanked her for the cake and put it down carefully on the white wicker table on the verandah. Then I hugged my grandfather.

"Can you spare one of those for your grandmother?" Gran asked, offended.

"Of course, Gran. I was just coming." I was an expert dissembler. "I couldn't hug you when I had your lovely smelling cake in my hands." I gave her a hug, aimed to have just the same firmness as the one I had given my grandfather, but this was hard to gauge because he was a small, trim man and she, a large, corseted woman.

"Please come in and put your things down," I said politely.

"I want to look around first," my grandmother declared. "It's not every day your father builds a new home and your mother cooks a meal for us. Where *is* your father?"

"Picking up Nan."

Silence. I knew what she thought of that statement.

My mother emerged. Politeness overcame her phobia about my grandmother's damp kiss and then she hugged my grandfather lightly. She showed them around the verandah, which was furnished with white wicker and green and white canvas. She took them into the living room making sure to show them the television they had given us. Then she showed them my parents' bedroom with its two ample beds and silk bedspreads. They admired the view of the hills out the window.

Then it was time for the dining room.

My mother grew visibly smaller as we entered it. "Look, Gran," I said, "we put the crystal ashtray you and Granddad gave Mamma and Dad for Christmas over here on the drink cabinet." I was hoping to steer her away from the obvious. She glanced briefly at the drink cabinet—its very existence an affront to her Scots Presbyterian nature—then turned her attention to the place mats.

"Are these the ones Ailsa sent from Scotland?" she asked my mother as my grandfather wandered over to the sideboard.

"Yes," my mother said with relief. "They're so delicately embroidered, aren't they?"

"Nice place for the clock," my grandfather said to my mother. Then he turned and walked briskly over to my grandmother before she could inspect anything else in the dining room. "Come along, Isobel—at this rate, we'll take all day." He took my grandmother's elbow in a way atypical of him and marched her into the kitchen while asking my mother, who was standing frozen in the dining room, to explain how the new-fangled stove worked.

We were seated on the verandah eating savories by the time my father returned with Nan. He supported her slow ascent from the car, letting her rest her bad feet on every third step. After she reached the final step, she let go of my father's hand, adjusted her expensive navy handbag on her good arm, and straightened her navy and white silk dress over her corset. "Everyone's at the trough and I'm still in the paddock," she said. "Hello, Isobel. Hello, Charles. Long time. Meg, help me into your mother's room, would you."

I kissed Nan on the soft, powdered cheek she presented and took her bag to my parents' bedroom. I put it on one of the two beds with their traditional, beautifully woven spreads made of some French material my parents had ordered. Nan took a heavy compact embroidered with petit point out of the bag and put even more powder than usual on her nose.

"Nan, your glasses are smudgy again," I commented proprietarily.

"Doesn't matter today," she said dryly but handed them to me anyway. I got out one of my mother's ironed handkerchiefs, polished her glasses, and handed them back to her. I could hear my father taking his parents through the kitchen to the back garden, which was still awaiting landscaping and, years later, a pool. The back garden looked out at the hills.

Nan walked slowly out of the bedroom and up to the living room. She ignored the television. (She'd had one for some time.) She patted the piano and then looked up at the oil painting she had painted as a young woman. My mother had apologetically asked my father to hang it; he had thus far been reluctant to put many nails in the pristine plaster and wallpaper. After a pause, Nan said the painting would look better lower. Then she slowly made her way down the corridor to the dining room and stood looking at the china cabinet.

"Bloody awful clock," she said to me. " Alex and I never did like it but it was all we could find during the war. I'd hoped the movers would drop it by mistake when you moved."

"Nan! You and Grandpapa gave it to Mamma and Dad for their wedding! They would have been very upset if that had happened."

"Doesn't make it look any better. It's still ugly. But your mother's attached to it so I don't say anything. Maybe it'll break all by itself one day."

Lunch went off perfectly. It was the first of many meals hosted expertly (albeit reluctantly) by my mother at a table that suited no one. The furniture makers had forgotten that dining tables with folding parts needed decent spaces for legs. My mother and Nan, seated on one side, rested their short legs on carved bars that efficiently blocked access to the floor; Gran, whom my mother had seated together with Granddad on the other side of the table, simply put both of her long, stockinged legs over the bar. My father, at the head of the table, didn't notice where his legs were.

To my relief, my father said grace. Then he poured a tiny bit of sherry for Nan and my mother and added a little to Gran's glass. He and my grandfather had a snifter of Scotch and soda. My mother looked wistfully at the Scotch and thanked my father for her sherry. I had lemonade in a crystal water glass. We all toasted the new house, most of which I could see from where I sat. My mother had put me at the end, facing the mantelpiece clock.

EIGHT

....

THE JUMPER

It was just an outing to the Princess Margaret Gardens and Zoo in the middle of a subtropical winter. Yet it had been discussed in the two fourth-grade classes for weeks. Roneoed letters in smudged purple print had been sent to each family and returned obediently by each student thus avoiding being sent to the headmaster's office for a caning. Each level had an annual outing on a bus hired for the day. Most of us had been to the gardens and the zoo lots of times but having the day off from school to go as a group in a smelly bus was special.

On the purple sheets sent to our parents (we all had two parents and if someone didn't, we rarely knew) was a paragraph explaining that pupils were to bring their lunches and wear either school uniform (optional in our elementary school) or "clothing appropriate to a town outing." There were no chaperones, only teachers accompanying us. Mothers neither worked nor volunteered then, which suited my mother very well.

The day before the outing, my father loaned me his old war camera and taught me how to use it. My mother examined my clothes, both the ones hanging in my wardrobe and the ones folded in my drawers. She said I could wear my good green long-sleeved, woolen jumper with its embroidered trail of red, white, and blue edelweiss across the front, along with my dark green pleated skirt. The color looked good on my mother but did not, I discovered later, flatter me. However, at the time, I thought I looked good in it. It was a Nice Outfit.

Clothes were chosen for various reasons in our family, mostly reasons with political or artistic loading. Nan, my mother's mother, having married someone who made money quietly, spared no expense on clothes. She gave herself, my mother, and me imported clothes for birthdays and Christmas and sometimes between. This pleased my mother and disturbed my father.

Gran and Granddad had enough money but not lots. They had put much of my grandfather's earnings into private school fees for my father and aunt and into extended trips home to Scotland for Gran. She, too, had good taste and wore dateless outfits bought when visiting her family in Edinburgh. The daughter of an upstanding, Scottish merchant, Gran had grown up in quiet, respectable, Presbyterian ease. Her clothes in the studio portraits taken of her in Edinburgh before she married show her in suits falling gracefully from her then-slim frame. When she married her good-looking Australian in uniform on one of his leaves, she did not marry into money so she bought one good suit for winter and one good imported dress for summer the rest of her days. She wore these for special occasions: church and morning teas, for example. She wore lighter, locally produced dresses around the house and to places such as the butcher, baker, and corner grocery store. She wore heels, day and night. I don't think I ever saw her in a nightgown or slippers until she was slowly dying.

She and Granddad were not often able to buy me imported

clothes for birthdays the way Nan could—a fact my father saw not only as a reflection on his capacity to provide for his family but also as a threat to my appreciation of his mother. He needn't have worried; I never could make myself like Gran, despite Granddad's loving her and my loving Granddad. I did love Gran but in a generic, unquestioning way that came from the fact that she was my grandmother.

The clothes my mother and Nan chose for me were classical, well made, appropriate to the occasion—and, usually, capable of being Grown Into. Nan also designed and made beautiful clothes. She loved to create subtle, low-key sartorial effects in both daytime and formal evening wear for herself, my mother, and me. I loved dressing up in old dance costumes she had made for my mother when she was young or in odd clothing Nan had picked up on the family's trip around the world in '38, things like the black Japanese kimono with cherry blossoms, which I later turned into a full-length evening dress.

The Good Green Jumper, however, had not come from Nan; rather, it had been my mother's choice, a re-evocation of that trip around the world with her parents. On that trip, she had fallen in love with all things German, Austrian, and Swiss. She had decorated our colonial home with a few discreet Swiss things that were not easy to find in '50s Australia. We had a small cuckoo clock (confined to a corner near the kitchen table), a wooden coffee grinder (also confined to a kitchen shelf), a chalet music box my father had given my mother (confined to her bedroom side table), and geraniums galore (which grew in brick flower boxes that the builder had constructed around the verandah when our house was built).

With my father's blessing, my mother had ordered the Good

Green Jumper for me at Robertson's, our only high-quality department store. She had seen it there, fallen in love with it, and had it ordered *in my size* from one of the store's southern branches where the weather stayed colder for longer. So the jumper was unusual not only because of its design but also because *it fit* instead of being large enough for me to Grow Into.

Both my parents had decided to give it to me for my birthday, together with the latest hardcover novel in the Chalet School series whose dustcover showed the series' multinational boarding school students, in elegant clothes and mitts, flying on skates across the ice.

When the day of our outing to the zoo finally arrived, I was relieved because it was cool enough to wear my jumper. In the subtropics, this time of year could be steamy, hot, and rainy or dry, cold, and clear.

I arrived at school armed with my lunch box and my father's camera. I noticed that only two other girls, two boys, and I were not wearing school uniform. I quickly cast back to the purple letter we'd been given and remembered that we were, indeed, officially allowed to wear our own clothes.

As we climbed onto the bus, Miss O'Reilly, fresh from Dublin and unable yet to get a position at one of the parochial schools, snapped down at me, "We've got airs today, haven't we?"

I didn't think it was a question, so I didn't answer. I didn't know if I'd done something wrong but, from her tone, I knew I'd better be my most respectful self. I smiled up at her and said, "Good morning, Miss O'Reilly."

I saw her looking at the flowers on my sweater.

"They're edelweiss," I explained, pronouncing the "w" as a "v" as my mother had taught me. I pointed to the little trail of flowers wandering uninterrupted across my flat chest. Miss O'Reilly shrugged, gave me a little shove onto the bus and settled herself in the front seat beside Mr. Kent, the other fourth grade teacher. All the girls had a crush on Mr. Kent.

As we lurched our way into town, one boy in the back seat threw up on the floor and another peed in his pants. Several of the girls, in their depressing uniforms that suited no one but showed little dirt, pointed at me and began to giggle.

I wondered if I had something on the back of my jumper or skirt. When they weren't looking, I felt all over but could find nothing wrong.

Only my closest friends spoke to me that day and even they spoke with careful friendliness that made me uneasy.

Three of us had cameras and took photographs of the class in front of the aviary, in front of the koala enclosure, and in front of the kiosk where Miss O'Reilly and Mr. Kent each bought themselves a cup of tea and biscuits. Miss O'Reilly was wearing a pink jumper (the elbows bulged) and a brown skirt. It looked sad to me, that combination of colors, especially with her white skin, black hair, and sharp blue eyes.

It was only when Arlene walked past me in front of the century plant I was trying to photograph, pulled at my jumper, poked at the embroidery across the front, and caught her short fingernail in an edelweiss, that I understood. "Miss O'Reilly told Mr. Kent you're showing off with big words and hairs."

"Airs," I said automatically, just the way my mother corrected me. Then I wished that either Arlene or I were dead.

"See-e-e-e?" she replied. She started a whispering singsong campaign: "Muggy uses big words, Muggy uses big words."

At dinner that night, after relating at length the details of the bus trip, the century plant, and the koalas, all of which we as a family had seen many times, I finally said to my mother, "I got into trouble for what I had on."

"Darling, why on earth?"

"The edelweiss jumper."

"The letter said you could wear school uniform or something appropriate for a trip to town. What you had on was appropriate for a trip to town. At least, I thought so."

"Miss O'Reilly didn't know the word 'edelweiss.' She thought I had 'airs.'"

"I'm so sorry, darling. It's my fault. I feel terrible." She hugged me and started to cry a little. I hugged her back, told her only a couple of girls had been mean, and that I didn't care about Miss O'Reilly because I hated her.

I felt bad that I had ruined my mother's evening and my parents' birthday gift. As I hugged my mother, I privately resolved never to make her unhappy again, never to use words I hadn't learned in school, and never to forget, as she had, that foreign clothes and foreign words could change one's life.

NINE

....

QUEENIE

The Royal Theater was on Charles Street—and still is. It was regal. Its curlicues were painted antique gold. Dark red carpet lined the foyer and wide staircase.

My grandmother Nan was a devotee of the arts. She might have become someone or done something serious in the arts. However, she was a good-living Methodist who had lost her mother at eighteen, gone to live with a married sister and found herself designing clothes. She allowed her talents to overflow into any medium and onto anyone. She drew detailed pictures of fairies and elves in inks and traditional landscapes in oils. She colored black-and-white photographs by hand. She played the piano by ear and by vamping. (She made even made a vamp card for her piano and perfectly hand-colored it.) Until my mother could do it better, Nan accompanied my grandfather on his mandolin and balalaika, two of the few personal possessions, apart from family photographs he had brought with him from Russia. Some of the dance costumes Nan had made for my mother were still hanging around the house and I would occasionally dress up in them. Later, Nan would take my mother and me to almost every performance that came to the Royal.

Our town was not a raging metropolis. We experienced an uneven range of performances, all of which had the same effect on me: unless I was offered a contrary opinion, which I often was, I was impressed by anyone who stood before stage lights.

When Grandpapa died, he left Nan even better off than they had been, so we went to the theater in quiet style. We went to Saturday matinees. Nan, living further out, would pick us up in a National taxi (she trusted them more than Townwide and all the drivers knew her.) She would wear one of the outfits she had bought in one of the few international shops or Robertson's Imports Department down south when she visited her brothers or sisters: soft leather handbags, fine gloves, a fur in winter, suits tailored to fit exactly, and feather creations made by a milliner to match each outfit and to fit a thirties hairstyle she wore until a new hairdresser eventually updated her.

Nan was beautiful and pretty—not a frequent combination. She wore both qualities well. Having grown up during the Victorian era, she had an antipathy to the sun and used an umbrella in rain and sun. Even in her nineties, her skin was unblemished, soft, and fair. She carried an elegant black stick and had her black shoes for her misshapen feet made for her when she went south. I sometimes helped her into her shoes, maneuvering the soft, stretched leather around large bunions while she sucked in her breath. Her feet were a physical trial about which she rarely spoke. However, I knew when they were hurting because she would lean heavily on my arm as we walked at a pace so slow and stately that it made me ache.

Her first comment on those Saturdays when my mother and I hopped into the taxi (all seated in the back seat because it was too familiar to sit in the front with the driver) would be to tell my mother to put more powder on her nose. Nan didn't like shiny noses.

I would wear some simple, expensive, often imported creation usually bought by Nan. I'd wear it with white socks, black patent leather shoes, white gloves, and sometimes a hair band. In retrospect, neither the hair band nor my batwing glasses nor the bands on my teeth were flattering to my face or ears but I thought I looked quite good. My mother would wear a dress bought by Nan for her or made by one of the high-end dressmakers in our town. She would coordinate it with matching accessories in the spirit of the fifties.

My grandmother, tyrannized by and tyrannical about beauty, must have been disturbed by my body's uncoordinated evolution. I was awkward in pre-pubescence. My best feature was my wavy hair. Photographs taken by the obsequious man in the foyer of the theater were later carefully "improved" by Nan's artistic ideas. Those black-and-white photographs of one, two, and three of us were variously transformed under her touch: my hair lengthened, my eyes brightened behind my glasses, my hips thinned, my mother's hair tidied, Nan's own shoes reshaped and made almost indistinguishable from the carpet by India ink. Nan was a slave to proportion as well as beauty. My mother and I inherited the obsession.

When we arrived at the Royal, we would make slow progress in the program queue. The same middle-aged, stout woman—with her blonde hair and nasal tone—would call out "programs-two-and-six-pence-programs-two-and-six." We would inch forward, getting silently excited as we moved closer to her. Some of the audience bought a program for their group. Nan, however, bought one for each of us. I felt special and glamorous when she did that, although those theater photographs reflect more of my awkwardness than my feeling of glamor.

We usually had several pictures taken by the photographer assigned to the program line. He would later send them in large envelopes to Nan's house. We would then find our seats. They were always third row, center.

Nan would be surprised to know that, in my mind, my rapt experiences of most of the shows we saw over all those years almost blend into a single experience now, decades later. The foreign folk dancers who never moved a facial muscle and danced as though they were on skates mix with *Oklahoma* and the other musicals. I knew the songs to all those musicals.

Two performers who stood out for me were Queenie Paul and Marlene Dietrich. I had been told that one was well known and the other famous but I made no such distinction between the two. They both performed on the stage of the Royal Theater on a Saturday afternoon with me in the third row; that made them pretty much the same. Looking back on it, by the time Marlene Dietrich performed on the stage of the Royal Theater, she might have been on a par with Queenie Paul.

Marlene Dietrich was at least in her seventies when I saw her. She performed in her iconic, gold, see-through dress. Both of my grandmothers were in their seventies by then, so it was puzzling to me that Dietrich did not look as old as they did. I thought all older women had bad feet, large bosoms, thick corseted waists and hips, false teeth, glasses, and ineffective hearing aids. Marlene Dietrich did not seem to have any of these. She leaned against a post on the right side of the stage and, riveted to the spot by the shining dress, sang huskily "Falling in Love Again." The audience went wild.

Later, I went backstage and handed over my program to some man for her signature. When he brought it back to me, she had signed it in a scrawl across her photograph. Nan was impressed.

Queenie Paul was, according to my grandmother and the program notes, a vaudeville singer who had been on the Australian circuit for a million years. I remember only her large size and her yellow hair, which was what made me recognize her on Charles Street one day when I was in town shopping with my mother.

I jabbed my mother and whispered loudly, "That's the woman from the show!"

My mother looked over. "You're right. Queenie Paul."

"I wish I could get her to sign my autograph book."

"You could just tell her you've seen her performing and ask her politely," my mother suggested.

Queenie Paul was walking slowly down Charles Street. She had been sparkly on stage, so I was puzzled by how slowly she moved now, her large body swaying from side to side in a fuchsia dress without a waist. She seemed lonely, which I was sure she couldn't be given that she was famous.

"I couldn't," I replied. "I'd be embarrassed. I'd interrupt her."

"You'd probably please her if you did ask, darling."

By the time I edged my way up to her, she had stopped at the entrance to Robertson's and was lighting a cigarette. Everything happened at Robertson's.

"Excuse me," I said, using my best manners. "I'm sorry to bother you but are you Queenie Paul?"

I waited for something awful to happen. If I was right, she might find me a nuisance; and if I was wrong, she might find me a nuisance.

"Yes, ducks, the one and only."

"My grandmother and mother and I saw you in a show. I wonder if you would mind signing my autograph book?"

There. It was done. I had brazened my way into a famous person's life. I waited.

Queenie Paul looked down. I noticed that her hair was grey at the scalp and her face had a lot more lines in it than I could see from our third row center seats.

"Happy to, duckie," she answered. "Got a pen?"

I was surprised she didn't. Surely famous people carried a pen to sign autographs. I ran back to my mother who produced her fountain pen. I ran back to Queenie Paul and handed it up.

She dropped her cigarette on the footpath and stood on it, extinguishing it with one move of her flat, white sandal. Then she took my white leather autograph book, with its alternating pale pink, green, and yellow pages, and my mother's fountain pen. Thus far, I had obtained the signatures of my grandmothers, my grandfather, my mother, my father, three school friends, and an honorary aunt. Queenie Paul looked through for a spare page and then, holding the small book with one hand and writing with the other, she signed her name with a slow script.

I have forgotten her performance but I remember the signature. She made the Q with an internally spiraling curve. The last part of the Q faded into the bottom right of the page with a flourish. It took her a long time to make that Q.

I thanked her politely. She drew her shoulders back, shook my hand, and moved on slowly.

I looked at her dyed hair, backlit as she walked down Charles Street, and decided that Queenie Paul was a nicer famous person than Marlene Dietrich.

TEN

THE EGG SHELL

My mother sent me off every day with Little Lunch and Big Lunch in a box. For all of us, Little Lunch consisted of small bottles of milk handed out by the school and sweet biscuits sent with us by our mothers. We consumed it on the gravel playground, during a half-hour punctuated by violent activity. If we didn't bring Big Lunch, we could buy it at the tuck shop, which sold sausage rolls, tomato or slimy ham sandwiches, cream puffs, and jam rolls. Mostly, we ate foods our mothers prepared. I don't remember what our lunch boxes looked like but I remember the wax paper that my mother carefully folded around the colorful mix of little foods.

When we ate, my friends and I often straddled the four crossbeams under the landing of the outside staircase. People thundered above us. It was one of the few shady places to sit.

The first time my mother sent me to school with a boiled egg, I knocked the shell against the buff-colored beam and peeled it with my ink-stained fingers. My mother had made a salt-and-pepper mix and wrapped it in a tiny packet that unfolded neatly. I dipped the shiny oval in the black-and-white mix and then bit the egg at an angle so that none of the mix fell onto the gravel.

That night, I heard my parents raise their voices at each other once again. I was working at the wooden desk that had been Mamma's when she was in school. I was coloring a map of Australia, one I had drawn for the third time (the first two versions had ink spots that added non-existent islands to Australia's territory). When I heard my parents' voices, I got up and crept to the door of my bedroom. I kept my hand on my closet door so that, if one of them appeared, it would look as though I were getting something from the closet, not trying to hear them more clearly.

My mother was saying it wasn't her fault. My father was saying she was being lady of the manor-ish. A familiar argument.

I went back to my desk and worked some more on the map. We were only allowed to use Derwent colored pencil sets for school assignments. These had, in my opinion, feeble effects despite intense effort. I used the pencils to laboriously pepper the innards of the map with tiny, pale yellow, sheaves of wheat; tiny pale orange pineapples with tiny, half-dead-looking, green tops (both drawn with the so-called *dark* green and *bright* orange pencils); tiny, grey, merino sheep (done with the black pencil); and tiny, beige cattle (done with the dark brown). I took each blunt, colored pencil from the Derwent box, inserted it into my small metal sharpener, and twisted slowly. dropping each curl of wood into the waste paper basket. I tried hard not to make the pencils too sharp or too blunt. Too blunt and my little drawings would be fuzzy and would earn me a 6 out of 10. Too sharp and I risked breaking the pencils and needing to sharpen them again. This was undesirable because, when lined up, the pencils already looked like a gathering of mismatched people: some tall and elegant, some short and stubby. As I worked, I put each pencil away, point up, in the brightly colored cardboard box with its hole cut in the middle to show most of the colors. I arranged my pencils in rainbow order. Their outsides looked good—strong and bright—even if they made pale illustrations.

Finally, the voices from the other room stopped. My father came in and looked at my map. He said the little pictures were well done and then asked me if I had called his parents today.

I said that I had called them yesterday.

He picked up my map and put it down parallel to the edge of the desk. "There are two kinds of people in the world, Meg: givers and takers. If a giver marries a taker and both agree, it's alright. But if the giver gets tired of giving … " He looked out the window at the pawpaw tree. The crickets started up. "Don't forget to say your prayers. Good night, Miggles." He left.

A little later, my mother came in. She heard my prayer, "God-bless-Mamma-God-bless-Daddy-God-bless-Little-Chang-God-bless-everyone-I-love-Amen," and tucked me in, neatly folding the edge of the ironed sheet under the mattress. She read to me and then whispered in my ear as she reached to turn off the bedside lamp, "Daddy's upset again. He wants me to have another dinner party. He doesn't understand why I find it a strain." I hugged her and kissed her cheek before she adjusted the mosquito net and left.

After a few minutes, the voices rose again, this time over the sound of rain. I slipped out of bed and under the net, careful not to let any mozzies in. I tiptoed to the hall and peeked around the doorway.

I heard an odd, rhythmic noise. In the shadowed hall, beyond the sideboard where the clock ticked, my mother's fist moved back and forth against the wallpaper. Her knuckles banged in a steady, slow thud. She didn't miss a beat.

My father's voice was low and pleading. "Luce, stop please. You'll hurt yourself. Please stop. I didn't say you *never* have people. I also said your dinner party was so lovely last summer that you could even use the same menu because this is a different group. We do have to repay some of the dinners we attend, I'm afraid. But for now, please stop. We'll talk about it later. Just go and play the piano. Please."

There was silence. Then I heard my father shifting papers in his study. Eventually my mother began playing scales: the major, the minor, then the same scales with hands in opposite directions. If she made a single mistake, she'd start from the beginning again. While she was moving through the scales in opposite directions, I fell asleep.

The next day at Big Lunch and just before I'd finished eating, the other girls left our crossbeams first to play ball against the wall and then hopscotch and knuckles. All our grandparents had been enlisted to collect sheep's knuckles every Sunday roast lamb dinner until we each had five to use for the game. When I heard my friends running, crunching through the hot gravel close to the smelly rubbish bin, I eased myself down from the crossbeam, planning to join them.

It was then that I looked down at the remains of my Big Lunch. Cradled in the crumpled, salty wax paper lay the broken shell of the egg my mother had cooked for me that morning. At this moment, she would either be waiting for the cleaning lady, doing the ironing, making tea for my grandmother, fixing dinner, or practicing the Sibelius. She had explained to me yesterday about Sibelius and the harmony of the spheres. It had taken her longer than she expected to explain this because I didn't even know there *were* different spheres, let alone that a composer knew how they sounded when they were in harmony.

I looked at the eggshell. I couldn't throw it away. I felt as though I would be throwing away a piece of my mother. So I folded it in the wax paper and gently placed it in my lunch box to take home. My mother would have to throw it away.

ELEVEN

RED CORDUROY

Rainy days in winter were a boon. They gave my mother and me an excuse to stay inside. Blue skies and hot weather somehow requested one's enthusiastic presence at some as-yet-unplanned, open-air event. We felt like wet blankets or unhealthy if we wanted to refuse an event even before it had been planned.

Sometimes, during our short if often sharp winters, my mother and I would get out the large square of red corduroy from the linen closet and pretend we lived in a northern climate. We would lay the corduroy over the end of the dining table and I would do my homework there rather than in the kitchen or my bedroom. My mother associated that particular red with all things Swiss and I, too, came to think of it as Swiss. I found it easier to do my homework when I became Swiss.

One winter day, I was lifting up a wing of the dining table in preparation for spreading the red corduroy when I heard my mother's voice above my right shoulder. A small woman, she was still a head taller than I.

"Darling, what would you think if Daddy and I were to get a

divorce?"

I was just above eye level with the tabletop. I looked at the dust that was beginning to accumulate in the intricately carved edge of the table, which my parents would end up using for another fifty years, and considered my mother's question. I liked to look at the complicated pattern of the woodwork. I took off my glasses and started cleaning dust out of the patterned edge of the tabletop, using my fingertips with their bitten nails. My myopia allowed me to see close-up things perfectly.

Long trained to direct my antennae outward, I actually didn't know how I felt other than a little sick and fuzzy, as though I were trying to look at something far away and poorly lit without my thick-lensed glasses. I needed time to come up with a good answer; anything I thought of seemed risky.

"Where would you live and where would Daddy live?" I asked, while I tried to think about how to answer her question.

"I don't know yet. We'd have to talk about it."

I went back to cleaning out the dust. "I think it's up to you and Daddy. I would love both of you either way."

I rather wished the table were the big old radio at our earlier home, a tall thing into whose varnished wood I used to sink my two front teeth during scary radio serials without getting into trouble. There were no precedents for this scene in any of the stories in *School Friend's Annual.*

"Thank you, sweetheart. Let's just keep this conversation between us. Daddy would be rather upset if he knew I'd mentioned it to you."

"Yeah."

"Not 'Yeah,' darling. 'Yes.' I hope you don't mind my reminding you about 'yes.' One does get into verbal habits. They're like grooves. Every time one uses a word or phrase, the groove gets deeper. It's just as easy to carve a good groove. Then one doesn't have to think about it."

"Yeah—yes. I see what you mean, Mamma."

"Thank you, sweetheart. I think you'll find the effort worthwhile. Let's keep that other thing between us for now. I just wanted to know what you thought."

She touched my upper arm tentatively with her long, tapered fingers. Though she kept her nails short for typing and piano, she still had elegant fingers, a trait we did not share. When she dressed for a ball, she would slip rings that my grandparents and father had given her over long, white-kid gloves and her hands and arms would become the most beautiful in the world.

Sometimes, if my hands were clean, my mother would let me try on her evening gloves. My short, stubby fingers didn't fill them and the tips flopped around. She would let me try on the rings, too—diamonds and sapphires in delicate settings—if I did so over her dressing table and in her presence. She would take the rings out of a box in the top right drawer of her dressing table and place them on the crystal tray. I would kneel on her dressing table seat and lean over so I didn't risk dropping one.

"Remember not to put any ring on the fourth finger of your left hand, darling. It's supposed to be bad luck before you're married," she'd say. "I know it's superstitious but one never quite knows."

Once, during a ring session, Nan called. My mother went to answer the phone. I slipped several rings on the fourth finger of my left hand. And I instantly knew, all through my body, that now I would never get married. I also knew that I had casually taken an irrevocable step that would affect my future. I could never tell anyone. They would be aghast, broken-hearted, that I had taken fate into my hands and ruined it. By the time my mother returned, I had placed each ring separately over a symmetrical cut in the crystal tray. Each shone in the afternoon light.

After she had asked me the divorce question, Mamma's hand slowly wandered from my arm. She picked up the mail sitting on the dining table. Together we spread the red corduroy over the surface. I still had homework to do. Sitting at the dining table when it was covered with the red corduroy did help me do my homework because of the Swiss thing—and it was a good change from the kitchen table or my small desk overlooking the valley and hills.

I worked on learning Wordsworth by heart: "My heart leaps up when I behold ... "

Once I got it down cold, I moved on to Composition. The choices were "Nature," "Native Animals," and "A Weekend at the Beach." I chose the first and, careful to stay within the horizontal lines on the pages, I wrote, with a freshly sharpened pencil, a page titled "Sunset over the Range." I only had to erase once in the whole page—when I put a hyphen in the wrong place. I included a good sound effect in the composition: I said that a kookaburra laughed while the sun sank slowly over the mountains. I concluded with what I was sure was a highly original philosophical reflection on the beauty of nature.

Later, my teacher would write "9/10" in her neat, red pen and "Excellent" at the top of my paper. I would think it unfair that I lost a mark for erasing. Later, I would show it to Nan, who would borrow it and slowly type a copy on heavy paper with her long, slim forefingers. She would write "Meg - Nine Years Old" on a tag, pin it to the top of the paper with a sewing pin, and keep it in her scented handkerchief drawer for years.

After I finished "Sunset Over the Range," I moved on to Social Studies, learning the gauge of the railways in each state for tomorrow's test. I had finished by the time my father arrived home.

"Did Dad call?" he asked my mother over dinner.

"No, but your mother did. She asked us for lunch Sunday."

"It's up to you."

"It's not up to me. You should decide. If I decide, either way I'll be wrong. If you have work to do and need to stay home and I've said we should go, I'll be in trouble. If we don't go and your mother feels hurt, I'll be in trouble. You decide."

My father took another bite of the rissoles and gazed over her shoulder at a place that didn't seem to match anything I could see.

"We might as well. It'll save you cooking and I can pick up the bookwork Dad's been doing for me." He looked tired.

The next night it rained again. After delaying my homework by brushing Little Chang until he squirmed away in boredom, I finally got out the red corduroy. My mother was practicing the piano and waiting for my father to come home. I had been assigned a chapter on Burke and Wills, early Australian explorers who tried to cross the continent from sea to sea. They didn't make it. They had to turn back and split up. They kept waiting for each other at lots of places but kept missing each other. Eventually, one missed the other by hours and died.

After I finished the chapter, I wondered why on earth they would include in our Social Studies book a story about something that didn't happen.

TWELVE

MORNING GLORY

Morning glories grew on the steep hill that sloped precipitously from our home to the Scots Presbyterian church my father and I attended. The hill was part of parkland that eventually led from the mountain range to the valley.

From third grade to sixth, I had to pass by the morning glories every day as I walked to the bus stop. The bus, speeding dizzily, would take me farther down the hill to my school. On the way back, it would groan and heave, weighted down with sweaty, elementary school students pushing, hitting, laughing, and fighting. At times, the bus would be so full that it couldn't make it up the hill even in the lowest gear. Those standing would have to get out and walk. The bus would wait at the top for the ones who had been tossed off. Once we remounted, the bus would continue on the high flat area to the tiny grocery store at the end of the main street. There the bus and I would part ways.

The next mile and a half was on foot—past the grocery store, past the red phone booth. Sometimes, I would dial my mother even though I didn't have a threepence to put the call through. I could hear her but she couldn't hear me. She would say, knowing the crackling silence was I, "Yes, Meg, you can play at Lynn's today for half an hour," or "I'm sorry, darling, but you need to come home. You have that composition to finish and a mental arithmetic test tomorrow," or "Nan is here waiting to see you."

After I passed Lynn's house, I would walk past the house with the stinking rogers (small marigolds that tumbled over the red brick fence in the front) and along a path where I had to step twice on each slab of concrete in order to avoid stepping on the cracks. Then I would cross the road to where the grassy footpath fell away into the morning glories and wound past our church hall. (I say church hall. I realize this sounds as though there was a church. The church hall *was* the church.) Besides the morning glory part of the walk, the only interesting things to note on the way home were the swimming pool where someone was supposed to have drowned, the two-storey house (the only one on the long main street), and a garage where someone was always playing the violin furiously. This part of the walk was a good time for thinking about all the funny and mean things that had happened during the day and about Serious Questions.

Walking home along that footpath every day, I became enamored of those morning glories. They were beautiful and terrible: my father had explained that they were poisonous and that I was never to pick or eat them. He'd said that if you ate just one, you might go mad or die. Eventually, I decided—and it *was* a decision—that a witch in a brown robe or perhaps a madman lived in the parkland beyond the church hall. In those days, there were no loiterers for any of us to fear so I invented two. As a result, I began to walk faster along this section of my trip home.

After the morning glory section, it was easy going until I got to the Catholic church, another area laced with danger. Presbyterians did not enter Catholic churches, nor Catholics, Presbyterian churches. The Catholic church and the priest's house overlooked the whole town. ("Catholics buy on hills" was my father's financial analysis.) Two streets beyond was our house. We overlooked the hills, river, town, and parkland, which sprawled between the houses below and whose tall gum trees grew close to our fence.

On Sundays, my father and I would drive to church, park up the road, and then walk down through the morning glories that trailed beside the wooden stairs down to our church. I would go to Sunday School in the basement and he would go to the main part of the church. On the Sundays when Mrs. Toomey was not playing the pedal organ at a pace worthy of a royal funeral, my father would bring his weighty, reel-to-reel tape recorder on which he had recorded hymns earlier in the week with the help of the organist of a stately, larger church. However, our congregation, lost in habit, still sang determinedly at their own pace, thus falling several bars behind the bright speed of my father's recording. Their pace was so slow that they had to take a breath every two words, no matter the phrasing. I knew all about music from my mother.

I could hear the singing from downstairs where we were creating Biblical scenes by cutting out figures in flowing robes from yellow, orange and brown felt. Our figures traipsed bravely across blue felt skies and yellow felt deserts, passing bright green felt palms. Then we would sing:

Jee-sus bids us shi-ine with a clear pure li-ight,
Like a little can-dull burn-ing in the ni-ight.
In this world of darkness, le-et u-us shine,
You in your small cor-NAH ...

[*Nah* was the highest note in the melody]
... *and I. IN. MINE.*

I did not feel as though I was shining in my corner. It was dark down in that basement. The organ was out of tune, the trees filtered out the morning light, and those steps needed to be negotiated past the beautiful, deadly flowers in order for me to get home again.

It was not in the basement of the Scots Presbyterian church but rather under the huge fig tree near the Catholic church that my first Important Insight about Life came to me.

I gained this insight on the way home from school. Having been one of the last to catch the bus, I had been one of the first tossed off the bus so it could climb the hill. I remounted, dismounted at the grocery store, called my mother, and heard her say, "Hello Meg. Darling, Nan's here." Then she would whisper an apology for depriving me of playing with Lynn.

As, without a threepence, I could not talk back, I hung up and left the telephone box. I crossed the road, stole two marigolds for my mother and Nan, and jumped all the cracks in the concrete footpath. As I wandered with terrified nonchalance past the morning glory slope, I saw a woman halfway down the purple-covered slope picking morning glories. I was too terrified of the witch I had invented to say anything to this woman: perhaps she *was* the witch, although she looked pretty boring. Anyway, I decided the woman must know something I didn't about morning glories. Adults usually did and, if she knew something I didn't, she would think me rude or silly to warn her away from those beautiful, dangerous flowers. So I walked even faster.

When I reached the priest's house, I rested in the cool shade under the large fig tree. I began to reflect on two questions, both of which I thought were fairly challenging: "How can I know Everything?" and "How can I be Good?" These were not rhetorical questions for me; I knew there *were* answers. I just didn't know the answers yet.

I decided the answer to the first question was, in fact, easy. All I had to do was memorize every fact there was—which crops grew in each nation, the capital of every country, the names of mountains and rivers, the lineage of the British kings and queens, and the names of everyone in the world and their family members. Then I began to wonder whether this task might be impossible, since I couldn't even remember the names and important dates for Australian explorers in our Social Studies book without my mother's making up rhymes for me about them.

The second question was harder. I was still considering it when I noticed, across the road and just in front of the grocery store, two dogs, one stacked on the back of the other. The dog on top was moving rhythmically. The dogs distracted me from my inner conversation and I felt an odd kind of sick excitement and surprise inside. As I watched, the owner of the store came out and kicked the dogs away.

Suddenly, I felt An Answer arrive. It flowed over me like late yellow sunlight filtering through the fig tree. It felt like rain breaking a heat wave after a beastly Christmas. The answer to my second question was simple! My parents knew *everything*, so all I had to do was everything they told me to do. Perfectly. Forever.

I felt free and light and happily superior to everyone in my Sunday School class who had not yet sorted this out.

The dogs skulked off in opposite directions.

I turned the corner, cut across the priest's garden, leapt over the Johansen's rose bushes (only knocking off one bloom), and raced into the house. As I ran down the hall with my leather schoolbag swinging, I made a scratch in the wallpaper—just a tiny scratch. Then I leaped into the air and landed exactly on the line in the carpet, tipping over Nan's expensive black handbag, the one in which she said she kept her life. I quickly stuffed the contents back into the bag: the heavy leather wallet, leather coin purse, petit point lipstick case with its little mirror, petit point powder case with its little mirror, leather address book, envelopes, heavy black and gold fountain pen, rubber bands, hairpins, handkerchiefs with embroidered edges, and another petit point photo frame, which held a photograph of me. In my room, I flung my schoolbag on the bed, ripped off my uniform, and dropped it onto the floor of my closet. I rooted through the third drawer from the bottom, the one with shorts and tops, until I found one of each that Nan had given me.

I headed toward the kitchen where I knew my mother and grandmother would be having tea and biscuits. I decided not to mention my important insights right then. Perhaps, I thought, I might even keep the Secret of Being Good to myself for a whole day, or even two, and then just tell my mother, much as I loved Nan. But I decided I would tell them about the dogs and the woman picking the morning glories because I had decided by now that the woman must be running down the street "in the nuddy," as Nan called it, and that she would probably be dead before we'd even finished afternoon tea.

THIRTEEN

PHAR LAP'S HEART

"It's simple really," my mother explained after she gave us one of the clues in her cryptic crossword to solve while my father drove us to the museum. "Just take it apart and put it back together again."

"You can't do that in life," my father said, as he drove past his old boys' private school, glancing up, loyally appreciative of its imposing architecture.

"It's not *supposed* to be 'like life.' "

"I know. I sometimes suspect that you prefer art to real life."

My mother gave a sigh.

" 'A prophet with a pen but missing letters can still make a flower.' "

My father and I were silent. He nimbly and unexpectedly shifted to the other lane. Granddad had once remarked about my father's driving: "You're quick but you're good."

"Well?" my mother asked patiently.

"Well what," my father said.

"Take the first phrase: a prophet."

"What about it."

"What's the name of a prophet?"

"Ezekiel. Isaiah."

"You couldn't have a word like that in a cryptic crossword. You're not trying."

"I don't have the concentration for it right now, Luce. I'm sorry ... with Dad in hospital and Mother away. When I drop you off and get to the lab, I should phone Duncan and ask him if he can run the committee tonight so I drive over and see Dad during Visiting Hour. Please don't go to the trouble of making something that can't be reheated. In fact, I'll just have toast and Vegemite when I get home."

For my mother's sake, I decided to try. After all, she was taking me to the museum. "You mean the words have to be simpler or shorter or something?"

"They have to make something."

"Amos," said my father and moved into the outside lane to miss the hospital traffic.

"I suppose," my mother said dubiously, "Amos could be in a cryptic crossword. It has 'am' and 'so' in it. However, I've not yet seen it used."

"Lucy, don't lean forward, please. I'm trying to see what's coming from the left. Meg, sit to the right or left, not right in the middle of the back please. It blocks the rear vision mirror."

I moved to the left so I was behind my mother. My mother sighed and quickly leaned forward to put her bag on the carpet before my father braked at the stop sign.

"Micah," my father said.

"You two aren't any fun to do these with," my mother said with disappointment. Then she added, "With whom to do them. No, that's not right either. It should sound simple. I know: I don't think you two have fun doing these with me and I don't have fun doing them with you." She sat for a moment. "That sounds accurate but rather declarative and rude." Neither my father nor I was listening. Clearly, this was one of the many conversations she had with herself.

We arrived at the entrance to the museum. It was an exotic place for our town. Built in the style of a famous building overseas, it had alternating light and dark bricks.

We stood in the entrance beside some squat, plump palms and waited for Nan to arrive. She was getting a taxi from town, where she had been to the chiropodist. I wandered around the other side of the palms. On a little podium, I noticed a black metal sculpture of a naked man. I stood there surveying and memorizing his form. I hadn't seen a naked man before and was curious about why he had not one but two things hanging down. They hadn't mentioned that in the sex book on my mother's top shelf. After a couple of minutes my mother walked around the palms to see what was fascinating me.

"Look," I said. "He's got two."

"Darling," she said in her gentle, remonstrating voice, "It's not really ... *proper* for a child your age to stand and stare at a naked man!"

"It's not a naked man. It's just a statue, a carving."

"Not a carving, a cast. 'Carving' means the sculptor cut it out of stone or wood. 'Cast' means the sculptor made a special version that he could then remake out of metal."

"Cast. But still, he's not real, so why can't I look at him?"

"You can. And you have, it seems. Who knows who walked by. It's still somehow ... too ... unusual ... for a nine-year-old to be staring at it so long. People could think you're precocious. Anyway, Nan will be here any minute."

"Precocious." This was proving to be a good day for words. I liked the sound of *precocious*.

"In this case," my mother said firmly, " 'precocious' is not a particularly good thing. Although," she added, faithful to accuracy above all else, "sometimes it can mean something good. It means 'ahead of where you are in life.' For example, a child who plays piano, sings, or dances like or as well as an adult. However, sometimes it can refer to a child who gets above herself in an annoying way or who could be seen that way even if she isn't—because of how she's acting."

I took one last lingering look at the black, shining statue. The things were glinting in the midday sun and made my eyes squint behind my glasses.

We went inside the glass doors to wait for Nan.

"What're the things called?"

"What things."

"The statue's ... the man's ..."

"Shhhh!"

"What's the name?" I whispered.

"Penis," she whispered back.

"Both?"

"Darling, do we have to have to discuss this now?"

"Nan's not here yet."

"Just the front one. Remember the kangaroo book?"

"How do you spell it?"

"P-e-n-i-s."

"It's a nanagram."

"I suppose it is. I wish I could find a seat. My back is aching."

"Snipe."

"Spine," my mother said, sighing as she sat and adjusted her back against the cold, beige concrete wall of the entrance.

"Pines."

"There she is."

Through the entrance doors, we saw my grandmother emerge from the taxi with difficulty and slowly. She was wearing one of her most elegant feather hat creations, which I preferred to the Queen Mother's, personally, because Nan used more interesting colors—not as bright either.

She paid the taxi driver and took my mother's arm as we made our slow progress.

"Do you need some tea, Mother?" my mother asked.

"No, I had a cup while she was doing my corns. Hurt like the dickens today. I've got cotton pads between every toe." She rested a moment and then looked at the statue. It held her gaze for a minute. "Small bloke," she said contemplatively.

"Mother!" my mother exclaimed. "Not so loudly."

"I was talking about how short he is," Nan replied, unperturbed.

We were going to see a special exhibit of musical instruments. We never got there. It was unexpectedly closed so we wandered through the permanent exhibits.

We reached a wall of glass bottles that had things in them that made me feel sick without knowing what they were.

"Mamma, look."

"What, darling? Mother, why don't you sit on that seat while Meg and I look at the bottles. We won't be long."

I took my mother's hand.

The wall was lined with creatures without any fur, all pink or yellowish, and in bottles filled with fluid. Big slim bottles, little bottles. A whole wall of them.

"They're animal foetuses, darling. It's what animals look like before they're born. Inside their mother. They're less than appealing before they're born, aren't they."

"I thought 'feet' was the plural of 'foot.'"

"It is. Oh, I see what you mean. This is spelled differently. These are f-o-e-t-u-s-e-s." We walked back towards Nan.

"Why does it have an o but it's pronounced with only e's?"

"It's Greek."

"It's all Greek to me," Nan dryly commented. "Let's go. This is boring."

"You can't make a nanagram out of 'foetuses.'"

"Probably not. We can try at home. Let's not talk about it now. I'm sure it's tiring Nan out."

"I'm not tired. I'm bored."

"Very well, Mother. We'll go now. We have to leave through this door. Take my arm. Meg, come on, darling. Nan's ready to go."

"I'm not *ready* to go. I'm bored."

Walking in slow procession on either side of Nan, we traversed the rest of the medical exhibit and came to a huge room. There, in the center of the room, was a full-size horse. In a giant, glass box. He had all his hair on. He was huge. He had a penis. He had a huge penis. P-e-n-i-s. Penis.

"He was a famous race horse," my mother explained as we continued walking.

"Too bad I didn't have something on him. His corns must have hurt after a race." Nan commented.

"How did they get him in ... there?"

"They stuffed him."

"They what?"

" 'I beg your pardon,' not 'what.' Taxidermy. Stuffing animals that have died in order to make them look alive is called taxidermy."

"You say you rang for a taxi?" my grandmother asked, sparking up.

"No, Mother. There's a taxi rank right outside. I was just telling Meg about taxidermy. The people who are trained to stuff animals are called taxidermists."

"What's that?" I suddenly asked.

It was in a jar.

"It must be part of the inside of the horse that they kept. It's in formaldehyde like the other foetuses you saw earlier. Formaldehyde keeps an animal or foetus or body part preserved."

"Alive?"

"Not alive. Preserved."

"Like jam?" I asked.

"Not really. Could we discuss this in more detail later, Meg?"

"We can get out this door," said Nan speeding up slightly.

"Mother, I'm sorry. We have to go out the other way. There's a sign."

"Got to get out by walking all round the back end of a horse. Fine way to treat visitors. Imagine what overseas people think."

"It's a temporary exhibit, Mother."

"Nothing contemporary about it. That horse is deader than a dodo. Good we never brought Serge to this museum," Nan commented.

My mother's back was hurting so she switched arms with Nan.

"Serge would've stayed here if you'd given him half a chance," Nan continued. "When he finally retired as a choreographer, he made a mint in London. Sent me a postcard from Madrid last month. Still asks after you. Never married. There again, he would have been gone all the time with the ballet company.... I'd give you and Michael more, of course, but you keep saying Michael wouldn't like it."

"I don't think Serge was the marrying type, Mother. Do you think we could talk about this later, please? I'm sorry you're upset about Michael. I know you mean well. He just takes pride in providing for us."

"I'm not upset. I just said it's a pity."

"Here, Mother. Here's a little bench."

"Mamma, what's in the form-and-hide?"

"Formaldehyde. F-o-r-m-a-l-d-e-h-y-d-e." I was in the running for a local spelling bee next month. My mother was a master at building on what she had already established in any situation, even when we were using the museum's powder room.

I had learned a new word and how to spell it: form-al-de-hyde. I was interested in the way the word sounded with its four syllables. I was also interested in the way it was spelled. It reminded me of "formal," but didn't mean that. It reminded me of "form," but wasn't. It sounded like hide and seek but wasn't. It sounded like the hide of an animal, but wasn't.

"It makes a nanagram. More than one." I explained my four words.

"Those words aren't anagrams," my mother explained, as we emerged and approached Nan who was leaning forward majestically on her elegant walking stick in boredom, "but thinking of them was clever of you."

"What's in it?"

"In what?"

"The form-al-de-hyde."

"The horse's heart. Here's the door, Mother."

His heart. They must have taken that big horse and cut him apart and then put cotton padding like the stuff between Nan's toes all through him. What did they do with the rest of him?

They cut his heart out.

We were walking at a slow rate of knots toward the taxi rank. I would never think about taxis the same way again. Clearly, they had some connection to what those people had done to the horse.

There were no taxis. Nan sighed heavily. My mother looked personally responsible for the absence of any taxi in sight.

"Mamma, I forgot the information sheet. I really want it. For school. I know how to get back. I'll just be a minute. Pleeeease? Please, you and Nan wait here, alright? I know exactly how to get back."

I ran as hard as I could. I could feel my heart pounding. Just as Phar Lap's heart must have pounded.

I read the sign. It said Phar Lap had the heaviest, biggest heart of any horse in history. A taxidermist had put it in formaldehyde. His heart was shown off to everyone.

I was sure he wouldn't like that. I stood there in tears in front of his heart, looking up at it. I couldn't imagine what kind of person would cut out someone's heart and then show it off just because it was big. I told Phar Lap I was very sorry.

I ran back and got away with having a wet face because my mother was helping Nan into the taxi, telling the driver that they needed to wait for her daughter who would be here in a moment but that her mother just had to sit down.

We went back to our place, had afternoon tea, and Nan went home in another taxi. Most of the taxi drivers knew her and didn't even need an address for the big house where she had lived alone since Grandpapa died. They all forgave her for closing her eyes so she didn't have to witness their fast driving.

My father arrived home late for dinner.

"Hello, little Meggie." He gave me a big, tired hug with one arm before he even put down the things he was carrying in his other. "Good time?"

"Yes, thank you, Daddy. Thank you for driving us."

"The musical exhibit was closed," my mother commented as she served dinner, which was rissoles. I loved her rissoles. So did my father. My mother found them boring to prepare and boring to eat but she liked pleasing us.

"That's too bad. Could I have the salt and pepper, please, Luce? So what did you do instead?"

"Looked around a bit and came home," my mother replied. "Mother's feet were bad and so was my back."

I sat there balancing peas on the back of my fork. Penis. Spine. Pines. They hid his form in his hide. They form his penis and hide.

"Meg, eat up. We've both finished and you're only half way through. I went to see Dad in the hospital. He was a bit better tonight. He said the doctor came this afternoon and was pleased with him, considering everything."

"I saw Phar Lap."

"Did you! I'm glad you saw Phar Lap. That was a good alternative, Lucy. He was the most famous racehorse, Meg. Granddad saw him once."

"Alive or taxidermed?"

"At a race. He outstripped the field by two laps. Phar Lap. His name means lightning in another language but it's also a kind of play on words: F-A-R and L-A-P."

Lightning. Far. Lap. They didn't even give him a proper name. They named him after how he ran and then they ran him to death, cut out his heart, and put him in a taxi to go to the taxidermist to put him in a form, to hide him, to stuff him. Granddad had had a heart attack. Someone had attacked his heart. That's why he had been in hospital. Would someone cut his heart out if he didn't get better and he died?

"You never figured out what the cryptic crossword clue was today," my mother commented to us over pears and custard.

"Just tell us, Lucy. I'm too tired right now for word games." My father lined up his knife and fork neatly. His eyes were dark underneath.

"One last try, Meg?"

"Micah," said my father as he put his napkin in the ring.

"John. Except it's without the 'h,'" my mother declared with satisfaction as she began to collect the dishes.

"I don't understand," my father said, pushing his chair back from the table and loosening his tie.

"The prophet is John and the pen is a quill. Together, they make 'jonquil' but without two letters. It's simple. I'll never make a crossword person out of either of you."

As my mother was tucking me in, I asked, "If you have a really, really big heart and you die, does it always get cut out and preserved?"

"No darling. Of course not. Well, hardly ever. Sweet dreams."

FOURTEEN

DEL

When she wasn't meditating before it was popular—let alone acceptable—in the colonial subtropics, Del shot snakes in the backyard. Her father owned the only gun shop in town. He was German. Del said her father was Jewish and her mother wasn't. Jews were rarely on our radar screen.

Del was a crack shot. In her '50s, New Look, thin cotton dresses with bare, tanned legs and plain sandals, she was different—and therefore of interest to my mother. Del was my mother's height, around five feet. This was before my mother developed scoliosis. A pretty, freckled woman with a gymnast's body, curly hair, and a bouncy, cheerful voice, Del was the closest thing to a casual friend my mother had. What this meant was that once or twice a year one of them walked the mile to the other's suburban house and had afternoon tea without dressing up.

Perhaps my mother felt kinship with Del because my mother's father was European too. He was Russian. In addition to sharing a part-European background, my mother was connected to Del by two things, both of which involved guilt. First, my mother once complained to Del that my father couldn't keep track of his socks and instantly felt that her confession was somehow dangerous evidence of sedition. Second, she secretly shared Del's interest in meditation.

My mother had several books on meditation on the top right shelf in the closet she shared with my father. They hid there with two manuals on sex and broken-spined classics and romances from her young adulthood. The sex and meditation books were neatly covered with brown paper, like my schoolbooks, so that if Someone should open the closet, the books would pass unnoticed. I couldn't imagine who might look: no one other than my parents ever opened the closet—and I was sure my father must know about the books. She used most of the right-hand side of the closet and organized her clothes by multiple sections such as Best Formal (including her fur) and Housedresses. My father's smaller section of the closet—the lower left—housed his reefer jacket, suits and two spare lab coats, a dinner suit, tails, a sports jacket, regimental dress, and slacks.

I knew about the sex books. I'd looked at them one day when my mother was practicing the piano. While my mother had worked on Scriabin, I'd climbed like a monkey up the heavy, built-in, solid wood drawers. Perusing the black-and-white photographs of wildlife in those books, I'd learned all that was to be learned about sex long before the books were brought down for my parents to show me. I then set my sights on the meditation books. Meditation was my mother's secret, so I considered these books far more dangerous and interesting.

My father liked Del, too. She was a staunch member of our Presbyterian Church and her daughter went to Sunday School with me. Del didn't drink or smoke or do anything unusual apart from shooting snakes. Her church membership and predictable life (except for the snakes) made her trustworthy in my father's eyes.

Del shot snakes because she, her husband, and young daughter lived on the main road to our house. Each of the houses backed onto a small canyon. This was where the snakes lived. Del wouldn't harm a flea but when it came to snakes her aggression flourished. She shot the lethal ones and the harmless ones. She didn't wait to check.

In pre-ecologically-aware Australia, most creatures that were unidentifiable or unfamiliar were deemed dangerous until proven otherwise. This informal policy did not distinguish much between two-legged creatures and those with more legs or fewer. It was not a bad policy as far as wildlife went. Despite the fact that koalas, kangaroos, wombats, and a few other harmless native inhabitants had caught the mythic imagination of the mostly English, Irish, and Scots immigrants, there were more lethal creatures in Australia than anywhere else—and a lot of them lived in the yard. Early on, we'd learned that the prettiest and most innocent-looking creatures often proved to be the deadliest. We'd learned how to run from the surf if the lifesaver blew his whistle and we knew to report a spider bite immediately. People were regularly eaten by sharks and crocodiles and died from snakebites. The local newspaper was always glad to feature a story, say, about a grandmother who killed a scorpion in her granddaughter's cradle. Her deeply creased and tanned face would smile grimly and victoriously from under iron-grey, permed hair on the front page of the next day's fish-and-chips wrapping. So Del wasn't unusual in her aggression toward wildlife, just unusual in her method of extermination, her accuracy, and her doing the killing in the middle of suburbia.

Del lived on the same street as the Macleods, whose house I passed on my way home from school. The Macleods lived in a large house and Roddy Macleod went to my school. Their claim to fame was twofold: Roddy's father was a barrister and the family had a Rottweiler named Jacko who surveyed passersby suspiciously from his one eye, the other being almost shut and sickeningly milky.

We had distant relatives further along. They shared our last name but I never did meet them. Most people assumed the name was Scottish so were not surprised when I told them my father and I went to the Scots Presbyterian church. The relatives I never met were Anglican.

The house next to the Macleods, owners unknown, sported a pet wallaby called Wally.

Then came Del's house. I would often wave at Del on my way home from school. I would also wave at Elly, her Pekingese, who would stand on the front windowsill and bark at me, her long tail-plume waving back and forth in time with the palms in the front yard.

Next to Del lived the Rosenwalds, who told everyone they were Holocaust survivors. What that meant I could not imagine and lacked courage to ask. I only knew what they did not do, which was to go to the local Presbyterian, Methodist, Anglican or Catholic churches. My father explained they thought Jesus was still coming. I wasn't any clearer about the Rosenwalds after he said that.

Ruth Rosenwald did things my mother respected: she played in a quartet, wrote poetry, and taught at the university when few women in Australia did any of these things. Her husband spoke with an adenoidal, atonal drawl, breathed heavily between sentences, and was our local doctor. My childhood doctor. I kicked him in the stomach once. He took out a wart on my foot and didn't use enough anaesthetic. It really hurt and my foot instinctively shot off the table and hit his white-coated stomach but he said and did nothing after I screamed. For the first time in my life, I didn't apologize for something I knew I shouldn't have done. I don't think he liked being a doctor much but my father liked him.

My mother preferred Dr. Ruben. She went by bus to the next suburb to see him and sometimes I went with her. Dr. Ruben had pale-blue eyes, a thatch of blonde hair framing a ruddy face, elegant summer suits, and a warmly laconic, solid manner that made all his women patients fall in love with him. This included my mother.

Ruth Rosenwald told my mother Dr. Ruben was Jewish. I knew she was wrong because one of his other patients had told my mother that Dr. Ruben and his family attended her Anglican church.

One afternoon, my mother and I converged at Del's for afternoon tea. She sat us down in the dim living room and explained that she had recently rescued Elly from a terrible situation. It seemed that several days before, Elly had escaped and been found by Jacko, who lost no time in "you know ... and Elly didn't like it. They got into a terrible fight, so I fired my shotgun in the air to separate them. The next day, we took Elly to the vet. She was still shaking. The vet asked me if I had any brandy in the house, which I do for emergencies."

My mother understood about brandy for emergencies. All self-respecting daughters of Victorian women understood about brandy in tiny medicine glasses for emergencies. My mother had a daily understanding about pouring a tiny medicine glass of brandy for emergencies because she usually had an emergency daily in the late afternoon.

"The next day," Del explained, "Elly was shaking again, so I gave a her a little brandy again. It settled her down. Then the next day, she was shaky again. Now every day at the same time, she gets shaky. Look."

Sure enough, Elly was shaking vigorously. Del went to the kitchen, got a piece of bread, and soaked it in brandy. Elly wolfed it down and stopped shaking. Soon she was curled up in the corner, snoring softly through her tiny, flat, black nostrils.

A little later, after we'd finished the pikelets Del had bought at the local corner shop for the occasion, she asked brightly, "Would you like to see the snake I killed this afternoon?"

We went down the back wooden stairs and respectfully surveyed the snake. It was lying in a peaceful, green heap at the bottom of the stairs. Del got a small pitchfork, deftly caught the belly of the snake with the spikes, and threw the snake into the air. It twisted heavily in the afternoon light and landed with a thump in the backyard incinerator that was out of sight behind a bottlebrush.

"I have to get rid of them quickly. Flies get them or Elly goes native and tries to drag them up the back stairs."

We admired Elly's aristocratic overestimation of her own capacities.

On the way home, my mother and I walked passed our church. Mamma explained to me again why she didn't go to services with my father and me.

"It depresses me somehow," she explained. "The music all

sounds the same to me: funereal. Many of the melodies are old German ones. And they will insist on playing them so slowly, with no phrasing. Then the prayers all sound like each other. I do feel guilty saying this. I don't want you to get the impression I'm disloyal to Daddy."

We passed the end of the church lawn. My mother added, "Even if it weren't joyless, I can't sit in the pews. They're impossible with my back as bad as it is." By this time we were passing the house with the violinist.

"I suppose my religion is inside. Daddy doesn't think that really counts as much. Granddad doesn't go with Gran so I don't know why it makes Daddy sad when I don't go. Nan was raised Methodist. While she doesn't go to church, I do think she believes in God though."

We passed the Catholic Church on the corner and entered the home stretch.

"Grandpapa and his family weren't religious. His stepmother was very religious apparently. Jewish. He never spoke about her to me. Nan told me Grandpapa never liked her. She said Grandpapa was an agnostic but became a Nominal Methodist when they got married. Of course, you don't need to mention Grandpapa's being an agnostic to Daddy's family. They just know Grandpapa and Nan were Methodists—which they *were*, strictly speaking."

As we entered the house, I decided I probably should not mention to anyone, including my mother, that I had read her meditation books and knew about Del's shared interest in the topic. I also decided I wouldn't tell my father that Grandpapa was really an Agnostic; in fact, I wouldn't tell anyone, including Del, that he was two religions: an Agnostic and a Nominal Methodist. Even if I did like the sound of "Agnostic," I'd never seen one of their churches or met anyone from their congregations. While people like Dr. Ruben or the Rosenwalds might be interested in my having a Russian grandfather even if he was dead, I wasn't sure they or Del would have heard of the Agnostic Church.

FIFTEEN

MASEFIELD

It was raining. Cats and dogs. We had planned to go to the beach on Saturday, but the weather forecaster on the radio said the rain was supposed to last through the weekend. My mother and I got the red corduroy out of the linen closet, lifted the sides of the dining table, swung out the legs, and laid the dark cloth over its regularly polished surface.

I spread out my homework in descending order of dislike and started from the top. There were the main crops of each state to learn, the capitals of ten European countries, ten "new" words (all of which I knew), and the first and last verses of a Poem of Choice from the Fourth Grade Reader. Presumably, the middle verses weren't important.

My mother struck a match and lit the stove, which sat in its low alcove. It was modern, that stove. Instead of standing freely, it rested on a wide shelf under which were built a set of cream-colored drawers. A small china dish, hand-painted with edelweiss, sat on top of the stove, neatly holding used "Redhead" matches. Even though it was only five o'clock, the sky was dark and heavy. Moving sheets of rain obscured the mountains out the side windows as well as the view of the city and bay from the front windows. My mother turned on the lights.

The phone rang. It was Nan. At least I was sure it would be. She always rang before the news came on.

"Darling, would you please get that?" my mother said.

"I'm in the middle."

"Please."

I went out to the verandah and picked up the receiver.

"Hello. This is Meg speaking."

"Hello, duckie," Nan's voice crackled at me.

"Hello, Nan," I said brightly, showing by my tone how pleased I knew I was supposed to be to hear from her. I mean, I was, in fact, pleased—except I wasn't. I loved Nan but I just didn't want to have to be H-H-and-T right then. "H-H-and-T" was my mother's and my abbreviation for Healthy, Happy, and Terrific.

"Sorry about my voice," she said.

"There's nothing wrong with your voice, Nan."

"Sounds like a load of gravel."

"Nan! It does not."

"Haven't talked all day." Nan was lonely but wasn't any keener on people as a species than my mother was. But she was keen on my mother and me. My birthday was coming up soon. Nan was already talking about it. She wanted to take us to lunch and buy me a new linen dress at Robertson's.

"Anything exciting at school? Probably not," she said with a flat finality, a quality she shared with her older siblings who still lived down south.

"Not really. Gareth McGraw tried to jump the fence and split his school pants."

"Lucky that's all he split."

"Do you want Mamma?"

"If she's there." As if she thought my mother would be elsewhere at this time of night when it was pouring rain, I was home from school, we had one car (all families had one car), and my father was due home from work in an hour.

My mother was looking slightly panicked as she pulled out a shallow metal cooking tray in the kitchen. She was not a natural cook, so she followed recipes to the letter, including measuring cooking times exactly using either a noisy alarm clock or a tiny hourglass with sand in it. Looking over at me as I sat in the dining room beside the phone, she made an expression with her eyes and mouth that meant, I knew from experience, *I really don't want to talk with Nan right now but I feel guilty that I don't want to talk with her but know it would hurt her feelings if she knew I didn't want to talk with her so I know I have to talk with her unless you can manage to head her off in a way that doesn't leave me feeling guilty you did it but I know you can't really do that so can you at least just give me a minute to finish this.*

"She's making shepherd's pie, Nan."

"I won't keep her."

I put down the phone and went through the dining room into the kitchen where my mother was now cutting potatoes with a complete absence of passion. She leaned back and held the middle of her back as I came in. The transistor radio was playing Beethoven. She turned it down.

"What did Nan say?"

"She said she—"

"—won't talk long," we finished together. My mother walked toward the phone and I went back to the Poem of Choice.

"Hello, darling.... No, I've a little time. I'm sorry. You caught me just as I'm putting the shepherd's pie together."

I must go down to the sea again, to the lonely sea and the sky,
And all I ask is a tall ship and a star to steer her by.

I knew all about tall ships. We'd done them last year. I'd drawn one on a blank page of my Botany Book. We did Ships after we did The Australian Sky. The best bit about the sky section was that I got to draw and color different kinds of clouds. I preferred drawing cumulus because I could make the edges curly but I preferred writing "cirrus." In Early Discoverers of Australia, we got to draw Captain Cook's ships. I went to town on that one. Nan got out her detailed sepia ink and watercolor paintings of tall ships and my mother looked up others in the encyclopaedia. I liked drawing the ones with three sails. I always put a cross on one of the sails. I made the sea look good, too, although sometimes it came out looking like my cumulus clouds because I used the same curl to make a wave.

And the wheel's kick and the wind's song and the white sail's shaking,
And a grey mist on the sea's face, and a grey dawn breaking.

This sounded depressing. I looked at the other poems in the reader to see if I liked another better. One was about a churchyard and another, about a wild horse. Might as well stick with what I had. At least I had one verse down.

"Oh, did she?" my mother said in a voice that told me she was in for the duration. "That's good. A postcard or aerogramme?"

I must go down to the seas again, to the vagrant gypsy life,
To the gull's way and the whale's way, where the wind's like a whetted knife.

I was surprised there were gypsies who sailed on the ocean. I thought gypsies used wagons and stole things. Spelling was strange back then. Why didn't the poet just say "wet knife"? Besides, why was it wet anyway? Maybe it was raining—in which case who'd want to go to the ocean? But who cared—all I had to do was stand up in class tomorrow and recite the poem. I repeated the poem to myself from the beginning and rewarded myself at the end of each line with a bite of SAO biscuit with butter on it. Chang wandered by, licked the crumbs that fell onto the pale carpet, and moved on to more fertile territory in the kitchen where my old baby blanket and a wicker basket served as his nest in the corner.

"Acapulco's Mexico, Mother."

And all I ask is a merry yarn from a laughing fellow-rover,

I had it. Mostly. The Hendersons down the road had a dog called Rover so I could remember that line by thinking about my getting the dog to tell me a story and the dog laughing.

"I have no idea why they'd moor there," my mother said with a tinge of resignation in her tone. The shepherd's pie was going to be late, but there again, my father would be late, too, from the lab.

And quiet sleep and a sweet dream when the long trick's over.

This last line's meaning eluded me. I couldn't imagine what kind of trick a British poet would play on whom, or why. But I had both verses down cold now.

"Poor Mattie! She must have been frantic. They never left anyone behind in port when Daddy and you and I were *en route*. Remember they'd blow the horn? I recall they even waited half an hour in Port Said when the Charletons' son got lost. There again, that's twenty years ago. They're probably stricter now."

The rain was coming down fiercely and had changed direction. Chang was curled up snoring. His little shih tzu nose never let him get enough air, so he snored. The potatoes were boiling quietly on a low flame. My mother, having anticipated her capitulation while I was stalling Nan, had put them on a low boil.

Having polished off the poem, I moved on with relief to memorizing crops. After all that loneliness and grey and mist that the poet thought was really poetic, memorizing Australian crops like wheat and pineapples and apples was more cheerful. I drew with my HB pencil a distorted map of Australia that left off Tasmania and Cape York. I then drew yellow long things, round green things, and yellow spiky things in the right states to help me remember. Then I moved on to the section of the social studies book titled Capital Cities.

The mantelpiece clock chimed three quarters. "Not too bad," I commented as my mother hung up the phone and returned to the kitchen. "Quarter to six."

"Darling, that's naughty to say even if it is true. You know Nan's been lonely since Grandpapa passed away. It's only three years. She doesn't get to talk all day. I'm it."

"And I'm 'it,' too. Except not as long."

"Yes, you too. But you have homework. Nan wanted to talk before the news." She took the potatoes off the flame and drained them. "How far are you?"

I told her.

She got out the potato masher. "Why don't you recite it to me?"

I stood in the doorway between the dining room and the kitchen, took a large breath right at the moment that Chang snored, and started: "I must go down to the sea again to the lonely sea and the sky and ..." (breath) "... all I ask is a tall ship and a star to stir her by and the ..." (breath) "... wheels stick and the wind sings and ... the white sails shake with grey mist on the sea and dawn breaking ..." (gulp).

"I'm afraid something is a little off, sweetheart. The way you're saying it doesn't scan." My mother wiped her hands and came into the dining room. The rain was creeping under the window making bubbles of water at the seams. A flash of yellow lightning over the city was instantaneously followed by a clap of thunder. "That was close," my mother said. "Did you hear how quickly the thunder followed? Help me find the towels to lay along the sills. The rain's seeping in already. I don't want it to run onto the wallpaper."

We put old towels—Chang's, mainly—along the sills. When the rain blew sideways, the windows let rain in even though they were still fairly new. The lights of the city were magnified in the sheets of rain streaming down the bay window.

"Why don't you say it to me a few times—properly—while I finish the potatoes."

"Can I brush Chang and then do it? Please?"

"You need to learn the words and to say it properly, darling." She looked at my scuffed anthology with its grey cover and dark green title. I had put a plastic cover on it as soon as we bought it. We all had to cover our textbooks with brown paper, or better still, plastic. My anthology had been fresh at the beginning of the year. In fact, when we'd come home from town in the bus with my new textbooks, they'd all seemed full of promise. Except for the mathematics one. At this point, close to the middle of the year, the plastic on the anthology was curling and the tape that kept the corners in place was losing its grip in the steady humidity. "Let's do it again."

I said it again, taking only one breath in the middle to get to the end.

"The first time, let's work on the right words and the pauses. It sounds much better to take breaths at the pauses. Poetry's like music. It has a beat. The rhythm often echoes what the poet is talking about. And you skipped the metaphor."

"Meta for what?"

"What do you mean 'what'?"

"What is 'a meta' and what's it for?" I enunciated patiently. My mother clearly must not have her full attention on me.

"Oh, I see what happened. No darling, *metaphor* is one word: m-e-t-a-p-h-o-r. A metaphor stands for something else. Here." She put down the potato masher, came over, and pointed to a line of the poem. "The sea's face. The sea doesn't have a face, but the poet gives it a face. For effect. You also left out the second *'grey.'* "

"The whole thing's 'grey.' Like tonight. Like Aunt Mattie. She always wears grey—and she has grey hair. She's like a cloudy day. The poem's depressing. I wish I'd picked the one about the graveyard. At least it has flowers."

"You're naughty to say that about Aunt Mattie. Right. But naughty. *"Grey"* is there twice because repetition creates emphasis. Repetition builds. It's similar to when you repeat a section in a piece of music." She spread the mashed potato on the top of the mincemeat.

"Repetition is boring. I'm bored saying this poem over and over."

"Recite it one more time, but this time pretend you mean it. Pretend you're an actress. Greer Garson or Vivienne Leigh or Ingrid Bergman—one of your favorites from television. Slow down. Look at the rain outside. Imagine you're an old woman down at the beach. You're walking by yourself in the wind—"

I grabbed an umbrella off the umbrella stand, bent my body over, and started limping. My mother made whistling wind sounds, which made Chang bark because he thought someone was calling him. We got the giggles.

"Emphasize and it will sound right. Emphasize it on the right beats—just like bars in music." She stopped. "I know. I'll make sea sounds on the piano." We raced into the living room. I beat my mother and turned on the chandeliers as I swung around the corner into the room. My mother sat down at the keyboard and made rumbling sounds in the bass. Chang barked. There was another flash of lightning and a thunderclap.

" 'I MUST go down to SEA again, to the LONE-ly sea and the SKY...' " I bayed like a wolf and we got the giggles again.

The phone rang.

"Oh bugger!" my mother exclaimed, and followed her exciting exclamation instantly with, "I shouldn't have said that. It just slipped out. Don't tell Daddy. I didn't mean to say it." She rose from the piano stool and went to answer the phone. There was no caller ID or answering machine then. The phone ruled.

"No, Mother, of course not.... Yes, it was loud, wasn't it? ... The whole street? Can you get to the candles and torches Michael put in the kitchen and your bedroom?"

I performed the rest of the poem to a rapt Chang who followed my crabbèd, limping progress across the wet sands of the living room carpet with large brown eyes. "I think Michael'd better pick you up and bring you here for dinner. He's running late and so am I, with the dinner, anyway."

I returned to the dining room and was looking up the capital cities. At the end of the chapter, the countries were on one page and the capitals were listed upside down at the bottom so we would have to work for the answers.

"Nan's coming for dinner," my mother added unnecessarily on

her way back through the dining room.

"Venice's the capital of Italy, isn't it?" I asked.

"No. What's another city you've heard of in Italy?"

"I don't remember."

"Yes, you do. You saw it in Audrey Hepburn. What rhymes with 'home'?"

"Rome. I thought Venice was. Nan showed me that picture of you and the man from the ship in a gongola. She said it was the nicest city in Italy."

"*Gondola.* Venice is a nice city and it *is* on the water. But Nan and Grandpapa and I didn't go to Venice on the ship we took to *England.* The fellow from the ship stayed in touch with Nan and we did all meet again in Venice. It was a pleasant coincidence. Probably better to not mention that photograph, darling. It was a long time ago and I wouldn't want to give Daddy the wrong impression—about that fellow. There was nothing—at least on my side. Daddy waited for me back here for all those months we were away. Will you please set the table? I must call Daddy and ask him to pick up Nan."

"He'll be cranky," I commented unnecessarily as I lined up the knives and forks on top of the squares on the tablecloth and pulled the table out to accommodate Nan, thus jiggling the knives and forks and requiring my realigning them.

When Nan arrived, she progressed slowly up the path with her black stick poking gingerly at the wet path. My father's large, competent hand was firmly under her elbow and he covered her with his umbrella. With the path slick, she moved more slowly than usual. By the time my father and Nan arrived on the verandah, there were dark, wet spots on one side of my father's suit. He guided Nan inside, shook out the black umbrella, and shut the

French doors. The verandah was rapidly getting shiny with wind and rain.

Nan sat down heavily. Her descent down two uncovered flights of stairs to her garden path, the five-minute trip in the car, and the ascent up our path had exhausted her.

My father gave me a firm, damp, tired hug and went to change. He was a good hugger.

My mother had dinner out.

"Too much food," Nan commented.

"Eat what you can, Mother. Do pull your chair in. You look as though you're about to run off and rob a bank."

"Too much trouble—and you can't push with your back how it is. The letter from Mattie's in my bag."

"After dinner."

Nan said nothing. She simply picked at the crisp, tanned potato waves that my mother had made across the top of the pie. This immediately weakened my mother's resolve.

"Meg, would you please get Nan's handbag?"

My father returned and sat down. "John rang today," he said. "He wants the committee to think about buying the lot next to the church."

"Is that good?" my mother asked, as she motioned again for me to get Nan's bag.

"He's phoning me tonight." My father took a bite of the pie, looked at his watch, and said more loudly so Nan could hear him, "I'm sorry, Nan, but I'll need to get you home either before or after a man rings me."

"My handbag, Luce ..." my grandmother said, appearing not to have heard what my father had said. Nan had sporadic hearing loss. It seemed to get worse at curious moments, I'd noticed.

"Dad, Gareth McGraw split his pants on the fence today."

"You told me," Nan said.

"No, Nan, I didn't say 'Nan.' I said 'Dad.' I was telling Dad."

"Poor kid," said my father. "Happened to me once. Your grandmother mended them. She didn't have the money to spend on new pants during the Depression. She did a beautiful job."

"Mother, I do think we'll enjoy Mattie's letter better when we can concentrate—after dinner."

"My bag's on the verandah, Meg," Nan said.

"In a minute, Mother," my mother said.

"Meg, eat your peas," Dad said.

"I have."

"I can see them under your potato. I don't like this fibbing you've been doing of late."

"Only a few."

"Fibs?" asked my father.

"Peas," I said.

"No," said Nan to my father. "I didn't say Kate. It's from Mattie."

"He didn't say 'Kate,' Mother. He said 'late.' Meg, just get Nan's handbag, please."

"After she finishes her peas, Lucy," my father said firmly. "First things first. I'm not the only one who sets standards here ..."

I shoved the peas more deeply into the mashed potatoes and swallowed them in a gulp.

"Don't take that attitude, Meg," my father said, turning to me.

"Daddy, I'm only eating the peas in one bite because you told me to eat them before I get Nan's bag."

"Forget the letter," Nan said flatly. "You're not interested."

"We are, Mother. Michael, strictly speaking, Meg has, in fact, finished her peas. Could she get the bag for Mother now? Mother, Meg's Going To Get Your Bag Now."

The phone rang. My mother sighed. My father rose quickly from the table and raced to answer it. He always raced to answer the phone.

"I told you he wasn't interested," Nan said as she pushed most of her helping to one side.

"The telephone rang, Mother. Michael went to *answer it*. Here's Meg with the letter."

"I would have heard the phone. He probably went to ring someone on one of his committees so he could escape. Your phone's always engaged when I try to ring you."

I handed Nan her navy leather bag. It was soft leather and weighed a ton.

"Get my other glasses out please, Meg," Nan said.

My mother cleared the table.

Nan, having finished all she was going to eat, pushed her chair farther from the table—dangerously so. Her plate of half-eaten food balanced on its fulcrum right on the edge of the nasturtium-patterned tablecloth. "Here it is," she said, and she put on her glasses. The lenses had her fingerprints all over them.

" 'Dear Kay. Greetings from New York.' They went through the Panama Canal. Did I tell you? 'Harry sends greetings, too. The ship stopped here for a day. We both went ashore on one of the small boats.' Probably like the ones we took ashore, Lucy. Only Mattie and Harry went Second Class. 'You and Lucy—and Alex, were he still with us—would have been interested in the canal. It took all day.

" 'I had quite an experience recently. We were in port. I went with other passengers to a market while Harry went on a tour of the area with some of the husbands. I lost the other girls.'"

"I didn't know she had children," I said.

"She doesn't," Nan replied.

"Then whose girls are they?"

"It's a turn of phrase, darling," my mother said. "Let Nan finish while Dad's on the phone."

"'I heard the ship's horn but couldn't find a taxi,'" Nan continued. "'I had to walk back and arrived just as the ship was pulling away. I had to go by land to Acapulco and stay overnight. All I could find was an elegant, frightfully expensive old hotel. I was horrified at the cost but there was nothing else. Thank heavens Harry has me always carry money for emergencies. The ship was due to dock the next morning.'"

Nan put down the letter and tucked into the tinned peaches and cream that my mother had put into bowls. My father came back from the phone and sat down. My mother served him.

"John," he explained unnecessarily. "We have to present to the committee tomorrow night. I have to ring him back to review the minutes. He's finishing them now. I'll ring him after I take your mother home." He turned toward Nan and enunciated loudly, "Nan. I'm. Sorry. But. I. Have. To. Take. You. Home. After. You've. Finished. Your. Dinner. I. Have. To. Ring. Someone. Back."

Nan had stopped hearing again. She was rereading the letter avidly.

My mother got Nan ready. Nan seemed to be taking longer than usual to put things back in her bag and do up her coat.

My father gave me a suspicious hug. He was still dubious about the potato and peas. "How did your homework go, Meggie?"

"Masefield, crops, and capitals."

" 'I must go down to the sea again.' One of my favorites since fourth grade. Masefield got that right. I think of it every time I go to Victoria Island. Which I've not been able to do since the new lab opened. Appreciate being young, Meg. I wish I were nine again. I was about that age when Mother and Aunt Sarah and I went to stay with the family in Scotland. Granddad was so good about sending us." I knew this. He had told me lots of times—before I turned nine and since. "I remember being on deck. The salt air, the boat creaking. I'd like to be that age again—but with no war ahead of me. All those years away—from your mother—from Mum and Dad—from Australia."

Nan pushed herself out from the kitchen chair, handed me Aunt Mattie's letter with an air of patient resignation and asked me to put her bag back on my mother's bed in the main bedroom. She would get no further audience tonight. My mother started to clear the table. She was playing a game with herself, I could tell. She was seeing how much of the table she could clear before she needed to go to the bay window and wave goodbye to Nan. She would wave until Nan and my father turned the corner.

Instead of taking Nan's bag to the bedroom, I took it to a chair near the front door. My father was in the hall making two fairly short—for him—phone calls. I heard him promise to phone back in half an hour. Then he put on his raincoat and went to pull the car around.

While my mother was cajoling Nan into eating a bite of pie in the kitchen and my father was outside, I read the last part of Aunt Mattie's letter: "I was having a cup of tea in the hotel lobby before dinner. A man asked if he might sit down on the long, leather couch beside me. It turned out he was a recent widower. Quite young for a widower. He was good-looking and spoke fluent English. He said he was in Acapulco on business. We got to chatting and when we rose to go in to dinner, the hotel restaurant said we could dine at the same table in the dining room if we wished. I didn't want to seem rude, so I agreed.

"I couldn't translate the menu so he ordered a lot of courses for us—and two different wines! I couldn't drink much. As you know, Harry and I never do. When we finished, he—Juan was his name—insisted on paying. The poor man then found his wallet had been stolen. As though he didn't have enough troubles with his wife passing away recently! I asked the manager to charge the dinner to my room. Juan was mortified—and most appreciative.

"He said I looked like his wife. It's odd, isn't it, the things we find ourselves doing in a foreign country. I mean, one thing just seems to lead to another and one finds oneself surprising oneself.

"The next morning, he asked the hotel manager to take a photograph of us before I left for the dock. Even though he, too, was a visitor, he seemed to know people and what to do. He had a business meeting so he couldn't go in the taxi with me to the dock.

"Harry was relieved to see me as you can imagine. He was shocked at how much the hotel cost but didn't say anything and I didn't go into details. Harry said we need to stay together at all times on the trip from now on.

"Do you remember Georgio—the Italian boy Mother wouldn't let me talk to? Juan looked like Georgio."

"Harry sends his greetings, as always. Affectionately, Mattie."

I folded the letter and put it in Nan's bag. Dad came to the door. He waited, ready to open the umbrella. Nan rose from the table with great effort. I had come back to the kitchen and was helping my mother clear the table. Nan turned to me. "Come along for the ride, ducks. I'll tell you the rest about Mattie. She had to stay at a grand hotel—alone—well, in a manner of speaking." She laughed.

My father looked worriedly at my mother. Nan's upbringing and experiences in the country, despite being raised Methodist, had inured her to some of life's rougher circumstances and unexpected outcomes. My father didn't like where this story was heading.

My mother knew better than to push her luck, so she sacrificed Nan's usually unchallenged wishes on the altar of my father's values. "Mother, I'm sorry. I'm afraid Meg needs to finish her homework. I know she'd love to go along for the ride but she hasn't finished yet. I am sorry. And I'm sorry the pie wasn't very good."

"It's the false teeth. Not you. Can't chew."

My father waited with the umbrella. His eyes looked heavy with weariness. My mother looked anxious. I knew it would not be a peaceful night after he finished those phone calls. Under my father's, mother's, and Chang's gaze, I kissed Nan's soft, freshly powdered cheek with what I thought was a good mix of love, secret regret, and fierce but reluctant determination to complete my homework. I handed Nan her big bag.

"If you're ready, Nan," my father said in the heavily careful way he reserved for his mother-in-law. My mother and I stood by the window as he held the umbrella at a forty-five degree angle to the rain. His other shoulder would get wet this time.

The rain was pelting sideways. By the time my father pulled into the drive again, we had new towels along all the inside of each windowsill.

I heard the car door and then the front door shut. I heard my father sigh loudly.

He picked up the phone. "The line's dead."

"Oh dear, what if Mother needs us. Were her lights back on?"

"Yes. Could you forget about your mother just for a moment, Lucy? I'm worried about John. He's waiting for me to ring. Meg, you need to be in bed." My father's lids were even darker now and his jaw was set in a certain way. He often got testy when he had dark lids and his lower jaw off.

"I was waiting to say goodnight."

"Did you learn the Masefield?"

"Yes, Daddy."

" 'For the call of the running tide is a wild call and a clear call that may not be denied ...' Ah, well. Now it's bills that call.... Good night, Miggledy-Piggledy. Here. Come let me give you a hug."

My mother picked up the anthology as I started to change into my pajamas. "Let me hear it one more time as you get ready for bed, darling." Hail started pelting the roof.

"Why do we have to learn it by heart?"

"So you'll remember it when you're older, I suppose. Daddy still remembers this poem and likes it. Remembering poems is like remembering words to songs: one recalls them later. Let me hear."

I recited it with emphases on the right syllables, ending with "and a quiet sleep and a sweet dream when the long trick's over."

"Mamma, why's there a trick in it?"

"It's a different kind of trick—"

My father walked past the door. "Phone's still dead. 'Trick' has many meanings—a lie, a joke, someone taking advantage. A trick in cards—"

My mother, always a stickler for accuracy, added, "There's 'turn a trick'—"

My father looked pointedly at my mother. "That is not pertinent to the poem—or to Meg. In the poem, Meg, it means time spent on watch or at the helm. Masefield's talking about responsibilities, about loneliness you think will end but doesn't."

My mother's shoulders sagged.

I went down the hallway, cleaned my teeth fast but left the water running so they'd think I'd cleaned them longer, and walked down the hall toward my room. My father was looking through the pile of today's mail on the dining table.

"More bills."

I hugged him. He was looking sad. My mother tucked me into bed.

"I must remember to ask Nan to read me the rest of Aunt Mattie's letter so I can make the right noises. I couldn't give it the kind of attention she wanted," she said.

"I know the capitals. Do you want me to say them?"

"I believe you, darling."

"None of them rhyme, except Rome."

"None of them rhymes. 'None' means 'no one,' which means just one."

"Rhymes. Except Rome. I read the end of Aunt Mattie's letter when no one was looking."

"Darling! That's very naughty. One should never read other people's letters!"

"Nan was going to read it to us anyway."

"That's different. It is her letter. What did it say?"

"It said she got stuck in a hotel and met a really nice man but he lost his wallet and she paid and the next morning they had a picture taken like the one you had taken in Venice."

"Photographs can be misleading at times, darling. I told you meeting that man again in Venice was a pleasant coincidence. Nan simply had that photograph—of me and the man—taken to commemorate the gondola ride."

She tucked me in. "I'm sure Aunt Mattie appreciated a kind man's help under the circumstances but you don't have to talk about it. It might be taken the wrong way. She's never been abroad before. Just forget about that old photograph of me. I don't know why Nan kept it. Also, you'd better forget you read Aunt Mattie's letter. It wasn't right to read it yourself."

She changed the towel on the window. It was soaking up clear blood from the sky that kept oozing into our home. The rain was more fitful now.

"Sweet dreams, darling. Put yourself to sleep with the poem!"

" 'I must go down to the sea again,' " I said in a sing-song voice and then made whistling-wind noises. My mother giggled and pulled the door almost shut so the light from the hall shone in a thin line across my dark blue carpet.

I lay there listening to the rain. I was not thinking about Masefield.

SIXTEEN

THE REVIVAL MEETING

I had long since decided that they were not telling me the truth. Not that they were telling me untruths. They just were not telling me everything because I was only ten.

The Sunday School teachers didn't understand that I was an only child and privy to information normally denied a child. We sat on the long wooden pew polished by generations of students and considered Ezekiel.

"Do you know what omniscient, omnipotent, and omnipresent mean, girls and boys?" Mrs. Baxter asked.

A magpie squawked in the bird sanctuary and Wicky broke wind. Ann twisted her snotty handkerchief. We could hear the choir singing the threefold amen upstairs. The service was over. There would be biscuits and lemonade soon.

"It means that God knows everything," Mrs. Baxter explained. "He is all-powerful. He is everywhere."

Finally, Mrs. Baxter had let loose a clue with which I could work. I watched the magpie fly from one eucalypt to the other. Then I followed the slow steps of the Sunday School director's wife, Mrs. Cameron, as she approached the tea urn, which was beginning to heat up.

My mind worked overtime. A few weeks ago, I had learned that God had appeared to Moses in the burning bush. We had even illustrated this story with an orange felt burning bush on the dark blue felt board. So I knew that God had appeared to at least one person. Now Mrs. Baxter was telling me that God was everywhere.

We began packing up our belongings so we could join the adults for morning tea in the hall. The older children started to scrape the pews across the concrete and pile them on top of each other.

So God knows everything. That has to mean He knows everyone as well. And the thing she isn't saying, I reasoned, *is that if God appeared to Moses, there's no reason He couldn't appear to me.*

"We need to move this," yelled Jimmy Baxter, tipping me off the end of the pew. I stood up, adjusted my blue-framed glasses, straightened my blue panama hat, and unstuck my blue and white linen dress from my seat to which it had glued itself with the humidity of a summer morning.

I added my hymnbook to the pile in the dark corner by the old pedal organ, which we gathered around to sing "Jesus Loves Me This I Know" every week.

And if He's everywhere, what happened to Moses could happen anytime. To anyone. It could happen to me.

I could hardly wait to get through the soggy biscuits, tomato sandwiches, and tea that had steeped too long so that I could get home to my blue-wallpapered room with its view of the hills, and consider my options.

Of course, I couldn't test my conclusions during the day, especially today when we were going over to my grandparents for

Sunday formal lunch. But tonight, I decided, under the mosquito net, would be a good time to try.

Eventually, I made it to bed. The polished wooden radio was playing muffled Mozart in the dining room. My parents were talking in uneasy peace. Having said good night three times to my mother, making sure I was the last to say it so she wouldn't think she loved me more than I loved her, I sat up in the dark, slipped out from under the mosquito net, put my glasses on, and looked out the window at the mountains and the low stars. I thought the stars might help. Then I closed my eyes and asked God to come to me, but not in a burning bush; someone might hear or smell and I wanted this to be strictly between Him and me for now. I didn't know what to do next but wait—because I reasoned that God was probably the one who should be talking, not me, despite my being quite a talker and despite all the practice praying aloud we had had.

Nothing. I opened my eyes. I closed them again. Nothing. Then I felt something soft on my right forefinger. I looked down. A moth had flown in the open window and landed on my finger. It sat there, still and silent. I watched its wings in the moonlight. Then my body took a big sigh, and I felt as though warm milk were flowing through me. I closed my eyes and sensed a Hand touch mine. Just as I felt the Hand, the mozzies discovered me. I climbed back under the mosquito net and sat cross-legged on the bed, silently asking the Hand not to think I was rude. I reached out my own hand. Once again I sensed something flowing up my arm and into my body. And I could have sworn something touched my hand.

Then there was nothing except the sounds of my parents, who had turned off the Mozart and moved to the living room where I could tell my father was giving my mother a long report on something in which, to judge from her tone, she was trying to show interest even though she didn't understand it fully.

Suddenly tired, I lay down and fell sound asleep.

Six months later, the Wyatt Evangelical Campaign, an American import, came to town. Some people from our church went for training with the Wyatt people. Soon after, our Sunday School Director Tom Cameron, a kind, dark-haired, round-faced man, invited us to come to a revival meeting in the hall. With the promise of pikelets and scones afterwards, we all showed up.

The meeting began with lots of hymns and prayers and little speeches by people who talked about God and Jesus far more enthusiastically than our understated church usually did. Then Mr. Cameron rose, adjusted the microphone downward to match his height (thus making everyone laugh), and said Now Was The Time. Now Was the Time To Profess Our Belief. If we truly believed in God, we should stand, walk down the center aisle, come up onto the stage (which blazed with special lights usually reserved for the Christmas pageant), and Be Counted. We started singing another hymn, "Now is the Hour." Some adults bravely walked up and stood on the stage with the lights glaring up at them from the floorboards.

"If you believe in Jesus Christ, our Lord and Savior, come up on the stage and be counted," Mr. Cameron invited, holding out his hands in a grand gesture no Australian man I'd ever met or seen on our black-and-white television had used.

I was in torment. If I went up on the stage and said "I believe," then I was behaving as though my night under the mosquito net hadn't happened. How could you say you *believed in* someone you *knew*—someone you'd met and shook hands with and talked to, for goodness sake? But if I *didn't* go up, everyone would think I didn't "believe in God," which was true, but not true at all. I sat there sweating at the end of the pew. I could be faithful to God and unfaithful to Mr. Cameron or unfaithful to God and faithful to Mr. Cameron who, after all, was one of my father's friends and worked on two committees with him.

I waited until the second-to-last verse of the hymn and then scuttled up the left-hand aisle and stood at the back of the stage under the heat of the lights. As we sang the last verse, tears began streaming down my face. Because I was standing at the back, no one saw that I was crying and probably would have thought it was because I was Believing.

It was not, as I thought then, the first betrayal. Nor was it the last.

SEVENTEEN

....

SLEEPY LAGOON

Nan was playing "Sleepy Lagoon" on the piano again. She played by ear. Her long, slim, wrinkled hands—rings now too loose—moved tentatively across the keys like daddy longlegs moving across the carpet.

My mother was cleaning up in the kitchen after lunch.

I was packing. Tomorrow we would go to the beach for two weeks. My mother and I would go; my father, needing to work would join us on the two weekends we would be away.

Nan always played the same wrong notes. She would correct them, of course, but I winced nonetheless. Not for myself, but for my mother because I knew it bothered her. I heard those wrong notes just as distinctly as my mother did but, because it was Nan playing, it didn't matter somehow.

I took an old suitcase that Nan had handed down to me and put it on my bed. Originally expensive, the suitcase was made of dusky blue leather with rusting gold closures, a dusky blue, slubbed silk lining, and four dusky blue, elasticized pockets on the inside.

I laid out my sandshoes, some shorts and tops, three sundresses Nan had made me, and my hairbrush on my bed so my mother could review them before I packed. I also put out the two new Chalet School books I had received for Christmas a week earlier and the *School Friends' Annual.* I had read most of the stories in the *Annual* already but there were some I wanted to reread.

Nan moved on to another favorite, mostly played on the black keys. They were easier for her.

My mother stopped making noise with the dishes and came into the hallway.

"Meg? Where are you, darling?"

"In my room. I've got everything ready to pack."

My mother came to the door of my blue-on-blue room and looked in. She was wearing a beige and white shirtmaker dress, in which she looked crisp, especially with her shorter pearls.

"Look," I said proudly.

She glanced down the hall in the direction of where my grandmother was playing. The mantle clock struck two. She came in.

"I'll only look quickly right now, sweetheart. I can concentrate better later. I do need to spend some time with Nan. I think she's a bit down at the mouth because we're going away tomorrow. I don't want her to feel neglected and wan this last afternoon."

"I told Nan I'd do her nails," I said to my mother. "As soon as I've finished packing." I showed my mother the piles on my bed. The wooden drawers in my built-in closet and my dresser were all partly open.

"That's lovely. You've made a good start. I'll get my list later—the master list by subject area. We can check it together."

"I've *got* everything!"

"What about underpants? Your swimming togs? Sandals?

Toothbrush? Hankies? Paints? Diary? I think we need to sit down quietly after Nan leaves and tick things off against the master list."

Nan stopped playing. I heard the lid of the piano close and the stool being pushed back with difficulty. My mother and I looked at each other. I could see myself in the mirror behind her. My glasses were askew and my white shirt was hanging out of my shorts.

"Darling, if you're going to do Nan's hands, now might be a good time. Daddy'll be home soon from Gran and Granddad's and he'll want to take Nan home right after dinner before he starts his desk work."

"Can I use your nail file?"

"May I use your nail file. Where's yours?"

"It's gone walkabout."

"Don't borrow the one with the grey handle. That's my best. It's the only one I've ever found that sits in my hand just the right way. I doom things. I just find something perfect and the shop that's selling it closes. I pity any store that satisfies me; it always goes broke after I find it. There *are* emery boards you could use. They're in my top left drawer."

I went into my parents' room with its two beds and subtle, gold, woven bedspreads, made for them when we moved in three years ago. The sunlight was flowing at an angle across the bedspreads and bouncing off the crystal on the dresser. I opened the drawer, got out an emery board and the clear nail polish, and went to the living room. Nan was sitting on the sofa with her head nodding. She didn't stir when I sat next to her; she didn't hear well and my movements didn't disturb her. Just then, my mother came to the door of the living room and said, "Mother, would you like a cup of tea and a biscuit?"

Nan stirred and looked around, momentarily puzzled. "What?"

"I'm sorry, Mother! I didn't mean to disturb you. I thought Meg was doing your nails."

"I wasn't asleep. I was thinking. About when we were in Lugano. You'd washed your hair and were drying it on the hotel balcony when that young Frenchman—"

"You were afraid I'd get a cold," my mother intervened deftly. "Would you like a cup of tea and a biscuit while Meg does your nails?"

"Two biscuits, thank you. What do you have?"

"Monte Carlos and Tim Tams. I just bought two new packets of each: some for us to take and some for Michael."

"One of each then."

I took off my pink-rimmed glasses and put them on the low table. I picked up the nail file. "Nan, give me your hand."

She let me lift her soft, elegant, wrinkled fingers onto my tanned thigh, which was covered in blonde down.

I started to file.

"Nan!" I remonstrated. "You've still got the clear polish on from last time I did them. Some, anyway. You promised you'd take it off after a week. It's yellow." Unperturbed, she looked down at me with her hazel eyes dim behind her smudged glasses. I wanted to clean them after I finished her nails.

"No one can see it," she replied calmly.

"I'll take it off," I said, and I ran into my parents' room and got nail polish remover and cotton wool from the back of a drawer.

Nan surrendered to my remonstrations with silent pride in me. We sat quietly as I took off the polish and began to file.

My mother brought the tea and biscuits. She had used the

kitchen china—white with a gold, wavy edge. Things were getting down to business in the Going Away arena.

Nan rested her left hand in mine and picked up the stainless steel spoon. She took two heaping teaspoons of sugar and dropped them into the tea without losing a grain, stirred carefully, then put the spoon back in the saucer. She picked up the cup and took a sip.

"The sugar bowl's almost empty and this isn't sweet enough."

"Meg, would you please get more sugar for Nan? I need to start ironing Daddy's shirts for the next two weeks and I want to spend a *little* time with Nan."

I went to the pantry. The Vegemite, honey, and sugar were all on a lazy Susan. I turned it around, got the spare sugar bowl, and brought it to Nan. There was one biscuit left on her plate: the Monte Carlo. She had eaten the Tim Tam first so the chocolate wouldn't melt in the heat. I handed her the sugar. She deposited a third, hefty teaspoon into the cup and stirred.

"When's Michael carting me off?" she asked my mother in a flat, dry tone after my mother had finally risen and gone into the laundry room to do my father's ironing. I knew my mother was dreading the question. Without saying it, Nan was implying that my father was wresting her from the bosom of her family and sending her into coventry for two weeks. This wasn't far from the truth but everyone, including my father, would have sworn it wasn't.

My mother sighed in the laundry where she was ironing. I heard her sprinkle water from the little bottle she used to dampen the clothes, and then the iron began to steam and hiss. "Meg, would you please tell Nan that Daddy will take her home before dinner?" she called out to me.

"Daddy'll take you home before dinner, Nan," I said.
"Ask your mother. I don't know."
"What? I just said: before dinner."
"How do you know?"
"Mamma just told me."
"She's in the laundry."
"She called out."
"You can't hear her in the laundry. She must have said it earlier," Nan said firmly.
"She did, Nan. Just now."
"No one could hear from here to there."
"Sometimes you don't hear everything, Nan."
"There's nothing wrong with my hearing. I heard you telling your mother you wouldn't come when your father takes me home. You were in the dining room and I was in the kitchen."
"But the door was open. And it's not that I don't *want* to go when Daddy takes you home. I love going to your place—always. I just haven't packed—enough, anyway. Mamma wants me to go through things with her master list. Can I put another coat of the colorless on?"
"You'd better come back from the beach or it'll go yellow again."
I heard my father pull into the driveway.
"There's Daddy."
"Where?"
"The garage."
"How could you see him from here?"
"I heard him."
"You can't have."
"Nan, give me your glasses. They're filthy. They've got marks

all over."

Nan obligingly took off her glasses with their marcasite tips and handed them to me. I took them into the kitchen, used soap on them, and brought them back gleaming.

Nan looked strange without her glasses. Her eyes had sunk in. Six years of wearing heavy prescription glasses had had the same effect on my eyes. I gave her glasses back. She put them on, careful to thread the arms under her hair. A small bead of perspiration trickled down the side of her face, taking some powder with it. It was over a hundred degrees outside.

My father came in the front door and dumped three paper bags on one of the canvas-backed squatter's chairs on the verandah.

"Hello, Nan. Hello, Meggie. Where's your mother?"

"Hello, Daddy. In the laundry room." I went out and hugged him, knowing that he would be uneasy if he thought I were giving Nan more time than I gave Gran.

"Gran sends her love. She's looking forward to seeing you tomorrow. She gave me a sponge cake she made today especially for you and Mamma to take to the beach. She won't have time to cook it before we drop in *en route*."

He disappeared down the hall to the bathroom. When he emerged I could hear him talking in what he thought was a whisper to my mother. He didn't know how to whisper. My mother did. He never did learn how.

Nan started to talk to me again. "Are you going to watch 'The Graham Kennedy Show' tonight?"

"Probably. If we finish the packing."

I hadn't known we were seeing Gran and Granddad tomorrow. I couldn't make out the words in the laundry but I recognized the content of the conversation by its cadence, rhythm, and phrasing, just the same way Nan knew how to play "Sleepy Lagoon" by ear. My parents would be talking about taking Nan home. My mother sounded plaintive. My father sounded defeated. I felt weird in my stomach.

Then the tones changed. My father adopted his informational tone and my mother sounded surprised, taken aback. She asked several questions. Nan was telling me about a skit she had seen on television. She loved television. She said it kept her company. My mother always felt guilty when Nan said that or when Nan answered my mother's daily calls by saying, "Haven't talked all day. Sound like a frog."

I made the right noises so Nan would think I was listening. I was—but only to her tone. My father's voice rose and I heard the word "Nan." Then I heard my mother say, "Your parents...." He said we would take Nan home now and would see Granddad and Gran tomorrow because they were on the way to the beach. From my mother's perspective, this meant they were getting more time than was their due.

Dad came to the French doors that led to the verandah. "Meg, do you want to come while I take Nan home?"

Somehow I didn't think, by his tone, that this was a question. Nan looked dubious, then pleased. I started to help her with her things. She had several Robertson's department store bags she had brought up to our place with things to show us from her archives as well as her heavy, navy leather handbag from down south.

"You've got the kitchen sink in here," I teased, using the words my mother always used.

"Your mother always says that," said Nan. "It's not heavy."

"You don't have a bad back like Mamma."

My father emerged with keys. Nan raised herself from the seat with difficulty. I handed her the ebony cane with one hand while I held the Robertson's bags and her great handbag in the other. I scooted my feet into my thongs. Chang wagged his tail.

"Come on, little boy," my father said warmly. "Do you want to go in the car?" Chang wagged intensely.

My mother came out and kissed Nan, apologizing for having perspiration on her face.

"I'll telephone as soon as we get down the coast—and when I can find a phone booth, Mother. We'll be sure to drive by the cottage at some point when Michael comes down again next weekend."

"Not much point. Not ours any more." Nan said with Cornish-Australian understatement and offered her soft cheek to my mother. They always kissed, never hugged. My mother said her side of the family didn't hug much.

"I'd still like to see it," my mother said, sounding slightly sad and apologetic.

The drive to my grandmother's house was only a few minutes. Nan sat in the front beside my father. Chang and I sat in the back. He pressed his firm body along my sweaty leg and I stroked his flat, furry head. We drove to the top of the street, took a few turns, then went down the long hill onto Bay Road and onto Nan's street. My grandmother's house was on the right, surrounded by imposing, manicured gardens with palms, a pond, and jacaranda trees. I remembered swinging on the green metal gate when I had been little and we had lived with Nan after Grandpapa died. My father pulled up on the white gravel driveway and came around to let Nan out.

"Would you just give the lawn a hose before you leave, Michael?"

"It's too hot now, Nan," my father replied. I knew he was right. "I could come down again later and do it." I knew he wouldn't want to but he would and then there would be talk behind closed doors at home after he got back. What did they think: that I was deaf? I could even hear Chang scratch the back door when I was on the front verandah.

"I'll do it later. Do me good," Nan replied.

My father didn't protest for once; he had come down often on hot days.

We walked slowly up the two-part, stone staircase that led to the main landing. I handed Nan her big handbag. She fumbled to find the key. The stained glass on the front door was dim. She handed me the key. I opened the door and couldn't see the dark interior for a moment. The grandfather clock chimed five-thirty sonorously and the stained glass in the window seat cast a rainbow of colors onto the mushroom-colored armchairs and over the piano. The vamp card that Nan had painted so beautifully was sitting on the piano keys.

I put the parcels on the bed and the groceries my mother had sent with us on the kitchen table. The house seemed big and empty. I wondered what my grandmother did all day.

"I'll just show you those letters from Mattie," Nan said. I knew my father wanted to leave. I knew my mother was feeling guilty about Nan. I knew Nan wasn't letting herself feel anything. She started looking under the newspapers on the window seat for the letters. Aunt Mattie, now widowed and an honorary aunt-by-marriage, was traveling again.

"Would you mind very much if I looked at them next time,

Nan? Dad has to get back to some paperwork and Mamma can't finish packing if I don't get home soon. She said she needs to help me. I'd love to see them but I'd better go. I'm really sorry."

Nan didn't say anything but turned slowly and walked to the front door. I gave her a hug at the front door. Her glasses were gleaming. Her hands felt smooth. I loved the way the tips of her fingers would stay in a big, flat dimple if I pressed them. They always took forever to plump up again.

"Take care of yourself," she said. "Don't go out in the sun. It'll ruin your skin."

"Oh Nan! Everyone does."

"Look at them. Look at me."

"You were born like that. You have beautiful skin."

"So do you. I've always worn a hat and used an umbergingum, rain or shine. Sit in the shade and don't go out at midday."

"Bye, Nan." I gave her silk waist a big hug and reached up—not far any more—to kiss her cheek. Her hand brushed past my ponytail and twisted the curl at the end between two fingers as I let go.

My father and Chang were already down in the car. I ran down the two flights of stairs taking them two at a time, which terrified Nan. I waved at the bottom, waved as I got in the car, and waved again as we turned the corner. I could see Nan slowly waving from the top step as we passed out of view.

"Nothing's enough for Nan," my father said. "Sad, really. Your mother does her best but Nan keeps her on a short rope. No need to tell Mamma I said anything. It'd upset her even though it's true. Help your mother when we get home. She has a lot to do before tomorrow."

We came inside and my mother came out of the bedroom. "How was she?" she asked me. My father had already gone to his study.

"She was going to show me Aunt Mattie's letters but she couldn't find them."

"I must remember to ask about them when I ring up after we get there tomorrow."

After a cold-cut dinner, the master list came out, all sorted by categories. There were hundreds of things I'd forgotten. My father disappeared into his study once again to work on bills and meeting minutes.

My mother and I took a break and watched "The Graham Kennedy Show." In the middle, the phone went. My father raced from his study down the hall to the phone, as he always did.

"You treat that thing like a Commanding Officer!" my mother would often say. "Why do you have to race every time it rings?"

He came into the living room looking vindicated. "It's Nan."

My mother rose. It was the commercial break. Nan must be watching Graham too.

That's good," I heard my mother say as I watched the commercials. "I wonder where the other is." She settled herself. "Venice? Of course I do.... The snap with your white fur or the black? ... Oh, *that* was a different day.... On the day we took the gondola, I was wearing the suit Daddy bought me in London." Silence. Graham Kennedy started again. "That's too bad. Did she see the doctor?" My mother was clearly in for the duration. Nan must be bored with Graham tonight.

My father walked past the living room, stood still for a minute, sat in an armchair, sighed, and rested his strong chin in his large, tanned, smooth-skinned hand. He, too, had soft pads on the ends of his fingers. I liked pressing his pads, too, but they didn't stay pressed in for as long as Nan's. By the time my mother hung up, my father had gone back to his study, and Graham was saying goodnight.

The next morning, we packed the car, waved at the house, crossed the Blamey Bridge, and stopped at Granddad and Gran's. Little Chang would spend the day with Big Chang and with them until my father came back in the early evening.

Gran had a cold but insisted on kissing everyone on the mouth. She said, as usual, it was an old wives' tale about kissing and colds. My mother discreetly wiped her mouth. So did I.

My father drove us to the hotel and, while we started to unpack, he went for a quick walk on the beach to "blow the cobwebs out." When he returned, he gave me a Big Bear Hug, called me "Miggledypiggledy," and he and my mother embraced. Their embrace had a kind of silent apology thing on both sides. I don't know how I knew that but I did. Then he gave her a second, normal, goodbye hug. My mother and I stood and waved until we couldn't see him any more. He kept one arm out the window waving slowly even though he couldn't see us. He was dining with Gran and Granddad, given it was his and Chang's first night alone.

My mother and I unpacked. The next day we went to the beach in the morning and the skating rink in the afternoon. I had my photograph taken in black-and-white by a photographer hired by the skating rink. My mother paid in advance. (We would pick up the photo a week later. In it, I had on my best top and shorts, my leg was stuck out the back, and my glasses were steamed up. I was smiling widely through my dental bands and some boy's blurry legs appeared in the background.)

When we came home from the rink, I had a funny feeling in my stomach. I went to the toilet and pulled down my white underpants. There was blood on them.

"Mamma."

"Oh darling, your first period! What a pity you've started so young! I'm sorry. It *would* have to start when we were on holiday. Poor darling." She walked the long block to the pharmacy and back again. I sat on the toilet watching the water get pinker and pinker between my legs, getting cramps, and feeling dramatic. When she returned, she showed me how to put on the twisty cotton belt that held the pad up. I had to change it every few hours. The cramps got worse. My mother gave me a Bex to stop the pain. It helped a bit but I was sick into a little paper bag, which my mother took away after she held my head.

I knew what It was. I'd had The Talk—with both parents present—either because my father had wanted to be part of my sex education or because my mother was embarrassed. I don't know which. My mother had told me that Nan had never told her anything. My cramps went away. Then they came back. My mother had been plagued by cramps all her life until she had things taken out when I was eight.

After I was over the worst of the cramps, she told me she should phone my father. We wandered—I waddled—up to the public phone on the corner. I stood in the booth with her while they talked. She told him my first period had come. I could feel the thickness of the pad. It was wadded between my legs and still clipped front and back, I hoped, onto the straps. I was worried my white shorts would turn red or blood would run down my leg. My mother got me a pineapple tartlet as one of my compensation prizes because I wouldn't be able to swim in the ocean until the bleeding stopped.

My father wanted to talk to me so he could congratulate me.

He said he wanted to take me out to dinner when he came down next weekend; we could celebrate my starting to "tick over."

I thanked him and felt shy and proud—and depressed that I couldn't swim until next week.

I handed the phone back to my mother and stepped out of the red booth. A dog was lifting its leg on the other side of the booth. I could hear the ups and downs of my mother's voice and caught a few words. She was sounding beleaguered again. My father was talking because there was silence at her end. Her shoulders started to droop. I caught phrases. "I wasn't going to ring Mother *just* about that ... I do see what you're saying, Michael. You're trying to be fair to both grandmothers. But it's difficult to ring you *then* Mother *then* your mother, too, from a public booth.... And what they don't know won't hurt them. At least, I hope not in Mother's case although she will think it odd later when I do."

A second dog came along and lifted his leg where the earlier one had been. My mother came out of the booth.

"Daddy's very happy for you darling. He asked me to tell you, 'I'm proud to have a grown-up daughter,' and to promise you we'll take you out for a special dinner on Friday night when he arrives. By then, you should have finished the whole messy thing.

"By the way, I don't think there's any need to tell Nan when I put you on to talk to her. Or Gran. I wouldn't want either to feel hurt if she finds out we told the other first—so it's better if you don't tell either. Daddy prefers to wait to tell them on the same day."

It had not occurred to me to tell either of my grandmothers and I was distinctly ill at ease with my father's overflowing pride. I looked down at my bulging white shorts and decided I could still roller skate even if I couldn't swim this week.

My mother picked up the black phone in the booth to ring Nan. "She'll be worried I haven't rung yet. I'll tell her the phone booth was occupied. It was—by us—so it's only a little white lie. Help me remember to ask about that other letter from Mattie."

EIGHTEEN

NAN'S PHOTOGRAPHS

My grandmother colored photographs by hand. She also arranged for sepia studio photographs to be taken of each of us annually. Even after color photography became common, she still took black-and-white pictures so she could color them. With her help, photos of azaleas in her gracious garden escaped from their monochromatic, deckle-edged prisons to appear in various hues of pink; tall palms swayed green against an evenly blue sky; and faces were delicately given life with a shade of flesh tone. Nan's fidelity and fierce devotion to her idea of beauty was unbending. Being unable to resist improving on reality, she often applied this aesthetic to her family: she would color my father's club ties, each with its strict, regulation colors, to match what the rest of us were wearing; and she would sometimes "put height on top" of my mother's hair, height being the rage at the time.

Nan applied this aesthetic especially to photos of me. I was the unqualified—at this point anyway, given my beloved batwing glasses, prepubescent shape, and banded teeth—heiress apparent to her throne of perfection. While she waited for my body to catch up with my hormones, she would tell me to take off my glasses for informal or studio photographs; as I grew older, she also used her sepia ink to slim my blossoming hips and shorten my pointy-toed shoes.

As she aged, her sight worsened steadily. At the same time, her pursuit of visual perfection in nature and in those she loved grew more relentless. Now, through the central fog of her vision, her tinting extended the stripes of my father's ties beyond their natural boundaries and into his lapels, turned my eyes bright turquoise, made my mother's cheeks look as though she were running a fever, and made my teenage lips look as though they had been stung by several bees at once. While she never worried about taming the growing pile of news clippings, magazines, old letters, photographs, and hand-painted cards (from me) that spread in comfortable chaos both in and on top of the window seat, she kept her paints carefully lined up and usually in the right rainbow order, on the verandah table where the light was best for coloring. She would hold a magnifying glass in her left hand and color with her right all the while wearing special prescription glasses designed for close work. Oddly, it didn't seem to bother her that her glasses were usually smudged.

Sometimes when she came to our house, which was at least once a week, I would remonstrate when the afternoon sun slanted unforgivingly across her regular bifocals and well-dressed, corseted form. "Nan, your glasses," I would say.

She would take off her glasses and hand them to me. I would take them into the kitchen, wash their delicate marcasite tips and increasingly thick bifocal lenses with soapy water, wipe them with a handkerchief, and return them to her.

"See how much better they are?" I would ask with my proudly

inherited belief that I could improve others for their own good. She would put them on and thank me. I suspected her of just being polite. She didn't seem to care that one could see perfect fingerprints reflecting tiny rainbows all over the surface of her lenses. Because she couldn't stand a hair out of place in a photograph and only bought the finest clothes and handbags, this puzzled me.

It was also puzzling that she did not take care of her hands. Of course, they managed to look lovely anyway; she had deep, oval nail beds and long, finely tapered fingers like my mother's. I would sit in front of her with indignant, bossy affection, filing her nails and painting them with clear polish. Being both myopic and artistically inclined, I did a good job. We didn't talk while we were doing this. Because Nan couldn't hear well, our conversations were monosyllabic but she and I didn't often need words to understand each other.

Nan generally presented her improved photographs to the family with both satisfaction and silent reproof. My mother and I would always tell her how lovely they were and how much better everyone looked. We would evince surprise when Nan told us that she had taken a few inches off my mother's hips, widened her own lips slightly, changed the color of a dress or tie, or painted in a potted plant to hide herself completely. She didn't like how she looked in photographs but sometimes, because of the positioning of the figures, she couldn't work out how to cut herself out.

"I wish she'd leave the bloody things alone. It's one more way your mother can't keep out of our lives," my father commented with mild irritation over lamb chops one evening. He had just glimpsed the latest pile of doctored photographs on the desk in the hall. "I don't know why I bother any longer to say anything."

"Michael, she loves doing it. She doesn't color the studio photographs—not often, at least, and only if they are her copies—but she loves coloring the home snaps. It makes her feel as though she's done something thoughtful for us as well as keep her busy. She's lonely. She does see people for morning or afternoon tea in town but she's had to find ways to keep herself busier since Daddy died." My mother's shoulders fell forward.

"Can I be post office, please?" I asked. This was the term I had invented for acting as a translator of feelings between my parents. I knew I could get the words just right and improve the exchange. They each looked slightly amused. "Nan is just trying to make things look nicer from her point of view—and keep herself busy, too. Dad, you like us just the way we are. Mamma, you want both Dad and Nan to be happy."

"You mean well, Meg," my father replied, spooning up some of my mother's dutifully made, excellent tapioca. "You'll understand later. Sometimes people don't know how to let their children have their own lives."

He finished the tapioca and put his spoon neatly aside. "Good pudding, Luce. Thank you. The dinner was lovely." He looked out the kitchen window at the grass. "I'll have to mow this weekend," he sighed and put his napkin in its wooden holder. "Luce, your mother's a good woman. Sometimes, I just have a bellyful. It's not just since your father died. She's been putting her oar in ever since we were engaged."

"What about *your* mother?" my mother said in indignation, sounding tremulous.

I could tell that this conversation was going to take longer than I originally thought. I rose, went to the fridge, and took out the condensed milk. I got out three clean teaspoons: two for me and one for my mother. When she saw me eating some, I knew she would want some too.

"What about her asking Mother whether I'd been baptized and insisting on it before we could get married? Wasn't that putting her oar in?" My mother folded her napkin neatly, refolded it so that the slightly creased corner was underneath, and slipped it into the ring.

I picked up our dessert plates, handed over the condensed milk and a teaspoon to my mother, and excused myself to do homework. I knew where this was going. It had gone there a thousand times before and it would end in tears and hours of silence.

The next morning, my father looked up from the paper and called me out onto the verandah. I was running late for the bus.

"Meg, I don't want you to form the impression I don't like Nan."

I had.

"That's not it," he added.

It was.

"It's just that your mother has always felt she has to please Nan, especially since your grandfather died. It's a pity Nan doesn't understand it's difficult for your mother. Nan just needs to let go more; it's hard for your mother. She feels responsible for Nan—*and* for us."

"I know, Dad. You're just worried about Mamma," I lied.

Despite his objections to Nan's improvements to the family photographs, my father didn't notice details about people. Over dinner one evening, my mother asked him what the church's new bookkeeper was like.

"She's a nice young thing. Right values. Good head on her

shoulders. Two girls. Husband's a solicitor."

My mother, well trained by Nan, always grilled him for details.

"Is she tall?"

"Average."

"You said 'nice young thing.' How young is 'young'?"

"Twenties, thirties, perhaps early forties."

"That's a wide range. Thin? Plump?"

"I didn't look."

"You must have noticed *something*."

He made an effort to be precise. "If I had to say, I'd say she reminds me a little of you or Mum somehow."

"You think your mother and I look alike?" my mother asked.

Realizing he had stepped into enemy territory between two bites of mashed potatoes, my father grew careful and testy. My mother didn't know when to stop.

"So she's not thin," my mother added, pushing a tiny escapee of un-mashed potato to the side of her plate.

"I told you all I noticed. She's pleasant and willing to help with some other responsibilities, too, while Del and her family are on holidays. I, for one, am grateful. It's more off my shoulders."

"I don't see why it had to be *on* your shoulders."

"I'm heading up the fundraising," he said wearily.

"Is she grey- or brown-haired? You might have noticed that at least."

"Grey," my father answered immediately. If my father were not so incensed every time I told him a lie, I would have suspected him of making this up for the sake of peace.

My mother said something about blood out of a stone. My father said nothing. We continued eating.

"Maryann said Miss Wentworth dyes her hair and has really

hairy legs under her stockings. She had to climb a ladder one day and the hairs showed." I contributed this tidbit from school as a peace offering to my mother for her inability to elicit visual detail from my father and to my father for his inability to notice and for having so much on his list.

A few years later, when Nan went to live at a gracious hotel where country people stayed when they came into town, she kept her house and gardener, took her best clothes with her, and presided over the hotel foyer chairs during the day. She was an endless source of delight to new guests, who loved her style, forthrightness, and clever way of pretending that her sight and hearing were not impaired.

My mother and I would join Nan for lunch at the hotel at least once a week. She would take us to the Palm Room, which had mirrored walls, well-lit booths, and two palms at the entrance. All the waitresses knew Nan and knew to serve her only half a portion because she disliked plates overflowing with food.

The same waitress in a crisply ironed, pink cotton dress usually took our order. Nan would often comment, in the way deaf people do when they assume no one else can hear, "Nice girl. We get on. Pity she's so *plain!*"

"Mother, *please* not so loudly," my mother would say. She didn't mind Nan's finding the waitress plain. She minded being associated with someone who might be seen to be impolite and she minded the waitress's possibly hearing. "She's part *Aboriginal*," my mother would quietly remind Nan. Nan was placidly immune to remonstration and, having grown up in a small country town where she would have been seen more Aborigines than we did in our big town, she was possibly oblivious to the reason for our cheerful, efficient waitress's dark, broad facial features.

"Mum, who *cares* what Nan says," I would say, trying to free my mother from her need to improve her mother. "They all know Nan and how she is."

When Nan entered a nursing home, she stopped coloring photographs. By that time she only had peripheral vision. I was in my twenties by then and living in another state, so my mother emptied Nan's house alone. All the things in the window seat. All the paints. All the photographs, documents, papers. All my Russian grandfather's papers and photographs from his family. All the sewing things.

"You don't know how much your mother suffered," my father later told me. "She was overwhelmed with everything there was to do. Fifteen crates. One day in the middle, you phoned long distance saying you were going skiing. She was pleased for you but she sat down and cried when she hung up the phone. She could have done with your help. She packed those fifteen crates by herself. Nan never let anything or anyone go, not even a newspaper cutting."

I don't know why I didn't fly up to help. Perhaps because my job didn't give me much time off. When I did go up later, I was glad Nan couldn't see how unaesthetic her expensive nursing home room was. My mother had been reading and recording, with her clear enunciation, cassette tapes of light novels. She had been doing it for a while. I thought it was a good idea so I did the same thing and sent them to Nan.

The last time I went to visit her, she told me she didn't know why God was keeping her here so long; that she missed Grandpapa, her brothers and sisters; that she loved only my mother and me in the whole world. When I had to leave for the airport, her nurse helped her move slowly to the door to say goodbye to me. I got into the taxi, wound the window down all the way, shouted Nan's name, and waved in big gestures. Nan waved in the general direction of my taxi as it drove away.

My mother kept every duplicate studio portrait and every photograph Nan had colored, including the ones with pink leaves, green flowers, and red cheeks. Even though she'd cleared out Nan's house all those years ago, she'd not thrown away anything since; she kept everything that had Nan's creative imprint on it, all the studio portraits, including the Russian ones with the unreadable Cyrillic on the back, and all Nan's family photographs, many of which had been hand colored by Nan. She didn't even know who most of the people were but she kept them. While she was oddly happy to give me three of Nan's exquisitely rendered pen-and-ink drawings of Victorian nymphs cavorting, she couldn't bear to give me any of the Russian things or any photograph Nan had colored.

"They'll be yours eventually," she would comment dryly.

Once, when I was visiting my parents long after Nan had died, I slipped into my mother's bedroom while my parents were out. I went to the closet where she kept the tightly packed and partially organized boxes of Nan's photographs. While there was only one copy of Nan's and Grandpapa's earliest photographs and formal portraits, the later ones—the black-and-whites—had been reprinted several times and each copy had been hand-painted. I found the copy of each in which Nan's coloring was most flawed and stole them. I left my mother with the black-and-white originals and the best-colored ones. She never noticed.

NINETEEN

....

THE LETTER

"Dear Miss Woodford ..."
I wrote the final version on my best paper: the pink deckle-edged. I wrote it in blue Parker ink with my Osmiroid fountain pen with the special nib. I had rewritten the letter six times on cheap, lined paper. I needed to ensure I had taken all steps to forestall her misinterpreting it. Then I copied the final draft onto the pink paper.

At thirteen, I didn't own much writing paper, usually getting only a box or two I didn't like from distant, elderly relatives at Christmas. But asking my mother for writing paper would require explanation.

I had been practicing Miss Woodford's elegant, upright script with its heavy down strokes and light, angled upstrokes. Long trained in adapting and blending in for survival, I was still surprised that visual imitation came to me easily.

"It's like looking at my own writing!" Miss Woodford would later exclaim.

My first paragraph was a poem I had worked on for weeks, even on the bus home, strap-hanging as we turned the corner past the C of E—Anglican—church.

I included the poem because I thought it was good and because it expressed my purest feelings. Consider its opening stanza:

When alone, my wandering soul
Whirls me away into unknown realms
Where I explore, finding there
Something new at every turn.

I liked the "wh's" at the beginning of "when," "whirl," and "where." A good start, I thought, to a poem written by a thirteen-year-old. Correction: I considered it an impressive beginning for any poem. I revised endlessly, changing punctuation, adding words that sounded more poetic than others. I was pleased by its depth. The poem said all I wanted to say but in a better way than prose. I hoped Miss Woodford, too, might be similarly impressed. I had to put the next stanza on the next leaf of paper:

Questions fill my days:
What is the meaning of life?
When will this misery end?
The joy, the bliss that I could know
If I could answer these!
Only then could my soul take wing
Only then would I have peace.

I knew I would need to use a second leaf because I had to use the right layout for a letter. My mother had shown me early on how to write letters putting the pages in the right order and using warm but not gushy phraseology, especially for the bread-and-butter letters to the elderly cousins who sent me the writing paper. So of course, in this special letter to Miss Woodford, I couldn't write on the back of the first leaf: the back of the first leaf would be for later, when I'd finished the first side of the second leaf. But how was one supposed to know how many leaves one needed unless one wrote a draft?

Now that the poem was down, I started the first paragraph:

"I have wonderful parents and everything a young woman could want. I wouldn't want you to think my home life isn't happy."

I decided that putting this in early would allay questions Woody might have about whether I was unhappy at home.

Even in the novel I had been writing, I hadn't said anything *bad* about my heroine Olivia's parents—and didn't want to. My fictional parents were talented, wonderful, and loving. I only killed them off so I could give Olivia the fateful encounter with her favorite teacher and the headmistress. This literary exercise gave me pleasure and comfort. It was, of course, a compelling invention—one that showed signs of heartbreaking brilliance. (I used both a pen name and a name for the heroine different from my own so that, if anyone read my story, they would not mistakenly think that I was the main character, Olivia.)

In the novel, Olivia goes to a really good private school and is a really excellent student, really popular with girls and teachers. However, the teachers—especially the Senior School headmistress, Miss Worth, and the Junior School headmistress, Miss Garson—can't show how much they really respect and really care about Olivia, of course, because it really wouldn't be fair to the other girls. But then Olivia is called away to Miss Worth's house where Miss Garson is also waiting for her. The two women really want to Break the Bad News to Olivia themselves because both of them really love Olivia and really want to be present when Olivia hears the news.

At this point in the story, I took inspiration from the penultimate scene in "Mrs. Miniver." We had watched untold hours of old films on Australian television when it had arrived five years earlier. Even now there was insufficient local programming. I loved the whole film but I especially liked the bit toward the end where Greer Garson is driving the car in the company of her beautiful daughter-in-law with saintly eyes. Bombs are raining down on the black-and-white English countryside. The car gets bombed. Greer (by now, I called her by her first name) looks down in flickering black-and-white at her daughter-in-law. The young woman is wounded but she doesn't appear to be. Nor does she seem to be hurting or know she's dying. But it's clear to all of us that she's dying. Greer looks down with fierce and tender love. The daughter-in-law looks up and looks saintly. She still feels no pain. Greer looks strong and loving and secretly heartbroken. She raises one eyebrow in anger against The Enemy and presses her beautiful lips together.

Woody could raise one eyebrow—and I had practiced in the mirror until I could do it, too. Strong women apparently raised one eyebrow when necessary.

I went back to the letter:

"Nor do I want to give you the impression I am depressed. I merely am concerned that my belief in God and my faith are not as deep as they could be and I hope you might be able to help me."

I was sure Woody had a deep connection with God although she had never talked about it, even when she led our morning assemblies with their hymns and Bible readings when I was in the Junior School. Perhaps after she got my letter, she and I could talk about God and the meaning of life. She would certainly be able to sort out all my confusions. But what if she was Church of England? I was Presbyterian. Would this create a crisis of faith in me? Perhaps I would feel called to become C of E—and then I would have to leave home because Gran and my father wouldn't approve.

In the most recent dream I'd had about Woody, she was singing in church with stained glass light falling on her face. The dream reminded me of the end of "Mrs. Miniver." Greer and her family, including her grieving, handsome son but minus, of course, the beautiful, young, dead daughter-in-law, are in a little village church with the roof blown off. They are singing a triumphant hymn. You know they'll have to triumph daily over sorrow and that they shall.

I got the second leaf to begin the next paragraph of the letter and crossed my fingers that the page numbers would come out right. I started the next paragraph:

"I am concerned about writing to you. I don't want it to affect any future position of responsibility if I prove worthy of being considered for one."

That pre-empted the possibility, I calculated and hoped, that she might see me as ambitious (I was), unfit for service (I wasn't), or not healthy enough for one of the school leadership roles I wanted badly (I thought I really was mentally healthy enough—but perhaps I wasn't—but perhaps all the girls felt like the way I did). I mean, I was genuinely worried about God but that didn't mean I wasn't a Good Sport, a Responsible Contributor, a Happy Citizen of the school community to which my mother had belonged, far less communally, before me. In short, I embodied as best I could—and wanted to be seen as someone who embodied—the values the school held: "Head, heart, and hand through the years."

I had the part about the head sorted out; I had the heart down, too, because I knew I loved my dog and my family; really, really liked my friends; and secretly loved two other people: Jurgen, a boy to whom I'd never talked and who took my same bus to his boys' school; and Woody, whose daily presence was now denied me since I had moved on, with an armful of prizes, from our Junior School and crossed the valley of sporting activities that divided Junior and Senior Schools.

However, I did wonder if anyone took the bit about the hand literally. Even when we were in Sick Bay, the most we got from any of the sturdy Mistresses-on-Duty was a quick, dispassionate pat on the forehead to see if we were running a fever. Apart from menstrual cramps, any other sign of weakness put one at risk of being seen as a "feeble flower" and therefore not fit for duty. Better to faint from practicing gymnastics than to lie on the Sick Bay hard leather couch for unknown reasons.

I set aside the pink letter and opened the exercise book in which I had been writing my novel in faint pencil. I was writing it in the middle of the exercise book so no one would find it.

Olivia looked across at Miss Worth and Miss Garson as they served her a cup of strong tea with milk and sugar (to help the shock she is about to experience). Olivia put her tea down carefully and said in a polite, even voice, "Is there something wrong, Miss Worth? I do hope your elderly mother is well?"

I set the story down again. I finally decided that I would include something in the envelope for Woody. I had lain awake at night debating the merits of this. It was daring, especially as I had to send the envelope to school, not having her home address. I was going to include my gold, heart-shaped locket. My parents had had it engraved with my initials and given it to me for my eleventh birthday; I loved it. I loved it even more when I put a tiny grey photograph of Woody in it. I had discovered this early picture of Woody in one of my mother's special Old Girls newsletters and I had secretly cut it out and put in the locket.

I was close to the end of the third pink page, having written on the back of the second, and was about to start the fourth page, which should get the letter to end at the bottom of that page on the opposite side of the first leaf.

"I wanted you to see this heart. I hope you won't take it the wrong way. You'll probably sigh and think, 'Another needy student in my busy day.' I am not sending it so you will worry. I just want to be truthful."

In the novel I was writing (I was up to page nine—almost double numbers—at this point), I had decided I should delay the climax slightly. Olivia's thoughtful question about Miss Worth's elderly mother was heartrending so I added, on a separate page, material I could insert later into the main story:

Miss Worth and Miss Garson glanced at each other across their teacups with stricken, yet silent emotion. Miss Worth, having seniority, said finally, "Yes, my dear," (I liked that touch) *"my mother is really as well as can be expected, thank you."*

After I had made a note on the page of the original draft about where this beautiful addition should be added, I resumed the main storyline:

"Olivia, I'm afraid Miss Garson and I have something difficult to tell you. There has been a fire."

"Where, Miss Worth? I hope no one was hurt!"

I couldn't resist. I took a break from the letter to Woody and reread the whole novel to date. I was moved yet again by its poignancy and inspired prose. Then I checked the letter to Woody four times for grammatical and spelling errors, put the heart in, sealed the envelope with saliva, and walked with Chang across the road to the red letter box. Chang lifted his leg efficiently against the box, the letter slipped from my shaking fingers into the dark hole of an uncertain future, and I went home.

A week later, Miss Colbert, our French Mistress, threw out casually at me as we were preparing to leave the classroom, "*Mme. Woodford voudrait parler avec vous.*" She always spoke French to me more than she did to the others. This embarrassed me but it was a fact that I understood what she said to me in French more easily than I understood what our mathematics mistress said.

"What's she want?" Miranda asked. We put away our French books and got out our Ninth Grade Physiology text. The Science Mistress would arrive any minute.

"*No* idea!" I replied carelessly.

I had to decide which lunch hour I would choose to walk down the long hill from the Senior School to the Junior School. If I went too soon, it would all be over. If I went too late, Woody would think I was rude or didn't care. I waited two days and then, on the third, sick with terror, I walked down the hill, across the playing fields, and up the stairs of the Junior School. At least she wasn't the Mistress-on-Duty that day, wandering through the grounds during our lunch hour, ensuring our safety, the grounds' cleanliness, and generally being available for crises that never happened. I distracted myself by smiling at the little Junior School girls, who still recognized me as one of their recent leaders, and reflecting on the next parts of my novel, which I pretty much knew by heart now.

Miss Worth looked at Miss Garson, love and pain filling her handsome eyes.

Woody came to the door of the Junior School staff room. She always took me off guard with her easy, athletic height.

"Meg! How nice to see you!" She acted as though nothing had happened. Perhaps she hadn't got my letter and this really *was* about something else. "Shall we go down to my office? We might find *some* quiet there!" she said, laughing at her own humor and the unlikelihood of getting any quiet at all. She walked briskly ahead of me, stopping momentarily to lift up and plump out daisies that had been shoved too far down into an old vase on a desk by the window. The flowers effortlessly rearranged themselves. I knew I would never be able to let flowers rearrange themselves effortlessly. I also knew that this would be a good detail to add to my novel. Where, exactly, I didn't know but now was not the time to decide. I was living Life.

Woody walked down the hall toward her office. I followed with a calm face making sure to greet the little girls in the hallway. They smiled shyly at me, one of their previous leaders.

Woody sat down. Her office was dark wood. Just to be in it again made my breath shallow. It was winter. I took my blazer off in the hopes that she might put it around me if I started to shiver but I was so awash with dread I couldn't even pretend to shake.

Miss Worth pressed ahead, her neat feet in their high heels placed elegantly together.

"*Your home caught on fire, my dear, and I'm afraid your parents were ... no one survived the smoke. They didn't suffer. There was no pain. However, they are with God now.*

Woody took my pink letter out of her top drawer. I sat unmoving—terrified, ashamed, and numb—as I watched the envelope emerge. She laid it at right angles to the blotting paper.

"This is like looking at my own handwriting!" she exclaimed with what seemed like admiration of my imitation of her handwriting.

She hated me. I knew it. In fact, she must hate me even more for imitating her writing. I had no right to copy her handwriting. And she must hate me for writing to her. I was sure she'd told everyone. My school career was a dust ball on her polished wood floor. At that moment, my blazer slipped off the back of the straight-backed, leather-seated chair on whose edge I was perched. It heaped onto the floor. I bent down, retrieved it with a clammy hand, and quickly hooked it over the back of the chair again. Thin, crazed lines of dust lay in different places on its dark felt where it had touched the floor.

"I'm sorry, Miss Woodford. I've made rather a mess of things," I said lamely.

"Now we shan't talk about this again. Nothing has changed between us."

I wasn't aware that there was anything between us before this or that there was anything to change. I didn't understand what she meant but it sounded both ominous and reassuring. I had risked changing for the worse something I didn't know was between us. But she had just said she wasn't going to let that happen. Perhaps she just meant she wouldn't hate me and wouldn't tell on me, thus ruining my school career.

Her black telephone rang. She apologized and said she must answer it. I stepped outside and waited while she spoke. I started shivering, looked down through the rippled glass at the distorted figures playing in the quadrangle. I felt too stunned to sort out what was happening, so took refuge in recalling my novel:

Hours later, Olivia was looking blindly into the middle distance, aware that Miss Worth and Miss Garson were sitting by her but she was unable to really see them. She realized she was in a bed in Miss Worth's house.

"You are going to stay with me for a few weeks until you are better, my dear. You fainted from the shock. Your parents left official care of you to us but you will visit your elderly grandparents, of course. We shall ensure you see them frequently. Sadly, because my elderly mother is coming to live with me, I cannot have you to stay permanently with me but Miss Garson would really like you to live with her."

"I'm so sorry," Woody said. "I had to answer that. Do come in again for a moment. Lunch hour is almost over, I'm afraid."

I sat down after she indicated the chair again.

"Now as for this silly thing," Woody said, withdrawing the heart slightly from my pink envelope and holding it matter-of-factly, "we shan't mention it again, either." She trickled the heart and chain carefully into the envelope and handed it to me firmly across her dark wooden desk with the scuffmarks around the legs. The envelope was empty of the dreadful letter.

"I'm sorry about the envelope," she added as I looked down at the tape crisscrossing the top of the envelope. "They seem to have opened it at the Post Office."

So now the whole town knew.

"On to other things. How are your classes? A's as usual?" She smiled at me.

I nodded. "Except for Maths. No matter how I try."

She laughed. "And your mother? I saw one of her articles recently. She's certainly a credit to the school. What a wit she has—and so astute, too. How is your father's lab?"

I answered somehow, pulling pat answers from somewhere. I put on my blazer and slipped the pink envelope into one of its pockets.

Woody rose. The interview was over. A small girl with red eyes and tears streaming down came to the door wanting to see Woody. I excused myself.

Olivia looked over toward Miss Garson, eyes brimming. Miss Garson's eyes were also brimming and she raised one eyebrow slightly. Then, she reached over and, because Olivia couldn't see properly because of the shock—temporarily, of course—embraced Olivia.

A week later, my father called me into his study. "Miss Arlington rang me today. She said she was phoning for my opinion on an agenda item for the next meeting of that joint committee we're on. But I'd given her my opinion at the end of the last meeting. She's not one to forget things."

I managed to stand there looking innocent and surprised despite my stomach's lurching.

"I repeated my position about the agenda item and then asked her if she was satisfied with you. She said you were a very good student and Form Leader. But then she mentioned something about how girls who've gone through the Junior School can sometimes find it harder to adapt to the Senior School than those who come only for the final four years.

"Why would she say that? I suspect she's uneasy about those new friends you've made.

"Then she said she wondered—of all things—if you were 'taking life too seriously' and if you were taking enough time to 'roll on the grass!'

"It seems to me you 'roll on the grass' a great deal and don't take things seriously *enough*. When I was only a few years older than you are now, I was away at *war*. We went off, and then years later—*if* we were lucky enough to make it back—we were expected to pick up life again without missing a beat. Your generation has it easy, young woman, thanks to those who fought so you and your mates can swan around.

"These Saturday mornings in town with your friends ... the day you missed the bus home and didn't even phone to tell Mamma you were taking the later one; your not calling your grandparents regularly; your not helping Mamma as much as you could. It's self first, school second, and home a poor last, as far as I can see."

I stood there at attention and tried to look straight at him. He sounded like an officer in one of the many British war movies I'd watched. I felt as though I were a deserter or had gone AWOL.

"Miss Arlington did finish by saying she was looking forward to working with me on the SU next week and thanked me for my input—but I know that's not why she was ringing."

"What's the SU, Dad?" I asked, stalling and looking for a diversion. It worked beautifully at school but less often with my father.

"Some university labs have established a committee with selected high schools," he answered impatiently. "She and I are both on it. You know that perfectly well. Are you trying to red herring me? Despite her comments, I'm not so sure about you. She doesn't see the other side as your mother and I do."

"I forgot the initials—SU." I reasoned that if I didn't explain and looked interested in something else, perhaps the bomb would miss me.

He looked suspicious but let it drop. "I don't think headmistresses have *time* to chat about individual girls unless they draw attention to themselves in a way not entirely laudatory."

"I don't know why she'd ring, Dad," I said, appearing confused.

After dinner, I went to my room to study. I couldn't get over Miss Arlington's comment. She never thought *anyone* was serious *enough*. I couldn't imagine *her* rolling on any grass, literal or otherwise. (She always wore high heels, even on school holidays. Some of the girls had seen her in town in a sleeveless sun frock but she still was wearing stockings and heels.) I couldn't even imagine what rolling on the grass might look like for me or why she would say it.

So, I reflected as I conjugated the French irregular verbs assigned for homework, Woody had told Miss Arlington—*something*. I was pleased, hurt, and scared. Woody must have been more worried than she had let on to me. I tried to imagine what Woody might have said. Whatever it was, Miss A hadn't told my father. Perhaps she didn't know anything. Perhaps Woody had just told her we'd bumped into each other and she'd found herself mildly concerned about me. Perhaps Woody had told her everything and they had both kept my secret.

I knew I could never do something so dangerous again and that—in addition to being a Good Student, Model Citizen, and Emerging Leader—I had better quickly and regularly establish signs of Rolling on the Grass. For a long time.

I took the heart from the envelope and pushed it under my mattress. I looked at the torn envelope and went to throw it out but did not. Apart from anything else, where could I throw it at home? My mother would find it. Then I noticed the tape with which the Post Office had resealed the torn envelope. Stamped over and over in dark blue capitals along the tape were the words: ... ANSIT DAMAGED IN TRANSIT DAMAGED IN TRANSIT DAM ...

I decided to keep the heart in the torn envelope; after all, her hands had touched it.

TWENTY

THE CAR RIDE

Finally, I saw her athletic figure dressed in silk with Italian shoes: Miss Woodford walking briskly up the hill from the Junior School where I had spent that charmed year with her. Now that I was in the Senior School, I had to wait days for a glimpse of her sitting in the headmistress's office or walking competently to the tram or on duty in the playground, her thick head of pepper-and-salt hair shining in the sun. Daily for three weeks now I had loitered in the Senior cloak room pretending to repack my books in my satchel and tidying my uniform, my hair, my hat, my gloves, my anything, in hopes of coordinating my departure from the Senior School with her long walk down the hill opposite our buildings.

I wrapped up my conversation with Gwenda, who was, in the cruel vernacular of the day, a "nothing" to those, like me, who had been voted to run the school at the student level. I was making Gwenda's day by showing uncommon, insincere interest in her when, out of the side of my new contact lenses, I was rewarded by glimpsing Miss Woodford descending the outside stairs of the Junior School.

I had long since calculated the number of times in a month we could accidentally meet on the way to the tram so that she would not feel stalked. I had done the same thing successfully with the boy who lived at the top of the hill: I permitted myself a certain random rhythm of "accidental" encounters. I had accidentally encountered Hugh on the bus home two days ago, so I needed to wait at least another four days before accidentally encountering him again. However, today was a green light day for Miss Woodford. I had waited three weeks. I would walk along the path, head down as though lost in thought. I would suddenly raise my head and say with surprise, "Oh, Miss Woodford! Good afternoon!" She would smile and reply, "Good afternoon, Meg," and then—. I didn't know what then. It really matter didn't matter what then because I could live on that alone for the next three to four weeks. I had already recorded ten dreams about her along with eleven dreams about Hugh. Everyone else fell far behind in the dream count.

I walked along beneath the jacarandas, which were casting lavender bells on the path. I lowered my head and stared at my polished, lace-up, black school shoes as I tracked Woody's progress down the road in my peripheral vision. She was now a few yards to my right.

As she approached, I looked up, startled, and said, "Oh, Miss Woodford! Good afternoon!" Just as I had rehearsed. I smiled at her through my new contact lenses. She smiled and replied, "Good afternoon, Meg" with a diffidence that implied, I liked to think, tender significance but that might have been, in my worst imaginings, dread of encountering me again. "How are exams going?"

I was pleased she was so interested in me so I regaled her with exact descriptions of the unfairness of some of the questions. We reached the bottom of the hill in five minutes. The walk was only half over. We still could talk all the way around the corner, which was another five minutes. If the tram wasn't full, I might even be able to sit opposite her if I didn't have to give up my seat to an adult, which all the girls from our school were expected to do when they were in uniform and even when they were not. This was a very, very good day. I knew that I would be up until after midnight recording the encounter. I would then reread it at disciplined intervals, alternating between it and the latest chance encounter with Hugh—until the next possible encounter I permitted myself with one or the other.

So it was with despair, shock, and rage that, as she was laughing at my description of our French exam and a blooper I had made, I looked down to the large iron gate and saw the ten-year-old Hillman sitting there with my grandparents in it. From my entry into my mother's alma mater years ago until now, they had never, *ever* picked me up. Here, on this long-awaited day, they sat waiting placidly. In my stellar career as "a natural leader, excellent student, and fine citizen of whom her parents can be proud," according to the headmistress on my most recent report card, this was the most embarrassing thing that had ever happened to me.

I panicked. I had to be nice to them. And I had to be with Woody. My grandmother was in one of her fine Italian knit suits with blue hair set firmly and sprayed. My grandfather was in one of his neatly brushed, grey felt hats, his handsome mouth holding a cigarette with an ash almost the length of the entire cigarette. As a child, I had watched his cigarette ash stay attached to the filter through red lights and green, through coughs and comments, never scattering on his perfectly creased trousers.

I was doomed. I managed to pull myself together enough to say to Miss Woodford in a normal voice, "There are my grandparents."

"How nice. They've come to pick you up," she commented with the wide smile that often broadened into a wink or raised one of her generous eyebrows a little. It was a trick I had practiced in the mirror until I could move the muscles separately. It came in handy years later when I was teaching.

I knew I had to introduce them. My worlds crashed together like passenger ships. I was drowning on the prow.

"Hello, Gran. Hello, Granddad. Miss Woodford, these are my grandparents." They shook hands through the window of the car. Miss Woodford made ready to leave. I was stricken as I got into the car.

My grandfather shook his ash out the window. He looked up at Miss Woodford, his deep brown eyes, faded to grey around the rim from the subtropical sun, meeting her dark ones. "Would you like a ride?"

I was torn between heaven and shame. My world, carefully calculated to ensure the occasional sacred encounter, had been hijacked by my grandparents in their old Hillman. The car had once belonged to my father. My grandfather had expertly repaired it himself.

Miss Woodford said it would be out of their way. They insisted it was not. She insisted that it was. They insisted it was not and she got into the back seat beside me. The powerful mixture of fear, intimacy, and shame I felt at sitting beside her in the back seat of the car with its sprung beige leather seats made me dizzy. I was having my most intense experience apart from encounters with God I had had while meditating in front of my bar heater in winter. It was also the most excruciating.

Woody knew now: she knew now that my grandmother but probably not my grandfather would have gone to a school like Newnham. Not all the girls at Newnham came from families who would have attended private schools. However, all Newnham girls and their families had ... something: connections, professions, money, tradition, mothers like mine who'd gone to the school, fathers like mine who'd attended the equivalent boys' schools. I adored Granddad almost more than anyone—but he did use odd grammar sometimes. And Gran was so blunt coming, as she did, from Scotland. Miss Woodford needed subtlety. If Granddad used odd grammar or Gran asked an inappropriate question in the car, my connection with Woody would wither instantly and my inner world would collapse on itself in a way I could not imagine.

We went over a bump. The back seat lurched. My grandmother apologized with her crisp Scottish accent so unlike my grandfather's Australian accent. My grandfather asked, "Right back there?" I stopped breathing.

Miss Woodford laughed and said it was the most fun she'd had in a week; her parents were ill and this was the first time she'd been able to go anywhere and even now it was just to the dentist. She then said how lucky she was that they had come to pick up Meg so that she could get to town faster as well as meet them. My grandmother asked Woody if she was English. Woody asked my grandmother if she was Scottish. My grandfather teased them both about their accents. It began to dawn on me that they all liked one another.

My grandmother asked Woody if she was a Newnham girl herself. I held my breath. There she was: my blunt grandmother questioning Woody's origins.

Woody said easily, "No" and explained she'd gone to a state high school closer to her family's home.

I'd never asked. I'd assumed, because of her accent, that Woody had gone to one of the girls' schools. Because of my blunt grandmother, I now knew where Woody had gone to school: a government institution known for its high academic standards. I wondered if I could get a transfer.

They moved on to other topics: street repair, the latest news, my father's work.

We let Woody out in Liverpool Street right in front of her dentist's building. Now I knew where her dentist was. I memorized the address. My heart went walking off to the dentist while my body sat in exposed silence while my grandfather commented on what a nice girl the teacher was. A bit long in the tooth, my grandmother added, but a nice type of girl.

That Christmas, Hugh and his parents moved down south, Gwenda gave me a handkerchief sachet with my initials embroidered on it, and Miss Woodford's parents died. She stopped walking to the tram and bought an eight-year-old Hillman with her parent's legacy.

TWENTY-ONE

....

THE STORY

Mabel Montgomery, my mother's childhood friend from Miss Ellery's Kindergarten, was in her forties when her mother died of senility. She lived alone in genteel poverty in Herrington House in Herrington Heights. Nan—my elegant, quietly irreverent grandmother whom my mother called twice a day and whom we saw twice a week—took Mabel under her wing, giving her leftover clothes, hats, and lunches in town. Mabel had no phone, no car, no newspaper, and no money. She had "friends in the country" whom she would visit annually for a week.

Every two months, Nan would write in her flowing penmanship on heavy cream paper to invite Mabel for afternoon tea and then to repair to the sewing room to try on Nan's exquisitely made castoffs.

To accept, Mabel needed to walk two miles from Herrington House to my grandmother's large house and gardens and slip her acceptance note, written in a large, round hand, into the letterbox, which was embedded in the brick wall and usually occupied by a tree frog.

They would meet at Nan's house. After Nan had fitted Mabel, Nan would alter the pieces and they would meet a second time—all arranged by letter, of course—for the transfer of the altered clothes. A third meeting would take place in the center of town so that Mabel could christen her "new" clothes. In a taxi, Nan would pick up Mabel at Herrington House. They would proceed into town—my grandmother seated in majesty in the back seat with her eyes firmly shut because of speed—and they would lunch at Robertson's.

My mother, who, when she wasn't feeling guilty about Nan or her in-laws or the washing or something she had said to the greengrocer, liked to be left alone indefinitely. Her best companions were her typewriter, the grand piano, a pile of German novels, Raj fiction, or books on eccentric topics she had ordered through the local library and which often required weeks to arrive from some library down south. However, she was regularly quietly bullied by her own guilt into inviting Mabel to afternoon tea. This was no was small thing. My mother loathed entertaining and found most people boring. Boredom made her back and legs ache. Despite her boredom and her dislike of entertaining, she did quite a lot of it on my father's behalf.

One afternoon, I arrived home from school with a pile of homework, including a short story due too soon. We were "doing" The Short Story and had been assigned to read several boring Australian ones, analyzing point of view and structure—exposition, conflict, rising action, climax, dénouement. Now we had to make a story up, filling in the blanks, and do it in a thousand words or less for submission at the end of the week.

I opened the front door, not to the sound of my mother's typewriter or of her piano but to Mabel's careful tones trying to penetrate my grandmother's deafness and my mother's voice offering more tea.

I walked in, said a polite hello to Miss Montgomery, kissed my grandmother on her soft cheek, and kissed my mother, all in the proper order—I thought. Maybe Nan should have come before Miss Montgomery but I'd done my best; I knew I should use my best manners, especially in school uniform, but couldn't remember whether Age trumped Visitor in the greeting rules. Personally, I would have hugged Chang first but I was being good: I knelt down on the Persian carpet and hugged him last, then went off to wash my hands and comb my hair before joining the adults, as I was expected to do.

I was resolved to be the perfect Young Person, the charming Only Child. However, the end of the day got the better of me. As I sat together with the three of them and began to make conversation, I heard myself using slang that lifted Miss Montgomery's thick grey, unplucked eyebrows a smidgen. The harder I tried to be formal, the more slang came out—school was "beaut"; our trip south was "fab"; some of our teachers wore "daggy" clothes.

My mother began to make frantic, miniature facial gestures at me—the kind she made when we played duets and she didn't want to stop the flow of the music but did want me to get a grip on the beat. We were having the regulation afternoon tea: pikelets, scones, and cake, none of which were made by my mother, who drew the line at foregoing the keys on her typewriter or piano in favor of the stove. I offered Miss Montgomery, Nan, and my mother—in that order—some of each of these and managed to remember; as the afternoon tea progressed, to leave at least one of each uneaten on the painted plates. Chang wandered around looking for scraps under the delicate side tables.

Finally, I excused myself and went off to work on a story.

"What happened?" my mother asked me later as she cut up meat for Chang and shelled peas.

"I've no idea. She's so ... depressing. She's just ... grey all over."

My mother giggled guiltily, agreed, and told me never to say that in front of anyone in case someone heard and thought we were mean. I went to the fridge and helped myself to a soft drink and a couple of Tim Tam chocolate biscuits lurking at the end of the packet. We kept them in the fridge because they melted on summer days.

Mabel had been sent home in a taxi, along with a pile of clothes and some cotton stuffing that Nan had advised her to stick in her petticoat "up top" to fill in the gaps. Nan had begun to play "Sleepy Lagoon" on the piano in the living room for the third time before dinner. Every time she missed a chord, my mother winced. I suddenly realized that this was how she must look when I was playing a wrong chord, which I did frequently. It was the first time I became aware that even I, adored by my mother in a sedate, objective way, had not avoided making her wince.

I was hoping Nan would stop playing before my father arrived home. She and he still saw eye to eye on little other than where my mother's first allegiance lay, which pleased my grandmother but not my father.

"You know the way you and I got the silent giggles in church at that funeral once?" I told my mother by way of explaining away my strange behavior with Mabel. "It was like that. I just couldn't stop even when I told myself to. I was watching myself. I did see you making those your eyebrow squiggles but it didn't help. Mabel's just so solemn and careful and correct that she makes me do the opposite."

The following week our stories and poems were due for submission to the school magazine. I submitted two sonnets and the short story I'd just finished for homework. I was pleased with them. One sonnet was about aspiring to be a veterinarian and the other was about feeling religious when I felt the wind blow. I thought them both pretty original and they scanned and rhymed. I was also so pleased with the short story, which I had worked on until one in the morning, that I didn't feel the need to sit my mother down in the kitchen and make her listen to every word, as I usually did. She was a good critic: fair, ruthless, honest, respectful. She didn't solve my school problems but would hint loudly and cleanly so that I got the point.

The next morning I turned in my submissions to Miss Fletcher for the magazine. Fletch was tripling her duties this year: Senior Boarding School Mistress, Religion Teacher, and Magazine Editor. She was a relentlessly pleasant, gentle woman whose chief claim to fame among the girls who boarded was that one had seen Fletch drying her hair one Saturday afternoon and it was down past her waist and grey and she had phoned her mother—reverse charge, long distance—with all the wet hair hanging down. We concluded she must have a wild side after all. Even though it was rumored she was a deacon in the church, she couldn't be all dull.

When I dropped the submissions off, Fletch smiled and looked pleased to have some from me. I walked a fine line managing to stay liked by my peers and by the teaching staff, most of whom were highly educated, single women.

I waited to hear something from Fletch about my brilliant work. Nothing came.

The following Thursday night, my mother told my father that

the headmistress had phoned.

"Miss Arlington? Again? What's wrong this time?"

"She didn't say anything was wrong," my mother replied. "In fact, she said that all was, as usual, 'quite in order with Meg,' but that perhaps you might find time to give her a ring in the next couple of weeks."

Later, my father walked into my room where I was working on another poem beneath my fat Chemistry book.

"Miss Arlington rang. She doesn't ring to pass the time of day," he said, his jaw set to the side in the way that told me he was sad or angry. "She's a busy woman."

I waited. He hadn't asked anything but my silence was considered an act of rebellion.

"Well?"

"I don't know, Dad." I scanned through the last weeks in my memory. Other than talking too much in Chem lab, I was sin-free to the best of my knowledge.

By the next afternoon, I had a hunch.

That evening, I listened to my parents' conversation through the wall that separated my bedroom from theirs; the most successful way to do this was by holding an empty water glass up to the wall.

"All she said was that she'd found herself thinking about Meg. I asked her whether something was wrong. She said nothing at all was wrong but she does keep in touch with involved parents. She told me she appreciated my unsolicited support at the last joint meeting. So that might have been why she rang. Something sounded off but I couldn't push it. You know what she's like."

After a moment of silence, he opened my door a crack. I'd turned the light out about ten minutes earlier so he did not see me slide the glass under the sheets. I pretended to be just waking as the light from the corridor slid across the floor.

"Meg, you've only just turned your light out so I know you are still awake. What's going on at school? Something's off and I don't think you're being straight with us."

I assured my father I'd been given good marks for all my homework (I'd even got an A- for the short story from our English mistress although she'd added, "Too ambitious for a first attempt. Write about what you know. Grammar and paragraphing good.")

I decided my father needed a bone to chew. I told him I'd only got 7 out of 10 for the Mathematics test but always managed to get an A in the final year exams even when my homework wasn't always good. I said sadly I just couldn't think mathematically. I asked my father if he could help me some time with Algebra. Caught up in my mythologizing, I also told him I'd tried out for running and ballgames but didn't know the results yet and was sure I wouldn't get in. I added, after an appropriate moment for reflection, that I hadn't got into trouble for talking in class since last term; after all, I was the elected class leader and knew I was supposed to set an example.

Finally, I decided I needed to close my musings down or they would never end: I "confessed" that what I was really worried about was the new history section; I didn't understand Canada. I asked if he could help me with that, too, on the weekend. He seemed mollified, kissed me on the forehead, touched the little hairs that grew at the edge of my hairline and were always damp, and pulled my door almost closed on the way out.

By this time, I was sure I knew what had happened: Fletch must have completely misunderstood my story. Just because I had written about a middle-aged woman who wears grey and takes care of her mother (who is senile and doesn't recognize her daughter) and the daughter, because she loves the mother so much that she doesn't want to see her suffer any more, puts a pillow over the mother's face one night and waits until the neighbors wake the next morning so she can ask them, with a radiant smile, if they would be kind enough to call the police to arrest her (because she can't afford a phone), this didn't mean I wanted to kill my mother, for heaven's sake.

I decided I'd better withdraw my story from Fletch and submit another—probably something about unhappy Aborigines—which I could whip up tomorrow night. Stories about Aboriginal children were always safe. I would submit mine to Fletch with the excuse that I thought it was better written than my other story.

TWENTY-TWO

....

THE MOTH

It landed on my desk one night about ten o'clock.

My mother had retired to the piano to practice Bach. Through the thick plaster of the walls, I heard her repeating a phrase in a prelude until her left hand moved with ease through the fingering. Again and again she would ask whether her playing late at night disturbed either my father or me.

"You go ahead, Lucy," my father had insisted on this particular night. "It's lovely. Ever since we were first married, it's helped me write reports. Makes me focus."

"Yes, Mamma. It helps me study better too."

"If you're sure ..."

It was a ritual conversation. We knew the rules but it was one of the few times we told the truth. The truth was wasted. My mother never fully believed us.

Shortly after this exchange, I heard my father speaking on the phone with his mother. He was on the verandah, speaking loudly so Gran—whose hearing was bad—could make out what he was saying. I was in my bedroom.

My mother stopped playing. She went to one of the French

doors that opened onto the verandah.

My father interrupted his phone conversation with Gran and turned his attention to my mother. "What, Lucy?"

"I'm sorry, Michael. I'm worried that I'm disturbing you. I can hear you raising your voice and I don't want to be a bother."

"You're not. I'll keep my voice down."

"Only if it won't interfere with your conversation. It is a little hard to focus ..."

"I'm sorry.... No, Mother, I was talking to Lucy. Go on. You were telling me about their finally calling the new minister."

My mother went back to the Bach and my father to his now-muted conversation. Soon he would return to his study and re-immerse himself in Philosophy I, Greek, Latin, and Ancient History, all of which he was studying in the time his doctor had ordered him to take off from his work in the lab. "Can't burn the candle at both ends," his doctor had remarked laconically. "Can't go through all those years in the war without a spot of bother occasionally down the line."

After that doctor's visit, my father put his senior man in charge of the lab and wrote up a detailed manual that, had it been a battle plan, could not have been more finely organized. Then he walked down the wide, sandstone steps of the lab for the last time for a year.

"You know what she asked us today?" he said at dinner. "That snip of a thing who's teaching Philosophy I? She asked the class, 'How do you know if the phone is ringing?' How do you know if the phone is ringing? What kind of question is that? *That's* why we give our students free university education? To sit around discussing whether the *phone* is ringing? The phone is ringing because it's bloody ringing and for twenty years that's meant work for the lab, for me, income, putting you through the best school.... That little snip with her short skirt and Ph.D. is about ten years old—and I think she might be a bit pink. Her husband's in the Political Science Department and I've heard he's a radical. They don't want children, either. Perhaps I'm too old to study what I always wanted but you two encouraged me and ..."

"Michael you had to do something. You were sick! You're still taking care of us financially even if things are a little different. We all agreed. Now you get to do what you really wanted to after the war."

"Play along with the snip, Dad. Just *ask* her something. Make her feel important. Or ignore her and enjoy the rest," I said, skilled in the art of darting invisibly around impossible teachers.

My father looked at me with a combination of shock, suspicion, enlightenment, and relief. The next night, his protestations subsided. We went back to the monologues that had characterized our nightly dinners for years. Where until recently my father's monologue had been about the people in his lab, now they were about the odd types he was meeting in the Arts Faculty. My mother's monologues tended toward the latest German novel she was reading, her bad back, her mother's health, some new successful band she had predicted would top the hit parade, her doubts about her latest article and about how she was sure she wouldn't be able to deliver it on time, a new show on television with some obscure actor she had seen in an art film ten years ago and whose career she had tracked, and back to her mother's health. My monologue leaned toward a daily *recitatif* of restrictive actions of teachers at my girls' school (some of which teachers had also taught my mother and my best friend Livi's mother); outrageous activities of my peers, such as wearing their school hat backwards in town and not getting caught; and school gossip. I kept my writing, my passions, my nightly experiments with mysticism, and my diary to myself—or so I thought.

After the washing up, we would each repair to our separate pursuits.

The night the moth appeared on my desk was balmy, one of the first nights of true summer and before it would grow so beastly and sweaty that I would have to do my homework under the mosquito net if I wanted to leave the window open. No one had screens then.

I had given up on my Physics homework but had left the large text open. I needed to be able to place it quickly over the poetry I was writing if someone came in.

The moth landed beside my fountain pen. I sat still, looked at it, and then looked out the window. Beyond and far below the yellow light from my desk lamp, the lights of the valley peppered the dark as far as the foothills. Stars rested along the undulating crest of the highest hills. A half moon was freeing itself from an indigo cloud.

I looked back at the moth. It lifted itself from the desk and placed itself on my fountain pen, wings folded.

When my father knocked on the door, I moved suddenly, always ready to present the right impression and so he wouldn't know what I was doing, regardless of its legitimacy. I covered my half-written poem with the Physics text, the moth flew out the window to somewhere inside the pawpaw tree just beyond, and I answered, "Yes Dad," all in seconds.

"Sorry to interrupt your homework but you should know that Granddad isn't well again. You might give him a ring tomorrow when you get home. I didn't call you to the phone tonight because you said you had a lot of homework. At least I assume that's what's you're doing."

"I'm sorry about Granddad," I said. "He's only just over the bronchitis. I'll ring tomorrow."

"How's Physics?"

I held my breath. If he decided to look, I was caught. The poem (written to and about him) underneath my textbook would be revealed.

He glanced down idly but with interest at my desk. "What are you on now?"

"The eye."

"Always interested me, the eye."

He bent over and picked up the book. Without looking sneaky, I tried casually to close the spiral-bound exercise book that lay underneath.

He looked at me. "You're devious, Meg. Your mother and I just begin to trust you, then you do something like this, and we have to start from scratch. I don't know what you were doing just now and I don't want to know but you clearly have been taking advantage of our trust."

"I was just taking a little break and trying to write some poetry." I made sure to look right into his eyes so I would look innocent.

"I said I don't want to know what you were doing. I already know what I need to know: you said you were doing one thing but were doing another. By being deceitful, you denied your grandfather the pleasure of speaking with you when he is ill. I don't know why we're sending you to the top school if you can't even be honest—or thoughtful. Giving is not all one way, you know. It's not easy to keep you at that school. I'm not generating the same income this year as I have in the past. You know I have to work weekends at present. I wouldn't be taking the year off if the doctor hadn't made me and if I hadn't sensed some divine intervention about it. I've put my foot forward in faith but I can't do it alone. You constantly let me—all the family—down."

"I'd finished my Physics, Dad—mostly. I was just taking a break."

He looked at the textbook. Unfortunately, it was open to the first page of the chapter on the eye and I hadn't underlined anything.

He looked back at me sadly.

"You've been swanning around for half an hour at least. You could have spent it studying and calling your grandfather. Those girls in your group are a bad influence. All that pointless gossip at lunchtime. You tell us about it every evening."

"They're not, Dad. Most of them get top marks." I decided I would never show him the poem I was writing, even though it was a special poem about him, and—I thought—fairly brilliant. "Livi's in the group. You like her. There's nothing wrong with them. Only a few aren't really good students. Anyway, I'll eat lunch with whoever I like. It's not the same as class and it's not home." I thought about this declaration. Two things were wrong with it: first, "whoever" should have been "whomever." Even in adversity, my mother's unfailing grammatical training did not desert me. Second, what I'd said, I'd said it to *him*.

"You bloody well won't, if I say so. I never spoke back to your grandfather. Didn't have to. We knew what he wanted without being told and we respected him. From now on, you leave me no option but to tell you to leave the door open while you're doing homework. When you prove yourself trustworthy—and I'll tell you *if* that day arrives—you can push it to again."

I knew my father's concern was not about my school performance. I had long since proven I was a good student *and* a leader. (Good students ran the risk of being thought "brains" by their peers, so they often lost leadership elections.) My father's concern was about my secrecy, my lying, my priorities.

The next night, the moth came again and sat on my fountain pen. It came the next night and the night after that.

On the fifth night, my father phoned from the booth outside the university library. After my mother assured him I only had an hour of homework, she let me watch my favorite television program, "Father Knows Best," and start my homework later. By the time I got to my room, it was eight o'clock.

The evening was still hot. I opened the window wide and started studying. With the door open.

The moth arrived. Tonight it did not sit on my pen. Rather, it sat on the windowsill for a long time and then flew at the hot light of my study lamp. With a hiss, it singed itself to death, falling away from the light bulb and onto my open French book.

I picked up its gentle, powdery, grey-brown body. I thought I might write a poem about it. Perhaps I would change it into a bird. A bird in a golden cage. A bird that was in a golden cage and died. (No one would ever think a poem about a moth was good.) The bird in my poem would never be seen by anyone. It would die without anyone knowing it. Writing the poem, however, would have to wait until later, when I was under the covers, the door mostly closed, and I, officially asleep. I would have to use my new pencil flashlight, the one my father had given me after my old one died. The new one was just like his.

Wing dust mixed with tears dropped on the left-hand page of

my French text, right next to the *Vocabulaire* list. *How stupid*, I thought. *I'm crying over a moth.* The tears even dropped onto the irregular verb conjugations on the right-hand page. I wrapped the moth in a piece of tissue paper and placed it in my second desk drawer.

I turned the page and began to review tenses and moods: conditional meant that something or someone depended on something or someone else; imperfect meant the thing wasn't over yet. We were supposed to review them as well as the simple past. I didn't get to the simple past that night.

TWENTY-THREE

THE ORDER OF THINGS

We lived in alternating controlled chaos and reparation. The reparation took the form of precise categorization. I was less naturally driven to the order end of things than my mother, so she was usually the instigator. I fell for it every time.

"Darling," my mother said from the kitchen one day, "I thought I might do out the linen closet this afternoon. It's so hot it's ridiculous for me to even try to draft the next article or even play the piano, let alone paint. Even the German novel I got from the library isn't very good." This was before we had the pool.

I heard her put on the kettle in the kitchen. I was in my room.

"Are you very busy or might you be able to help me get things from the back of the bottom drawers? I want to use the little cut linen afternoon tea cloth Nan gave us—when she comes with Mabel tomorrow. I've taken a cursory look. It's not in the front."

I added a word I'd just remembered to the poem I was working on. A good word: "penumbral." I thought it went well with "longing." I had come across it a week before in the novel we'd been assigned for English. We'd been given the whole academic year to read it (it didn't do to hurry anything in '60s Australia) but I'd read it in an afternoon. It was one of those early novels—sincere, self-conscious, set in the gold fields. It was considered not only well written but potent with capacity to awaken interest in early Australian history among young readers. There were scads of references to early discoverers, gold fields, food, respectable characters overcoming colonial odds, all covered with a kind of unending heat and dustiness. Even spending a single afternoon on the whole thing had bored me silly.

"I'm sorry, darling," she said, coming to the door of my blue room; I still loved the ice-blue wallpaper and deep-blue carpet I had been allowed to choose when my parents built the house several years earlier. "I didn't know you were in the middle of something. I am sorry. Did I ruin it?"

"Don't be. Sorry, I mean. How were you to know? And no, you didn't. I'll be there in a minute," I added. She smiled ruefully, knowing what my minutes were like.

I was working on a religious sonnet. I planned on entering it for a State competition. It started:

My hair blows like my virgin thoughts ...

"Virgin" made me a little uneasy but this was poetry and if Keats and Shelley and other people could do it, I could. I was having a hard time finding a rhyme for "virgin" but I didn't want to give up the word. And the line didn't scan. It wasn't iambic pentameter yet. I needed to add a two-syllable word. Finally, I decided, in the interest of completing a first draft, to redefine it as blank verse. Then I could work in "penumbral longing" somewhere without worrying about beat.

"*Which* cloth? There're a lot of them," I called out, buying time. I crossed out "penumbral" and replaced it with "last light's." This seemed more banal but I liked the alliteration in "last light's longing."

"The one Aunty Lou gave Nan—with the cream roses trailing down the corners and the tired-looking scalloped edges."

"Bottom shelf."

"I know it's in the bottom, darling. That's why I was wondering if you could help. It's where I can't reach. I feel guilty now."

So soft and silky, glints before my eyes

Now that was iambic. Maybe it could be a sonnet after all. If I added a beat to other lines ... but what about the rhyme?

"Aunt Lou's dead, Mamma. And Nan doesn't care. Or are you having an attack of guilt about asking me?"

Before the trees, before light dies

Maybe I could do rhyming couplets. The rhymes were coming pretty easily now but I seemed to be losing the point I had wanted to make. I couldn't remember, in the mounting heat of a February afternoon, the particular suffering that had led to this inspired piece in the first place. Perhaps I was supposed to succumb to the muse and let it take its course. I scratched out "unfold" and substituted "untold."

A crow squawked outside my window and landed ungracefully in the pawpaw tree. The air was gold with heat and the hills were mauve instead of blue-green. The private-school twins in the house around the corner were yelling politely at each other as they played cricket. Next door, Aiden was practicing "Für Elise." He still stalled on the first trill but plodded determinedly onwards. He stopped playing when he got to the middle part with the repetitions and broke into "Chopsticks." I heard Mrs. Trembath say "Aiden" in a civil, firm voice from their back landing. The left hand of "Für Elise" started up slowly again.

"Aiden has no ear," said my mother. "Poor thing. He can't even hear it's a waltz. They could get him a metronome. I feel guilty now; Nan gave Lou's cloth to me because she thought it was pretty and I'd like it but I've just said mean things about it."

I decided to give up the sonnet *cum* rhymed couplets *cum* blank verse for now.

"Being nasty now doesn't count if you are very nice about the thing later. Especially when Nan's here. You can show it off to Mabel. Tell her it came from Nan's dead cousin. That'll make Nan happy and Mabel will think you're being spontaneous and confidential because it's about the Family. Hold on. I'll crawl into the back and get it."

"But darling, you're writing. I just registered what you're doing."

"It's not working."

"That's my fault."

"It's. Not. Your. Fault." I was now half in the linen closet and half out. It was cool down there and smelled of starch and unpainted wood.

"If I hadn't gone on about the tea cloth, you'd be finished."

With my bottom stuck out into the hall, I kept handing out impeccably ironed cloths to my mother. Some were yellowing at the folds.

"I do wish Aiden would at least move on to the Scarlatti," my mother said. "He does sound a little like a drunken koala at times. There I go again. And it's not strictly accurate because I've only heard a koala's cry on the radio. I'll never learn to be *naturally* nice. I also used a poor simile. Koalas don't get drunk so how would one know what they sound like drunk anyway?"

"They do howl though when they're trying to get sex," I added as a consolation prize. "They sound *awful*. We heard one on that zoo trip. Mamma, you'd be boring if you were nice all the time. Your articles aren't *always* nicey-nice but people still love them. You're never publicly nasty at someone else's expense. I think that's one of the reasons they keep publishing you. Listen: I. Wouldn't. Have. Finished. The. Poem! I was too hot. Please let's just do the linen closet. It'd give me a sense of satisfaction to have finished something. Then we can watch 'Mrs. Miniver.' It's on again tonight."

"Only if you're sure. I would appreciate it. I know: you and I could play being at the Chalet School and the maids have the day off so ..."

"I'm a little old for Chalet School, aren't I?"

"What's that make *me*, then?"

"Alright," I said. "But *you* be Jo. I'll want to be Miss Annersley today. I feel like being headmistress. But first we have to think of why we are at boarding school during the summer holidays." I passed out more folded linen tablecloths and handkerchief-linen, hand-embroidered hand towels to my mother.

My mother paused for a moment and then said confidently, "Jo's cousin in England is unwell and Jo's sister has to accompany her husband to a conference in Canada. So Jo can't spend the summer with either of them. Because she's an orphan, she's going to visit her other cousins in Italy soon. However, until she leaves, she's stuck at school. Miss Annersley, who privately has a soft spot for Jo—as we know—has taken her under her wing and will stay at school until Jo leaves for Italy. She will take Jo to Italy via Lugano where Miss Annersley has distant, interesting relatives. She will even smoke in front of Jo because she trusts her. Jo won't be allowed to smoke, of course. Miss Annersley is also delighted for Jo because she knows that the mistresses and students have voted Jo in as Head Girl next year but she can't tell Jo. It's a secret—except to the teaching staff and to millions of readers.

"Miss Annersley tells Jo that this afternoon she would prefer they could go hiking but she has to prepare to entertain Someone Important who's arriving by train tomorrow from Interlaken. Jo cheerfully offers to help Miss Annersley."

"That's a lot of background for one pathetic little afternoon tea cloth."

"I *had* thought that perhaps we might even manage more than one shelf of the linen closet." My mother had the grace to look shamefaced. "The length of the tale is, I admit, unintentionally proportionate to the number of shelves." My mother looked like my shih tzu when he was caught chewing on the furniture.

"Jo," I said, "would you kindly take the ironing blanket off the kitchen table? We'll sort the linens there. Do be a dear girl and make us some tea too, would you?"

My mother trotted off happily to the kitchen to reheat the water she had been heating before we started this whole thing.

I pulled out everything on the bottom shelf. One hot-pink, tired, rubber, hot water bottle; several scales that said one weighed more than one was convinced one weighed; a shoebox of shampoos used once and rejected for inability to control waves or create bounce; and three large shoeboxes of linens that did not belong on the upper shelves.

"Are these all the nasty ones?" I demanded as I loaded all three boxes into my arms and walked carefully into the kitchen, "or are there *more?*"

"Careful! You might drop them. Then I'd have to wash and iron them again. I mean, the school maids would have to wash and iron them again when they return."

"You don't *ever* use them. I've never *seen* half of these!"

"That's not the point. They'd still be dirty. You're not being Miss Annersley."

"Sorry. Thank you, Jo, for being so concerned about the health of the girls. However, I think that the maids, being Swiss—as you well know—thoroughly cleaned the polished floors so we need not worry." I dumped the three tired boxes onto the kitchen table.

"Miss Annersley doesn't get crabby with girls without good reason. You're being crabby."

"Yes she does. Miss Arlington at real school does, anyway. She even gets crabby with some of the Form Mistresses in front of us. Livi loves it when she does that."

"English headmistresses of Swiss boarding schools don't. Not the headmistress of the Chalet School anyway." My mother sighed. "This isn't fun any more. I thought we could do this together and have fun." She sank onto the kitchen chair whose cushion was covered with Swiss edging she had ordered from down south. She took a small, sad bite of Scotch shortbread and sipped her tea.

"I need a Bex," she said wearily.

"Where are they?"

"You don't want to do this closet. I know you don't. *Please*, go back to your writing."

I went to the kitchen cupboard and turned the white lazy Susan, upon which everything was placed according to function and alphabetic order. B. Bex. I got a glass of water, opened the fine white paper folded lengthwise, then across. The powder stayed in the fold while one poured it delicately onto one's tongue without breathing so heavily that it sprayed all over one's face or choked one. My mother took it delicately, deftly, expertly. She downed the powder with minimal water and went back to the tea.

"Let's start over." I said, relenting. "Jo, I'm terribly sorry to disturb you when you're concerned about your cousin but I do need a little help to prepare things for tomorrow. Could I possibly trouble you to help me?"

My mother brightened, straightened her back, and smiled. "Of course! I'd be delighted. I have an idea."

"Yes, Jo?" I managed to say without too much suspicious resentment leaking into my tone. My mother, with her preternatural ear for anything less than full-bodied acquiescence, looked up. I quickly assumed an air of authoritative inquiry and started to line up the three boxes at the end of the table. Out of the corner of my eye, I could see my mother settle again.

"Let's put them out three different ways: by color, then by Unlovable to Truly Loathsome, and then by People Alert."

"Define 'People Alert.' "

"If Nan's coming, we can be on the alert to get out her things; if Aunt Vee's coming, we get out hers. We can decide which method works best."

The afternoon sun was beginning to slant at the depressingly oblique angle that heralded the onset of a summer evening of mosquitoes.

Clearly nothing less than complete approval of Jo's idea was going to pull off this venture. "Excellent, Jo. Let's begin."

For over an hour, we played musical chairs with the unused linens. Jo was undecided about which system was most effective. I was reminded more than once by Jo that her cousin was seriously ill and that Jo needed tender handling. Finally my mother decided on the categories: Unlovable but Passable; Unlovable; and Loathsome. She thought more than three categories might confuse her if she were in a hurry. We agreed to pin little notes cut from lined paper in an exercise book and written in Jo's neat, flat script onto things that had "sentimental value." These would also list the name of the person who had burdened my mother with the gift.

By the time we'd finished the little notes, it was time for my mother to have a cigarette, so we had to switch roles because only Miss Annersley—not Jo—could smoke. We decided that tomorrow we'd spend an hour doing a box from the next shelf up.

"That's a difficult box. We have to decide if anything can go to Second Life. They're coming next week to pick up the old table downstairs."

"I'll be Jo tomorrow."

"As long as you don't bully me into making decisions to give things away when I don't want to."

"You don't need umpteen guest-bedroom dresser cloths, Mamma! We don't even have a guest bedroom."

"I asked you not to bully me tomorrow and you're already starting today."

"I. Am. Not. Bullying. Merely pointing out you don't need them."

"It's your tone. This is supposed to be fun."

"Alright. Let's do that batch tomorrow. As long as I'm Jo."

"You can be Jo. You can set the time we do it and how long we spend doing it. I do appreciate your help, you know. You're a 'Good Daughter.'"

"I know. Now can I go back and finish what I was working on?"

"Of course, darling. Daddy won't be home from the board meeting until after seven so you can have a whole, perfect hour undisturbed."

I retreated to my room. I closed the windows and turned on the desk lamp in that order so the mosquitoes wouldn't all come in to accompany my resumption of work on the poem.

I sat there looking out across the Trembath's garden to the valley. Aiden was playing ball under the back steps. A dog barked. The lights were beginning to come on in the valley between our house and the high hills.

I thought about my mother's need to have everything just so, her conviction that things had a perfect place, that tones had a right way of being delivered, that the afternoon tea had to be perfect for Nan—and for Mabel, for heaven's sake, who was lucky to be invited anywhere, given she was so boring and spinstery. I kept trying to tell my mother it didn't have to be perfect but she never listened. Our lives were Swiss order or chaos with nothing in between. It pained her to see or hear or sense imperfections.

I knew I was not like her. I looked around my room. A mess. The dressing table was perfect only because we'd done it together last week, including washing my hairbrushes and repapering each drawer. But the rest—clothes hung the wrong way, shoes on top of each other in the built-in wardrobe, underclothes mixed in with shorts and tops. Diaries concertina'd between cardigans to hide them. The mess did bother me but it didn't bother me a lot: that was the difference. I felt sad for my mother and relieved for me.

I grabbed Chang and hung him over my lap. He hung, limp from heat, like an old rug. I reviewed the last version of the poem.

My mother, having put the potatoes on to boil for a potato salad, had gone to the living room to practice Beethoven. I heard the metronome. This was one of her favorite pieces. I hummed along automatically as she played. I liked the repeating s's in the first two lines;

Fluted silence stands,
And sings to me.

Those s's. I had discovered that some part of me understood an invisible order I hadn't known was there—"silence," "stands" (two s's), "sings (also two s's). Now I found myself changing the next line to begin with "seeking" without my even intending it:

Seeking truth in the park

And then another two s's in the next line:

Is life green shimmer, merely mirage?

A rhetorical question. That was good: I knew there was, indeed, a meaning to life but I knew I didn't know it yet so this was a good way to express the depth of this painful state attributable, doubtless, to my age.

And now, if I really, really didn't try, the next line might begin itself.

Would I could know!
If I but knew the answers
To these penumbral longings.

No, I'd changed that in version four to last light's longings.

Repeated l's. Overall, this was becoming a good, deep poem. I seemed to be using poetic techniques and a kind of discovered order without even trying.

I read the tenth version out loud as the light faded outside and the sky bled. A solitary mosquito had found its way in and settled its proboscis into my tanned, left arm. I held my breath as we had taught each other to do at school: if one did this, one could trap the enemy and it couldn't escape. Sure enough, I tickled the mosquito and it squirmed helplessly. I slapped it to death and flicked it onto the mounting sheets of paper in front of me.

I closed my door and read the poem aloud again, standing in front of my dressing table's full-length mirror. My delivery was improving each time. I loved the way certain lines rolled on my tongue and showed the depth of the pain in my soul: the whole poem was deep but some bits were deeper than others.

Having written it out in my best penmanship, which had won me prizes at school, I pulled out the rules of the competition from my drawer. There were three categories and limits to the number of words.

The first category was Sonnet. My poem didn't have fourteen lines, iambic pentameter, or a sonnet's rhymes, so it didn't fit in the Sonnet Section. The second category was Rhymed Verse: General. My poem didn't have all lines rhyming and I didn't think they'd count internal rhymes so it didn't qualify for the second section. I reviewed the last category: Blank Verse. It qualified.

However, I knew what would win: some poem about Aborigines. (We had never seen any, really, except for those on the corner near a central suburb we passed on the way to school.) Or some boring, nationalistic thing about the beauty of a jacaranda tree in bloom or the travails of Captain Cook.

Really, there was no point in submitting my poem. In fact, now that I looked at it again, it wasn't even good enough to submit to Miss Bowen for the school magazine. The last time I'd given Bow'n'Arrow (Miss Bowen, by any other name) one of my poems—a full-blown sonnet about Truth and Love—it was good. Very good in my opinion. It scanned perfectly, rhymed perfectly, and had Depth. I had shared my most intimate thoughts with her in that poem! And what did I get back? She had scanned one line incorrectly through her thick glasses, having clearly put the emphasis on the wrong syllable, and she had handed it back to me together with my regular homework without so much as "Good effort" or "Promising first attempt" written on it. All she said was "Line 11 fails to scan correctly." That sonnet wasn't even required homework!

I read my new poem, which I had titled "Silent Song" one more time, this time quietly sitting at my desk rather than standing in front of the full-length mirror as I had done earlier. What I had loved looked foolish, dusty, flawed. I had fallen out of love with it although I couldn't bear to throw away the earlier versions: there might be one or two good phrases I might want some day. But the poem itself was a flop. It didn't sing any more. I looked out the window. I could see myself in the reflection, except for where my fingerprints and a dead mosquito blurred my vision.

My mother was practicing a transition in the Beethoven. I could tell she wanted to play that section just once without error. Suddenly, she stopped, banged the keys impatiently and discordantly, closed the piano, and went to check on the potatoes.

TWENTY-FOUR

....

COMMUNION

The Reverend Duncan Needham spoke his written sermons slowly and punctuated the end of each sentence with a long pause. He spoke his unwritten ones even more slowly. My father had long since developed the admirable habit of appearing awake during sermons when he was actually sleeping—a habit he maintained for decades.

Reverend Needham's sermons were so slow that I had time to parse and repeat each of his sentences inside my head. I had also discovered that, if I repeated them in the voice of Claude Rains, Robert Young, or Alec Guinness—whose movies were shown repeatedly on early Australian television—the sermons sounded more interesting.

Take the sentence: "And if it was good enough for Jesus Christ to forgive a sinner like the woman at the well, we would do well to forgive those who trespass against us." Mr. Needham sounded as though he were reporting the cricket score. Sharing the announcer's horror of intruding on the game with personality, he eschewed emotion in favor of even-toned interest. Any greater display would have earned distrust. However, Claude Rains repeated the sentence to me as though it were a password into the underground. (I had read the story of Violette Zsabo, the underground resistance worker, so passwords appealed to me.) Robert Young said it to me as though the sentence were kind advice to his daughter before he went off to his doctor's office. And Alec Guinness said it to me standing on a bridge, calling out over the river, and defying all odds in khaki.

I liked my sound game. When I played it, Mr. Needham—tall and thin, with his patchy grey hair and bunch of blue-ruled papers pinned together with a sewing pin—became personal and his words plumped up with meaning and promise.

At the end of the service, we would line up to shake Mr. Needham's hand. In fact, I would shake Robert Young's hand with my gloved one, smiling up at him innocently underneath my wide-brimmed hat.

At night, after my parents thought I was asleep, I often read under the sheets with a small flashlight. I was currently in the middle of *The Nun's Story*. Well, more accurately, I had read it in one night and was rereading it page by page over a couple of months. I had found a battered copy of it in the top of my mother's closet next to where she kept her meditation books, sex books, and *The Well of Loneliness*. I had decided to sneak *The Nun's Story* into my room after my mother's old ballet mistress met me outside Robertson's, took me to morning tea, and then to see the film. I was never able to work out why she did that. She didn't know me and it was the only time she ever did anything with me. She disappeared from our town with her husband and mother soon after; no one ever found them.

As I took communion classes with Mr. Needham, sitting through his wandering explanations of "The Meaning of Becoming a Communicant," I also planned my entry into the Carmelites. The thing I liked best about *The Nun's Story* was that, after giving everything away—including her hair and her good grades, because the Mother Superior asked her to get bad grades in order to make some old nun feel better—and after about umpteen million years carrying heavy keys on her waist and not looking in the mirror as she walked through the asylum where she was nursing, Sister Luke was so silently heroic and tired that the Mother Superior called her into her office, spoke kindly to her, and told her that she was to get her wish to leave Belgium and go help lepers in the Congo. The Mother Superior was also so perfected as a Living Rule within the Order that she was permitted to break the convent ban and "venture the human touch" to Sister Luke. Sister Luke lived for years on that gesture—the Mother Superior's two-cheeked farewell—until she decided she had to leave the order to work for the Resistance, like Violette Zsabo. If I were to become a Carmelite, I would be perfect, too, look like Audrey Hepburn, and the Mother Superior would venture the human touch. Later, I would *be* the Mother Superior and *I* would venture the human touch. Usually, Mr. Needham's classes were nearly over by the time I had reviewed this plan.

At my private school, Morning Assembly was led by the headmistress, Miss Ruth S. N. Arlington. A straight-backed, handsome woman, she stood behind a carved lectern in corsets, linen-and-guipure-lace dresses, and high heels. She would say a prayer, do a reading (usually from the New Testament), give a two-minute address on something like "The Journey of a Thousand Miles Begins with the First Step," and then we would sing a hymn that somehow reflected her address as much as any Scottish or German hymn from the nineteenth century could reflect what was relevant for young women in the '60s. One of the senior music students would accompany the hymn with boredom and confidence on the organ. Then we would file out past the Head, who would stand still until the last ninth grader had crept past her and into a classroom, and the day of lessons would begin.

Miss Arlington was called "Miss A" by the well-behaved girls and school leaders, "Toothy Ruthy" by the majority, and "Snarly" by the rebels who defiantly stuck their school hats on the back of their heads en route home through the town center, talked in uniform to boys, and got Cs.

Sometimes when Miss A read the scripture for the day—especially after her elderly mother and ailing sister-who-smoked came to live with her at her residence—she sounded as though she were keeping Emotion out of her voice. The Senior Mistresses, all of whom had preceded Miss A's arrival and had been at the school since my mother's time there, would flick glances at each other, amassing—in silent complicity—confirmation of Miss A's social unfitness for her position and their deep suspicion that she might, in fact, even believe what she was saying. They feared she was treating the school as a church-based institution rather than as the finest girls' school around, which just happened to be governed by a consortium of Protestant denominations.

I would join my friends in gossiping about Miss A's emotional tone on morning break but, in the quiet of Algebra, I would imagine Miss A as Mother Ruth, the Mother Superior and, because I had abnegated so much ("abnegate" was a recent addition to my extensive vocabulary), Mother Ruth would call me to her office and venture the human touch.

My communion lessons with Mr. Needham continued weekly over the spring. Meanwhile, I practiced wrapping a pillowcase around my face, making the corners into wimples, and crossing myself nightly under the mosquito net. I also made up prayers to Mary. I felt awkward doing this. Mary wasn't someone to whom I'd been formally introduced by Mr. Needham or with whom I had been taught how to converse. Nonetheless, she and I got to know each other a little and I did like blue a lot, which I had heard was supposed to be her color.

At the end of the lessons with Mr. Needham, I wore my best white linen dress, stood up at the lectern, read the Apostle's Creed, and was proudly served the communion grape juice by my father who was a church leader. After the service, we went outside, and lined up in the queue to shake hands with the minister. That morning, Mr. Needham shook my gloved hand particularly vigorously with his hairy, freckly, thin, bony one.

Later that week, the newly elected school leaders of each level were announced. I, being the leader at my level, mounted the shiny wooden steps onto the stage with the other leaders so that Miss A could pin my badge to my uniform. We faced the assembled girls and teachers and Miss A, her neat and corseted back to the crowd, moved along the line of leaders. Her groomed hands, adorned by a single pearl ring, neatly pushed the pins through the lapels of my peers' uniforms. She followed each pinning with "Congratulations," a small nod of her head, and a firm handshake. The mounting applause would then become raucous as it erupted from the restless student body, glad of a legitimate reason to make noise in the Assembly Hall.

Finally, Miss A reached me. She pinned my badge neatly to my uniform. As she did so, the pearl in her ring brushed the left side of my neck. As the applause mounted, she murmured to me in crisp, low syllables, lips barely moving, "Still determined to wear those silly contact lenses, I see."

"Yes, Miss Arlington."

"Vain puss," she whispered. Her left eye dropped in a half-wink behind her glasses. Then she smiled slightly before she stood back and firmly shook my hand.

TWENTY-FIVE

....

SLEEPWALKER

Livi's brother Pete sleepwalked again that night—around the ledge that separated the ground floor from the upper storey of their big house. It was a hot night in the hills his family owned. Livi's older sister, Gwyn, was away with friends; her brother Bertie was off staying at the beach; the others—Roddy, Trish, and Pete—were at home.

Before Livi and I went to bed in her room on the ground floor, her seven-year-old sister Trish climbed in through our window, crying and talking through her tears and snot until we finally deciphered what she was saying: "Roddy threw me out of his room—through the window."

Livi let Trish sit on her bed. We listened to her tale, which concluded with her crying, saying she also had bumps that hurt. Livi gave her about two minutes, then amiably pushed her out the door, thus producing a howl of indignation and a bang on the door from Trish.

We resumed our talk about sex and fell asleep, Livi in Gwyn's bed and I in Livi's, imagining acts we had never seen or read about.

We awoke to thumping. Rod wandered past our room in his pajama pants. When Livi called out to him, he answered casually, "Pete's sleepwalking again. Dad's having a cow. Maybe Pete'll fall this time. That'd be good."

Livi rolled over and went back to sleep. I did, too, after listening to distant voices and bumps for a while. Having no brothers or sisters, I was unused to family noises in the night except for my father's snoring or my parents' talking quietly or uneasily when they thought I was asleep.

The next morning, Livi's parents invited us into their bedroom while they had coffee. Mrs. Stonington was wearing an ice blue confection. Its front fell like a bishop's stole. It was also elaborately embroidered at just the right spots to cover her. She bade us sit on the bed and asked me to tell her all about myself. Livi said Mrs. Stonington liked me; she and my mother had gone to the same girls' school that Livi, her sisters, and I were attending. Mrs. Stonington also thought, according to Livi, that I was clever, pretty, and polite.

"She doesn't have time to really notice us," explained Livi. "She wants to but she can't. They're too many of us. When you're here, it's good. I get more time with her." Livi and I had been separated when we graduated from the Junior School to the Senior. Livi had been put into the "less academic class," which today would be called by a euphemism; I had been put into the "brainy" class. We still ate lunch together and were now considered grown up enough to meet alone in the city to go to a film together. We had recently wept our way through "West Side Story." Livi had taken my hand in the middle of it because she was crying. I thought this was brave of her but I didn't quite know why: something to do with honesty. I sensed an honesty in Livi that would have been dangerous had I tried it.

Mr. Stonington came back from the bathroom in silk pajamas, slapped Mrs. Stonington on what I presumed was the top of her leg through the expensive bed sheets, and crawled back in beside her.

"Bet you're teacher's pet," he barked at me with a large laugh. "Livi'll never be teacher's pet. She's not brainy. You're brainy. I bet even that dried up old maid of a headmistress likes you." He laughed.

"Jack!" Mrs. Stonington remonstrated, laughing gently. Livi laughed, too. I was relieved when Mrs. Stonington and Livi laughed because I hadn't known what to do. I was sure Mr. Stonington couldn't have meant what he just said.

"Livi's one of the most popular girls in our year, Mr. Stonington," I replied loyally and accurately after the laughter faded. Livi and I were by then sitting on the hand-tapestried *chaise longue* beside Mrs. Stonington's dressing table. A string of heavy pearls and two rings with diamonds and sapphires lay on top of the intricately carved, slightly dusty dressing table. A dog or child had chewed one of the delicate claw feet on the table. The tapestried flowers were scratching my tanned, newly shaven, slightly nicked legs. The morning sun was streaming over the Stonington's hills and through the balcony doors. I pulled my shorts down to cover my legs a little and to make the couch less scratchy.

"Livi'll never be Head Girl like her mother. She's not as pretty—or brainy," he said loudly. Everyone laughed again. The laughter began loudly with Mr. Stonington and was echoed faintly by Mrs. Stonington, who added, "Livi would make an excellent Head Girl, Jack! So would Meg." Livi gave a short laugh. I gave a little laugh. I had learned how to cue to save one's life in a small family and suddenly realized I could use the skill in a larger situation as well. Mr. Stonington patted Mrs. Stonington again, this time high up on her thigh, letting his hand rest there for a minute while she put down her transparent porcelain coffee cup. She smiled at me and asked me about my mother and which newspapers she was writing for at present.

"I hate him," Livi later said calmly, after we had compared menstrual pains. "I bet Mum hates him, too, but she doesn't say. Roddy said Dad keeps poking her when she's asleep and that's why there're so many of us. He gives her diamonds every time she pops another one. She's got lots of diamonds."

I thought I hated him, too, but couldn't work out if it was disloyal to think or say this about one's host. It was almost time for me to leave. I packed my small suitcase of clothes including the pink shorty nightie Nan had given me last Christmas (I wished it were ice blue) and shoved my toothbrush inside my sandshoes. I had forgotten toothpaste so Livi had told me to use any of the tubes in the second bathroom. I'd never stayed in a place that had two complete bathrooms before. None of the other girls at school, even the ones whose families had big, gracious, colonial houses, had second bathrooms.

Mrs. Stonington drove me in her giant car from their place back to my place in the afternoon. No one I knew had two cars except for the Stoningtons. Livi said it was because they lived so far out, went to different private schools, and the live-in help couldn't lug them all in one car every morning and afternoon. Mrs. Stonington was late for a luncheon at her club. She was dressed in crisp, navy linen and was wearing a different strand of fat pearls from the ones that had been on the dressing table. Her prematurely white swathe of hair matched her French shoes and handbag.

Having waved goodbye to Mrs. Stonington, I walked in the front door alone. My mother emerged from her afternoon rest, having set aside the next hour to listen to my lengthy tales about the weekend while she had tea and a cigarette. She had written neatly on her daily list: "AT, M. 60." (This meant she had allocated afternoon tea to listen to me for an hour; I knew I'd have to talk fast.)

Later, when it cooled off, I helped my mother decorate the Christmas tree. The tree was important to finish because my parents were having a small sherry party the next night for the members of their world events discussion group. My father had gently nudged by my mother into hosting it. She acquiesced and then felt guilty about regretting her acquiescence. She preferred to read good novels.

My mother and I were undecided about what should go on the top of the tree. She wanted to put the fairy with the sparkly skirt that Nan had made for us. My father, just home from ten hours at work, said Christmas was a religious holiday and perhaps we could, for a change, observe the true spirit of the season by putting a star on the top instead of Nan's fairy.

My mother looked crestfallen and panicked and said she could but that she was worried Nan would feel hurt.

My father said, "Nan, Nan." He retired to his study in a quiet way that presaged several days of silence interspersed with verbal parsimony, which would prevail until after Nan left on Christmas afternoon. I knew he would chat, of course, at the sherry party, would be kind on Christmas morning, speak pleasantly at our lunch for Nan on Christmas Day, and again, but with loving enthusiasm, at his parents' house on Christmas afternoon. But I felt an invisible shadow.

We planned to pick up Livi after Christmas. When that happened, things would improve all around. Livi would come to the island with us. My parents, used to one child, would ask her questions about herself. She adored them and their questions. I didn't like their questions unless they were questions I wanted to be asked, such as what happened about the stuck toilet at school or the girl who passed out in the corridor and was caught by her school tie by the headmistress, in which case I gave generous, detailed answers that, oddly, my parents couldn't always remember. My father would feel he had a real family with two children instead of one—a fact he indirectly attributed to my mother, at least according to her. Having two of us would cheer him up and the shadow would lift.

But for now, there was silence. My father could be silent more loudly than anyone I knew, even our Form Mistress, who specialized in Wordless Sarcasm.

I sat in the living room looking at the forlorn tree with its bare top and feeling sick in my stomach. My mother had disappeared into the kitchen to have a cigarette. She said it calmed her down.

The phone rang. My father raced to answer it. He always raced and the phone was always for him, unless it was Nan or Livi ringing. He called me, big hand over the receiver, and said in a low voice: "It's Livi. Don't stay on long, please. I'm expecting a ring from the head of the fundraising committee."

"Hi."

"Hi."

"Can't wait to go away with you and your Mum and Dad," Livi whispered.

"Me either," I replied.

"I'm busting to tell you what Lizzy told me about her mother. She said her mother had a kid—*before*."

"Before what."

"Can't say now. Next week when we're away—if I don't get the bloody chicken pox and you don't. That's what Trish's bumps were. She wasn't kidding. Peter's got it now too. Shut UP, Roddy! I can't hear Livi! Shut UP, Pete! Fall downstairs somewhere else! The doctor came this afternoon. Bugger OFF, Pete! So has Mum, even though she's had it before. Dad's having a cow. I'll have a cow if I get it and can't go with you. I'll tell you if I get it but don't tell your parents anything yet. Promise?"

"Cross my heart. What're you doing?"

"The usual. Except Mum's in bed. Trish's in bed. Someone else has bumps, too. I've forgotten who. The cooking woman isn't allowed to come because she's preggo and doesn't want to catch anything. I'm supposed to help fix dinner but bugger them. Bugger Trish. Bugger Peter. Not bugger Mum. Dad's the biggest bugger. What're you doing?"

While Livi talked, I imagined Mrs. Stonington's beautiful hair, beautiful clothes, beautiful jewelry, and beautiful car. I imagined her lying in bed with a fever and wearing ice blue lace to keep herself cool. I imagined bringing her a cup of coffee. I imagined Mr. Stonington patting Mrs. Stonington on the thigh to cheer her up and buying her more diamonds because she was sick.

When Livi hung up, which was soon because none of us had more than one phone or extensions, I sat in the living room by myself. Chang hopped up in my lap. His shih tzu fur had picked up pine needles and old tinsel was dangling from his thick tail. He lay on my lap panting away the heat of a silent pre-Christmas night.

I could smell cigarette wafting around the side of the house and through the open window. My mother was having a cigarette outside under the eaves.

The sky started to spit. A storm was coming.

I wondered if Pete would try to sleepwalk with chicken pox in a storm. I scratched myself on the arm. There was a bump. I wondered if I had chicken pox and would be sick in bed. If I were, my father would cheer up, take care of me, and start talking again before Christmas—and we could avoid the whole day, sort of, but I'd have to get better just before we left for our holiday with Livi.

I looked down at my arm where there was a thin line of blood. A mozzie bite. I must have killed a mozzie; I didn't have chicken pox.

Then I decided to think about the star and the fairy—and work out how I could fit a fairy *and* a star on the same high point of the tree.

TWENTY-SIX

THE BOAT

It wasn't that all the girls were going. It was just that all the girls I cared about were. To the island, that is. On Emma Gardiner's boat. Well, her father's boat, to be exact. For the weekend. That included overnight. I had offered to visit my grandparents, washed the dishes by myself four nights running, and got top marks in all my homework so that my father would be in a good mood and my mother would feel she could advocate for me with impunity. It worked.

"It'll be great," Dee declared over sandwiches at lunch that Thursday when the Mistress on Duty had moved past our group. "We can tell all the sex stories we know."

"Including Em and her dog," added Rachel.

I was one of the "in" group and I nearly risked my status by asking "What *about* Em and her dog?" However, I was rescued from needless embarrassment and possible excommunication by Christina. She opened her hazel eyes wide through the red hair that was falling into them, took a large bite of her ham and cheese sandwich, and said, "Whaaboudemanerdog?"

Everyone giggled. I giggled; although I had not a clue what

they were talking about, I knew it was what we in the "in" crowd were supposed to do. Rachel took pity on Christina and whispered in her ear as Christina was wolfing the last, generous portion of her sandwich. Christina looked startled, then alarmed, then intensely preoccupied and vague. Everyone laughed.

"You're fibbing," she said.

"Yeah, and Woody doesn't dye her hair black either, dumb-dumb."

"As a matter of fact," said a charming voice above us, "she doesn't—but don't let on you know."

Everyone froze. Who said that? Then we knew: it was Woody herself. Miss Woodford had returned unexpectedly from her lunchtime rounds as Mistress on Duty. Everyone liked Woody. Unlike the other mistresses, she wouldn't make us suddenly get up in the middle of our lunches and pick up all the papers underneath a tree or something. She'd just idly say something in parting, such as "… and clean up that disgusting stuff under the tree before you play softball, would you?" as though we were her equals.

We looked up. Woody was standing there, lean and attractive in summer silk and Italian weave shoes. She was smiling amusedly. The sun backlit her thick, black hair cut with its big waves falling away from her handsome features.

"I'm sorry, Miss Woodford," Dee said meekly, aghast she could find no place to disappear.

"Nothing to apologize for, Deborah. After all, you've promised not to tell so there's nothing to discuss. Now what *are* you girls doing for your class's flower show stall? Have you thought about it?"

By the time she had finished discussing the flower show with us, we were almost back to normal except for Dee who still was slightly hunched and uncomfortable in her winter school uniform.

"Well, I can't stand here all day enjoying this elite company," Miss Woodford finally said. "I have duties to perform. Good day, girls."

"Goodbye, Miss Woodford," we chorused.

We sat in horrified silence.

"Anyone except Woody," said Livi. "Anyone ..."

"Do you think she'll hate us? I mean forever?" asked Dee.

"She was laughing," Rachel said but her voice was flat.

We wrapped up our lunch remains in silence.

"I know what we can do on the boat," said Hil, brightening considerably. "We can have one of those séances you're always talking about, Meg. After we do sex stories. After Em's father goes to bed."

Our parents each drove us down to the dock on Saturday morning. None of us had slept much the night before.

Em and Hil had the best clothes. They always had the best clothes but I tanned best, which gave me a leg up on being "in."

We moved smoothly across the bay singing all the folk and popular songs we knew until we reached the island. Great, white sand hills slid effortlessly and without shadow down to the beach and the turquoise shallows. It was midday.

Dr. Gardiner moored the boat close in, told us we could wade ashore, and reminded us to be back before lunch. He said he would collect us, moor further out, and then we could swim by the boat for the rest of the day.

In the blinding sun, we climbed the sand hills. Someone noticed Hil had a dark stain spreading across her white shorts and told her she had "Jack." "Jack" was our name for menstruation. Someone came up with a sanitary pad and Hil ran off into the shallows. She washed her underpants and shorts, then returned with shorts in one hand, dripping and less stained. She had wrung out her underpants and put them back on—damp, salty, and bulging with the pad.

Rachel got a nosebleed and swore professionally about it. We looked at her soaked handkerchief with respect. She usually used nosebleeds to get out of Algebra but this time we were up close and realized that sometimes she really did have one. She snorted for a while and then lay back with her head resting on a bottle of lemonade until it stopped.

Em lay tanning—looking cool, calm, and athletic. Her freckles were getting darker. She told us all there were wild pigs in the bushes.

"There can't be," Hil retorted. "Not in sand dunes."

"There are. Dad told me. My sister—the one before the sister before me—the one who let the St John's Prefect go all the way—well, almost all the way—saw one once when we were here."

We looked around.

"What do you think pigs look like when they slide down a sand hill?"

"Like Jimmy Fitzgibbon's chin. Pink and raw!"

"Who's Jimmy Whatever?"

"The boy who takes the bus with Livi when she doesn't get driven."

"Livi! You didn't tell!'

"There's nothing to tell. He's Roddy's friend. My brother's."

"Come on."

'He's Roddy's. He just talks to me. Sometimes. Anyway, he's

shorter than me and he's pimply."

"What if we see a wild pig?"

"Why do you think they're pink and raw?"

"Because they'd have to slide down on their behinds!"

"Like this!" said Dee. She suddenly took off her shorts, ran up the hill, and slid down naked.

Thus dared, the rest of us—except for Hil who had to keep her salty underpants on—shed our clothes and ran to the top of the hill so we could slide down naked.

The sand stuck to my sweating legs. I was grittily uncomfortable. However, I had earned my stripes with the group again. I was glad I had had my period the week before.

"Up the dune!"

"What?"

"A *real* pig!"

There were screams. We all grabbed our clothes and fled. Hil left her shorts behind where they were drying off under a scrub. We flew down to the water's edge with the cross pig making its way into its domain with threatening snorts.

We stood naked in the shallows, hoping Dr. Gardiner would stay on the other side of the boat when he picked us up.

Hil said weakly, "How am I going to get on the boat? I don't have shorts."

"Take mine," Rachel offered. "I've got my swimsuit underneath."

Hil was plump. She couldn't fit into Rachel's shorts, especially soaking wet.

"Take my blouse," offered Rachel. "Put your legs in the armholes."

"They're smaller than the legs, stupid," commented Em idly.

We put on our clothes as best we could and stood around in the shallows for a while.

After soggy consideration, we decided Em would get on board first and distract her father with questions about wildlife on the island during which time the rest of us would climb aboard while surrounding Hil in her soaked underwear.

After we maneuvered our way on board, we headed for the cabin below deck. Hil, being the only one of us to have ventured into tampons, disappeared into the toilet. The rest of us soberly changed and decided to stay close to the boat for the rest of the day.

"See any pigs?" Dr. Gardiner asked.

"Just one up top," Em responded suavely. She was the fourth sibling and had honed parental management skills early.

Dr. G. cooked sausages for dinner and served them with doughy buns. After cleanup, he took refuge in his cabin.

We drew straws over who got which bunk. I got a bunk with a porthole, which I was to share with Livi. The two who got the prow spent the night groaning because the tide created gentle, rocking motions that made them feel woozy.

While the others settled in below to exchange sex stories, Livi and I stayed on deck.

"I don't want to talk sex," Livi commented as we sat there trying to spot reflections of the southern stars in the moonlit water. "Roddy says it's all Dad thinks about. Must be—there are so many of us. Roddy says every time he even thinks about it, Mum's preggo."

"You told me. That must be hard for your mother. I saw a dog doing it with another dog once," I offered, knowing nothing of my parents' sex life and never having thought to be curious.

"They've got a pink thing that comes out. Chang tried it once with the poodle next door before she was fixed. The neighbors were mad but nothing happened. Look at the moon on the water."

Livi looked.

The full moon was shining high above the now-indigo sand hills of the island and floating lopsidedly in the water near the boat.

"What do you think about God?" Livi asked, kicking the side of boat with a bare foot.

"I think there's one." I was risking my status in the group but Livi and I predated the group so I took the chance.

"Do you think he's like Dr. Gardiner?" asked Livi. "Or your father? I hate mine."

I thought about mine. I didn't think God would look like Dr. Gardiner. God had looked more like my father when I'd sort of seen Him sometimes—God, that is—in the dark before I was going to sleep. However, I instinctively held this observation back. "He's probably more like Dr. Gardiner than your father at least," I said. "He's probably kind and knows everything. But He seems to have different rules for different people. Take horrible illnesses like Rachel's mother's. Or my grandfathers'. Or wars. He can't have made them up. It's confusing." In fact, I had spent hours and hours thinking about, and hanging around until I felt His Presence—but I wasn't going for broke in this, our first, conversation about God in the four years we'd been friends. Livi's parents didn't go to church.

"Think they're done talking sex yet?" asked Livi, bored with God.

"How about I teach us all how to do a séance?"

Livi stopped kicking. "Let's go. The mozzies are biting me."

We went below deck. Soon the letters were written on small pieces of paper and the water glass upturned.

"Someone ask a question."

"Out loud?"

"No. Don't say it out loud. We have to keep it scientific."

"D...O...G."

"Definitely Em's question!" Dee said.

"Someone else go." Em said. "Dee."

"P...I...G."

"Sex with a pig, Dee!" We all giggled.

"Rachel next."

"P...I...N...K."

"Must be about your behind, Rach! Next."

We were moving around the circle from left to right. It was Hil's turn.

"S...E...X."

"Whatcha ask, Hil?"

"Second last," replied Hil, refusing to answer and pointing at me.

"G...O...D."

"Meg the deep thinker," said Livi, good-naturedly.

"Last one. Livi."

"Y...E...L...L."

"Livi's father," I said and grinned at Livi. She looked sad.

As we bunked down, I whispered, "Did I hurt your feelings?"

"Yeah. You know I hate my father. Yours talks. Mine yells."

I thought about the battles at home and how I had promised never to talk about anything that went on. I stayed silent.

"*Your* father never yells at you or your mother."

"I'm sorry, Livi. I didn't mean to hurt your feelings."

"Do you think Woody really doesn't dye her hair?"

"I saw the roots once when she was sitting up the front. They were dark."

"You know the other day I told you I had to go to Sick Bay?" Livi tried to roll over but the bunk was too narrow.

"Mmm." I spat on my finger and tried to clean the porthole. It made it worse.

"I didn't have to," Livi said.

"You weren't sick?" I asked, trying one more time to clean the porthole with my shorts.

"Nup," Livi said quietly.

I knew she had forgiven me.

TWENTY-SEVEN

....

BLACK AND WHITE

"Why exactly do you need to leave so early tomorrow? Saturday? The eight-o'clock bus?"

My father was calling me from my grandfather's house. My grandfather was in fragile health and currently living alone because he had given my grandmother a trip to visit her family in Scotland for several months. My mother was cleaning up in the kitchen. I was in the middle of ironing my new dress.

"Because we've promised to help set up the stalls, Dad."

"What stalls?"

"The Junior School stalls."

"You're Senior School."

"They asked for volunteers. Livi and I volunteered."

I could feel the line tighten and my heart start to flap like a mackerel being reeled in.

"Why are you proposing not to come home until six?"

"Livi's mother said she'll take us over to the boys' school fête for an hour late afternoon. Two of Livi's brothers are working at it."

"Well, your mother's worried. You are only just over the flu and are proposing a long day. You're giving her unnecessary worry, especially when she's still getting over the flu herself."

"I feel well, Dad. I've been back at school for a week."

"Then, if you are feeling so well, you'd make a more loving contribution by leaving early, visiting Granddad, and then getting back to your mother. Granddad's ten minutes from school."

He repeated the words I had heard before: "As far as I can see, it's self first, school second, and home a bad last."

Reeled in, I lay flapping on the deck.

Silence. Finally, I said with respect and false calm, "I'm sorry, Dad. I'd change my plans now but I promised. I also promised the teacher in charge of the white elephant stall that I'd follow through and help unpack all the things you donated."

I thought providing him with logistical details might help, together with a strategic infusion of family solidarity in the form of "following through"—a favorite phrase of my father's, with his own donations.

"If I don't do what I promised, I'll let Livi down, too. She said she wouldn't go without me. Besides, Mrs. Stonington arranged to take us." (I did not yet know enough to give only one reason.) "I'm sorry. I should have checked with you first before I promised to work." I gave a miniscule of emphasis to the word "work." I didn't want to wake his indignation that I would call this "work" but I also wanted to point out that I was trying to be a Good Citizen.

I paused. If I took a loud breath, it was all over.

"You can leave on the 8:30 bus. That's early enough. Be ready—at the entrance gate—for me to pick you up at a quarter to six."

Hook released. I flipped off the deck.

Livi and I met in the locker room and hung up our dresses. My dress was beautiful—round-necked, long, off-white linen with two black-and-white-spotted thin stripes sewn down the front. A rolled, black linen frog marked the division between my expanding breasts in their new bra. The two lines of black spots parted at the knee and marked the edges of a finely sewn, inverted pleat ending mid-calf.

I would have sewn it myself. I could have. I was a good seamstress. However, this was a birthday present from Nan. Nan had good taste and—since not one of my grandfather's Russian relatives could be found by the Red Cross after the war—money. I was her only grandchild.

The shoes, which followed the dress, were from Robertson's, where all good clothes originated—except for those made by a few of the town's dressmakers. As it was early spring, white shoes and slightly tan-colored stockings were *de rigueur*. My demure inch-and-a-half heels were attached to pointed-toe pumps with a neat strap over the instep. A white leather bag (Nan's gift from my last birthday) completed my outfit and it was altogether as nice as Livi's navy linen outfit, which she, too, had carried to school. We had arrived early to help out with the Junior School's activities and we were not planning to put on our best clothes until the traditional flower show, with accompanying stalls and events, officially began. This was one of the only days in the school year when we got to wear anything other than our costly, dark, tailored summer or winter uniforms. We were excited at the thought of transforming ourselves.

"Let's find Woody," Livi said unapologetically. It would have taken me half an hour to work up to suggesting we find our jointly adored ex-teacher from Junior School days. Livi always said the impossible without apology. I decided that her ease around saying the unthinkable was something to do with having so many brothers and sisters, none of which I had. At first I'd thought she was brave; after I had stayed with her family a few times, I realized she could be brave because no one listened to her.

We headed down the hill and found Woody. We helped her for a while, then pitched in with other Good Citizens until it was time to go upstairs and transform.

Before we did, we sat down to share the lunch that my mother had prepared for me. Livi had forgotten to pack lunch. I offered her half my sandwich and half my peach. Woody wandered by, cool and tall in bone and white silk, with pepper-and-salt hair shining and good quality shoes newly whitened. Her handsome face was a feminine version of my father's.

"I hate to mention it, my dears, particularly as you are now Senior School and therefore far beyond my care," she said dryly, "but that peach does look rather unripe."

"Does it, Miss Woodford?" I asked, surprised and secretly delighted that she would care enough to speak to us specifically, let alone worry about what we were eating. However, I was sure my mother would never let me eat anything she thought might be bad for me.

"I could well be wrong," Woody added with a wry smile and a wink of one of her brown eyes.

Livi and I looked at the peach, then at each other, and immediately thought about the pieces we had already eaten. We looked up at Woody with alarm. We were sitting on a bench in the sun. We could see the shadow of Woody's petticoat backlit through her silk dress.

"Never mind. You won't feel the effects for another few hours," she quipped, "By then I shan't be around to pick up the pieces! Go right ahead!" She laughed lightly, patted me on the shoulder, and walked on.

"She likes you better than me," said Livi.

"Don't be stupid."

"Course she does. She patted your shoulder."

"When we were helping today, she talked about how you could swim really well in second grade."

"That was years ago."

"It still counts. Besides she's known you longer. And she got ice and put it on your ankle herself when you had that sprain and limped into her office in seventh grade."

"I fibbed."

"She didn't get ice?"

"Yeah she got ice. I fibbed about the ankle."

"You're kidding."

"I usually fibbed about being sick. Especially in spelling. You know that."

"I didn't. Even if you were fibbing, she still got you ice."

We walked up the wooden stairs worn down by thousands of feet ahead of ours, including our own mothers'. In fifteen minutes, our transformation was complete and we emerged.

Livi's mother was waiting for us. As my own mother, still recovering from the flu, would come later—one of the many annual sacrifices she made out of love for me—I hung around with Livi and her mother. The three of us wandered around the Flower Show in the School Hall.

Livi's mother's name was on the Honor Board. My mother's wasn't: her honors had come from extracurricular achievements, with her having written her first published opinion piece for a newspaper under a pseudonym when she was fifteen. Livi's mother and my mother were both beautiful. But somehow, Livi's mother exuded confidence whereas mine—despite outer achievements that, looking back on it, outweighed Livi's—did not. Livi wanted to look like her mother when she grew up. I wanted to look like Livi's mother when I grew up. Everyone wanted to look like Livi's mother when they grew up. Her beautiful hair was better even than Miss Woodford's and she wore terrific clothes that she and her husband had bought on their frequent trips overseas.

"Look at this," Mrs. Stonington declared. We stood in front of a mauve rose in a tall crystal vase. "Melinda's mother," Mrs. Stonington said. "How lovely." The rose was sporting a blue ribbon. Melinda's mother provided the best flowers for the headmistress's office. My mother, while pretty, dressing beautifully, being a kind of public figure, and a faithful attendee of school events, did not grow cutting flowers for functions. I trotted her out proudly as a respected national figure and Old Girl of the school but not as the perfect school mother.

I left Livi and Mrs. Stonington and wandered down to the sandstone library where the Art Show was being displayed. It was for all grades from Kindergarten to Seniors. I'd sneaked in before we were officially allowed and discovered that, of the five paintings I had entered, four had been hung and three had First Prizes. I had spent weeks of Saturday afternoons on them. As a non-art student, I was surprised, oddly guilty, embarrassed, puzzled, and pleased at having won so many prizes. The school had thought me too bright to settle for art and the arts, so I had been fated to struggle with Physics, Chemistry, and advanced Mathematics for more years. My father had concurred. "Everyone should have a grounding in the sciences. No matter what you do later, you need to know how the world works," he had declared.

Miss Arlington, the headmistress, had warned my parents that I might not shine in the sciences. "Imagination, so helpful in the arts," she commented in her beautiful script on my last report card, "is destined to wait for the higher realms in the sciences to spread its wings." She lightly linked the last letter of each word to the next in an elegant, positive backhand in inverse proportion to the views she expressed about us in our daily Morning Assembly. "Meg's results would indicate a leaning toward the arts."

I had won First Prize for my lettering—an Old English masterpiece done in sepia with flourishes and pale flowers that embellished the quotation,

This Above All:
To Thine Own Self Be True.

I had filled in each letter with graduated yellow and brown ink, something I'd learned to do from Nan. I had also won first prize for a black-and-white, laboriously rendered, pen-and-ink portrait of my dog titled, originally, "Chang: My Dog." And I had been given First Prize for an oil profile of a classmate; the background was a depressing brown grey because I didn't know what to do with the space between where the classmate stopped and the canvas stopped. But it still won the prize even though it was my first attempt at an oil.

After I helped out with the afternoon tea in the boarding house, a colonial mansion with stained glass windows and black-and-white tiled floors, I wandered back down to the library, artlessly following Miss Arlington at a careful distance. She was in a black and white silk suit with pearls, white gloves, black and white hat, white handbag, and white high heels. She was accompanying a member of the school board, one of many attending and all of whom were tall, thin men. I knew who this man was because my father was on a joint committee with him. I slipped behind a pegboard and listened.

"A pleasing turnout," Miss Arlington commented. They moved along a few steps and I slid down on the opposite side of the pegboard accordingly. I was used to making myself invisible while listening on the other side of barriers; I needed to stay abreast of wars and *détentes* at home and abroad. "This girl isn't even an art student and she has won several awards," Miss Arlington added in her precise accent. "Her lettering here is carefully executed, wouldn't you agree?" I heard a murmured assent from the trapped board member. They moved on toward where Chang was hanging on the pegboard.

"So many lines," she said. I was surprised that all she commented on was the number of strokes I had made but gratified she had commented.

My parents arrived around three. My father had gone home, got through some paperwork, and picked up my mother. She was feeling better. I took them both straight down to see the art. It was my third trip of the day to the library.

"Wonderful, Meg. Congratulations. We're proud of you." My father looked handsome, although his eyes were shadowed. My mother, who had made me hundreds of cups of tea and admired each stroke as I painted, was equally pleased, especially since my art capacity seemed to come from her side of the family. After they admired my work, they greeted other parents, congratulated Miss Arlington on a fine Flower Show, and left. My mother, still weak, was beginning to perspire from post-flu weakness. My father decided to drive her home so she could rest, visit my grandfather, then pick me up on the way back.

Livi's mother took us to the boys' school fête as planned. Livi and I each met boys we had seen at a party the week before and we each bought something from their stall. Then Mrs. Stonington, having bought a lot of things at stalls where her sons were working, took us back to our school in her large black car.

While I waited for my father to pick me up at 5:45, I sat under the jacaranda and reflected on the day. I had escaped by the skin of my teeth with my father the night before. It had been close but I had pulled it off. I had not only pulled it off but Livi and I had been told seven times we looked lovely in our new outfits; we had got to spend time with Woody who had teased us about the peach, which meant she really liked us and was treating us like true Senior School girls; I had been awarded more art prizes than anyone in either the Junior or Senior school and I didn't even take Art; I had talked to a boy in front of girls from my class who were also at the boys' fête; and I had worn my contact lenses all day. My life was finally beginning.

My father was five minutes late as usual. When he did pull up where a few other fathers were still parked waiting for stragglers, I greeted him and begged for two minutes to retrieve something I'd forgotten. This was a lie. In fact, I wanted to spot Woody once more; we rarely saw her now that we were in the Senior School. I'd glimpsed her leaving the Junior School just as I was walking out to the entrance to wait for my father. I needn't have lied; I ended up spotting Woody's athletic form from a distance as she walked briskly to her old blue car. I managed the whole maneuver in less than four minutes, raced back to the family car, and sat in satisfied silence.

My father hardly spoke on the way home. I thought he might

be upset about my grandfather so I decided to chirp. Sometimes chirping worked. Sometimes it didn't. When he was in a dark mood, I always felt I was to blame; however, I knew I couldn't be on the hook today because there was nothing to be on the hook about.

When we reached our house, he parked the car and walked up the driveway. I followed him in the dusk onto the verandah. He took off his sports coat and turned to me. His eyes were sunken and his jaw was clenched to the side—always ominous.

"You were an embarrassment to your mother and me today," he said.

I stared at him. I ran through times, places, and rules, and could find none I had officially broken. I also knew that our white lies about helping more than one teacher were watertight.

"You won prizes, Meg. That's a source of pride and pleasure to us. We want you to do your best and receive the recognition you deserve, always. But you failed in life today. Firstly, that dress: it's too long. It looks silly on a girl your age. Secondly, those shoes are too high. You can't walk properly in them and your stockings were wrinkled when your mother and I walked behind you in the art section. If you want to play grownup, you have to act the part with dignity and appropriateness. You looked like a tramp." (I'd known my stockings were wrinkled but I couldn't find anything to hide behind in order to pull them up.) "And lastly, you wasted time swanning around St. John's with the boys when you could have been helping your grandfather—or even getting home at a reasonable hour to keep your mother company, especially since she made the effort to come to see you.

"Love in action. That's all that counts. You disappoint me more than you know. I think it's time you started teaching Sunday

School. Do something for someone else for a change. Be a giver, not a taker."

He stood up. "Stay there a minute," he said and went away.

I sat there holding Chang who was depositing hairs from his tail all over the creased linen of my skirt. One of my pointed white shoes had been scuffed by the door when we were getting out of Mrs. Stonington's car. I wondered if the scuff would come off with cleaner or cover up with whitener. It wouldn't look the same if I had to cover it with whitener. I wondered if I would ever wear that pair of shoes again.

He returned with a book. "I want you to read this."

I looked at it. It was *Stories from the Bible* by someone I didn't know. Kahlil Gibran.

"As you read it, write out what kind of woman you want to become and give it to me when you've finished. Now get that outfit off and help your mother with dinner. She could do with it, too. Those teachers aren't the only ones deserving of your time and attention."

I did not catch my mother's eye. If I had, I knew she would have seen how hurt I was; then I would have distressed her as well as having disappointed him.

I went to my room and took off the dress. I remembered how tired my father was from helping my grandfather these last weeks. My mother had told me. I could see it in his eyes. I decided that possibly he was correct about my outfit but then I changed my mind. I still liked the dress. I laddered the stockings as I took them off.

After dinner, I excused myself to do homework, went to bed early, and cried myself to sleep for two hours.

At midnight, I woke with stomach pains. I was violently ill for two hours. My mother blamed herself; it must have been the dinner she had cooked or she had given me flu again. My father told me I had overdone it, just as he had anticipated. I blamed the peach but knew I could never tell my parents because my mother would definitely feel to blame and my father would think I was "passing the buck."

My father slept at the door of my room all night. He held my head when I threw up, emptied the bowls, and put a cold washcloth on my head hourly. He knew just how cold to get the washcloth and just where to put it. I felt guilty for being so sick and contributing to his weariness, as well as guilty for all the ways I disappointed him and made his life harder. Chang slept in my room with his lush head on the point of my new white shoes lying pigeon-toed in the corner. My dress hung lopsidedly on a wire hanger like a tired fish.

In the morning, my father made me a soft-boiled egg and dry toast for breakfast. He put it on a tray with a fresh tray cloth and brought it to me in bed, arranging my pillows in just the right way. He told me to remember this lesson in overdoing. I apologized for causing more trouble. He said my artwork was good and when I put as much time and attention into my family and grandparents as I did into my art, I would grow into a well-rounded person.

A week later, the art exhibit came down and I got my pieces back a little the worse for wear. The picture of Chang and the piece with the lettering both had pinholes in the corners where they had been put on the pegboard.

I had a drawer my mother and I reserved for Sentimental Things. (I wrote little signs for each of my drawers in calligraphy.) I put the paintings in that drawer together with the blue ribbons

I'd won and the peach pit. They joined every card I'd ever got from my parents, grandparents, and anyone else who'd ever sent me a birthday or Christmas card, as well as postcards from each grandmother when she had been traveling.

Later that year, I added a deckle-edged, bread and butter note I'd received (and kept under my pillow for two weeks). The note came to me at home during the holidays, which made it even more special. It was from Woody, thanking me for my end-of-year gift. She added that it was delightful to "stay in touch with girls who have gone on to bigger and better things." I took that to mean me. She thanked me for the finely embroidered handkerchief I had given her for Christmas and for the card I had painted of a peach. She didn't comment on its being a peach. I wondered if she'd forgotten her special conversation with Livi and me.

As Christmas presents for the family and for Livi that year, I painted mauve roses. I made a little assembly line, adding a petal to each miniature painting until they were complete. I put the cards on top of small gifts: for my grandmother who was back from Scotland, my grandfather who was better, and for Nan, who later framed hers. For my parents and for Chang, I painted black-and-white miniatures on cards I cut myself. I painted them each a shih tzu. The paintings ended up looking like a dog in a sideshow mirror. I couldn't get the angle right and ran out of time on Christmas Eve. My father kept his painting in his top drawer with his good, ironed handkerchiefs. My mother kept hers in whichever library book she was currently reading. The miniatures weren't half as good as the original big one but it didn't matter; I had done something everyone liked.

TWENTY-EIGHT

BUILDING MOUNT EVEREST

What served to torture me later in my life was a joy in childhood. The joy was predicated on my belief that I could make things better.

Our lives were Swiss: my mother had the brilliance to turn our daily activities into a game; not liking parts of the life she had, she would schedule regular departures from it, entering—often with me—into a carefully researched and constructed world of imagination, play, and creativity, all founded in order and living in Europe.

She was a natural, patient, determined, and imaginative educator, and she was blessed with a quick and adoring student in me. She taught me her passions well. All stayed mine as long as I still lived at home; most stayed mine even after I left.

One of her passions was for all things Germanic.

In 1938, when she was eighteen, Nan and Grandpapa took her around the world. They traveled in quiet luxury arranged by Thomas Cook. Apart from my grandfather's having been denied permission to visit his family in Russia—a disappointment he expressed, according to my mother, only briefly in words and more fully in his trip diary—the trip had been gracious and unmarred.

During their leisurely journey through the European capitals and countryside, my mother and her parents encountered Hitler Youth groups, blonde and handsome, singing folksongs as they hiked mountainous roads in spring. Sometimes, smart, handsome, German guards would mount the First Class compartments of the trains in which the family traveled and ask for their passports. Grandpapa recorded in his diary his distaste for these handsome, youthful guards and their convictions.

My mother saw the guards as enchanting. She did not know about Grandpapa's Jewish stepmother, whom he disliked, until long after my mother had married. Nan said he disliked Extremism all his life.

From the time I was six, my grandmother would show me, often at my request, albums of that trip in 1938—black pages filled with small, deckle-edged photographs of elegant people standing in front of elegant buildings. The photographs, slipped into black corners glued carefully onto the pages, included descriptions that Nan herself had written in white ink: "Alex, Self and Lucy in Budapest," "Lucy on top of Mount Pilates," "Lucy and Self outside Folies Bergère." My mother's favorite photographs in these albums were of her standing on the top of mountains. She loved mountains.

When I was seven, my mother decided we would follow the adventures of Hillary and Tenzing as they ascended Mount Everest. We caught the bus into town one day and walked to the main library where we wandered the stacks finding a surprisingly good selection of books on mountain climbing, the Swiss Alps, and mountains in general. Several books had specific information on

Everest. We brought home a stack of books with photos of Everest and reviewed them carefully. Then we built Everest in the back garden of our rented house. A cliff, which bounded the garden on one side, provided us with clay, which became malleable when we added water. Each time Hillary and Tenzing set up the next camp, we'd add a flag to our mountain.

There must have been other children in our town who did things like building Mount Everest in the back garden but I didn't know them. My friends and I didn't talk much about what went on at home although each of us secretly thought our mother was the best one. I just knew I happened to be right. I frequently told my mother how I felt about her—in handmade cards; in horrible, handmade presents; in little notes of apology when I imagined I had hurt her feelings; in small rhymes (she taught me how to rhyme early); and by aligning perfectly with every belief, passion, opinion, interest, and emotion she had. Her growing success with her articles for papers and magazines fueled my conviction that she really was the world's best mother.

My mother loved everything about libraries: the promise of discovery, the smell of books, the luxury of checking out many books at one time. In addition to the main library, she belonged to a private library, the only one that loaned foreign language books. This library was exotic because it was in a basement under some shops. We didn't have many basements in our town. The ones we did have always seemed to be inhabited by interesting Europeans: the "Parisian," a morning tea and luncheon restaurant, was owned by Kati Fodor; the "Venezia," a dinner restaurant, was owned by Italians; and the foreign library was owned by Czechs.

We left our clay Everest behind when we moved from our rental home to our newly built house later the next year. By then,

Everest had melted to the equivalent of our view of the hills we could see from our new house. My mother had always wanted to live up high so my father had bought that architecturally challenging block of land on the crest of a hill with a wide view of hills and valleys, the town, and the river.

In the new house, my mother taught herself to read, speak, and write German. Although she learned it perfectly, she never wanted to speak it in public. She was sure she would make a mistake. Occasionally, she was backed into using it in conversation if my father invited German-speaking colleagues to dinner. He would cajole my mother into speaking German with them. They invariably commented, with surprise, that she spoke without an accent. She didn't believe them.

Perhaps her language ability came from her Russian side. Grandpapa was musical and Nan told me he spoke and wrote several languages—although he never taught my mother Russian or languages he had collected en route to Australia. In those days, when colonial assimilation was unquestioned, successful immigrants took pride in speaking English well, not in being bilingual, let alone multilingual.

By the time I was ten, I was better at and more interested in Germany and Switzerland and Everest than I ever was at naming the primary products of Australia, information considered essential in the elementary school curriculum (why, we were never told).

I was captivated by the Chalet School novels by British author Elinor Brent-Dyer. The novels were set in a trilingual boarding school in Switzerland. The publisher cleverly established the Chalet School club, which one could join by mail and which I did, of course, join. So, between accompanying my mother to the library where she checked out books written in German to improve her reading, pouring through others about Switzerland and Austria, which my father ordered her for birthday and Christmas presents, and burying myself in the latest Chalet School novel, I was increasingly at home with the geography and vocabulary of the region—Bern, Lauterbrunnen, Oberammergau, the Eiger, and the Jungfrau were as familiar to me as *edelweiss, danke schoen, bitte, föhn,* and *entschuldigen Sie mich.*

During long school holidays, I helped my mother with the housework. To alleviate the boredom of making three beds, polishing furniture, cleaning, washing, and ironing, my mother and I became Chalet School characters. Whenever we played this game, it turned out that all the maids had the day off and we, becoming, in turn, various teachers and students, had to "pitch in" and do the work. Mostly I was Jo, Head Girl for a few novels. As Jo, I became tall, athletic, and fierce, with lingering but nonthreatening health issues from childhood—just enough to make me quietly heroic when I did something ordinary: my hair also became dark brown and long and flew out behind me. However, rather than skating or skiing as Jo so often did, I ran around with the vacuum cleaner.

My mother usually became Miss Annersley, the smart, slim, wise, kind headmistress who understood what it was to be a girl still growing up yet knew when to use her authority judiciously. I loved the confidence my mother exuded when she was Miss Annersley. Instead of being subject to the autocracy of her fears, my mother walked around the house with a clarity I never saw at any other time. Long obedient to the pervasive power of her emotional and physical fragilities, I delighted in her firm, pleasant commands when she became Miss Annersley. I also liked inventing a bunch of sibling-like people to have around.

"Now girls," my mother, Miss Annersley, might say, "I'm afraid Elsa and Heidi have gone to Oberammergau to help their families prepare for the Passion Play. It's up to us to get this place shipshape. Jo, do show the younger girls how to make the beds, would you? Mitered corners, smooth pillows.... Come along, girls. We all have to pitch in." Miss Annersley and Jo would make their way steadily, with their invisible gang of young boarding school helpers, through all the tasks of running the house. My mother and I were in love with each other and with our Chalet School world. These were some of our happiest times.

The Chalet School books, impossible for me to give away, eventually took up dignified, affectionate residence beside my university texts. After I graduated and earned some money, I—and most of my fellow graduates—traveled overseas. I visited all the places I had promised myself I would visit. I sent postcards and letters to my parents, to Nan, Granddad, and Gran—and even, occasionally, to friends. Stamps cost money so we had to ration the postcards we sent. I saved most of mine for my family and my boyfriend, who was still studying at home. I made especially sure to send them to Nan and my mother from Interlaken, Oberammergau, Bern, Wagner's house, Pilates, the Eiger, and the Jungfrau. I loved retracing parts of the journey that my mother, Nan, and Grandpapa had taken, even though Grandpapa was no longer alive to know I was traveling with a rucksack on my back and staying in youth hostels instead of having a Cook's guide to meet me with a porter at each station.

A few years later, my father was invited to give lectures at two conventions: the first, in London; the second, in Zürich. Since my mother was going to accompany him, he offered to pay my flight from Toronto. I had returned home but had, by then, gone to Canada to do a post-graduate course. He offered to cover hotels and trains. I would only need to pay for a few meals, he explained. We could make a memory as a family, as he put it. I had little money but bought a new all-purpose coat and happily flew over to join them.

If my mother had been blind to the world she saw when she traveled through pre-war Nazi Germany, I was equally blind to how this trip would change my view of my mother's world.

After spending a few days in London, we headed to Zürich. Carl, a colleague of my father's who had frequently visited us in Australia, had invited us all to spend Christmas with him and his wife, Lisa in their village, which was close to where Carl taught at the university.

During our visit, we took walks in the snow, rode trains to different cities, and caught funiculars up mountains. Although Carl and Lisa, like most Swiss, were not religious, we decided to go to a candlelit, midnight service on Christmas Eve at the local Lutheran church. I was so tipsy from *glühwein* that I was convinced I could magically understand German—at least the hymns and most of the sermon. In fact, I might have: the order of service was so similar to the services from my childhood Presbyterian church. Moreover, it was Christmas so the message was predictable. My mother, knowing German, did indeed understand the hymns and sermon. They bored her, as always. Like her parents, she was not a churchgoer. What captivated her were the *real* candles on the fresh-cut, fragrant tree to the left of the pulpit. She lingered behind us in the freezing, clear night as we all wandered back to the house between deep-blue snowdrifts on either side of the road and beneath a full moon illuminating the mountains.

The day after Christmas, Carl and Lisa invited us to visit Lisa's sister in a charming town an hour away.

My mother begged fatigue. She enjoyed Carl and Lisa: they were talented, beautiful, educated, irreverent, kind, and multilingual. Moreover, Carl played the piano expertly, each smoked and drank moderately and enthusiastically until late at night, and they vacationed in Spain and unexpected spots in Europe. They had always interested my mother and they, in turn, had always found her fascinating when she and my father had entertained them. But people exhausted my mother, even interesting ones. She needed a break. While she was at home being interviewed on live, national radio about her magazine or newspaper articles, she rarely enjoyed facing people even in small numbers—and then only for a limited time. So she excused herself from the day trip with many apologies, claiming tiredness.

Carl remembered my mother's shyness about playing the piano in front of others from his visits to my parents in Australia. My mother had also confessed to him over the *glühwein* that she was as unable to tolerate making errors in German as she was making musical errors in public. Carl understood this; he was a perfectionist himself. He had been pleasantly outspoken from the day we arrived about the order he liked in "his" kitchen. My parents and I were privately afraid we might hang a kitchen implement the wrong way thus making Carl and Lisa regret urging us to stay. Informal meals with them could be, in fact, more stressful than times when Carl, a fine cook, was alone in his kitchen preparing something or when we insisted on taking them out for a meal. So when it was decided that my mother would not accompany us on the trip, Carl ordered her to spend time playing his grand piano while we were gone. He knew she wouldn't touch his grand unless she could be alone and unless he firmly commanded her to do so.

On the morning of the day trip, we all had breakfast together. As breakfast progressed, I realized I preferred to stay with my mother. I announced to the breakfast group that I "had slight sniffles" and wanted to avoid coming down with a cold. In fact, I had waited twenty years to hear my mother play the piano in Europe—ever since I'd seen Nan's photograph of my mother playing the piano at Wagner's house during their 1938 trip. My mother and I waved Carl, Lisa, and my father off, and they drove away in Carl's clean little car.

My mother and I went inside. To my surprise, she sat down in the dining room, lit a cigarette, and wrote two postcards. Why hadn't she sat down at the grand? After all, only we were left.

Finally, she rose and went to the piano. She sat down and cautiously looked through Carl's alphabetized cabinet of music, choosing some. Placing her fingers on the keys, she started to go through her scale routine to warm up. I was ecstatic but I said nothing, fearing I would make her self-conscious. I wanted her to enjoy this. *I* wanted to enjoy this. After all the times we had pretended to live in Switzerland, on this one glorious, sunny, snowy morning, with the Alps gleaming down at us, we didn't have to pretend.

"Darling," she said, stopping the scales and turning to me, apologetic. "I do hope you don't mind but I'd like to *really* experience this and I just can't when anyone else is around. Even you. Even half an hour would suffice. I know how you love to walk. The weather is perfect this morning so perhaps it might be good for you to take advantage of it. You're not hurt, are you? Please don't be hurt."

"Of course not, sweetheart," I assured her. I wasn't hurt. I was stunned. I didn't know I was "anyone else."

"When I feel self-conscious, I make mistakes playing in front of *anyone*, even you. Home's different. It doesn't count, somehow. You do understand, don't you?" she asked twice, anxiously. As I pulled on my coat, she suddenly exclaimed, "I'm sorry! I forgot! You're fighting a cold! You mustn't go for a walk!"

I found the right incantations. "I was lying, Mamma. Truly. I'm not coming down with a cold. I just felt like ... being here. I'd enjoy a walk, in fact. That's a good idea. I just wanted ... not to be with them. You need to be by yourself and I need to be by myself. It's perfect, you see? I truly do understand. And the light is perfect right now. This will work out just right. We can each do what we want. I'm so glad you thought of my taking a walk. I can take some photographs too." I had found the right words to convince her that her needs had not, did not, and would not hurt me, that her needs were my needs, that her needs had always, in fact, been mine, and remained so. Calmed, she smiled and waited patiently while I left the room.

"Please don't listen outside. I'll sense it," she called out timidly. I could tell she was still afraid that I might be "making the right noises" as she called it. (I was.) She was fearful of hurting my feelings. (She had.)

After repeating my incantations, I carefully closed the front door with a firm click—loud enough for her to be sure I had gone but not so loud that she might think I was upset. (I was.)

I sneaked around the wooden balcony to a side of the house where, through the window, I could see her playing but she could not see me. She was lost in a Bach fugue, her head bowed in a way that told me, from long experience watching her play when she didn't know, that she was utterly absorbed.

In the clean pane of the great floor-to-ceiling glass that divided the piano room from where I was standing on the balcony, I could see my mother clearly. A reflection of the Alps overlaid her image on the glass. To my surprise, I began to cry. I didn't know why I was crying. After all, I had wanted this moment for years, never imagining it could ever happen. Now that it was happening, I felt ... nothing. I wiped my eyes with a paper napkin I'd stuck in the pocket of my all-purpose coat after a snack at some coffee shop. Then I angled myself so that my mother could not see me and quickly got out my camera. I knew I could never show this photograph to my mother or even tuck it into Nan's old album from 1938. Were my mother to find it, she would know I had silently intruded on her and betrayed her wishes. I would have to keep this Swiss game to myself.

I aimed the lens. From where I was standing, my mother looked as though she were playing a grand piano on top of the Alps.

TWENTY-NINE

....

CHANG

Chang died in the middle of the night. That's what my parents told me the next morning; given how they looked, I had every reason to believe them.

Eight years earlier, we had driven south on a Saturday to pick Chang up. I was ecstatic. We had spread newspaper on the floor of the back seat and he delighted me by peeing all over the pages. The moment I picked him up, I loved him—instantly and totally. I held him along the length of my arm with his satisfying, small head resting in the crook of my elbow all the way home. His eight-week-old shih tzu teeth and tongue locked onto the inner skin of my arm and sucked. I felt an unfamiliar, vertical delight flash through my ten-year-old body. I was too young to know it then but Chang was the first male to waken both my sexuality and my maternal feelings. "He's sucking my arm!" I exclaimed to my parents who were sitting in the front seat.

They laughed. I didn't tell them how it made me feel.

We called him Little Chang to distinguish him from Chang, my grandfather's dog, who then became Big Chang. My mother gave Little Chang three-course meals at least once a week. On

Sundays, he got a miniature roast with lamb, roast potato, peas, and gravy. My mother prepared all his meals from scratch or we bought meat from the butcher across the park.

Living on top of the hill, overlooking hills to the back and the town and river and parkland to the front, we had no fence. Chang needed to be let out daily—and, of course, at night. Moonlit and moonless nights were alike: Chang would scratch to go out and I would shiver on the front stoop in my dressing gown in winter or in my short, cotton nightie in summer watching as Chang lingered thoughtfully, assessing the front lawn for just the right spot.

When Chang developed an eye infection, we gave him ointment. He went blind in that eye anyway. Chang and I shared something special then because neither he nor I could see properly. I would close one eye and pretend I was Chang walking around the house with my thick lenses and bumping into things. This was before I got contact lenses. Chang just adapted to his limited vision.

"I'm going to be a vet," I informed my parents. This decision followed fast on the heels of my decision to be a hairdresser.

One day Chang escaped. It was the height of the hot, rainy season. The rain was driving down the hillside from the saturated, sultry sky. My mother and I walked the streets in our raincoats looking for him—I, in my bare feet. We went from door to door and called his name between houses: "Chang Chang! Chang Chang!"

We finally found him safe and dry, visiting with the bishop's wife only a few doors down from our house. She had not heard us the first time we'd rung her doorbell. This became one of our favorite family tales.

Chang slept beside me after I had foot surgery. During my recovery, he slept along my bare legs while I read him Chalet School novels and watched replays of black-and-white movies from the forties.

I brushed his long, silky coat daily. When my mother and I washed him, his favorite game was to hold onto the end of his blanket or a towel and let me swing him around in wide circles.

One day after church, my father decided to take photographs of Chang and me with his best camera. Chang and I played on the front lawn. I had on my batwing glasses, tartan skirt, and navy sweater, and Chang was newly washed and brushed. Of all the photos saved in my boxes from childhood, it is one of only three that show me laughing, not smiling: the two others are a photo taken at the beach in which my father is teaching me to swim and a photo of me playing with all my grandparents at my mother's parents' beach cottage.

Chang slept in the laundry room in a basket with my old, cream-colored baby blanket, the one with the satin edges. He was the only member of the family who liked me no matter what and into whose miniature mane I could cry or whisper the truth without worrying about repercussions or dividing family loyalties.

I don't know why my parents didn't wake me the night he died. I think they were being kind and it happened quickly. They came into my room just before I rose to get ready for school. And told me something had happened to Chang in the night. They told me that they had heard him walking up and down restlessly in the hallway instead of being, as he usually was, curled up in a basket in the laundry room. My father had risen and taken him out in case he needed to lift his little furry leg. Afterwards, Chang had settled right in to his basket. When my father had risen to check on him an hour later, Chang had seemed listless but by the time my parents returned to him after my father had woken my mother, Chang was dead. In those days, one didn't take animals to the vet often, especially in the middle of the night.

I went into the laundry room and knelt down beside him on the green-and-white checked linoleum for a long time. He was curled in his basket with his eyes closed. He looked alright. I stroked his ears and brushed him a little. But when I stroked his silky tummy, his belly felt bloated and hard. Apart from my Russian grandfather who had died when I was too young to understand what had happened to him, Chang was the first being I had loved who had died. And he was the first whose lifeless body I would touch.

My parents told me I could stay home if I wanted that day. I went to school. I felt it was the brave thing to do: to swallow my grief. If Sister Luke in *The Nun's Story* and Violette Zsabo in the war could brave impossible things, I thought I should at least go to school. I went through English, French, and Ancient History imagining Chang at home, in his basket, still, waiting for us to bury him that evening when my father got home.

That afternoon, we had our weekly Religious Education class. The School Chaplain was a mild-mannered fellow whom we felt free to ignore completely. I mostly ignored him but managed to never give him the impression of ignoring him. Rather, I'd ask questions—just enough to convince my friends that I was covering for them so they could catch up on overdue homework but not so many that they would think I was serious. (Religious Education was a good class time to catch up with Physics in particular.) Long practiced in the art of appearing interested in and liking someone with whom I had nothing in common, I gave Mr.

McDonald the impression that I liked him and listened to him. Secretly, I did. I told my classmates I was just pretending to like him and pretending to be nice but I was, in fact, pretending to pretend. In truth, I felt sorry for him. Mr. McDonald had no idea of our capacity for cruelty or of what went on in our teenage minds. His gentle inquiry into our spiritual wellbeing was generally harmless because it touched on nothing of import. He had a daughter our age with whom I would much later share a one-room apartment for a few, undisciplined weeks in Copenhagen.

This particular day, Mr. McDonald asked us—for some reason—to discuss whether we thought animals had souls. I was uncharacteristically quiet. I didn't trust myself to speak. Those who heard the question began to take pleasure in voting against the idea. I thought of Chang, lying in the laundry at home, being voted on.

Miranda nudged me. "Are you alright?" she said with her usual, diffident kindness. I was aware of feeling dramatic inside and acting just the opposite outside. I wanted no one and everyone to know about my loss.

I nodded without speaking. Always free with words to the point of being reprimanded for talking in class until these last two years of high school, I couldn't even whisper to Miranda. It was too personal, too fresh. Chang was still in the laundry. I wrote her a note and passed it to her. She looked over with horror and raised her eyebrows. "That's *awful!*" she mouthed. I nodded and opened my Physics book.

That night, when my father got home and before we all had dinner, we wrapped Chang in his blanket and carried him down to the lower terrace, one of his favorite places. We laid him with his collar on top of the blanket. Then my father told me to go upstairs and be with my mother. She didn't say anything but finished getting dinner ready. We didn't talk much during dinner. We each were glum in our own way: tears fell on my plate but I said nothing; my mother rose in the middle of dinner and disappeared into their bedroom, reappearing with a red nose and a damp handkerchief; my father looked dark under the eyes and said he'd just have to give the spade back to Mr. Johannsen tomorrow because it was late now. After dinner, I did my homework, went to bed early, and cried myself to sleep.

When I went into the garden the next morning, there was fresh dirt where Chang had last lain. My mother had already planted a red geranium on top of him.

I won a Religious Education Prize that quarter. We had had to write only one essay all year to pass the class and I chose to answer the question "Do animals have souls?" It was an embarrassment to get a Religious Education Prize. People might think that one Meant It—and that could dampen one's reputation as a school officer and risk status with friends. But knowing how to satisfy major opposing parties was my specialty so I managed to sidestep the usual consequences.

When a new retaining wall was built next to the pool the following summer, I had bad dreams. I didn't know if Chang's small frame, his collar, nametag, and the blanket buried with him would remain intact or whether the workmen would part some of what was left of him from other parts. I didn't like to think about it and I knew my parents didn't want to think about it either. So we didn't.

Later, when I moved south and my parents came to visit Andrew and Olivia and me, my mother would gingerly put the back of her hand (being more afraid of germs than ever) on the silky spine of my latest dog and say, "Another one. I don't know how you do it."

"I love dogs. I love *this* one," I would answer.

"But he'll *die*," my mother would say each time.

"Yes, he'll die," I would say, touching the head of our latest dog as I said it.

"When Chang died, I never got over it," my mother said matter-of-factly and sighed. She always said this. She never repeated a single story except the one about her time after Chang. "For days and weeks I walked around ... you and Daddy were out all day ... You were at school and he was at work so it wasn't the same for you. I was used to spending every day at home with Chang. I never got over it. I missed him most because I was with him most. I couldn't go through that again. How can you?"

"I love them each."

"But what about when this one dies—like the last one and one before? You can't have loved them *very* much."

At this point in our ritual conversation I would always arrange my latest dog along the length of my arm and rest his head on the crook of my arm. I would stroke his brow and long ears while he snoozed and say again, "I love him to bits. And I'll love the next one to bits, too."

"Why would you choose to love something you know will die?" my mother would say. Then she would pat my most recent dog again with the back of her hand, stand, go to the nearest basin, and carefully wash her hands.

THIRTY

....

FLOWERS

The problem was this: my mother didn't grow flowers. She had a green thumb and she grew plants. But she didn't grow flowers. Well, it's not correct to say she didn't grow flowers. She just didn't grow the right ones. She grew nasturtiums and freesias and azaleas and night-blooming cereus—which bloomed, obviously, at night, but went to sleep during the day as faithfully as a koala. She also grew flowering ginger but it withered if you cut it. So did the hibiscus, the geraniums, and usually the hydrangeas, which a neighbor called "hy-geraniums." The jacaranda tree bloomed, pale mauve against the darker mauve of the hills across the valley, and the yesterday-today-and-tomorrow bush—one of Nan's favorites—had white, light lavender, and purple flowers. However, neither the jacaranda nor the bush flowers survived long in water. Our garden—divided into levels because my parents had bought a precipitous piece of land on top of a hill with views all around—was full of flowers. But they were the wrong ones. They weren't for cutting.

"Except for flowering trees and bushes, the flowers I grow turn up their toes and die. And the flowers that do grow seem to need to be red to thrive at our house," my mother observed, accurate and despairing. She was right. My father had taken her to different nurseries. Each time we would come home with something new. Everything grew fast in the subtropics although I didn't know it was fast compared with other places; I just thought it was the speed at which plants grew. However, after an enthusiastic start, many of the plants would slowly lose spirit and, while not usually dying, look as though they were not having a good time at our place. Eventually, my mother would ask my father to pull out the sad, little creatures and they would wither with the spiders in the compost heap behind the swimming pool change room. Flowers in the red range, however, not only took root but produced vast quantities of blossoms. They would spread themselves around like Romans at a feast. Even when my father pulled them out, they would reestablish themselves.

However, regardless of color, few were suitable for use inside. I didn't care what color the flowers were as long as they could be used in vases. Our garden's couldn't. We had no traditional cutting flowers: no roses, no chrysanthemums, no dahlias, no carnations, no geraniums, no sweet peas—nothing that looked good in a vase for longer than an hour.

As one of the Senior School leaders now, I was responsible for flowers for the headmistress's office for one week every month. I had tried bringing flowers from home but nothing survived being cut at dawn, wrapped up, and carried to school in the same school-gloved hand that carried my heavy leather satchel with its patina of years spent on buses and in smelly cloakrooms. I had to keep my other hand free to pay for the bus ticket, put away my money, pay for the tram ticket, put away the money again, and strap-hang if anyone even a week older than I stepped on the bus or tram. In such situations, the honor of our school was at stake: anyone in the public could report us to the school for not giving up our seat to an elder. I also needed that hand to read whatever I hadn't finished reading the night before.

"Melinda's always got the right flowers," I commented uncharitably to my mother as she was setting the table for dinner. My father would be late as usual and in a rush to eat dinner so he could arrive on time for one of his many civic meetings.

My mother looked at the tablecloth dubiously. It was red-and-white checked. "Somehow the red-and-white check doesn't look right for tonight. It's ... picnic-y. Not right for a stormy summer night. And ... hot looking. Could you please fold and put it the linen closet, and get out the green-and-white stripe? No, the ivy. You know the one. The green napkins, too, darling, please. What were you saying about Melinda? I'm sorry. I heard you but I didn't register."

I pulled out the ivy tablecloth, resting neatly on top of the kitchen tablecloths in the linen closet. Each cloth had been ironed dutifully by my mother on the ironing machine, folded in half lengthwise and rolled through the machine, folded in half lengthwise once more, and then rolled one more time through the machine to sharpen the creases. I flung the ivy cloth open into the air, just missing the stove. It caught its own breeze and settled, like a wave, on the laminated table.

"Darling, do be careful. You don't want to set yourself on fire."

"She's *always* got the right flowers."

"Right for what?" My mother handed me the cutlery across the servery. I laid out the cutlery, ensuring it was parallel. "Bread and butter plates, too," she added.

I went around the end of the servery, swinging by one arm on the pole that supported the edge. "For Miss A's office. We all have to take turns—the leaders—Miranda, Henny, Lou, me...."

"I'm sorry, darling. I didn't know you'd need cutting flowers for the headmistress's office when I planted things. What shall we do?" Her shoulders drooped a little as she went over to the stove to check the cauliflower.

I pulled down the bread and butter plates and set them on the table. As I went to the fridge to get out the butter, I looked over at her. The back of her hair was catching the late afternoon light. Her hair was the same as mine. Everyone admired our hair. My mother insisted hers was shiny because she brushed it one hundred times on each side each morning. I thought mine was due to genetics but brushed it the way she showed me anyway.

As she stood at the stove with her back to me, I thought of all the meals my mother had cooked my father and me and of what a strained, dutiful relationship she had with that stove. It didn't help that her mother-in-law was a fine traditional cook— puddings, cakes, roasts. I felt guilty. If my mother's heart wasn't in cooking, it certainly was in her garden. I had made her feel as though it was disappointing. I loved our garden, too, but it did disappoint me in this one respect.

I decided I had to undo the damage I'd done before dinner was served. I had to plan my remedial action carefully. Whatever I might say to undo my thoughtlessness couldn't be said too soon or my mother would suspect. Nor could it be said too late or she'd suspect. It also had to be delivered with the right touch of idleness. So I constructed a scenario: I would offer to get mint for the lamb. That would take me into the back garden. Then, in the rapidly growing dusk, I would choose some random, flowering plant as *the perfect thing*—the flower I needed, the one I'd forgotten that Mrs. Foote, Miss Arlington's secretary, had, in fact, told me Miss A liked.

"I'll get the mint," I said, trying not to sound too bright or eager as I disappeared out the door. After all, my mood couldn't change so suddenly. Chang followed me, waving his long-haired standard of pomp. Until he died a few months later, he was my faithful companion in crime.

I could hear Aiden in the house below playing "Für Elise" yet again and I glimpsed Mrs. Johannsen in the other house pruning her roses in the front yard with pride. I bent down and picked some mint. Several mosquitoes, annoyed, started dive-bombing me. I slapped at them angrily. The moon emerged above the high hills and low clouds, and a bird caught a quick dip in our swimming pool.

I looked around for a willing culprit. I spied a fern that my mother had grown from cuttings from Nan's house. That would do.

I walked back to the house, Chang following with his small furry legs moving like a duck in water. I leapt over the bushes, thus bypassing the path to the back door, closed both halves of the Dutch door after me, and turned the big metal key. I could smell the lamb. My mother was nowhere to be seen.

"Mamma?"

I heard a tap on the window. I peered through the green and white curtains to the side patio, a small space outside enclosed by a green trellis. My mother waved a little wave at me. I unlocked and opened the Dutch door again and walked outside. Chang stayed behind in the kitchen smelling the smell of heaven.

My mother was sitting on the tiny, white chair that had been mine as a child. She liked it. It fitted her small frame. I sat down in the green, canvas-backed director's chair beside her in the dark. She was nearly at the end of a Craven A. She had her special ashtray, which spun and made ash disappear, on the bench beside her.

"I thought I'd bring Daddy home," she whispered. She didn't want to talk any louder in case Mrs. Johannsen heard her. "You know he always arrives when I have a cigarette. He's running late so I thought I'd bring him home. He has to go out again, too. Another Management Committee meeting. I don't know why he needs to serve on *so* many committees."

"I had a fab idea," I said, as I watched the moon slide behind a storm cloud.

"About bringing Daddy home or something else?"

"I was getting mint when I suddenly remembered something I heard Mrs. Foote saying on the phone. She said Miss A liked ferns and something about her father's having grown them." I was warming to my topic. "You have hundreds of ferns. I can use them! They last, too." I stopped. My mother had an artist's unerring sense of cadence. My story needed to ring true to topic, be a perfect counterbalance to the intensity of my earlier disappointment and to the level of satisfaction I knew I needed to exude in order to satisfy her that *I* was indeed satisfied. It also needed to stop before it became suspicious.

Chang scratched at the back door and we heard my father's car pull into the driveway. My mother quickly extinguished the last of her cigarette. She had her medicine glass beside her.

"My tummy was a little rumbly, so I had a tiny sip of brandy. You know it always settles my tummy. Even Dr. Ruben says it's good for rumbly tummy. Nan even used to keep a thimbleful in the house for when I had cramps." She efficiently disposed of the ash and the cigarette in her mechanical ashtray. "I think I must have been more upset than I know about the flowers. I wasn't aware I was but I think that I must have been. I don't blame you of course. I know you didn't mean to upset me deliberately."

"Well, you can sin in peace now. I've got the flower thing solved. I'm just sorry I didn't remember what Mrs. Foote said earlier."

"Are you sure that *ferns* are satisfactory?"

"I even heard Footy say Miss A *prefers* greenery sometimes." Now I had gone too far. We closed the kitchen door behind us and locked it again. Chang licked something from the floor under the servery.

"Why would she prefer them?" My mother was precise and literal.

"No idea. Here's Dad. Run and clean your teeth so the ciggy doesn't smell. I'll hold him off at the pass."

The next morning, I went out in school uniform and bare feet to the back garden. I had made my garden bed. Now I needed to lie in it. I cut some fern fronds and made an elaborate display of putting them in damp newspaper and a plastic bag so they would stay fresh. Then I gave my dark brown, school uniform shoes a quick polish, shoved them on, and tied the laces. As a school leader, my duty was always to set a Good Example. It was our duty, too, to fine offenders whose shoes did not look shiny, whose hair was too long for their collars, whose gloves were missing, or whose hats were angled too far on the backs of their heads. I ran out the door with satchel and ferns.

I turned where the road on top of the hill veered and waved at my mother who was standing at the verandah window, watching. She waved back. I waved back. We each always wanted to be the last. Needed to be the last. I felt guiltier than she did this morning, which was quite a feat, so I made really sure I had the last wave before I disappeared from her view. I ran to the bus stop and just caught the bus.

In fact, I was even guiltier than my sin from the night before warranted. I had told yet another lie. This morning. I had told my mother I was taking the early bus because I needed to get to an extra swimming practice. I even remembered to say "extra swimming practice," because my parents knew which days swimming practice was.

I got off in the city, ferns in hand, and walked quickly down Victoria Street to Oxford Court. I turned left and walked past where my father's old lab used to be. Then I turned left again, and walked into the building next door—Oxford Florist.

"May I help you? Oh, for heaven's sake! *Meg*?"

"Hello, Mrs. Rydall."

"Ernie, look who's here! Michael's daughter! All grown up! What a lovely surprise. All in a Newnham uniform, too. How are your parents?"

My heart was pounding. I had never engaged in such calculated deception before—but it was too late now. What if the Rydalls phoned my father to tell him how nice it was to see me? What if they reached my mother by mistake?

The Rydalls and I talked a little. They seemed under the impression I had come just to see them on my way to school between bouts of public transport. Now I was going to hurt their feelings, too. But I was desperate. Glancing at the large clock above the flower-arranging area in the back and realizing that I soon would miss the last tram that could get me to school in time, I said, "Mrs. Rydall, I'm sorry to be rude but I have to get to school, I'm afraid. Do you have any roses?"

"Yes dear, we do. But they're expensive, I'm afraid. They're from down south. Do you have somewhere to keep them at school until you get home? We could save them in the big fridge and you could pick them up on the way home, if you like. That would be better for them. Mother having a dinner party?"

"No," I replied to all her questions at once. My hands were sweating in my navy gloves. "The ... school secretary asked me to get some flowers for the headmistress on my way through town. It's a long story." I pulled out my purse. It contained half the money I had saved over the last year. I knew I would have to buy flowers monthly for the next ten months. I began calculating.

"Well, dearie, the reds are all we have. How many would she want?" I made rapid calculations based on dividing my savings by ten, keeping some out so it wouldn't look suspicious, and then dividing that by the cost of the individual tall buds.

"Could I have one please?"

"Just one? I thought she wanted more."

"She did. Well, the secretary did. But I know she—the headmistress—will be happy with one."

"We could put fern around it, wrap it in tissue, and tie a bow. That way, it will look nice by itself."

She waddled into the back room, followed by Mr. Rydall. I looked with despair at the clock. I had seven minutes to walk up Victoria Street and get the tram. My heart was pounding.

The phone rang and I could hear Mrs. Rydall pick it up. She began to take an order.

Mr. Rydall finally came back with the single rose. With exaggerated surprise, I looked at the clock on the wall and exclaimed, "Oh, I was having such a lovely time talking with you both I had no idea! I must run or I'll miss the tram. I'm really sorry."

I gave him an inordinate sum and fled. I did not explain what I was doing with a bunch of additional ferns in my hand. In retrospect, I realized it probably helped my story. They doubtless assumed I must be something like Flower Monitor.

I staggered up onto the tram and sat looking with horror at the overwrought splendor of that single rose in its trappings. Masses of pink tissue surrounded the bud and marked the Rydalls' devotion to my father as a former professional neighbor. Somehow I had to get rid of the tissue. And the Rydall's ferns. The whole thing looked too professional.

I already knew there was nowhere between the tram stop and school to do the dumping. I would have to get off the tram, dump the stuff, and get on the next one. At the next tram stop—in a grimy, homeless neighborhood—I got off. A couple of Junior School girls who had been sitting behind me on the tram looked at me with curiosity but, out of deference, said nothing. They knew from all the badges I wore and from my embroidered blazer pocket that I was one of the goddesses of the Senior School.

I walked quickly down a side street and around a corner. There, leaning against a telephone post, was a swaying, barefoot, Aboriginal woman dressed in a flowery, shapeless dress. She looked at me and I, quickly, at her. She breathed with difficulty and I could smell the alcohol from where I was. I couldn't see how I could pass her without having to talk and didn't know what to say, so I acted as though I were looking for another street and turned back toward the corner. Having put some distance between us, I sat down on a couple of stone steps that led up to an unpainted door. I pulled the pink tissue and ribbon away from the single stem, undid the newspaper, discarded several ferns, nestled the rose amidst the rest, and rewrapped the newspaper around them. I was about to cast aside the orphaned ferns and pink tissue when I felt someone beside me.

"Wassyersdoin?" she asked me, moving back and forth on heavy haunches. "You go to that high an' mighty school up the road. Waddyersdoin here? 'Snot safe. I could rob ya. Anyone could. Ya stick out in yer bloody uniform. Get a move on. The next tram's almos' 'ere."

I glanced up at her, looked at the rose and ferns now secure in the newspaper, and then looked at the ferns and tissue I was about to discard into the gutter. I stood up and held out to her the extra ferns, now sprouting from pink clouds of tissue.

She stood there with her arms crossed. Her blood-red eyes met mine. She knew I was up to no good. She knew everything about me. She knew I was deceiving someone. She knew I was scared, not of her, but of something. She kept looking and kept her arms crossed.

I dropped the ferns and pink tissue, picked up my satchel, and ran. The satchel was heavy because we had Chemistry today and the Chem text was a whopper. I just made it to the tram before it took off. As it lurched forward on its rails, I looked back and saw her leaning against the post again, the ferns tucked between her breasts and the pink tissue adorning her dark, dull hair. She did not smile.

When I got to the school stop, I jumped off, ran up the hill, dumped my satchel in the cloakroom, ran upstairs to the Main Building, bounded up the main staircase two steps at a time to Mrs. Foote's office, and stood outside trying to look calm and composed. Mrs. Foote was on the phone.

"Good morning, Meg," she said as she put down the black receiver. "Isn't that lovely! Your mother must have a green thumb. Miss Arlington will be pleased. She hasn't had anything in her office for the last week. Louisa was out, as you know, with the measles." Mrs. Foote looked at me confidentially and lowered her voice. "I couldn't tell most but I can always trust you: Miss A's had difficult things to handle the last couple of days, so this will be very welcome. I'll be sure to tell her you brought it. She always likes to know who brought the flowers. I know she'll be particularly pleased this was from you—and your mother, of course."

By this stage, I didn't know whether I wanted Miss Arlington to know or not.

A month later, my mother showed up at the Annual School Flower Show. All the other mothers had arrived early, but my mother came just as the flower show officially opened. She looked beautiful in navy and white linen with pearls—and I could tell she felt exhausted in advance by the studied, relentless conviviality everyone was about to exercise. My father, like most of the other fathers, was absent; the lure of flowers and daughters sometimes successfully eluded them.

Dressed in a new spring outfit, which fit the school regulations for mufti on site, I was helping at a Lucky Dip stall when I saw my mother come in. I decided to take time off to walk around with her. As we stood admiring a particularly attractive arrangement, I noticed, with horror, Miss Arlington, in beige linen and pearls, walking toward us with neat, high-heeled intent.

"Good afternoon," she said with a pleasant smile, holding out her neat, beige-gloved hands to my mother. "Good afternoon to you, too, Meg." She turned to my mother again. "How kind of you to come. You must be meeting other Old Girls from your era."

They exchanged pleasantries while I stood with a smile fixed on my face. After a few minutes, I sensed Miss Arlington was readying herself to move on to the next mother-daughter duo, continuing her royal progression. I felt my tension ease a bit. Then, as an afterthought, Miss Arlington said to my mother, "I hope you exhibited your flowers." My mother looked fleetingly guilty. Without waiting for an answer, Miss Arlington continued, "You must be one of the few people to grow Osirias up here. One usually sees that rose only in the south."

My mother looked confused. "I'm sure you're right," she replied dubiously. Sensing something incomplete, she added in affable agreement, "As long as they're red."

Miss Arlington looked at her. Then, in the spirit of the Queen protecting a subject from making a fool of herself, she smiled serenely and excused herself to view the orchid winners.

"I wonder why she said I should grow roses," my mother mused, when Miss Arlington was out of earshot. "That came out of nowhere."

"Who knows!" I said with such heartiness that my mother asked me if I were feeling unwell.

The Saturday after the flower show, I received a letter in the postbox saying I'd won the prize for my section in the State Poetry Competition. The prize-winning poems and honorable mentions, together with the judge's comments, were in the next day's edition of the paper.

As my mother got out a Swiss tablecloth for lunch to celebrate, my father read aloud the critic's commentary on my poem. The paper had chosen a critic from a southern university to be the judge.

" 'Night Wanderer' takes on the long-ignored plight of displaced Aborigines. The poet is commended for looking beyond her own life with the help of research and imagination. The metaphor of the disrupted walkabout is sustained well."

"She sounds a bit pink to me. If some of those ivory tower types spent as much time going to bat for returned soldiers as they spend talking about Aboriginal rights—. Still, Commie or not, she certainly thought your work was good, Meg. Congratulations. What will you do with the $15?"

"I'll have to think," I lied. I knew exactly how I would spend it and over how many months it would have to stretch. I cut into another slice of the lamb, garnished with fresh mint from the garden.

"What made you write about Aborigines?" my father asked, pleased with my success.

"Stuff about Aborigines usually wins," I replied smoothly and bit into the baked potato. I dropped a little on the floor and Chang licked it up.

THIRTY-ONE

THE FEVER

My grandfather slept, breathing steadily but with effort. Winter sunlight slanted across his bed through the bubbled pane in the lower half of the windows that opened onto the long backyard with its sweet peas and empty chicken coop. The pale-blue, wooden walls were almost white in the afternoon light.

I sat beside him, alternately reviewing "Beowulf," "Le Misanthrope," and *The Australian Aborigine* as he slept. Even asleep, he was a naturally neat man in his ironed, striped pajamas. The neighbors next door were laughing in their kitchen. A magpie called from the great mango tree beside the back door.

My grandmother was visiting family again in Scotland for several months. (At that time, one rarely entered or left Australia for less than months.) Gran still was stoically, silently homesick occasionally—even though the cause of her departure from a respected, affectionate, Edinburgh household had come handsomely packaged in a Australian Flying Corps uniform in the First World War. My grandparents loved each other deeply, and my grandfather quietly admired Gran's courage in having overcome private fears and tears to make the best of her new land for decades.

Granddad had first sent Gran back to Scotland with her two young children when my father and aunt were seven and eight. They spent a year there. Years later, he had sent her again. Most recently, fifty years after that first return, he'd given her an anniversary card that read "Dear Isobel, Happy Anniversary. My present to you is a trip to Scotland. Love, Charley." An intelligent, steady, quiet-hearted man, my grandfather did not waste words.

So when my father asked me to be a little less self-involved and to help more with care of my grandfather while my grandmother was away, I caught the bus from the university's Botany Building, walked a winding shortcut through a neglected cemetery, crossed a main road, and caught the next bus to a stop ten minutes away from my grandparents' house. I walked along a couple of streets, past colonial houses in the older suburb in which my grandparents still lived, and reached their house.

I walked up the back stairs and peeked into his room to see if he was awake. He was in bed dozing with the newspaper folded vertically on his chest. I laid my books and purse on the telephone table and tiptoed into the kitchen across the squeaky floor to make myself a cup of tea.

Chang, Granddad's elderly shih tzu with his pepper-and-salt mane, followed me into the small blue and white kitchen where all was clean and orderly. I bent down and kissed Chang on his cold, black nose and stroked his luxuriant coat. His furry spray of white tail moved quietly back and forth. The kettle suddenly started to scream. I quickly took it off the stove.

"Hello," my grandfather called out.

"Hello, Granddad. Want some tea?"

"No, thank you, Meg. No appetite. Some pies cooling in the

fridge if you're hungry."

"Granddad! You're not supposed to be cooking! Dad told me the doctor said. You have plenty of food from our place!"

"Doctors don't know everything."

The first time my grandfather had ever said that to me—about a decade ago when I was eight—I'd begged him to put on my clip-on roller skates and show me how he used to figure skate. "Don't tell anyone. Doctors don't know everything," he'd said, smiling a little smile. Then, having adjusted my skates to his shoe size, he'd clipped them on and elegantly skated in a circle around one of the poles that kept all traditional colonial houses one floor above ground and thus cooler. He had skated over to an old chair, done a half turn, come to a neat stop, and sat down carefully. After taking off my skates, he had reached out his smooth-skinned arm for the key so that he could readjust them to my smaller size.

I looked in the fridge, spotted the small, newly baked pies he had made, went in to kiss him, and then ate a pie as I sat with him. Even though it was winter, he was wearing his thinnest pajamas and was covered with his lightest wool blanket. I worried he might be running a fever.

"Have you heard from Gran this week?"

He pointed to his desk on which a fountain pen, blue ink, an aerogram, and postcard were arranged neatly on the blotter. "You can read them." He lay his white, combed head—damp, I noticed—on the ironed pillowcase and fell into a light sleep. I read Gran's aerogram and postcard. The postcard had the same view she had sent me.

Just as I was reading the second act of Moliere, my grandfather's eyes opened. He stared at his hat, which was hanging behind the door. He started to murmur. I sensed he was not really talking to me.

"Church ceiling. They talk and laugh. On and on. Sleep up top. Stars. Moon on hills. But not home. Want *Home!* He shivered.

I realized, with silent concern, that my grandfather was indeed running a fever. Sometimes when he ran a fever, he dreamt strange things. Once, he had told me odd stories from a dream and the next day he had been admitted to the hospital.

I sorted out what must be happening. His fever was merging two periods of time: periods on leave from the war when he had regularly gone with a friend to a Scottish farm, met a young woman from Edinburgh visiting cousins, and married and the period in which he had sent Gran, my father, and aunt for a long visit to Scotland eight years after he brought her to Australia. These must have merged: his missing Australia when he was at war and his missing Gran and the children.

My grandfather stopped talking abruptly. Hoping this was just the fever, I put my hand on his forehead and said it must have been a lovely view. Then I kissed him on the cheek. He pressed my hand beneath his soft, tanned, flat fingers and slipped off to sleep. I was pleased that I'd had the presence not to correct him.

That evening when I saw my father, I told him about my visit and about the fever but I decided not to tell him about my grandfather's wanderings. Somehow, it felt ill-timed and unnecessary. I also felt as though I were telling on my grandfather as well as worrying my father unnecessarily.

Later, when my father telephoned my grandfather as he did each evening, I heard one end of what seemed to be an ordinary conversation. My father was saying things that told me the doctor must have come after I left. I was glad I hadn't said anything. It saved my grandfather his dignity during a moment of confusion and was a small moment of intimacy between us, even if it was a moment shaped by fever.

When my father hung up the phone, he told me that the doctor had said my grandfather was a little stronger and could get up more.

Immersed in my own life, I didn't sit alone with my grandfather again, though of course I saw him and my grandmother as often as my university studies permitted. Our studies were undertaken, as everyone's were those days, while we lived at home. Only country students stayed in special colleges near the university or took correspondence courses.

Two years later, my grandfather died. Soon after, I left with friends to travel and work my way around the world for a year as all new graduates did then.

My father had told me that Granddad's father and his family, all thoroughly English and xenophobic, were on holiday from England. They met a Greek family at a hotel in the south of France. Their son married the daughter against both sets of parents' wishes. They went to Australia. Granddad's father sent his wife and children to Greece once to visit her parents. I knew nothing else. After Granddad died, Gran found a photograph of Granddad's mother. Granddad had written her name and town on the back. I was curious. Granddad had never shown interest in his family history and never talked much anyway. I had sensed, too, that it was better not to ask him. Now I was free to inquire. I addressed a letter from Edinburgh using the family name and the name of the town in hopes that some family with the same name might still live there.

On the day before I was due to leave London to travel slowly across the continent, I stopped one last time at the bank to pick up mail. There was a letter from Greece in graceful English. I immediately replied, telling them when and where I would be staying in Athens.

I eventually arrived in Athens shabby but neat and clean and still with one good outfit.

The morning after I arrived at my Class C hotel, my distant cousin's driver met me over breakfast and, despite my protestations, took me in the back of a lonely black Mercedes to stay at the old family home. Elegant, kind, distant relatives offered me thick coffee and cigarettes on a silver tray in a large room. They moved gracefully among different languages according to whether they were speaking to the old ones, the maids, or me. I was glad I was wearing my good outfit.

They told me that the old ones remembered my grandfather and siblings coming for a summer. The room in which we sat had a fluted ceiling that looked like a church.

They claimed me without reservation. My English and Scottish and Russian sides were of no import to them. I was their beautiful Antonia, returning from being lost to an Englishman and a primitive colony. I sensed my "return" was of more import to them than would be the return of the Elgin marbles.

After a late dinner and much wine, they led me up an outer staircase to the roof. The children, they said, always liked to sleep up there at night in summer. I saw stars above dark olive groves and a moon rise above distant mountains.

Despite their repeated invitations, I stayed only three days. We talked late into the night.

They embraced me quietly as we said farewell. My curiosity was satisfied. I liked having "foreign" relatives—and I liked them. They overlooked my colonial background and lesser education.

What I realized too late was that my curiosity had cost them: the old ones were once again grieving the loss of their beloved Antonia to a lesser land.

THIRTY-TWO

KNITTING

When I was five, Nan taught me how to knit. I learned mainly by watching. Her needles were at my eye-level when I stood. She showed me how to purl and how to plain. She showed me how to do Fair Isle, using some old brown and green wool. When I knit, I held the needles close to my eyes because I couldn't see them clearly otherwise. I don't remember Nan knitting in later years. Sewing beautiful clothes but not knitting.

For most of my childhood, both my mother and I were knitters. We avoided knitting nasty things like tea cozies, although I still have the moldy green and yellow remains of one I had to make in Craft Class. We also avoided knitting baby clothes. We weren't close to many babies and those to whom we were close were already equipped with exquisite outfits, knitted in complex patterns by distant aunts on sheep and cattle properties. Besides, my mother wasn't interested in making things for anyone other than the three of us.

My mother and I would knit in winter—whatever winter we had. (It wasn't long.) Her mind was step-by-step, orderly. She liked to follow directions. Mine worked from the big picture to the details and I was strongest on general operating principles. I soon outstripped her. I liked to extract the directions from the shiny page and wing it from there while watching reruns of "Leave It to Beaver," "Pick a Box," and old movies. We knitted Fair Isle jumpers—sweaters—for ourselves and a plain jumper for my father: a cheery cream thing made with merino wool. It kept us busy through an entire season of "Father Knows Best." While my father was a trim man, he was certainly bigger than we were. We were using fairly small needles, so it took us a long time. We had to redo things, too, because, with my mother's knitting one of his sleeves and my knitting the other, they came out uneven.

Then we moved on to the big stuff. Not cable. Cable was too hearty, too Irish, too Scottish, and too traditional. Instead, we moved on to ski jumpers. The latest jumpers for skiing, to be worn under one's jacket, consisted of two large knitted squares with a Fair Isle design across both and drop sleeves with the same complex design around the top of each.

Of course, knitting ski jumpers required that one find a way to head south to go skiing but that's another story.

We would head for the second floor of Robertson's to get patterns and wool. On one occasion, I remember that we couldn't find anything in a color combination we liked. Disappointed, we'd gone home on the bus. However, the next day, when my father decided to take a cousin visiting from Scotland out to the animal sanctuary, I cheered my mother, depleted at the thought of smiling and being friendly to a stranger all day, by suggesting that we look at combinations of colors in the birds at the sanctuary to see which we liked. She cheered up.

My father picked up Hattie from my grandparents' and

brought her back to our house. Having lost the battle about why it wasn't "really necessary to spend the entire day with her, Michael. You've never met her before," my mother put on a jumper, skirt, and blazer, and became her most gracious self for the occasion. I was tied by withies of love to my mother's view of life so I, too, resented Hattie's intrusion into a perfectly good Saturday when I could have painted, knitted, read, written poetry, and even summarized the endless chapter on the Age of Pericles for Miss Calder; she had a double degree from Cambridge and a low tolerance for our being ill-prepared.

"I feel as though a big white bird is coming to land on our weekend and smother it," my mother commented to me with a sigh as we put out the china for afternoon tea, which we would have when we returned from the animal sanctuary. We renewed our determination to find the perfect knitting colors based on the birds.

When Hattie walked up our brick path between the ferns and stood smiling palely at us in a muted brown cardigan, sedate burgundy lipstick, brown skirt, and sensible brown walking shoes, we knew instantly we couldn't share this aviary goal with Hattie. Something made her tick but it wasn't color. That was clear.

When we arrived at the animal sanctuary, we became perfect hosts and she, the perfect guest—that is, except for when my mother and I deserted my father. We left him to take care of his cousin (for my mother, and therefore I, thought of her *not* as our cousin) in the wombat and emu enclosures. We took a risk: we asked them both, without much interest in our voices, if either wanted to see the birds; if not, we would just stop by them en route to the restroom (which, we had secretly noted, was close to the birds).

Hattie looked questioningly at us, waiting for a cue, so I gave her one. "They're not very interesting and you said you've seen parrots and kookaburras. The wombat and emu enclosures are very interesting and there's good shade on that path." I could see that she was carefully trying to avoid her first sunburn, white skin already pink in the shade. My comment would seal it.

She and my father walked on, speaking of relatives and wombats.

My mother and I beetled back to the wooden hut with the carving of a female koala on the door of the Ladies side. The koala's femininity was designated by a little carved apron painted pink. My mother and I got the giggles at the sight. We ducked inside quickly so we wouldn't have to lie about having stopped at the restroom.

"Don't sit on the seat," my mother said automatically as we went into adjoining stalls. I could hear her pull off two pieces of toilet paper to make into a seat and a third to drop into the bowl to combat splashes. I had long since outgrown this ritual and had graduated to squatting a few inches off the seat and aiming.

"Come on, Mamma, or we shan't get there and the whole plan will have been wasted!" I said as I waited impatiently outside the stall, already having washed my hands in the steel sink.

"Whisper! Someone might be outside!" she hissed *sotto voce*, adding, "The water splashed me!" I heard more toilet paper being pulled. "This is the shiny, government-issue kind." More pulling. Soon she was going to have that thing overflowing with brown toilet paper. She finally emerged looking embattled.

"Come on," I pleaded.

We went from the sickly sweet darkness of the restroom into the blinding light of mid-afternoon and down the short path to the birds.

I grabbed a notebook out of my handbag and looked up. There, behind the wiring, was what we had come for: birds, each with its unique mix of colors. The parrots were the finest, of course, and we jotted down the colors of the males with care.

"They're rather garish," my mother commented.

"No, they're not. We don't have to use all the colors, just a couple." I didn't want our outing to lose its zest.

"We can't both use the same colors. We'll look like one of those horrible hair ads, 'Which twin has the Toni?' People will see us together and think how sweet that we are wearing Mother and Daughter outfits. Ech."

"We are sweet and it would be lovely—but I can't wear your colors anyway; our eyes are different colors."

"Your eyes are blue, too."

"Not blue-blue like yours. Mine are green-blue and I have darker skin, remember?"

"Ever since you were born, I've clearly been under a misimpression. I thought you had blue eyes."

"They are blue. I didn't mean it like that. They're just not cornflower blue like yours. They're *sea*-blue. And as I said, my skin's darker."

"I've never forgiven your aunt for saying you were sallow once when you were little."

"I am sallow."

"She didn't have to say it. What color do you think you can wear?"

"Dirty dove."

We rejoined Hattie and my father. Both were more than ready to forego more mammals in favor of afternoon tea.

It was another week before my mother and I could get back to

Robertson's. Shops closed at noon on Saturday and weren't open on Sunday.

My mother chose green and red yarns, plus off-white for the background.

"That's not from one of the birds," I said accusingly, as we counted skeins.

"I just left out the gaudy colors, as you suggested."

"It looks remarkably like all the pictures of alpine hikers in your Swiss books," I said suspiciously.

My mother said nothing and went on counting skeins.

"What about you?" she countered when she had finished counting the plump skeins of each color sitting beside each other on the glass counter.

"Dark grey, medium grey, and light grey up top on a dusty pink background. I said 'dirty dove' and I meant it. I'm a dove named Hattie. If I fly over you, watch out."

"That happened to me once," my mother responded.

"On you?"

"When I was trying to learn to drive. Nan was so against my learning. I took lessons. In the second lesson, a bird dropped white and yellow all over the windshield. I couldn't see properly. Then the instructor started talking to me at the same time about something unrelated and I couldn't reverse park. It all seemed like a sign, particularly when I got home and rang Nan who said she'd been worried silly because it was raining. That's when I gave up learning."

I arranged the skeins deftly on the counter, quickly counting them. I was two short.

A small, wiry woman of indeterminate age, dressed in the regulation Robertson's black skirt and white blouse, came up to us. "Meh ai help yiu?" she asked in her best artificial British accent, something many of the assistants in Robertson's adopted. (The elevator woman was especially Shakespearean.)

"Yes, thank you. I can only find three balls of this light grey."

"May I see the pattern directions?" she asked.

I handed the booklet over to her, turning it upside down so she could read it from her side. She read it with an expert eye and then looked dubiously at the front cover.

"Are you sure you want this one? This calls for eight skeins of two colors, not three."

"I'm changing the pattern and putting grey in the middle."

She looked suspicious.

"I got my inspiration from a bird at the animal sanctuary," I added, my better self abandoning me. "Nature really has the best ideas." My mother quickly mustered interest in patterns on a shelf because she was getting the giggles and felt sorry for the woman, who, we remembered, used to work in hosiery and was used to a smaller range of colors and choices.

"We'll have to order it up from down south. We don't have demand for heavy wools up here."

"How long do you think it will take?"

"A fortnight."

I smiled bravely and said, "I'll just have to knit slowly." I caught my mother's eye. She was peeking out from behind the pattern stand, looking gently reproving. It was time for me to stop showing off. My mother put both her wool and mine on the family account. The sales clerk whooshed the invoice up to the accounts department along the wire in its metal tube.

By the time the balls arrived from down south, I had knitted everything I could. My mother was halfway up the front side of her jumper, having had to undo about four inches to catch a stitch she had dropped while watching a rerun of "Three Comrades."

By the time we went skiing, we both had finished our jumpers. My mother was more impressed with her sweater than with mine. I was more impressed with mine than with hers.

The first day we went skiing, people stopped us and asked if we were sisters. My mother preened happily. We preened until the afternoon when someone remarked that we looked so sweet in our mother-daughter jumpers—and asked us where had we bought them.

"They're not really meant to be mother and daughter jumpers although they are handmade. I just thought of using birds for colors," I explained.

"If you keeping saying it that way, people will think you knitted them both," my mother said, sounding justifiably injured. I made sure that, for the rest of the week, when we would meet at lunchtime—I, from my intermediate lessons and my mother, from her beginner's—that I said, if asked, "We each made our own. We each chose colors from birds." My mother was happier getting her rightful credit.

When I left home, I left four ski jumpers behind, some knitted in bird colors, some in Swiss, in the top closet of my old room. Years later, when I was home helping my mother do out closets, we came upon a box my mother had labeled "sentimental." The category was not helpful: for my mother, most inanimate objects fell into that category. I opened the box.

"Mamma, look!" I exclaimed in self-admiration. "The ski things I made."

"I knitted *one*," she said suspiciously.

We examined them all, each with its different set of colors, each made from the same pattern, each the same size, each pressed and folded neatly.

"I think it was this one." She held up the dove grey.

"You did *not* make that. I remember specifically: I made it look like a dove." I admitted to not being absolutely certain who made the others: the ones in shades of blues on white or red and green could have been knitted by either of us.

"See the way I sewed the sides together? That's me," I said, indignant.

"You probably sewed up the sides on one of mine because you were always better at that. I'll look it up in my diary."

"Please don't do the diary thing. You'll have to go through about six years'. Look, it doesn't matter. We were both brilliant, then we got bored. They're all lovely and we both know you knitted one."

"It does matter. One day you'll forget and say you knitted them all. I want it on record that I knitted at least one good one. You owe me fifty cents if I can find the reference in my diary while you're here."

She disappeared to the back room, which was her war room. In it, she kept all her cassette recordings of Michael Jackson, video releases of films like "Lawrence of Arabia," craft supplies, and a diary for each year of her life from age thirteen on, minus my childhood years when she was too busy to keep one.

I had been looking forward to playing piano duets with her until my father came home from the lab. Now that I lived a flight away, we didn't have a chance to play often. But my mother hunched over a pile of dark blue journals, each the same size, turning pages as she smoked Craven As using her black, filtered holder.

"Mamma, who cares?" I said, trying to draw her away from her obsession with accuracy and into what I hoped would be a musical feeling for the moment.

"I care!" she said, not looking up and with a suspicious tremor in her voice. I decided I should back off. Clearly, this was a question of public record.

An hour and a half later, she emerged, triumphant, holding open a journal at its mid-point.

"Here. July 7."

I knew what was needed.

"What does it say?"

" 'Meg and I to town. Bought wool—red, green and white. Expensive but should be lovely. Meg to university ball with John McA.' "

"Who in hell was John McA?"

"The fellow from the biology department who used to phone you too early in the morning."

"No memory. What wool did I buy?"

"I don't say."

"You put yours down but not mine?"

"I can't put *everything* in the diary. You owe me fifty cents."

Decades later, when I was cleaning out the upper reaches of my mother's closet, amidst seventy-year-old silk evening gowns made by Nan I uncovered a clear plastic bag.

"Look," I exclaimed to my old friend Livi, who was helping. "She kept one of the ski jumpers I made." Livi looked at me and I, at her without speaking. We sat down to look.

We opened the plastic bag. Its innards were wrapped in tissue and carefully folded with mothballs. I took out a single sweater, still colorful from years in the dark. On its green and red front was pinned half of an index card. It bore my mother's neat, flattened printing: "THIS IS A JUMPER THAT I MADE." "I" was underlined three times.

THIRTY-THREE

THE RIBBONS

The day after we celebrated my grandfather's birthday and a few months before I graduated from university, Granddad went into hospital again. My father visited frequently, despite the long drive from the lab to the hospital on the other side of town. We spoke with my grandmother daily.

One evening, I arrived home from classes and opened the front door to a ringing phone. I lived at home. In that period in Australia, we almost all lived at home when while attending university. When I picked up the receiver, I heard my grandmother's voice.

"Your father said you're going over to the hospital to see your grandfather. I wanted to ring before you left. Big Chang hasn't been eating much lately. He didn't even eat the baked dinner your grandfather cooked for him last weekend. He died today. He was fifteen. It was to be expected. Your father can bury him tomorrow. Don't say anything about Chang to your grandfather. No need to bother him in hospital." I don't think she cared much for Chang but she had kindly tolerated him and my grandfather's passion for dog shows by ignoring both the dog and the shows.

Big Chang had outlived my dog, Little Chang, by several years.

I loved Big Chang. I felt tears coming but I didn't tell my grandmother. I was used to her telling me that everything was a secret so I paid no attention to that but I also happened, for once, to agree with her.

That afternoon, I caught three different buses to see my grandfather. We had one car. Everyone had one car.

My grandfather was sleeping when I entered. The ward was divided into four low-walled sections, each of which held six beds, three facing three. So the ward could accommodate twenty-four old soldiers. My grandfather's bed was closest to the hallway, which ran down the middle.

As fastidious in illness as in health, my grandfather slept neatly, his thick white hair combed back from his smooth, tanned skin. His light blue-and-brown-striped pajamas had been washed, starched, and ironed by my grandmother, and a nurse had secured them to within a button of the top. His hands, so like my father's, were folded on top of the sheet, which was tucked in tightly at the sides.

A metal cup sat beside him on the side table. When I looked into it, I had to fight the desire to dry-retch. Having found that I was not squeamish about much, I was surprised that my stomach lurched at the sight of green phlegm. With emphysema and pleurisy, my grandfather needed the cup often. I disapproved of my own reaction and summoned up inner discipline in order not to show it.

I picked up the single, straight-backed, wooden chair and gingerly placed it down beside his bed. The elderly man in the next bed moved his hand slightly in greeting. I smiled back and gave a wide, silent wave. I never knew how much the men could see and wanted to be sure to acknowledge his effort to greet me. Many of them had no visitors.

I don't know how long my grandfather and I sat like that. I watched Granddad's face for a while, his profile like my father's: good bones, large thin nose, fine nostrils; pepper-and-salt eyebrows; well-shaped mouth with a touch of generosity at the sides of the upper lip. His skin was pallid beneath the tan he always had from gardening.

"Hello, Meg," he said as he stirred. "How's Uni?"

I bent over the bed to gently embrace him. "We have two weeks' holiday soon."

"I thought you'd just had holidays." He lay still as he spoke. His brown eyes, circumference bleached to grey by the sun over the last seventy-five years, rested on my face. My grandfather was as effective with his gentle, silent authority as my father was with his frustrated, forceful eloquence.

"That was May, Granddad, the last one."

His hand lay palm down on the sheet. I took it. His skin was always like silk. For a man who, after having worked at a desk all his life then spent years gardening, cooking, and repairing things, his skin was surprisingly un-calloused, soft, and pliable. The pads of his square fingers gave beneath my touch; anemic blue veins mapped the top of his hand, almost casting shadows in the late afternoon sun. I could watch his slow, weak pulse in the largest vein. I looked at my own hands: like his, my teal veins lived close beneath thin, tanned skin.

"We get two weeks in August, too. I've a pile of papers I have to finish before."

"You can only do your best, Meg. You can only do your best." His heavy eyelids—a bruised, brown color—closed for a second as weakness competed for his attention.

I held his hand as he slept. This was my secret: I had felt a larger Presence underneath my mosquito net years earlier, so I thought I might at least call on It to bring my grandfather strength. I sat there not moving. I imagined a stream of—of Something—healing, flowing through my palm and the tips of my fingers into his hand and body. If he got better, I would know Whom to thank.

I had to leave. I was behind in my papers. I hated to wake him.

He sensed my inner movement and woke. He reached for the metal cup, finished his hacking, and lay back exhausted.

"Goodbye, Meggie. You have to go."

"I just heard, Granddad. I have a job after I finish Uni. Teaching."

"That's good, Meg. Good for you."

"Mamma and Dad send their love. Dad said he'll be over tomorrow evening. He's working tonight."

"That's good. Give everyone my love."

Despite a harmless C of E upbringing and years of passive cooperation with my Scots Presbyterian grandmother, my grandfather was not a churchgoer. However, he was naturally religious; when my father had taken me as a newborn to visit my newly minted grandparents, I apparently had flooded my grandfather's best trousers through my clothing and his.

"She just wet you all over!" my father had exclaimed, perturbed.

"Honey, Michael. Pure honey," my grandfather had replied, unperturbed.

He had tended his garden and cooking as quietly and carefully as he had his grandchildren. He had plucked his strawberries with unexpected dexterity from such square fingers; he had squatted beside me to show me chickens; had held my hand in his large one and let me collect eggs when no one else trusted me with them; had rolled up his trousers so he could wade in the shallows so I could splash on the side of the creek. And he had washed, brushed, and unfailingly walked Chang, his shih tzu—Best of Show—long past Chang's show status and into a slow, waddling, dignified old age.

"I'm sorry, Granddad, I have to go. The last bus leaves in ten minutes. Everyone sends love."

"Goodbye, Meg." He raised himself up a little as I kissed his soft cheek and he kissed mine. "The nurse said Gran rang but I was asleep. Have you talked to her? Did she say anything about Chang? He hasn't been eating."

Chang. I had promised myself and Gran (in that order) that I was not going to tell Granddad about Chang. I couldn't bear to think of his going home to find Chang dead and buried without even a headstone, just some of Granddad's sweet peas that had turned brown covering his little grave. I couldn't bear to think of Granddad's knowing I had known and lied. Although we had never talked about it, he and I understood each other's love for Chang better than anyone.

"Gran said there's no problem with Chang's eating now," I prevaricated.

My grandfather's head sank back on the regulation pillow but he kept his eyes open until I got to the door of the ward where I turned and waved. Four elderly men waved back.

When I got home, I called my grandmother to tell her what I'd said. I enlisted her cooperation. More used to declaring the details of secrecy than being handed them, she nevertheless agreed not to contradict my invention.

My grandfather died the following week, in the early morning. The hospital phoned my father. He retreated to his study. Three days later, we went to the service at Victoria Street Presbyterian. My mother wondered what to wear. I couldn't cry.

My grandmother, who had come to stay with us for a while, stayed for two weeks. Then she rose one morning, said it was time to go home, and disposed of my grandfather's clothes and few effects quickly. She loved him greatly but she didn't keep things. All she kept of Granddad's things were his grey felt hat behind the door, his retirement watch, his World War I medals, the big war portrait, his fountain pen—still clean and functioning after forty years—and Chang's many show ribbons.

"Take them. They're no use to me," my grandmother said as she fiercely prepared tea and scones in the kitchen where my grandfather no longer stood beside her pickling his onions or making his coconut ice.

I took the ribbons. Long practice had made me a skillful liar for my own and others' benefit but I had never lied to my grandfather until Chang died. There was no such thing as absolution in our sedate Presbyterian Church. The ribbons were my absolution.

Later, I hid Chang's Best in Show ribbon under my academic robes as I went to my graduation ceremony on a sweaty, midsummer night.

THIRTY-FOUR

HIS HANDS

What I most like to remember about his hands is how they taught me to swim. He took my mother and me to the beach as often as his work allowed. The beach was safe. He and my mother didn't disagree at the beach—at least not often enough for it to burn into memory. He would take me into the tepid shallows of the Pacific and float me with his broad hand underneath my round, firm, little belly in its pale turquoise, boucle bathing suit. I would kick and splash and he would encourage me. I'd hear his voice close by above me: "Go on, Meg, I'm holding you. Splash with your legs. I'm right here holding you. That's it!" I would splash and kick, knowing that at some point he would lower his hand just the tiniest bit so that I had the sense of swimming without his support but always knowing his hand was just below me.

There was his hand in punishment. I don't remember the things I did to warrant reprimands but there were regular punishments—all predictable, all infringements of rules that, looking back, had a military quality. He had not fought in the war for years for nothing. As a young officer, he had had heavy responsibilities. One mistake would have cost lives. There could be no errors, so he had made none. So later, a five-year-old's mistakes seemed not so different to him after his officer training at Duntroon and jungle warfare. He would still jump when my mother or I slammed a door unexpectedly.

When he was a child, his mother used to chase him around the garden occasionally, trying to catch him to spank him with her umbrella when he'd been bad, he once told me, laughing. He also said he never gave his father reason to spank him, except twice: the first time, he rode too close to a bus on his bicycle, hit the bus as it stopped suddenly, took himself to the hospital, and came home with a mended nose; the second time, he almost made his mother miss the ship that would take her, his sister, and him away for months to stay with his grandparents in Scotland. "One quick tap on the backside each time," my father explained. "That was all. He never needed to spank me again."

I knew I must have been very naughty to oblige him to spank me as often as he did. He told me he hated doing it. He said it hurt him more than it hurt me. He had a large hand. It was firm. I cried when he spanked me. He told me that if I could be good, he wouldn't have to suffer so from having to spank me. Usually, I would tell him what I had done. The number of smacks would be proportionate to my infraction. It still puzzles me why I told him. If I'd had siblings, perhaps one of them would have clued me in earlier to the virtues of lying. However, my father had an uncanny way of knowing the truth, no matter what I said. It was not until twenty years later that I realized my mother, who secretly came into my room to comfort me after a spanking, had given him the information that helped him appear uncannily accurate.

"You were dumb" was Livi's good-natured assessment of me

one day. I was staying with her for the weekend when we were about to turn thirteen. Her father had been in the war too. He was a daredevil pilot according to Livi. She and her siblings were proud of who he had been but hated him for how he acted with them. "My brothers told me how to avoid Dad—most of the time."

My father consistently said that if I'd had a brother or sister, I would be expected to do this and this and that and that. While washing up the dinner dishes with my mother one evening, reason finally spoke through me. I answered back. I pointed out that if I had a brother or a sister, I wouldn't have to do the drying up *every* evening. My logic was not appreciated.

One of my father's consistent spankings was for nail biting. I bite them still, on occasion, to this day. My father decided I had picked up this habit from his cousin's wife, whom we saw infrequently. Her background and religion were different from ours. So she was suspect. She dyed her hair and bit her nails. I bit my nails. Therefore, I must have picked up this habit from her and he needed to break me of it.

He painted NoBite, a quinine-flavored mixture, on my small, stubby fingernails. It was a failure so spectacular in its paradoxical effect that even he was impressed: I liked the taste. Keeping his sense of humor, he sent in a "tidbit" to the local newspaper recounting that when he painted NoBite on my fingers the first time and asked me how it tasted, I thought he must not know how good it was and politely stuck my finger in his mouth.

After this, he took another tack. He and I agreed I would tell him how many times I had bitten my nails during the day and he would give me an equal number of smacks. Because he said he was doing it to help me, I told him the truth every time. He persevered because he loved me more than he could bear and because he saw it as his duty to discipline me and teach me self-discipline.

I didn't tell Livi I used to do that. She would have thought I had been really stupid and I didn't want to lose her as a friend. She had so many brothers and sisters that no one noticed whether she was even there, let alone whether she was biting her nails. Besides, she thought my father was terrific, not like hers. I didn't want to spoil her view of him.

My father's hand on my brow was different. When I was running a fever, he was not low of spirit, irritable, exhausted, worried, preoccupied, or buoyantly enthusiastic, each of which he could be at other times. He was *still*, economical in his movements. His deep brown eyes would focus on the thermometer and then he would take a better reading of my condition by putting his hand on my brow. His fingers, broad and silky-skinned, applied just the right amount of pressure and exuded love. I suspected him of praying at those times. He would fetch a wet washcloth, cool it off by flapping it neatly in the air several times, and lay it on my head to cool me. When I had a cold, he would prepare a hot lemon drink—a squeezed lemon, boiling water, and lots of sugar. He would give it to me with the strict instruction to drink it all down at once. The strictness of his tone at these times was the strictness of the healer: he was working magic. When I slipped under my blue-and-white-checked merino wool blankets up to my nostrils and sweated, as he had told me I would after the hot lemon drink, I knew I would be better. And was.

Some nights, when he needed to feel my forehead or tend me frequently, he slept at the foot of my bed all night so that he could be there when I woke.

My father's hands were like my grandfather's, which, I was told, were like his mother's. It was she who protected my father from his mother after he cheerfully cut off his younger sister's blonde curls at her request. That was one of those times his Scots mother came after him with the umbrella. According to him, his grandmother hid him behind her skirt as his mother flew by, justifiably outraged and indignant, with the umbrella.

The first time my skin became my own beneath my father's touch was when he spanked me in front of the sideboard. I was ten. As I lay across his lap in the dining room, it occurred to me that if I appeared not to hurt, he might not be as interested in spanking me. He might reassess spanking as less than effective. So I decided I would not cry this time. Whatever I had done must have been a considerable infraction; it was a carefully delivered, extended spanking. After it was over, my skin burned. I stood up with difficulty but walked away at a normal pace, without shedding a tear, deliberately looking as though I were trying not to be bored but really was. It was the second-to-last time he hit me.

We each threw a few boxes on the floor over the next ten years and we each frightened my mother by yelling at each other a lot, mainly over curfews, schoolwork, and what he deemed were my failures in family responsibilities.

The last time he touched me in anger was by the pool. I'd arrived home late, the day before my mother's birthday. I had spent the weekend at the beach "with university friends." In fact, I had spent most of the time with my boyfriend. My father liked Stephen but he and Gran thought Stephen was the wrong religion and therefore, unless he converted, unsuitable in the long run.

It was just before dinner. I was exhausted. I decided to go down for a quick swim. I needed a little time alone to absorb having spent so much intimate time with my love before joining my parents for dinner. Later, I would wrap my mother's presents and telephone Nan to arrange to pick her up for our tiny lunch celebration the following day. My mother didn't like parties or surprises.

I'd been swimming for about fifteen minutes when my father came down to the pool. He was upset about my being late and delaying dinner. As I answered his accusations of selfishness, I felt at one remove. He could feel this and it infuriated him. I seemed impermeable. I was, in a way. He sensed, without knowing it, that my heart and attention were still with Stephen.

For once, I answered his accusations coolly and minimally. My logic—my best defense—was the thing that infuriated him most. He voice grew louder and then he unexpectedly placed his hands firmly on my arms. Still wet, I involuntarily stepped back, banged into the brick wall beside the pool, and landed on the ground.

I knew I had not hurt myself badly but something went cold in me. For the first time, I had no wish to make up or apologize. I sat there, ungainly, a few seconds longer than the physical hurt warranted. I noticed that I wanted to frighten him, which surprised me. I also wanted to wait, somehow, until I felt like getting up. Both feelings were new and surprised me.

I walked upstairs without speaking, dried and dressed myself, hugged and reassured my mother who had seen what had happened and was panicked and terrified, picked up my handbag, assured her that her birthday celebration would happen as planned the next day, went down to the old car my father had helped me buy, and drove away.

I'd be leaving in a few weeks anyhow. I had been accepted into a short course overseas and afterwards planned to travel on a shoestring with friends. It had never occurred to me to simply walk away without a plan—until then.

I drove to a friend's house. She made me tea and played me LPs of Monty Python, putting on one scratchy recording after another. She sat beside her record player, laughing and tossing her straight black hair with its few strands of grey. I laughed when she laughed, but I didn't find them funny. She was the first person I ever told about the incident with my father—and the last.

After a few hours, I went home. I could think of nowhere else to go that would not involve telling my hosts the facts. I was frightened by my lack of desire to resolve anything. I soon I would be gone anyway. My mother came into my room, put her arms around me, tried to comfort me. My body stiffened—for the first time—against her embrace. I would not let her make it all better.

The next day, I picked up Nan and she, my father, and I celebrated my mother's birthday with champagne as though nothing had happened.

A month later, my parents waved me off. My father wrote in his letters to me, in his beautiful penmanship, for which I so longed whenever we received mail at port, that he could hardly bear to pick up and throw away the sewing threads I had left everywhere on the beige carpet from my last-minute sewing frenzy.

THIRTY-FIVE

LAVENDER

My mother disliked lavender. She said it was an old person's fragrance. It depressed her the way closed curtains and late afternoons depressed her. All these, she said, reminded her of Victorian women. When her mother came for afternoon tea, Nan would walk around our hilltop house and close all the curtains. She felt exposed to the world, she said. Nan had firm views on everything, with most of which my mother agreed. Except for the curtains. My mother would walk around a polite half-hour later and open all the curtains, letting the subtropical light flow across the carpets and up and down the traditional furniture. I liked to follow it. Sometimes it set fire to the heavy glass ashtray my mother had brought back from Venice and that sat on a side table in the living room; at others, it would slide along the piano keys. Sometimes, it bounced off keys on my mother's typewriter in the main bedroom.

Lavender and closed velvet curtains on a hot day also reminded my mother of her Scots mother-in-law, who also had firm views on everything. I think the only things my grandmothers agreed on were their belief that their daughter or son could have married better, their love of me, and closing curtains. Gran never changed her mind or was indecisive. She had firm opinions on the right religion, Presbyterianism; on the risks of putting men on the moon; on how to cook pikelets, sponge cakes, roasts, and fruit cakes; on how many sixpences went into a plum pudding; on whom her children should have married; on how often grandchildren should visit; on not wearing makeup to church; on wearing corsets; on which gloves went with which hats and with which formal suits; on a fine education; and on which household duties were done on which days.

Nan's humor was dry and Australian. Gran was bossy but she loved a good laugh if the humor was Scots-derived. My mother and I had the same sense of humor, which differed from Gran's. It was an effort to look as though I was having fun with Gran but most of the time I pulled it off.

My mother had firm views on everything, too, but her everything did not intersect with her mother-in-law's. She had firm opinions on how often she should call Nan during the day; on whether the reviews or articles she wrote for the papers were good or just workmanly; on how often to practice the piano; on which songs should be at the top of the "Hit Parade"; on how essential it was to avoid chatty people; on the torture of church pews; on how unremarkable Isadora Duncan's work was when you boiled it down; on how electrifying Vaslav Nijinsky was; and on which side of town she wanted to live.

According to her, she had been—and still was—indecisive about almost everything else. She would even ask me to check her bread and butter letters—although she had been the one who had taught me how to write a good one, making sure to include something particular about the gift or recipient. She simply asked me to check hers because she needed another eye to reassure her she'd not forgotten anything or given inadvertent offense.

When Gran asked me one day, "What is your favorite color?" it was quite an original question for her. In fact, her asking me anything other than "How is school?" was unusual.

"Lavender," I answered, slightly embarrassed by the blunt intimacy of her question. Color was important to me. I was fussy and fickle about it. At eight, "lavender" was the word and the color of the week, not even of the month. For years thereafter, Gran gave me not mauve but lavender gifts: lavender-colored shorty pajamas in frothy but modest design (Nan gave me risqué ones in ice blue, my only steady favorite color); doll's clothes in lavender and white check (I wasn't keen on dolls except for porcelain Celeste with her real hair and whom Nan had given me); and hand cream with a lavender label (it didn't match the lining in my dressing table drawers, so I put away in the bottom drawer until it went hard). I loathed lavender by then, of course, and I had never really liked lavender anyway. Still, I dutifully kissed Gran on her fair, wrinkled cheek, long ruined by the coarse sun, and unfailingly wrote her and butter letters that mentioned something specific, all the while silently railing against her assumption that she knew anything about me.

I had inhaled my mother's inability to really like Gran. It stemmed apparently from an early incident during which my mother's future mother-in-law expressed a firm opinion about Russians. "They're plain people," Gran had apparently said one day as she served the engaged couple, later to be my parents, a light, warm sponge cake. My mother—half-Russian and far from plain, to judge from photographs of her youthful, beautiful self draped in expensive clothes or from Nan's stories of principals from the touring Russian ballet languishing in her daughter's wake and later of unhappy ship's officers—was offended.

"Was she implying I was plain?" my mother asked indignantly and rhetorically when she told me this story. "Or that my father was? He was a handsome man—beautiful blue eyes, fair curly hair. I would never say 'Scottish people are boring' to her, no matter how much I might think so. Between us, I *do* rather think many are—not your father of course. At least, a lot I've met to date appear to be." Then she added as we washed dishes in the twin stainless steel sinks of our new house, "At best, she was tactless."

Shortly before Gran died in her nineties, I flew up to visit her in the nursing home. She was no longer the large, corseted authority figure of my childhood. Her weathered, northern hemisphere skin had dried out in Australia and was stretched over her small, bent skeleton. Her hair was thin, curled within an inch of its life, and blue from the rinse she had had applied by the visiting hairdresser. Her teeth were in and a nurse had added a little lipstick to her mouth and powder to her nose, powder now too pale for her once white skin. I knew she hadn't chosen the lipstick; it was bright. She was sitting straight in her fake leather armchair beside louvered windows in her spacious room. It opened onto the slightly under-watered lawn. There hadn't been much rain this season. Around the lawn's concrete edge, a nurse's aide in pink was pushing a wheelchair.

Gran had told her nurse to prepare her for her granddaughter's visit. The nurses—mostly Scots—didn't seem put off by her brusque orders. They would tell me they often "had a good chat and a laugh with your grandmother. She's a lovely "per-r-r-son," they would say with their strong accents. "Such a good outlook.

It's good talking to someone from Home. ..."

As I entered the room, the nurse on duty waved to my grandmother, promising to return with a cup of afternoon tea as soon as she had changed the bed for another resident. Gran looked up at me with her faded blue eyes. I bent down and kissed her cheek. She stabbed a weak, wet-at-the-corners kiss on the side of my mouth. Her speech was slightly slurred, perhaps from a tiny stroke. The medications she was on made her daffy occasionally. She slipped in and out of the present without notification.

I sat on the edge of the bed and took her hand.

"Hello, Gran."

"Where's your father?"

"Outside. He wanted to give us time together."

"How was the trip?"

"Delayed but I'm here. That's all that's important."

"They shouldn't allow it. You should tell them."

"Gran, you've traveled a lot. You know things happen." I decided to change the tone; we were already slightly at odds. "I still have every postcard you sent me from port when I was little."

"When I asked you what you wanted, you said postcards. So I sent them. Every port. Every capital. You didn't seem interested. Now here you are, living down—"

"I wrote you back, Gran! I remember Mamma bought me cards to send you in Edinburgh when you were with Ailsa. I couldn't answer your postcards from Europe because you were always on the move. I still have all your postcards somewhere."

"You're thin. How's your mother?"

"She's alright. She had to wait for the house painter but sends her love."

"It's not the painter. It's her back. I know."

"It does continue to give her trouble."

"She got it when you came along. I never had any trouble."

"That's good," I said. A change of topic was in order. This could lead into territory whose emotional ownership was still under dispute. "That nurse, Elspeth, seems pleasant. She likes you. She said you and she and the other nurses have good talks and that you keep them laughing."

I made sure to speak distinctly and slowly. She was deafer than ever.

I heard my father talking with the nurses at the nurses' station. He always talked to the nurses, whom he described to my mother as "nice young things," and he often brought them sweet biscuits or chocolates. They thought he was wonderful because he came to see his mother every other day, usually to feed her lunch. My father's comments about the nurses gave my mother the wrong impression about the nurses for a long time. There was, in fact, only one "nice young thing" and she didn't last long on the unit because she was promoted to Activities Director. The rest of the nurses were middle-aged, plump, mostly attentive, and kind.

My grandmother lifted her eyes with difficulty as my father entered the room, crossed the tiled floor and bent down to kiss her. His thick, pepper-and-salt hair blew out of place as he walked in front of the fan fixed to the brick wall. It was a beastly hot day and few in our town had yet installed air-conditioning.

"Hello, Michael. Say 'how d'you do' to Dr. McGregor."

"Mother, he was your doctor when you were a girl in Edinburgh," my father said with kind, exasperated resignation.

"Say 'Good morning, Dr. McGregor.'"

Seeing that it was beyond my father to address Dr. McGregor's presence where it hovered on the wall alongside the fan, I looked in that direction, smiled, and said, "How do you do, Dr. McGregor? My grandmother has spoken so much about you." There, I had embroidered on her fantasy and felt more thoughtful than my father for a change.

My grandmother smiled when I said it. It seemed to satisfy her. She turned to my father. "Where's your tie? Your father never let himself go, even at the end. The first time I met him, he was neat as a pin in his Flying Corps uniform. On leave but still neat as a pin. He was neat as a pin to the day he died. Of course, I always starched his shirts and his pajamas. Pity women don't use starch now."

"It's unusually hot today, Mother. That's why I didn't wear a tie." My father looked worried, as though he needed to carry her across a stream and didn't know how to get her on his back. He kissed her cheek, patted her hand, and quietly started to put away the clean washing he'd brought from home. Sometimes he did Gran's washing and sometimes my mother did. More often, he did it because my mother's back was bad.

My grandmother's pale eyes narrowed. She looked at my father. "Say good morning to Dr. McGregor. He takes care of me."

"He was a good doctor, I'm sure. He's been gone a long time," my father said with a hint of weary, gentle protestation.

"Be polite to him. You wouldn't be here if it weren't for—"

"—Mother, I do remember your telling me about him, you know. He was your doctor when I was born and his son fought near Dad." My father was beginning to take her confusion personally. This was not going well.

"Dad, he's here as far as Gran's concerned," I said *sotto voce*, knowing my grandmother's inefficient hearing aid would not catch my tone. "Who cares? Just go along."

"Don't tell me what to say, Meg. You're not here enough to know. I need to keep her in touch—for her sake. Dad asked me to take care of her. I have and shall."

"She thinks wearing a tie on a day in the hundreds is for *your* sake."

"Don't be flippant, Meg. You have a sharp tongue."

"Wonder where I got that?"

"That's enough," he snapped quietly. I hadn't even been there a day and we were slightly at odds.

"Go to the second drawer," my grandmother slurred rapidly at me.

"Yes, Gran."

"Something for you."

"Gran, you shouldn't be worrying about me." I walked out of the stream of the fan and opened the second drawer of the small, fake wooden chest of drawers beside the sink.

"You don't come up enough," she said as my back was to her.

"I know, Gran. I'm sorry. I only have a certain amount of time off."

"I don't know why you keep her away, Michael," my grandmother said. Then, before my father could protest, she added, "On the left."

In the drawer were a spare set of false teeth that didn't fit; a small, black, suede-covered Bible, eighty years old, with thin gilt pages well thumbed; a dark blue hymnal carefully thumbed; a small address book; two ballpoint pens; postcards from Scottish relatives; and letter from friends made on trips through Europe in her seventies ("I count everything before I get on the bus and before I get off. I've never lost a thing ..."); and a thick handkerchief sachet.

"Take the sachet. You need it on all that traipsing you do," my grandmother said reprovingly.

"Gran, it's yours," I said, neither wanting it nor wanting to offend. "You should use it."

"Never go anywhere any more except with your father to look at the bay sometimes. There's a Christmas gift from Ailsa in it."

"I'll take it out."

"Keep it. Lavender makes handkerchiefs smell good. Put it in your suitcase." The nurse appeared at the door with tea in a heavy white cup and saucer with a plain, sweet biscuit accompanying it. My grandmother took a sip and said, "It's cold. You can't be from the Old Country!" She looked back at me as the nurse laughed and went away to ask the kitchen if they could make the tea hotter please. My father followed the nurse with apologies and offered to bring the hotter tea back himself.

I took the sachet. It had a slight smear of ballpoint ink on the corner. I took it over to my grandmother and put it in her now small lap.

"Here, Gran. You can give it to me officially."

"Don't be daft. I've just given it to you."

I opened up the handkerchief sachet with embroidery of heather on the flap. Inside was another sachet of fine muslin. Firm and gritty in texture, the lavender seeds inside it emanated perfume into the humid heat. I kissed her on the cheek and put it with exaggerated care into my leather handbag.

"There'll be something more for you one day if you're not in Timbuktu," she added.

My father returned from his odious mission. He loathed asking for special treatment but a hot cup of tea was a hot cup of tea and he had already given offense to Gran by failing to wear a tie in the middle of summer. He looked at me and made a slight apologetic motion, indicating his watch. He had a committee meeting followed by a university dinner. Despite his plans, as soon as I had arrived and changed from my traveling clothes, he had wanted to take me for a short visit with Gran because, as he always said, "You never know."

"We have to go now, Gran. I'll come again tomorrow. The sachet is lovely. Thank you very much for it."

"Don't lose it. Agnes gave me the sachet and Ailsa sent the lavender for Christmas. You've always liked lavender. You don't write to your cousins. You should. They might be in Scotland but you never know. Say goodbye to Dr. McGregor."

She stopped talking a few days after that. The last time I went to see her alone, I took a taxi. I sat beside her bed looking at her transparent, mauve skin and eyelids. Bruises spread across her arms and inert hands. Her mouth hung half open.

I said hello and kissed her on her dry forehead. I was in charge of the kisses now and I wasn't going to kiss her on the mouth. She didn't respond. I said hello to Dr. McGregor. I told her that he was taking good care of her and that I was taking good care of the handkerchief sachet and lavender. She didn't respond.

Finally, I decided to recite the Twenty-Third Psalm—her favorite—and to sing her some of her favorite hymns. I was surprised how easily the words returned to me after so many years.

Later, I took a taxi back to my parents' place.

"How was Gran?" my mother asked.

"Not talking."

"That must have been difficult."

"Not really. I didn't have to carry both sides of the conversation any more." I didn't tell her I had sung to my grandmother.

She might think I was switching sides.

My mother smiled sympathetically.

Later that month, I flew to London to finish up a project. Then Andrew joined me for ten days. We returned to Provence. Lavender curved in rows over the hills, scented cakes of soap at the village market, and even colored the soft grey, early morning mist. I chose a few postcards with highly colored lavender fields on the front and wrote my grandmother simple messages. I posted one card a day. My father told me later that, although the cards arrived in a clump, he read them one at a time to her to fill the time he sat with her.

She died at the end of that week. My father called our hotel just as we were leaving Aix-en-Provence to return to London. I ordered flowers through an international floral service. Everyone was at the funeral except for me—and my mother, of course, who excused herself because of her decades-old declaration that pews made her back much worse. The small service was, of course, Presbyterian.

When we arrived home again, my father posted me the spare order of service and a sealed brown envelope that just said "Meg" in my grandmother's rounded, flowing script. In it were flat, brown sprigs that had stained the tissue in which they were wrapped and a wad of ancient postcards from unspecified places in France. The earliest were signed, "Yours Faithfully, Duncan McGregor." The last, a black-and-white card captioned "Eglise Historique, Somme" and dated June, 1916, read, "Dear Isobel, We hope to see some fun soon. I am in good health and spirits. No word from you. I continue to hope you will make a favorable decision. Until then, I remain always, Your Faithful DM."

THIRTY-SIX

....

DRIVING INTO TOWN

On the way into town we passed St. Bernadette's on the hill. Its forbidding, red brick siding spiked into the intense tropical sky. Being Presbyterian, we would never have stopped to look inside. My father shifted gears as we climbed the hill.

My father drove me everywhere when I was home. I offered to get taxis but he protested. I refrained from replying that sometimes arriving in one's late twenties at friends' houses with one's father felt a little awkward. He was always careful about heading off immediately despite entreaties from my friends who genuinely wanted to see him. Everybody loved my father. Years later, by the time I cherished the experience of being driven by my father again, Andrew and Olivia and I—or I, flying up to see my parents alone—could easily afford to hire a car.

We passed the gracious, sandstone building that housed an extension of the university. For the umpteenth time, my father said, "Your mother's father owned that whole block of land over there."

"Yes," I commented, trying to hit a tone between knowing, which would make his comment seem irrelevant, and not knowing, which would make me seem oddly ignorant. He was really talking to himself.

We reached the top of Curtin Hill. My father continued this old family story but this time in an idle tone that put me on high alert because it usually meant he was working up to talking about something difficult.

"He was a good man, your Russian grandfather. Tough but fair. Didn't mince words. He wasn't going to take me on faith as his daughter's suitor. Over the years we came to respect each other. He helped me paint the first lab."

"I wish he hadn't died early. I barely remember him."

"He loved you. He used to love having you down the coast at 'Samarkand'—the beach cottage."

Sometimes I thought my father believed I had erased my own history. I knew what 'Samarkand' was.

"And you, little devil, you used to take the hose and spray everyone in the front yard of the cottage."

"I'm surprised I could see to aim."

"Your sight came from your maternal side. You never gave us any reason to think you couldn't see well. Not until second grade anyway. When we found out, we took care of it right away."

"I didn't mean it like that."

"I never spared expense on your health. Your teeth, your eyes...." He waited for the light to turn.

"Your grandparents adored you. Your grandfathers thought you could do no wrong. They were good men."

"I'm glad I knew them both."

"I never spared expense on your mother's health either."

I began to ease off high alert and settle in to my seat. This was a clutch of family stories I knew intimately, including how and when to comment. I could tell the stories myself with the same intonation, adjectives, and trajectory. I liked most of them.

Soon I would hear how he sent my mother and me to the top nursing facility where women whose husbands could afford it stayed for two weeks to recover from childbirth. It was a story I disliked because it included his longing to hold me but having to wait until my mother and I finally came home.

He always sounded wistful when he talked about those weeks and I would always hurt inside. He didn't get to do it again with another child. I somehow felt responsible for his wistfulness. However, by this stage, I had also realized that, instead of listening to him shift deeper into wistfulness—into what I called his *ubi sunt* mood—I could divert our conversational direction with memories of special things he and I had done, which was happier for both of us.

I watched the ice skating rink pass my window and the view of the hills unfold. I waited for the nursing home story.

"She never was strong. I didn't realize that she had an artist's temperament for years. She should have been living in Europe or down south where she would have had more liked-minded people around her."

This was a minor variation on the theme, I noted peripherally. Usually this reflection belonged with the collection of his reflections about the reasons my mother didn't go to church or about his late understanding of why giving dinner parties was a trial for her—she was really a writer and pianist, not a housewife.

"But she wanted to be the best mother she could be—and she was. She was always there when you got home from school. She was a natural teacher."

"She was an excellent teacher," I responded as usual and truthfully.

"Your mother and I have had our differences over the years. All couples do. But she was a wonderful mother to you. I hope you appreciate her."

"I always thought she was the best mother in the world."

"I wanted you and her to have the best I could give you—of everything."

"You did, Dad: the best school, the ski trips, the orthodontist, the contact lenses ...."

"I saw less of you because of the long hours at the lab but that's what fathers are for."

"I always knew that's why you weren't home as much as you would have liked."

"I wanted her to have the best. Like the convalescent home."

Here it was: the convalescent home story. I liked the part about the whiskey he'd shared with his father when the hospital had phoned to say I was born. I braced myself for the part about how he would have been at the birth, had they allowed husbands those days, and for the part about how he'd longed to hold me after I was born.

"She wasn't strong. I gave her the best."

This was another slight departure in the narrative. But I knew he was headed somewhere in my direction, some place where I needed to be more sensitive, more thoughtful. Like the day he told me the jury was still out on whether I would receive any inheritance because he hadn't finished taking his measure of me yet. That was also in the car, opposite the new shopping center.

My mother once told my father that he and I should talk about things only in the car because it was where we had our best talks. Translation: when he had to concentrate on driving, neither my father nor I could respond with as much intensity if the conversation did not move as we wished.

"She had the best the medicos could offer." This heralded the beginning of the story about my mother's pregnancy. She had the best obstetrician around—which my father could ill afford having only been able to start tertiary studies after the war—but upon which he had insisted. My mother had confided to me that she had disliked the specialist.

"He was a cold fish," she'd once told me, as we made the beds and listened to Chopin. "But Daddy was so pleased he could send me to him and he certainly had the best reputation. We didn't risk having a child during the war. Daddy worried he might be killed and I'd be left to raise it. After the war, he wanted to start a family right away and also had to do his degree while he was working. He'd lost the war years was how he put it. I just wanted to spend time together as a couple before we had children. We'd never really lived together. We'd had times, of course, when he was on leave but, for most of war, I was living with Nan and Grandpapa. Between the war and getting settled after—that's why it was a few years before you came along. When you did happen, you were planned. We wanted you.

"Daddy was so excited. He wanted me to have the best. He thought the obstetrician could do no wrong. So I didn't say anything about not liking the fellow."

I would always answer, "I can understand your wanting to wait," and then I would tell her, "You were good to continue to see the doctor even when you didn't like him."

"I didn't want to hurt Daddy's feelings," my mother would reply. "The doctor had the best reputation, too. I was afraid if I chose someone else, I'd choose the wrong one and it would be my fault if something went wrong."

My father and I passed St. Matthew's, the central Presbyterian church.

"Your mother and I were married there."

"It's a pretty church, isn't it," I said, both to avoid pointing out that I knew this perfectly well or giving the impression that I knew nothing about their history.

On the opposite side of the square from the church where they were married was the Catholic cathedral into which my first love and I had slipped often to pray. Unlike the Presbyterian church, which was closed all week and only open during Sunday services, the cathedral was open all day. People could kneel in front of a weeping Mary, her hands over her bleeding heart, which was broken in two by a jagged depression and line of black paint on the red porcelain of her heart.

While my father drove, I remembered holding Stephen's hand as we sat in front of the statue, each praying for the same thing.

"She understands how we love each other," Stephen had said.

"I like talking to her," I had replied, "but I don't know her very well. She's yours, not mine. Do you think she thinks we're too young to decide?"

"Nope," he'd whispered breezily, tenderly, confidently. "She thinks twenty and twenty-one are just the right age."

"Then ask her to put a word in our parents' ear."

"Do you think I haven't daily?" Stephen retorted back in a whisper. I'd leave by the side entrance so no one would see my leaving a Catholic church; Stephen would leave by the front. Later, we'd meet up at the university library.

"We were young," my father continued as he waited at the stoplight. "Twenty-one and twenty-two. But it was wartime and I had leave, so we got married. We'd been engaged for a year. That's what couples did: get married when the husband could get leave. Your mother was special. She was gifted, different. Looking back, I was innocent. Very innocent. I thought all women were like *my* mother."

I knew where my father and I were headed again: into the stories of the honeymoon cut short, the brief times of respite when my father on leave, my mother's moving back in with her parents while he was fighting overseas. I knew the rhythm of his recall and could safely attend with half my attention and think about Stephen with the other half.

"So when the doctor said she needed care, I told him to do whatever was best for her."

"It was a pity you had to wait so long to really have me home properly as a baby," I said to make sure he knew I was listening.

My father braked at the next stoplight in his customary, crisp manner.

"You have a habit, Meg, of interrupting. I'd be surprised if Andrew weren't bothered by that. It's not becoming. You jump in. You might not mean it but you come across as impatient and dismissive."

"I didn't mean to. I'm sorry, Dad. I was just trying to let you know I was listening and that I do remember things you've told me. They're important to you so they're important to me."

"It doesn't come over like that."

The light near the main post office turned red. We waited.

"If you'd listen for a change," he said, "you might learn something—that is, if you want to know."

I'd slipped. It was not that my comment was wrong. It was that my timing was off. It was also as if my father sensed—in that way he had of knowing when my family allegiances temporarily slipped—that I had been thinking about Stephen.

"I do want to know, Dad. You were talking about getting Mamma the best care and—"

"So when the doctor said she needed care, I did what he said. He was the authority after all. I'd been gone for five years on and off at war and finally, we were starting real married life. We moved out of her parents' into a little flat. But she couldn't make decisions: whether she wanted children ... where we might settle eventually ... even what to cook for dinner. She was frightened of making a mistake. It happened just after we moved into the flat.

"He was the best specialist—the *only* one those days. He said a hospital stay at a special hospital down south would help so I told him, '*Do whatever she needs.*' After she was there a few days, he rang up and asked me to approve more treatment. I had to say 'yes' or 'no.' It was terrible, really. Husbands were the ones who had to make the decision."

He started to negotiate the underground parking lot. A weekday, it was full on the top floors. We cruised the floors slowly, descending anticlockwise. It was the only large parking garage in the town then.

"I asked the doctor if it would affect her writing or playing the piano. He said he doubted it—just recent memory. I could never have forgiven myself if she hadn't been able to write or play again. That would have been the worst. Thank heavens, that didn't happen."

This was not part of the narrative. I had no prepared responses.

Had my mother asked him to tell me? They would have agreed beforehand on what he would say. They did not believe in having secrets from each other (even though they had a lot of them). Certainly, they kept no secrets from each other about me when I was growing up. I now realized that the times my father had said, with intensity, that "someone had seen" me going into the cathedral with Stephen, the "someone" was my mother, in whom I had confided and who had sworn to me that she would not tell my father. So when my father told me about her treatment, I knew that either my mother would have asked him to tell me or that he would tell her he had. He also would tell her exactly what I would say.

"That must have been a dreadful time for you—each—and an awful decision for you," I offered in the warmest, most neutral tone I could manage. I began to feel carsick in the close air of the underground parking lot as we spiraled down to Floor 6.

"It was a terrible thing to have to decide. Husbands had to sign then."

"Could she ... was she better ... after?"

"She'd didn't remember much about it but she was writing and playing again soon. We eventually moved into a rented cottage. Later, she decided she was ready to start a family. So along you came."

He pulled into a parking spot on Floor 6, turned off the engine, and said, "Your mother knows I'm telling you this. There's no need for you to go over it with her at length. I'd suggest you just say I told you, give her a big hug, and leave it at that." Once again, my role had been scripted. There would be no deviation.

We got out of the car. The escalator was broken. We walked up the twelve flights of concrete stairs into the blinding summer light a block away from the Catholic cathedral. My father was off to the dentist for an emergency appointment for a crown that had fallen off. He was leaving me in town first to shop and then later to meet Livi and one of her daughters for tea. We parted—he, to walk down to the arcade above which the dentist had his office and I, to go to Robertson's, which still had the best clothes in town.

However, once I had watched my father turn neatly and briskly into the arcade, I decided that I would go first to the cathedral. I wanted to see if the weeping Mary with the broken heart was still there.

THIRTY-SEVEN

FAT BRIDES

Fat bride photographs were among my mother's favorites in her collection of scrapbooks. She started collecting fat brides late in her life. She was particularly pleased with newspaper photographs of brides bursting out of strapless dresses. Her aesthetic sensibility, well trained by my sartorially exacting grandmother, was so surprised at the pride with which these women wore their ample flesh that her judgment was momentarily suspended and replaced by amazed, frozen observation. She would show me the latest additions to the scrapbook when I visited her.

"Look at this one!" she exclaimed one day, handing over the scrapbook for a moment before taking it back, bored with waiting for me to be done looking at the first page. "Wouldn't you think she'd want to hide those hips? Those big arms. I wonder what that little man will do with all that flesh." She paused for a moment, and then continued. "How old fashioned of me. This is not the forties. They probably have two children who were their flower girls. Can you imagine taking her to bed?"

It was important that I not try to hold the pages or move

through them at my own pace. Doing so took all the pleasure out of it for her. She wanted to scroll through them in her own time with me as witness. She would review the early pages and then continue on to the new.

The Fat Brides scrapbook had replaced the Big Toothed Smiles at Cocktail Parties scrapbook in my mother's affection. The cocktail partygoers clearly had been told by the newspaper photographer to open their mouths wide, separate their teeth, and look surprised.

"All the men stand behind the women and have their arms wrapped around and folded over the women's chests. Often, the men are almost touching their breasts," she said.

Open-mouth photographs, still appearing on the paper's society page, were so frequent now that my mother had lost interest in collecting them.

The Big-Toothed Smiles scrapbook and the Fat Brides scrapbook were filed beside a spiral notebook titled Unusual Surnames. The sole criterion for entry was that the name in question had to have a meaning. Each name was written in my mother's neat, flat, round script and put into a category such as Fruits, Places, Professions, Colors. There was also a section for people whose names either fitted or were particularly unfit for their professions: Sharp, a surgeon; Woodman, a carpenter; Lively, an undertaker. A perfect aesthetic—and its antithesis—were equally compelling for my mother.

She turned to a full-page, color spread of a popular singer spilling out of her gown. "Strictly speaking, I shouldn't have this one in here. I didn't find it myself. Daddy saw a woman reading the magazine at the supermarket checkout and bought me a copy. I try to only count them if I find them myself but I didn't want to hurt his feelings—and it was such a good picture. The groom's huge, too." She lingered a moment, flattened a corner, and turned the page. "When will your book be out?"

"November."

"This woman's name is Little. So it belongs in two categories: I can put it in the Unusual Names collection as well as in here with the fat brides. Look how big she is. Do you think I should put it in with the names or the photos? I have a category for adjectives...."

"Whatever, Mamma." I was hungry.

"I *do* dislike that word. People use it all the time now. I don't know where it originated. You didn't have to say it like that. You could have said it nicely. You know I don't mind what you say as long as—"

"—I say it nicely."

"Exactly."

"I'm sorry," I said evenly. "I just meant that whatever you eventually decide will probably work out well." I got up to get myself some cheese from the kitchen. The food on the plane north had been awful and I was hungry.

"Please use the open Camembert on the left, not the one on the right. I'd like to know what I just did wrong. I was trying hard to do everything right so we wouldn't have a row this visit and now I seem to be in the poo. Again."

"You are *not* in the poo."

"Yes, I am. You're cross."

"I am *not* cross. I'm hungry and I need a bit of cheese before we continue. That's all." I walked back with the cheese on a plate.

"My legs are aching. I need to lie down anyway. You do whatever you want to, except please don't look through the scrapbook, especially with cheese on your fingers. You're not genuinely interested in it anyway. I can tell. Play the piano if you like. You won't disturb me. I just need to lie down for a while."

My mother went off to her bedroom.

She emerged an hour later. "I'm sorry if I upset you before," she said, as she padded out in bare feet with prettily brushed hair and a fresh dress on. I could tell she was starting from scratch with me. "I didn't mean to upset you."

"You didn't upset me, darling. I was hungry. You know what I'm like when I'm hungry."

"You *sounded* cross. You were *moving* as though you were cross."

"I wasn't cross with you, I promise. I'm very sorry if I upset you. Could we finish up the scrapbook—which I do thoroughly enjoy, by the way—and then I'll pour you a Scotch and we can watch the news."

"We might even have time for the shoebox before the news. Could you please get it from my desk? It says "Cuttings to show Meg" on the side. I still have to sort them. I haven't had the energy. I've been saving them for your visit." We laid out the red corduroy tablecloth and sat down at the dining table side by side. My mother put her feet on a footstool while I straddled the table's uncomfortable legs. She carefully took out each clipping.

"Another bride. Lovely dress, but lost in the lard. Gran was upset that I was married in civilian clothes. She was concerned people would think her son had to marry me. You know. I found out later that she was married in civilian clothes *too* because she got married in the war, too! World War I, of course, not II. It was thought more appropriate, somehow, during the war, to get married in civilian clothes." She set the fat family aside and picked up a neatly clipped advertisement. "Petrol. His last name is Petrol and he works at a car repair shop. Why don't you get the Unusual Surnames notebook and we can put it in right now. Then that will be done and I can throw away the advertisement."

I went over to the shelves in her workroom, took out the notebook, and brought it to the dining table, flipping through as I went. "Peacock. That's a great name. Where does Mrs. Peacock work, I wonder.... Gran was silly to say that to you. You looked lovely in your wedding suit."

"You're in the wrong list. I asked you not to get ahead of where we were. You're in the Bird section, not in the Professional section. It was a lovely suit."

"Did Nan make it?"

"No. 'Peacock, Peahen, Pigeon, Plover.' I've alphabetized them."

"I see."

"You can't possibly see from that angle."

"It was a figure of speech."

"I included 'Plume,' even though it isn't a bird. I couldn't decide on a more appropriate category and didn't want to start a new one. I do have a category for Body Parts but I've only included human. Perhaps I should extend the category."

"What did Nan wear—for her wedding? I've never seen a wedding portrait of Grandpapa and her."

"I believe they had a private ceremony," my mother responded evenly, with a hint of formality.

"No photo?"

"I never saw one—even when I was clearing out the house."

"She was such a one for photographs," I said. "She kept the marriage certificate at least, I expect. She always kept everything."

"It's in the bank. Look. Mr. and Mrs. Arm. The Legs and their children. Of course, if one wanted to include other languages, one could go crazy. It's a pity Grandpapa never taught me Russian. However, in those days you were only supposed to speak English to be a good Australian."

"Why the bank? Yours is in Dad's files."

"Why this sudden interest in Nan's birth—wedding?"

"I loved Nan. I'm interested."

"More interested in that than in the Fat Brides, apparently. I'm sorry. This must be boring." She lined up the left and bottom sides of the cuttings we had not yet gone through. "Look, there *are* things I'd tell you but you'll ... tell Andrew—or Olivia or someone."

"I won't," I lied.

"I'm not sure at all about that."

"I promise."

"When Nan and Grandpapa were married ... I was ... I was already around. Nan kept it a secret all her life. Grandpapa came up here first. Nan came later with me. They got married up here. Privately. I always wondered if he married her because she had a pretty photograph taken of her and me and sent it. It just says, "For Alex" on it. No one knew them here. Nan's sisters down south must have known about me. She kept it secret all her life. Perhaps that's why her hair got thin and she wore a wig. Stress."

"No one cares any more," I said.

"Nan cared. She never told me until she was in her nineties. When I was growing up, I found their marriage certificate—and my birth certificate—in the window seat. When the places and dates didn't add up, I wondered if Mother had ... if Daddy wasn't.... I was sure I had to have been adopted. It's odd: I'd always secretly wondered if I was adopted even *before* I found the certificates.

"When Nan was in the last nursing home—that one your teacher, Miss Woodford, was in but you found out too late—anyway, back to the topic: I said one day, 'Mother, you *have* to tell me. Was I adopted?' I begged her. I told her I didn't mind if I was.

"She said I wasn't but that she'd never said anything to me or anyone because she'd always been afraid I wouldn't love her if she'd told me I arrived before they were married. She cried. She said Aunt Marion took care of me until Nan and I joined Grandpapa up here. Nan cried so rarely that I didn't ask her anything else—I felt cruel but I had to know. I told her I'd always loved her, that it didn't change anything. I think she heard. She was so deaf at the end. She stopped crying. I think she heard.

"It was a pity really: all that time she thought I wouldn't love her if I knew and all that time I spent wondering. Of course, in her day.... In *my* day! Even in *your* day! All those years I was worried I was adopted and could be sent back if I did anything.... I needed to ask, finally, although I did feel terrible about upsetting her. We never talked about it again. The next year she passed away. Otherwise, I'd never have known."

She shifted position in the chair to ease her back. I put a cushion low down between her and the back of the chair. The grandfather clock struck the half hour. "Now don't tell Andrew or Olivia—or anyone.... Here's a Dr. Foot. He was a podiatrist in London in the thirties. I found that one in an old dance magazine. And here's a whole wedding party—all seriously overweight, including all the tubby bridesmaids and the round little flower girls."

I put the cuttings aside and took a bite of the Camembert. I suddenly felt tired. The long day must be catching up, I thought.

I'd lectured in the morning and then caught the afternoon plane.

"You're not looking properly at the cuttings. You keep picking them up and setting them aside instead of letting me tell you about each before I show it to you. It takes the fun out of sharing them."

I handed her back the ones I'd mistakenly picked up before she'd introduced them but she set them aside; they had been bleached of import.

"I wish I hadn't told you—about Nan. I felt backed into a corner. I know you. You'd worry at the topic like a dog with a bone. I didn't have the strength to resist after our earlier row. Now you'll tell Andrew and Olivia as soon as you fly home."

"Mamma, I won't. I'm sorry you and Nan couldn't talk about it all those years. You were a love child."

"That's somewhat melodramatic. Although they did love each other from what I remember and letters I found when I was doing out the house.

"I feel guilty for telling. Furthermore, your time here is … the copybook of our time together has an inkblot now. Two, in fact. I wanted to do something simple: just show you the brides and names. I've added a lot since you were up last. I've given up on the smiles scrapbook. I told you that on the phone."

We got to the end of the shoebox.

"It's all over," she said with a sigh.

"What?"

"The cuttings. Plus we had a row. Plus I feel guilty about Nan. It was her secret all her life." She moved, uncomfortable from sitting so long. "I've been saving the cuttings to show you for a month. It fell flat."

"It didn't fall flat, sweetheart. I truly was interested. And Nan's story just ... happened. I promise I won't make too much of it. I'm more interested in what you want to show me. I love how you collect things."

I tried to remember if anything else needed to be undone. If she got to worrying, she would not sleep and then her carefully orchestrated heart medications would go haywire and she could end up in the hospital again. Everything had to be undone.

"I won't tell anyone. I certainly won't tell Dad or Andrew or Olivia what you told me. I don't think you were disloyal. We just had a little conversation between mother and daughter. We both loved Nan."

"The night before I got married, I said to Nan, 'Mother, you have to tell me something.' I think she'd been afraid the same thing could happen to me. Poor thing."

"Did she?"

"Did she what?"

"Tell you!"

"Not much.... Here's the one I really wanted to show you—it was stuck next to this other one: a fat bride with the big smile. Her name is Jennifer Counter and she married this short fellow named Arthur Point!"

"I suppose if she didn't know what to do on the first night, she would have—"

"—missed the point," we concluded together and laughed.

"Oh, it *is* nice to have you here when you're being pleasant." She patted my hand before taking the clipping away from me. "I need your opinion on which category I should put it in. I can't decide whether to put it in: big smiles, fat brides, or names." She seemed weighed down by the decision.

"Let's make a photocopy. You can put the original in one album, the copy in another, and enter the names in the notebook. Then we can cross-reference them."

"That's a good idea. That's my girl.... I wonder which album I should put the original in."

THIRTY-EIGHT

....

MAMMA, MAHLER, AND MANN

I'm so glad you're here—I've been wanting to show you 'Death in Venice.' I finally found the video I bought. I've just finishing rereading the book, too." My mother read Mann in the original, having taught herself to read German fluently decades ago.

"I'm glad I'm here too, darling. It's felt like a long time between drinks. I did watch the video once with you, you know—a long time ago."

"Not recently. There are things I noticed last time I watched it that I hadn't noticed before. I want to show you."

I walked around the kitchen making a cup of tea. I still was not fully used to the new kitchen in the retirement villa.

"The mugs are in the cabinet to the left, if you prefer a mug."

My mother didn't like mugs. Having grown up on endless cups of white tea with two teaspoons of sugar every other hour, she did not find a mug aesthetic. "A mug is so … dominant," she would say.

"I do prefer a cup and saucer," I said, "but I might just get one of the mugs because I can keep track of it better and it carries more fluid. I'm still a bit weary from the trip."

I waited for the kettle to boil. Then I poured the water onto the Bushell's teabag, walked to the fridge, and carefully took out the whole milk, which my father had bought for me along with other food oddities I had requested by email.

"Daddy got you the fat milk, I think," my mother said from the living room where she was sitting in one of the armchairs that had been with them ever since I was eight, updated now with plain covers replacing their old tapestry ones. I'd been home on a visit when they'd chosen the new upholstery, timed for their move to the retirement home. I'd made a good argument for plain upholstery by buying interior design magazines and tearing out illustrations of traditional furniture updated.

My mother's bare feet rested on the footstool; it, too, had accompanied them for over forty years. While she still kept two pairs of elegant high heels, purchased in New York in 1938, on the top shelf of her closet beyond her reach, her feet had flattened— first, from ballet when she was young; second, from inheriting Nan's feet; and third, from standing in heels at undesired dinners, cocktail parties, weddings, and functions for my father's multiple civic activities. Even when she played the piano, she had done so barefoot for at least fifteen years, her once-dancer's feet pressing pedals unconsciously, expertly.

When visitors came, which always delighted my father and exhausted my mother, she would put on shoes in their honor. She tried, too, like her mother before her, to get shoes made. However, Nan spent a lot of money on her shoes and was both successful in getting them made exactly to measure as well as stoic about where they hurt; my mother, neither willing to spend Nan's considerable legacy on the best handmade shoes nor a stoic, was less successful.

Whenever I would fly up for a visit, she would have me help her try on all her shoes. She never gave up hope that she could find something that would not be excruciating. We would group them: the "Doctors" group had to be relatively comfortable because she had to walk to the waiting room; the "Visitors" group did not have to be comfortable because she would just sit in them; the "Need Alteration" group required elastic lengthened, tiny spots flattened, a finish redone; the "Winter-House" group comprised a kind of sock with leather bottom; "Hospital" included slide-on slippers in white. She didn't like pink or blue for slippers. Every time I came to visit for a few days, which was every four to six weeks, we would review the shoes and move some from one category to the next, mostly downgrading, occasionally upgrading, adding notes such as "Put small buckle here" for the shoe repair man.

I took the tea in and sat beside her. My father was in his study working on the computer, catching up with speeches and investment research he couldn't do easily when I wasn't there. My mother's health needed frequent help.

She cast her blue eyes over the mug I had carefully placed on top of a pile of magazines, which obscured the woven cover protecting the small table that had belonged to her parents. Then she sighed and resolutely looked away.

"What?" I demanded. I looked at the mug. I had made it worry-proof. The mug was on a neat pile of magazines, for heaven's sake. I'd even made sure the magazines were flat, and the cover of the top one in the pile wasn't shiny.

"I haven't read those. You'll think I'm silly but if the magazines are squishy or have depressing circles on them, somehow all the life goes out of them—"

"Like Grandpapa's drawing in the new notebook he gave you when you were little and then you didn't want to use it because it was already written in?"

"A little. I still feel awful about that. I didn't look as pleased as I should have when he did that little drawing. He was just trying to be nice and the drawing was only small and just on the inside of the front cover. But somehow the notebook felt walked on—like the beach when you think you're alone in the early morning but then see big male footprints with lolloping paw prints beside them. Someone's already been there."

"So that's why you collect notebooks and hate to use them," I said. My mother looked attacked. I heard my tactlessness and decided to defend her from me. "I always loved Nan's saying she wanted to read her magazines before anyone else read the 'snotty guts' out of them!"

"Don't quote her on that even though she's dead. It was funny but it wasn't for other ears. She must have heard that phrase growing up in the country."

"Nan had wonderful phrases. Remember her saying she felt as though her atoms were all running in different directions if she didn't get her millions of cups of tea on time?"

"Darling, I'm sorry but I would appreciate it if you don't put your mug on the magazines. Could you at least put it on last week's television guide? I don't care about that."

I sighed slightly. My mother, always preternaturally sensitive about being annoying—which made her annoying—heard my sigh.

"Now you're cross. You and Daddy," she said. "I'm always getting into trouble for something. I try *so* hard. I wouldn't worry about the magazines but I have to go to real effort to get them.

Some of them Daddy has to order on his computer from London and others, I have to order by mail from Germany."

"Mamma, it's fine. I'm moving the mug and I'm not upset. Besides, I've almost finished so there's not much to spill."

"It's not just spilling. The mug perspires."

I didn't answer. I wanted to scream: I have come miles to see you and you only care about the circles on your magazines. I didn't say this; the fallout would have been worse. If I had said it, she would have had to take a pill, lie down, depressed because the visit had already gone wrong. There would be a blot on the copybook, a pawmark on the sand. I picked up the mug and held it. Why was it impossible to feel what was my real love for her in her presence?

I was still thirsty from the flight up from down south. Andrew, who usually made me early morning tea before he left, had had to go to chambers early about a case; Olivia had sped me to the airport in her little car before going off to her beloved architecture lectures; somehow, after giving my lecture and answering student questions, I'd been so harried by the time I reached the airport, I'd forgotten to grab anything to drink. The tea in the plane hadn't done the trick. This mug of tea—yet another diuretic—was no solution either and I had drunk it fast. My back was hurting in the armchair. I pulled a cushion from the sofa and put it behind my back.

"Is your back hurting? Are you feeling off color?" My mother sounded both anxious and disappointed.

"No, I'm feeling well. You know how it is when one's been on a plane. Just a bit stiff." I was aching.

"Perhaps this isn't the right time to show you the film."

"It's an excellent time. It's too hot to go out and Dad's busy."

"It's just that if we don't do it now, the time will get chewed at the edges. Right at this moment, the time's still stretching out—clean and unsullied. Soon your friends will start phoning on that new mobile phone to which you're in thrall and joined at the hip."

"Mamma, it's my only number when I'm here. I don't like to give people your number. Dad would be running to the phone all the time or having to take a message for me or call my hotel. How else are they supposed to reach me?"

"I wasn't trying to start a row."

"I'm not either. I just don't want you to think the time's all chewed up and in the rubbish before it's even happened."

"You have something tomorrow already and something the day after."

"Tomorrow I have coffee with Livi at 9:00. You said you didn't want me to come around from the hotel until 10:30. The day after, I'm seeing Miranda for morning tea when your cleaning lady's here."

"Let's not talk about it. I'm getting an upset tummy. I wasn't trying to start a row. All I wanted was to have some days that were clean—shiny and blue—with you. I've been saving all sorts of things for you. I've put the video in the player. Would you please hand me the control? Are you ready?"

"I'm ready."

She turned on the television. It blasted into the living room at a high decibel level. I put my fingers up to my ears. My father emerged into the hallway, looking startled. My mother pressed the volume button on the remote furiously. The sound lowered.

"You can take your fingers out of your ears now," she commented dryly. "You both act as though I do it deliberately."

My father returned to his office. Now the sound was too low.

My mother was testing me. I heard a crow outside.

"Can you please turn it up a little?"

"Could you please turn it up a little?" my mother said automatically. How many times had I done the same to Olivia.

"Could you please turn the thing up a little?" I said, this time grammatically.

"There must be something wrong with your hearing," she said ungraciously.

I decided to be morally superior so I simply replied, "Yes there is. It's just beginning. Just like you and Nan and Gran and Granddad."

She turned it up.

"What's the music?" I asked, raising a white flag.

"I told you earlier: Mahler's Fifth. The 'Adagietto.'"

"That's right. You did say that."

"We'll have to start again."

"Why?"

"Because you—we—were talking."

"I was listening as I spoke."

"You can't talk and look and listen all at one time."

"I can, darling."

"I can't."

"Sweetheart, it's not the first time I've seen it, you know," I said gently. "We did look at it once—in the big house. I thought it was beautiful. I'm happy to see it again."

"You haven't seen it on this size screen. It was lost on the small screen." She pressed the freeze button. "I don't know why I care."

"Please, Mamma. I just meant I *am* truly interested and you've made a good point: now we can see it on the bigger screen. I just meant I liked it so much the first time that it's not as crucial if I speak or move occasionally this time round."

"But *I'll* miss something. It interrupts my concentration."

"That's another matter altogether," I conceded. "I promise not to talk or move if I don't have to. Your concentration shouldn't be interrupted at all." Usually one for hearing irony where there was none, this time my mother missed my ironic undertone. I was hurt. Wasn't she interested in pleasing me? Her daughter? Didn't she want our time together to be a shared experience? I was always astonished, in the first forty-eight hours of a visit, by the strength of the emotional cocoon she could spin, by the fragility of the glistening thread with which that cocoon was attached to any equanimity, and by her fierce protection of that cocoon.

I was a prop. She had already staged the scene and written the lines for us. I was supposed to go on stage and, no matter whether I was tired or hurting, I was supposed to say my lines perfectly and not move downstage when I was supposed to move upstage. I was also supposed to say my lines with perfect intonation and feeling. I also had to act as though I were trained as a method actor: if I didn't fully embody the feeling, she caught it every time.

I had worshipped her when I was growing up. She could do no wrong. We had been best friends. Now we couldn't even seem to have a conversation about how to watch a film together.

She rewound the video to the beginning. I assumed she would then fast-forward to a particular point but we started at the beginning.

I settled as well as I could into the armchair. The upholsterer had restuffed the furniture with woodchips from what I could feel. We started to watch. And listen. My mother was right as usual: the film, two decades old now, was perfectly pitched.

My mother had read all of Dirk Bogarde's autobiographies. Once she had any research bit between her teeth, she never let go. Obscure books from around the world would arrive and her delight in opening them would rival her initial pleasure in my regular arrival. But while she could pick up or put down a book, I was a big, ungainly bird flapping around in her orderly space, even though I now stayed at a hotel. Thinking I couldn't hear because she herself was deaf, she had suggested to my father the visit before last that it was silly for him to give up his bedroom and that it made more sense if I stayed elsewhere. She told him that he should tell me when we were in the car sometime because we always talked best in the car. So I moved to a hotel when I flew up, worked in the early hours, called Andrew and Olivia, saw old friends, and then spent from mid-morning through dinner with my parents, bringing things of my own to occupy me when they took naps in their separate rooms.

After fifteen minutes, I quietly rose, slipped behind her chair, and—still watching and listening—moved to get another mug of tea and a biscuit.

The screen froze.

"What happened?" I asked.

"You got up."

"I'm getting myself another cup of tea. Do you want any? I would have asked you but I didn't want to interrupt."

"It has to be watched without any interruptions if you're going to get what I'm driving at about the film. You have to hear—see—how the music and the images are perfectly coordinated. It gives me goose pimples."

"Mamma, I *can't* just sit. I have to move around. I never just sit at home. It's always driven Andrew and Olivia crazy so it's not about this film or you. I just feel physically better when I get up and move around. I also concentrate better, oddly. I walk up and down when I lecture, too. Probably drives the students crazy."

"I can understand the lecturing and moving. But I don't see how it's possible to concentrate *on* something like a film when you're moving. I'll wait until you sit down again."

"I really can see and hear well from here."

"I can't concentrate when you're moving around."

"The jug's just boiled. I'm coming back."

"Seeing we're interrupted anyway and the water is hot, would you be a girl who'd get me a hot water bottle? There are lovely, thin, old towels beside the two hot water bottles in my bathroom. You can wrap one in one of those. This cotton dress is too thin. I'll burn myself."

"Gladly. You have two? Maybe I'll fill the other one for me." I had forgotten for a moment. I felt her alarm and fear from the kitchen.

"Daddy probably has one he could lend you."

I knew exactly what the problem was but I was caught in a web of my own making. I decided to play dumb and cheerful: it was a way to torment her yet remain blameless.

"I don't want to disturb him. He's on the phone with Robert Brown. They've spent the last twenty minutes solving the church's problems and have now moved on to the world's."

"I said you weren't concentrating on the film."

"Mamma, I couldn't help hearing them. *And* I heard the film. You can't hear Dad in his study. I can. Hold on. I'll just get the two bottles in your bathroom, the thin towels, fill them in the kitchen, and bring them out for us."

"Meg, I hate to be dog-in-the-manger-ish but Daddy had to

order those hot water bottles from England. It's impossible to get the ones I like here anymore. I just—it's often so hard for me to get the things I need and it takes forever. I had to ring all kinds of people to track them down but I finally found the British distributor. I—don't want to use them up. They have to last me a long time. What's wrong with Daddy's? I'm sorry. You don't like my saying 'Daddy.' Your father's. His is probably in the cupboard under the sink in his bathroom."

I did this. I started the whole thing. I felt mean and horrible.

"Mamma. I don't really need one. I truly don't. I just thought it would feel good but I don't *need* it. I'm standing up, the water's hot, it's easy for me to get yours, and I'll get the thin towel. I'm sorry your back is bothering you."

"It's not for my back. It's for my tummy. I have the rumbles. I don't know why."

I knew why: I had deliberately made her feel dreadful. I knew she was unable to lend or give any of us—even Olivia—anything other than a birthday or Christmas present. "I missed the Sharing Lesson at Miss Elery's kindergarten," she once said dryly.

It had taken me years to understand that her insights into herself didn't ease her pain and that my insights into her didn't ease mine. So why did I return to these crossroads again and again? Why was I compelled to set up a test that only I knew was taking place—a test whose rules were private to me and unbendable for her? I was pitching the strength of her fear against the strength of her love for me. Why? I knew I would always lose in my own secret competition because I always chose a language she could not speak. Why did I do this?

I went through her bedroom to the bathroom. The white towels—old because she only liked thin towels—were neatly stacked.

They were not fluffy because my father didn't believe in using the dryer, preferring sun and subtropical breezes to crisp them on the clothesline. There were two rubber water bottles with their rubber plugs. One was a nasty mushroom-pink. The other was a depressing, pale teal. I chose the teal and grabbed one of the thin towels. When I got back to the kitchen to fill it, my mother was standing there taking a tablet.

"Pain?"

"Nerves."

She came back and sat down. I proceeded to be overly solicitous. I had been torturing her. I was enraged at myself for permitting myself hope once again and enraged at her for being unable to let me use one thing of hers to ease my pain.

"Now I'm worried about *you*," she said as I handed her the bottle. She placed it on her stomach. "What's wrong with your back? Have you seen the doctor? It's nothing—serious?" More fear.

"Promise: nothing serious." On matters such as this, I could not torment her. "Same stuff as you. I inherited your body. It's a nice one, thank you, *and* my spine goes out of whack the way yours does sometimes."

"What about seeing Jacob? He's so helpful to me. His appointments person is very kind to me when Daddy takes me over. I'd love you to meet her."

"I tried him once, you know. His work is too strong for me. Let's just watch the film."

"I'll rewind."

"Mamma, we don't have to start all over again. We've watched twenty minutes, some of it twice—not counting the original time."

"Don't yell."

"I'm not yelling."

"It sounds like yelling."

My father emerged from his study having just hung up with Arthur, a longtime board member who was united with him in their conservative views, views of the minister, and plans for generating finances for the Building Fund. "It's lovely to see you both out here together. I can't believe it's really you sitting there. It makes me happy to see you having mother-daughter time. It's wonderful when the three of you come up but there's something special about just having you here alone."

There was a pointed silence emanating from both my mother and me, a silence to which my father was oblivious.

Looking at the scrapbooks, he continued, "Are you diving in already? Mamma's been so looking forward to your coming. She's been saving all sorts of things to share with you. I'm glad you're getting on with them before people begin to make their demands on you. I like seeing you both out here relaxing."

"We're having a row," my mother said flatly. My father looked taken aback. "Firstly, Meg doesn't want to watch the film. Secondly, I'm in the poo because I'm worried about using up those hot water bottles that were so hard to get. You know: the ones I got from England."

"Mamma, we are not having a row."

"We could have fooled *me*."

I was aware of my father's mounting anxiety. When he and I were having one of our *contretemps* despite my having learned to avoid most topics that could set us off, he felt in charge. When my mother and I were having an altercation, he felt helpless. "We do want to watch the film," I said, "and we are not mad at you about the bloody hot water bottle."

"See what I mean?" My mother looked over at my father.

"Take my hot water bottle, Meg. I don't use it. It's Gran's old one. It's under my sink."

"Thanks, Dad. I'll keep it in mind and get it if I need it."

"I'll fix it for you now if you like."

"No, thank you. Getting up and walking around helped. I'm better now and I don't need it any more. But I'll certainly ask for it if I need it."

"Help yourself. Any time. Or ask me and I'll fix it for you. I'm sorry you ever have need of one." My father looked concerned. He was entirely unaware of the pain he'd caused me during our earlier battles royal but he could not bear to know I was in pain from something that had nothing to do with him.

"I was trying to show her 'Death in Venice,' " my mother said, "but everything went wrong. I was trying my best. I thought 'This time, I'm going to avoid all rows.' I won't do anything to upset her. But I'm already in the poo."

"You are not in the poo."

"I'm going to lie down."

"Please don't, Mamma. Let's watch a bit more."

"Your mother has a rest every afternoon, Meg. She's not as fit as she used to be. Because you live down south, it's easy for you to miss."

"You can play the piano if you want," my mother said flatly. "It won't disturb me." She unwound herself from the chair and held out the hot water bottle for any hand to take and carry for her.

My father gesticulated madly at me while she was turning around, with difficulty, to pick a fine handkerchief from the corner of the seat where she always tucked it. He pointed at her bedroom, pointed at me, made walking steps with his forefinger and middle finger, pointed at me again, and then put his head on his folded palms as though in sleep. He pointed at me again, then at her, and finally pointed to his heart with his broad fingers, nails filed neatly short. It was amazing to me that he could type on his computer with his fingers: the tips were so squishy, warm, dry. Why was it that my mother's needs always took precedence? My protection of my parents backfired sometimes. When I had a skiing accident the first time I took Olivia years ago, I'd kept most of the details of my slow recovery from them. I downplayed my injury in order not to worry my mother into a frenzy and not to give my father cause to say, "You've moved, you see, and it's terrible for us when we know you aren't well but we can't just drive over and help you." It was a decision I now sometimes questioned.

I didn't nod enthusiastic affirmation at my father but I did stand and say to my mother, "Darling, let me help you in."

My mother handed me the offending hot water bottle in its thin, white towel nightdress, and I followed her into her white bedroom. Her cream, Irish mohair knee rug was spread neatly across the end of the bed. Without turning, she said, "I'm going to the 'loo first. Could you please pull the blinds and tilt them. I don't want someone gaily looking in."

She disappeared into her bathroom. I walked over to the blinds, passing her desk. Her daily planner and a large sheet of paper were on the desk. She had neatly ruled the sheet into columns and rows. At the top of the columns were the days I would be there noted in blue pen in her neat hand; red rows denoted hours in each day. Beside the planner, exactly parallel and on a sheet of paper, were some of her characteristic lists, all under the heading of "Meg's Days."

"Before Arrival" had a column all to itself. Then to the right were four additional columns under the general heading "During Visit." The four columns were labeled: "First Priority," "Second Priority," "Do If Time/Well Enough," and "Extras." Each title had been underlined using a wooden ruler that I knew her father had owned. Nan's sewing box sat on the floor beside the desk.

I skimmed the lists, curious to see what she wanted to do with me and what was most important to her. The "Before Arrival" list included:

Reread *Death in Venice*
Look for "D in V" video
Check "D in V" video rewound to beginning
Sort newspaper articles by topic
Find funny social column for M
Take Valium
Put away brandy
Sort shoes for sorting
Tidy dolls
Tidy desk
Find duets
Phone Exeter's—order Mahler sheet music

Under "During Visit - First Priority" were:

Watch "D in V" 2'10"
Show news cuttings 2'30" with tea break
Watch favorite programs 2-10 hrs
Show additions to scrap books 60"
Show early photos - dance festival 30"
Sort earrings?
Around the world photos – 1938 – new system?
Russian box/collection

Sort sculpture tools - Meg can do while I'm resting
Play duets - time to be determined
Play latest 30"
Organize books on top shelf 120" in two 60" slots
Phone May? (May was a cousin she dreaded calling—and to whom she thought I could speak better on the phone than she.)
Drive to bay - if sunny and tide in 1'30"
See old house 1'30"
Go to nursery - new geranium? 1'15"
Show M new art gallery - just the second room
Show awful new house painted purple and red - 5" en route to nursery
Art gallery at nursery - Nice? Nasty? 10" or 60" depending on answer
Take Valium on waking

My mother came out of the bathroom, took off her television glasses, and folded them neatly on the white bedside table. She started to arrange herself on the side of her body on which she now always lay. I went to sit down on the end of the bed and then remembered she didn't like me to sit there because it upset the mattress. I sat on the glory box, reupholstered by her with a piece of French tapestry she had bought on one of their overseas trips. She had folded the edges rather than cutting them, in case she didn't like the outcome.

"This is so pretty, Mamma. The glory box cover. You really have a good eye."

She looked happier.

"You've made a pretty room here. I do think the white is more cheerful than Nan's furniture you used to use."

I had ruined the trip. I had already blotted the clean-lined page of her hopes for our time. Was it so hard for me just to sit there and watch? Who *was* that creature who couldn't do it earlier this afternoon?

"I think it's fresh and uplifting," she said in a weary but more energetic tone. In order to avoid her serious food allergies, she lived off camembert and crackers, small amounts of excellent food cooked by my father, a severely regulated (by her) amount of Scotch and potato chips; the occasional medicine-glass of brandy; and seven cigarettes a day. Mostly, she lived off compliments.

"It's unsullied—it leaves one room to think." I replied. "I like where you've put the thirties-style illustration—the man playing the piano, the woman looking out to sea."

"It's tacky but it's pretty. I had a 'good' painting up there for a while—that gum tree looking wan in the late afternoon light. Daddy was presented with it when he finally retired from the Ethics Board. It just looked sad in here. Late afternoon light has always made me feel sad. I bought this thirties print at the local craft store. It's cheap and nasty but the colors are right."

"They are," I said brightly, feeling that I might still redeem her lists.

"Did you see where I put the dried flowers—the ones you sent from France?"

"Oh, there! What a good spot."

"I would have put them on the Greek embroidery Olivia sent last summer but the embroidery was blue and white."

"No, you did the right thing; it wouldn't look good at all. You can always take turns putting things out or not. I promise I won't be hurt. Neither would Olivia."

"I worry you'll think I don't appreciate them if they're not out."

"You mean like those 'Nasty Loathsome' objects we used to

bring out when the people who gave them came for afternoon tea or dinner?" I laughed.

"Of course not," she said, caught red-handed.

Something that had been between us floated out of the room on a ray of long afternoon light. I felt lighter. I picked up the mohair blanket.

"Do you want this over you?"

"Just my feet and lower legs. They get cold. I don't know why."

"Like that?"

"A little less tightly please if it won't hurt your back. I get cramps if it's too tight. Daddy always puts a little towel at the end so the blanket doesn't weigh on my feet."

I went to the bathroom and got the only thick hand towel I could find, rolled it up, and tucked it under the blanket.

"You didn't use one of the thin ones, did you? I only have enough to get me from one washing day to the next. I don't want to bother Daddy to do a wash in between. Those theses he reads don't get done as soon they could, mostly because he puts my needs first. But it's not *all* my fault. He will insist on talking to people on the telephone for so long...."

"I used the thick yellow towel with the horrible red L on it. Where'd that come from?"

"The cleaning lady. I have to keep it in there. It bothers me every time I see it but I'm afraid I'll forget to put it out when she comes and then she'll be hurt."

"You could blame it on me. Say you loaned it to me. Say I took it home by mistake after my visit."

"Oh, I couldn't do that. She might see through it. Could you please hand me my reading glasses? They're in the top drawer right here."

I opened the drawer. There was a neat, ironed stack of handkerchiefs, and a half-full bottle of two-milligram Valiums with several pills cut in two. She rationed the Valium perfectly. Like the Scotch and cigarettes. On top were several novels in German, a book on Taoism, and her Russian father's copy of one of Dostoevsky's novels in English. Reading in English had been one way he had learned it so quickly and so well, Nan had told me.

"Our generation never threw things away. You never knew when you'd need something," my father had said many times by way of explaining my mother's perfectly organized boxes of buttons, elastic bands, pins, rubber bands, and paperclips sorted by size and function. However, there was a difference: my mother's parents had not been directly affected by the Depression. Quite the opposite in fact. However, both Nan and Grandpapa had struggled separately in the decade before they married: my grandfather's leaving Russia for Australia; my grandmother's mother's early death.

My father's parents, however, had been affected by the Depression although my grandfather's government work continued and they managed to keep their son and daughter at private schools. However, one only had to look at the difference in the jewelry on his parents in early photographs and what was left to know that sacrifices had been quietly made. However, careful budgeting and the fear of there not being enough—of anything—had been sustained notes throughout each of my parents' lives no matter how financially secure my father's work and my mother's inheritance had made them.

"Would you be kind enough to just get me the paperback in the second drawer." I opened the drawer. There was her battered copy of *Der Tod in Venedig* on top of *Der Zauberberg*, also battered.

Each was carefully taped along its sides and the top one held a hand-painted bookmark.

"That's pretty," I said, finally getting in the swing of what it was that worked without fail: praise.

"You made that."

"I did?"

"For Nan. One Mother's Day or Christmas."

"I was better than I thought! Rest well, darling. When you wake up, we'll watch the whole thing from beginning to end before dinner. There'll still be plenty of time before dinner. I promise not to move!"

She looked mollified and dubious.

"I want to share it with you," she said wistfully. "There's a particular place where the music changes into the minor just as a shadow falls across Bogarde's face—it's perfectly timed." She moved her hand a little. I reached out and patted it gently. I gave her a kiss on the brow where her still-mostly-brown hair was falling in orderly, natural waves that resembled the hand-colored studio portrait of her at twenty that had hung at my grandmother's house for so long and now hung in my mother's closet. Our hairlines were the same.

"Don't let me sleep too long. No more than half an hour or there won't be time to watch it before dinner."

"I promise."

I went to the piano and sat down, flipping through my mother's practice pieces: Chopin, Bach, Beethoven, Scriabin, Debussy, Mahler. Being as musical but less trained than my mother, I started with the Chopin pieces I could manage, then tried the Mahler—clearly a new copy. I fumbled my way through a wide spread of chords and then worried that this might deflate my mother because I was reading the "snotty guts"—as Nan used to say—out of the music that we would shortly hear again in the film. So I went back to the Chopin, at which I wasn't too bad. My neck tired quickly so I stopped.

I sat down in the living room. My father was down the hall in his study on the phone again—something about a virus and a computer program. Despite my university work, my father was far more computer savvy than I. I felt at loose ends. The remote was lying on top of the pile of magazines. I turned on the television, muted it quickly, and was about to flip through channels when I realized that the video was still set. Keeping one ear open for stirrings from my mother's room, I turned the sound to minimum. The walls were thick and my parents were deaf as well as now otherwise occupied. I took off my glasses, sat down on the floor two feet away from the screen, and pressed Play.

I watched until my back ached. At a precise moment, the key of the Mahler became minor and a shadow fell across the face on the screen. I found my eyes flowing with tears. I felt guilty, unkind, wrong—and mildly annoyed because the film had produced in me a complete capitulation.

I quickly wound the video back to the beginning, rose, used my father's bathroom to wash my face, and walked back towards my mother's bedroom. Her tiny form, foetal under the cream mohair blanket, was cut by long, slanting rays of late-afternoon sun that backlit each of the fine hairs on the mohair and fell across her profile, which lay next to the half-open, battered book.

She stirred, took off her glasses, and moved the book from her pillow. She felt my presence at the door. "Why are you watching me?"

"I'm not—but you do look pretty, lying there in the sun. I just came to wake you as promised."

"What time is it?" she asked suspiciously.

"Still time to watch."

Not fully trusting me and always preferring objective data points, she consulted one of the three clocks she had in her room. She decided I was right.

"You didn't cheat and watch, did you?" she said as she struggled up and put her bare feet on the carpet.

"Why would I? I want to watch it—anew—with you."

"Do you *really* mean that or are you being nice?"

"Why would I lie about something like that? I did play the piano—mainly Chopin."

"Do you approve of the tuning? I had it tuned last week. It's not bright enough for my ear but I asked him to do it the way you like it—for when you came."

"It was lovely. The action is easier on your piano than on mine. Did you hear me?" I said, worrying she might have heard me playing the Mahler, thereby draining it of its life.

"Just some Chopin. Then I must have fallen asleep. You're quite good, you little devil, for someone who doesn't practice. I often feel sorry that I didn't realize you were as musical as you are. You did take that first part of the prelude a little fast, galloping through the easy bits and slowing down in the difficult. You might try practicing with separate hands and then with the metronome if you want to get it moving smoothly. I suppose I shouldn't have said that."

"Of course you should. Thank you for telling me, darling. I like getting the benefit of your knowledge."

"Now, of course, I feel as though I've made the film with my own hands and shall be responsible if you don't like it this time.

I've been looking forward to this for so long that it has to fall flat now. I try never to look forward to things because I jinx them. I've probably jinxed this."

"We have twenty minutes before we need to start watching in time to finish before the news comes on. There's shade on the back garden bench now. You could have a cigarette in the cool—guilt-free. The wind's changed direction. Dad won't smell it. Take your time. I'll make us some tea. Then we can start all over again."

THIRTY-NINE

....

TREBLE CLEF

"Of course, it was I, but I didn't know that when I first woke." I hear my mother shift on the unforgiving hospital bed and maneuver tubes. "It was a kind of dream, I suppose. The blood was going in and out of a violin shaped like a clef. Every time the blood pulsed, there was pain. I didn't even realize at first the pain was mine."

"Oh, darling. How awful. I'm so sorry. It's irrelevant, I know, but you have such vivid dreams: was it a treble or bass clef?"

"Treble. It looked like a *violin*. A violin couldn't look like a *bass* clef." I hear doubt and panic in her tone—and uneven breathing. She suspects I have not been listening carefully or that she is boring me. Neither is true. Either is dangerous.

"Of course! That was silly of me. I was focused on your pain, not on the form of the clef. *You* were clear. I just didn't construct the visual." The danger passes. I hear her breath return to its current, normal breathlessness.

She moves the phone. I wait while her breathlessness eases and I try, by breathing effortless patience into my silence, to prove to her it is fine for me to wait. If she imagines she hears impatience in my silence, she will use breath she doesn't have to apologize.

"I'm sorry to keep you waiting, darling. I had to change hands," she says. Then she adds, in the studiously polite voice she has always used when she is clinging to form as her only defense against disintegration at the thought of dealing with a stranger one on one, "Could you just hold on another moment? Someone's coming to do something." Then, *sotto voce*: "You know I can't concentrate if anyone's around when I'm on the phone—even you or Daddy."

"Take your time, darling." I watch the gardener below us climb the coconut palm, wide black belt binding him in a temporary marriage ritual to the palm, machete in hand, spikes on his shoes. A bird alights on the white railing on our front balcony.

"Thank God. He's gone," says my mother's voice, still breathless from terror at possibly having erred in a social interaction. "It's worse than Victoria Station here. I was telling you the dream. There were giant cryptic crosswords. All night. I was walking around in them but couldn't solve a single one."

"What a dreadful nightmare, darling! Did you turn the light on and read or watch television? At least you've a private room."

"I can't read. I can't even watch television. I don't know why. I have several books I ordered waiting at the library. Even if I felt like reading, I wouldn't have the heart to ask Daddy to go and pick them up. He's been so kind. He washed and ironed my nighties and brought them this morning. I don't want to ask him to pick up *library* books. Last night I did watch "Australian Idol." For some inexplicable reason, they're making contenders do songs from different eras. Most of the contenders are so young they don't know them and haven't taken the trouble to find out what the original sounded like. I'm sorry. I'm keeping you. Or at least boring you."

"Don't be silly, Mamma. You are never boring. You know I love your keeping me up to date about the latest in contemporary music. Especially since you've not been writing articles recently.... You've always picked up-and-coming people. I still brag about how you know instinctively. I get lots of currency with my students, too! Just be sure to save your energy and not overdo it. I can ring back later if you like."

"They bring the dinner so early I'd be worried you'd ring in the middle."

"Then I'd just hang up."

"I'd feel awful if I had to ask you to do that."

"Then we'll talk briefly now and I'll ring again tomorrow. Then it's only two days and I'll be up."

Under no circumstances must my mother even suspect that what she is giving me is not exactly what I have always wanted. Two days ago, when she was admitted to the hospital, I went out and bought a top quality mobile phone that gets good reception and does everything but fly me up to see her. Since then, I have felt its sleek, menacing presence in my pocket, ready to explode at any moment.

"I'm sorry, darling, I do need to hang up. The phone's heavy. But I want to tell you one last thing—and I can only tell you. Yesterday, one of the hospital chaplains came to offer me unwanted solace. I did what you suggested: I told him I was sorry I couldn't talk because the doctor said I had to sleep. Then I said faintly, just the way you suggested, 'Perhaps you could just say a little prayer.' I made my lids heavy and closed my eyes. He said a little prayer. He couldn't remember my name and didn't want to get up and look at my chart in the middle of the prayer so he filled in the blank with 'our dear sister in Christ'—but then he went away! I was so guilty and proud."

"Proud, yes. Guilty, no, Mamma. You're the one in the hospital bed!" Even now, all these years later, I have not managed to stop trying to take away the pain she feels compelled to inflict on herself.

"Hold on," she says. "I have to change hands again."

While she arranges the phone on her hospital pillow, I am suddenly still young and living at home. I have either just walked home alone from my local Presbyterian church (with its somnolent hymns full of passionate words we sing without passion) because my father has stayed on for a meeting or I have just got off the bus from school. I tiptoe up the path to the front door because I can hear my mother playing the piano, perhaps Debussy's "Pavane pour une Infante Défunte." Or I hear her typewriter hesitating over just the right word for an article that is due. She thinks she is still alone. She types or practices the piano with disciplined abandon. It is the only time she is herself.

I wait at the front door, unwilling to enter, stunned into the spell of a love whose tidal swell never fails to unmoor my heart from its tenuous anchor in my chest. The second I turn the key, she will close down like a sea creature into which I have carelessly plunged my curious finger. She will make us lunch and then she will give me a music lesson, teaching me how to read and play music, how *not* to play solely by ear (despite my penchant for mimicking), and how to notate it. I practice writing clefs over and over. I like the bass clef better than the treble: the curve comes out better. My mother comes from the kitchen often, interrupting dinner preparations, gently correcting my mistakes. The sound of an incorrect note is unbearable to her.

I snap back to the present, hearing my mother's heavy breathing on the phone.

"Mamma, congratulations! You have a new profession as an actress. I'm proud of you! There's more than one way to kill a cat, as Miss Arlington used to say!"

"I do feel guilty. You must promise not to tell."

"Promise," I reply. I tell her I'll ring her tomorrow and be up on the weekend—and that it won't hurt my feelings if she can't talk because they are doing something to her or because she is tired or because she can't breathe or because someone is in the room. I assure her that it will not bother me at all to ring back; all she has to do is tell me. It won't work but I'll try anyway.

I watch the palm tree fronds fall through the humid air and thump, broken, on the ground fifty feet below the pruning man. He chops off anything that is an older branch. A crowd gathers just beyond the danger cones surrounding the base of the palm. The gardener must not be disturbed and the observers must not be hit by falling fronds.

As we finish the conversation, my mother starts worrying, as she always has. Despite what I have said, she says she is worried she might not be alone to talk when I ring tomorrow and she'll feel rude. I tell her that either way is alright, that everything is alright, that she doesn't have to make a decision because we'll just experiment, which is perfectly alright with me as I have only one lecture to give early morning.

I wait until I hear her—breathing laboriously and heavily—place the heavy hospital-phone receiver back onto its cradle. My phone goes silent. I hang up and put the mobile in my shorts pocket again.

As I watch the pruning man rappel down the palm trunk to collect the fronds from beneath our balcony, I think about my own dream last night, from which I awoke to the sound of rain beating lightly on ferns, just as I used to hear it as a child. In my dream, a woman is dying. Another says with tenderness, already mourning her before she has died, "She was my Sabbath."

FORTY

....

THE DOLL

I have the shoes, too: the shoes she was wearing when she bought the doll on the streets of Budapest in 1938.

I might have more than one photograph of that moment if we could find the two-by-three, black-and-whites that my grandfather took of my mother and Nan (and the ones that the Cook's agent or strangers must have taken of the three of them). Now, when I travel, I carry my digital camera and my iPhone with me so I can capture anything, everything. I rarely print them so I miss holding them as I can hold that one of my mother in Budapest.

It's unlikely there are more photographs of the moment. As I remember from seeing my grandmother's "Round the World, 1938" album when I was little, there tended to be one photograph per event and each was usually orchestrated. The two-by-threes, slipped into black corners that were, in turn, carefully glued onto the black pages, were in a single, thick, leather album. Each photograph was carefully labeled in white ink by Nan:

"Lucy—Radio City Music Hall"

"Lucy & friend—deck of the 'Mauritania' "

"Alex, Self, & Lucy"

"Lucy playing Wagner's piano"

I would sit astride Nan's lap with the album in my lap. I could feel Nan's stockings sturdy beneath her beautiful silk dresses. Nan would turn the pages and tell me about each photograph. I don't remember if the photograph of my mother buying the doll was in that album. It must have been. In those things, Nan was orderly. In fact, in all things aesthetic, she was orderly. Her newspaper clippings, scrapbooks, other albums, and family memorabilia were all piled in the window seat in quiet, loving chaos.

Sometimes, when I was little, I was allowed to open the box and look at the doll. After my mother shut down Nan and Grandpapa's house and stored so many packing boxes to be laboriously sorted over several months, my mother must have taken that photograph out of the album and put it in the box with the doll.

Years later, when my mother would bring out the doll, she was always anxious. "Careful, darling," she would say as I took it out.

"Mamma, I've never hurt her all the times I've taken her out—even when I was little and Nan let me do it."

"I know but she's lasted over sixty years and—. She's probably worth something now."

"You *could* give her to Olivia. I know Olivia's grown up but she *is* your granddaughter and she'd adore it. *I'd* love to have her if it comes to that."

"You'll get her eventually. When I'm dead. She's in good condition. I wish I could send her to 'Antiques Roadshow' and see if she is, in fact, worth much."

"I could ask my allergist. She collects dolls." I fingered the doll's boots. "I've always loved her red boots—the real leather, the way they slip on and off the stuffed cloth feet. And her hair.... The plaits—they're silk, you know."

"I don't know how you know these things," my mother said, touching the hair gingerly.

"One can feel. I probably just picked up how different materials feel from Nan. She always knew fabrics and things by feel."

The long box with its faded-flower paper wrapper and soft tissue inside: it is a gentle coffin for a moment in the street, a street in Budapest. What street? Who painted the doll's face? Who made the apron, the headband of minute paper flowers, the blue ribbon around the transparent apron, the yellowed tulle under the midnight blue satin skirt? Those who sewed those stitches: all dead, I'm sure. The young woman in the photograph is a little older than my mother was at the time. I wonder if her grandchildren have any of her dolls. Or were they lost, perhaps, along with their maker, in the war?

In the photograph, my mother is standing, slim and straight (so straight then). Her dancer's legs are in elegant silk stockings. She is smiling. She is reaching for the doll. The doll is sitting on a tray suspended by a wide band around the street seller's neck. My mother is in a suit. The black-and-white photograph doesn't tell me the color but I know my mother's tastes—the same all her life. The suit is medium dark in the photograph so it wouldn't have been beige or cream. It was navy or brown. She is carrying a leather handbag. Leather gloves. A light-colored crepe de chine dickie underneath the suit.

"Meg, it's time," I hear from the kitchen.

"Coming," I call out.

My mother's profile is clear in the photograph. She is smiling her eighteen-year-old, effortless stage smile. I imagine my grandfather saying, "Lucy, stay there for a moment." My mother's straight nose, her Margaret Sullavan profile. She went through phases of looking like different well-known people and becoming well known herself for her syndicated magazine and newspaper articles. Eighteen was her Margaret Sullavan phase. I watched "Three Comrades" with her once. I tracked the film down for her on the Internet and, when we all flew up that year for Christmas, I gave it to her. On New Year's Day, when everyone else went out to dinner, she and I watched it together. My mother fell in love with her black-and-white young self again. I did, too.

In the photograph, Nan stands slightly to the side of my mother. Their profiles are the same. She, too, is smiling. This is what my grandfather would have seen on April 17, 1938, just days—according to his travel diary, written in elegant English—before he was denied entry to Russia to see his family again after so many decades.

Nan, too, is elegantly dressed. She is wearing a fur collar, leather gloves, a bag darker than my mother's, and laced shoes (Nan's feet troubled her even then; my mother's years of ballet exacted their price later). How tiny they each were. Their petiteness does not, however, show in the photograph. The woman who sold the doll must have been tiny as well because she is their height. A worker in uniform, blurry in the background, has stopped to look for a moment at the woman selling the doll to the well-heeled travelers with a Cook's guide standing, doubtless, with my grandfather as he took the photograph. The worker must be long dead, too. In the photograph, he looks to be in his late thirties.

"What are you doing?" I hear again from the kitchen.

"I'm coming."

The shoes. My eye rests finally on the shoes. High heels. Brown leather. Of course. Bought in New York after they had landed in Los Angeles and traveled First Class across the country by train. The shoes are made of soft leather, with bands an inch wide, gathered and tied flat. I have the shoes up in my closet, together with the dickie.

"Meg," Andrew says gently, barely masking his discomfort, "Radiation said they run on time. I don't think it's politic to be late for your first treatment!"

Having refused Andrew's offers to drive me several times, I drive myself to the hospital. I put on a CD. It's only twenty minutes from our house. It's an audible book because my mother is dead and I dare not risk listening to, let alone playing, any music that she played on the piano for so many years.

I lie there not moving. I am told that the beams and angles move until they line up with the tiny tattoos I now have. It is important to kill correctly. The attendants disappear. It's a room in which I shall lie alone for weeks while my flesh is burnt. I am relieved Olivia is in mid-coursework in London despite her many offers to come home. I want her here but I don't. She's my daughter; I love her but have no energy to give her or anyone else and know she would boss me about in her attempts to be helpful. Besides, what would she do when I sleep so much?

The next day, before I leave for the Radiation Lab, I lift the doll out of its delicate coffin, take off one shoe, then the other, and put them back on again. The tiny red boots slip over the cloth heel just as easily as they did when I was five.

I lift up the blue satin skirt. The cloth underskirt and underpants lie against the firm, slightly shaped, limp cloth legs. No dancer's legs, these. More like my mother's legs in those last days when I sat beside her as she lay inert in her hospital bed. Her legs were bruised, swollen. Not the legs that walked the streets of Budapest, that sat at Wagner's piano, that stood on top of Mount Pilatus, that waited on the deck wondering if there would be a letter at the next port from the nineteen-year-old who would later become my father. No, her dying legs lay beneath the pale-blue cotton bedspread with "St. John's" woven into the fabric so that the cross-fibers glinted in the late afternoon sun as it finally reached her southwestern-facing room. By then, she wasn't aware of the absence of the angled view she'd had of the blue-grey hills in her earlier room, of the absence of direct light, perhaps even of the absence of light.

After the Grand Tour, Nan, Grandpapa, and Mamma returned to their gracious, quiet home on the outskirts of town on the top of those blue-grey hills. "At lunch, when I was small and walked to school, I always used to look at the house to make sure it hadn't burnt down for some reason," my mother once told me.

When she married, the doll and the photographs lived with my grandparents and then just with Nan. Eventually, they came—packed in one of those many crates—to live with my mother. As I sat with my mother in St. John's, hour upon hour, her legs looked like the doll's legs without the boots.

When my mother was in her box, I stroked her hair, still mostly brown despite being eighty-five. I didn't touch her skin. However, I did replace the fuchsia lipstick. She would have loathed it. I didn't look beneath the box's lower lid. I didn't want to see her feet. Her face didn't even look like a good doll's face, really.

I thought about all that during the service. I thought about how she would have been bored in this church with its ascetic walls. However, while I think she might even have managed to forget her dislike of all church pews, which she declared to be "punishment pews," when she heard excerpts from her most loved articles, so un-church-like, read aloud and echoing off the cold stone walls with their brass plaques memorializing Those Who Served, including my father, like Margaret Sullavan in *Three Comrades*, she would have preferred to have perished in black-and-white in the snow.

We stood nearby, as the attendants slid the box my father and I had chosen for her into the long, black car. The box was rosewood, like the wood on the fine Mehler furniture with which she had grown up. My father and I had chosen it after passing over a shiny, yellow box—one her beloved Michael Jackson might have admired. My father and I imagined how amused she would have been if we had chosen that horrid yellow thing because the whole idea of death depressed her no end. Decorum prevailed.

My father and I watched the black car pull out into the midday traffic—no cortege to accompany it. We let her go alone to be burnt up. We didn't follow. All that care she had taken of the Hungarian doll—and there we were, standing properly, watching her stuffed-doll self decorously carted off into traffic to wait at traffic lights. Alone. To accelerate. Alone. While we made small talk in the church hall with those who stayed. Presbyterians believe in but don't often let themselves grasp eternal life: the kind the doll has, the kind my mother gave that doll despite my deepest wish to have and to hold it. They're not too good on the death bit, either. We could have gone out to the crematorium and watched the doll box disappear. Instead, we had to turn away and greet those who came. As though the doll box weren't in traffic being passed by a Honda. It was a full church so it was a good thing the church women's Refreshment Committee had made lots of little triangular sandwiches and brewed great urns of tea.

FORTY-ONE

....

PIANO LESSONS

In the Bach preludes. There was a symbol—I never noticed it until I started to play it for her. It means 'hold this note longer.'"

"You probably mean a *sostenuto*."

"That wasn't what the teacher called it."

"It depends which edition you're using."

"Schirmer's. But the teacher said the Schirmer's wasn't very good."

"Did I suggest it?" my mother asked.

"No, I bought it because it was the only one the shop had."

"I have others. Personally, I prefer the urtext. Just a moment, darling. I have to put the phone on the other ear. My shoulder is hurting from holding it. I'm sorry."

"Don't be sorry. I shouldn't be keeping you."

"I shouldn't be keeping *you*."

"You're not keeping me. I like talking to you. You know that."

"I prefer the urtext."

"Pardon me!" I said with a little laugh to ensure she knew I was giving her a compliment.

"I didn't mean it like that," my mother said.

"I know you didn't. You just sounded effortlessly esoteric, that's all."

"I didn't mean it to *sound* like that."

"I *know*. That's what makes it perfect."

"Nor did I mean to criticize your copy."

"You didn't."

"I need to stand for a minute. Can you wait? I'd like to see which is my favorite edition."

I heard her heavy breathing as she moved slowly around the room, rifling through the piano music. No sound of shoes. She never wore them except to the doctor's or for a drive with my father. The grandfather clock sounded five. Its chime had been drunkenly uneven for several years. My grandfather, the Russian one, had ordered it from Germany in the early thirties and had shipped it to Australia. Its slim, rosewood case, having spent its years in dim corners where its clusters of carved grapes and leaves caught dust but no direct light, had not faded in the harsh, subtropical sun.

"I can't talk long, darling," my mother panted as she returned to the phone. "I'm sorry. Please don't think I don't want to talk to you or that I'm not interested in talking about the music. I have to take the blood thinner and other medications on time. I'm sorry."

"Don't be sorry, darling. I know you have to. That's why I'm just giving you a little call now. I don't want to delay your tablets or your Scotch."

"You make me sound like an old soak."

"I make you sound like someone out of the Raj, not an old soak."

"Same thing," my mother retorted dryly. "Just a minute. I have to put the phone down again. I don't get on with this receiver. Daddy loves it because it's so light. He thought it would help me because it's so light. I'm afraid I haven't made friends with it; it feels like a little silver fish that can slip out of one's hand at any moment."

She put the phone on the top of the piano. She had long since sold the baby grand Nan had given her. She'd waited until Nan died to sell it. Its tone was not to my mother's liking.

Once, when I was visiting from down south, I joked that perhaps she could give me a piano for my fiftieth birthday the way Nan had given her one.

She looked at me blankly and replied, "I earned that."

"I always thought Nan gave it to you."

"In practical terms, she did. However, I like to think I earned it—by taking care of her all those years."

"Mamma, Nan had more than enough money from Grandpapa's estate. She wanted to give it to you because she loved you, not because of anything you *did!*"

"She said she loved me once—shortly before she died. That time I begged her to tell me whether I was adopted and she finally said she and I joined Grandpapa up north and then they got married privately." She stopped talking for a minute to catch her breath, which grew shorter and shorter. "They did love each other, I think. She was sad for years after he died early. Things are different now. One didn't *say* things such as "I love you" when I was growing up. Ask Daddy. No one *said* 'I love you.'

"I know Nan and Grandpapa thought I was pretty. And Nan put every article I ever published in scrapbooks. They did love to hear me play the piano. Nan liked making clothes and ballet costumes for me. Still, I prefer to think she gave me the grand because I took care of her all those years after Grandpapa died."

As I waited on the phone, I could see in my mind's eye the

long, last rays of late-summer light slanting across my parents' cream carpet, zigzagging across the dark arms of the chairs in their retirement villa, and onto my mother's scoliotic back.

"I've got the Bach drawer in front of me. Which prelude were you referring to? Correction: to which prelude were you referring?"

I told her. I wished I'd never mentioned it. I wanted my piano lessons, resumed after a forty-year hiatus, to be a subject my mother and I could discuss, a topic about which she would be more knowledgeable than I. In fact, there were few topics about which she was not quietly more knowledgeable than I. I didn't resent this at all; she was so uncertain about herself that I couldn't resent it. I still loved to learn from her. I didn't want the piano-lesson conversations to be something over which she would labor. But hardly anything was light work for my mother, particularly at this point in her fragile life. This bar of the Bach prelude was no exception. I could hear pages of music turn.

"Oh, *that*! That's just a held note."

"I remember your teaching me about held notes. But the teacher used some other word."

"I wasn't a good piano teacher for you. I should have made you stay with it. If I'd known your talent, I would have bullied you."

"You were a good teacher! You kept my love of music alive. And you had the wit to send me off to someone else when you noticed yourself running in to correct my mistakes when I was practicing and you were fixing dinner."

"I didn't realize you were so musical. Until recently. You have more talent than I."

"Don't be silly. Darling, I'm going to let you go now so you won't feel bad about hanging up on me. I'm going to be the one to hang up this time. It's my turn to feel guilty."

I hung up, replaced the music on my grand, and went to feed the dog. Olivia would call soon from London. We missed her badly but were ridiculously, quietly proud of her being awarded the scholarship.

It was when I was feeding the dog at the same time two evenings later that my father called and told me my mother had been taken to the hospital. She had lost half her blood supply.

"Don't ring her yet. Please tell Olivia not to ring either, although she could send a postcard. Your mother won't feel she has to respond to a postcard but she'd worry about how to ring Olivia from the hospital. I'll ring you on my mobile during visiting hours. That way I can tell you if Mamma's up to talking or not."

My father called me the next afternoon towards the end of the visiting hours. I rang back immediately. "I've been upset about what I said," my mother began, in a muffled tone that told me that she had little voice, less energy, and a bad hospital phone. "I didn't mean to criticize your edition of Bach or your piano teacher. After we hung up, I was worried that you might have taken what I said the wrong way."

"I didn't take it the wrong way, darling. We were having an interesting discussion about things I've never been educated enough to discuss with you until now."

"If you're sure...." She stopped talking. She had run out of breath again. Then she resumed. "The regular nurses are pleasant enough. Hold on a minute. Daddy's just leaving."

I waited.

"There's a new young thing from England this time," she continued. "Perfect skin, apple cheeks. Also a new Patient Visitor—the kind who wears uncrushed linen and pearls and smiles too widely. She pats my arm and alternates between "one" and "we."

You know the kind. I pretended to be sleeping today when she came. At least she doesn't pray over me.

"Last night was the night from hell. There was a temporary night nurse and she wouldn't give me my Valium. I specifically asked my doctor to put it on the chart, which he did. Daddy didn't like my asking because he thought it might be construed as interfering. However, I wanted to sleep so I asked the doctor politely and he agreed. The temporary said I couldn't have one. I told her to look at my chart. Finally, she brought me *something*—but it was different packaging. I realized she was giving me a sugar tablet. I refused it. I asked, 'Is the Valium on the chart or not?' She got quite cross. Went away. I heard her on the phone to my doctor. When she came back, she gave me a tablet in the right package. I wasn't going to let her get away with being so horrid earlier, so I said, '*Is* it on the chart or isn't it? I'll only take this if it's on the chart.' She had been unfair so I turned the tables. She finally showed me the chart and harrumphed off. It was right there, listed. I got it eventually but I shouldn't have had to work so hard."

"You dot one," I said. The story of my taking an unauthorized apple from the grocery shop, hiding it in my perambulator, and declaring with satisfaction en route home—to my mother's horror—"I dot one" was apocryphal.

"I always worried the grocer would think I'd tried to get away with it by putting the apple under your blanket. I took it back immediately!"

"I'm sure he didn't. Don't worry about the piano thing yesterday, Mamma. I enjoyed our talk."

"Luce, your afternoon tea's here," I could hear my father say clearly. One of the very few ways he showed he was now an octogenarian was that he still didn't realize that new phones picked up every sound within yards. I didn't tell him more than once because he would have been offended at my implying he wasn't on top of technology, which he generally was, and because, for fifty years, it had been vital to my survival to overhear to my parents' *sotto voce* exchanges. "Drink it while it's still hot, Luce. Meg will understand. She can ring back. You're the one in the hospital."

"Meg darling, my afternoon tea's here. I'm sorry. I did just want to tell you I dreamt about you and Nan and me last night. Mother and I were on a train trip. Two boring women in dowdy dresses got on the train before us. I worried they'd take our seats but they got off again. We were just going to board when I woke."

"You said 'you and Nan and me' but you didn't mention me in the dream. Where was I?"

"You were seeing us off. You were joining us later."

"Hang up now, Mamma. I'll ring tomorrow—but I promise to do it before afternoon tea."

"The tea doesn't always arrive at the same time," she replied anxiously.

"If I gate-crash afternoon tea, I'll ring back."

A year later, as Sarah, my piano teacher, leads me, as usual, to the upright in her small house, I take note of her outfit. Sarah is the essence of music teacher: navy dress with black cardigan over a thin body, black sensible shoes, thin black hair. I immediately want to ring and share this living cliché with my mother as soon as I arrive home.

Sarah runs me through some scales. I apologize each time I make a mistake. "I'm sorry," I hear myself repeating.

Sarah looks gently puzzled at my constant apologies.

"My mother's high standards—for herself," I explained. "I

picked it up. I can't bear it if I make a mistake when I'm around anyone."

She smiled and then said, "Let's give your neck a rest. I noticed you're rubbing it. I don't want this to cause you pain. It is supposed to be fun. You're not trying to be a concert pianist at your age. You said right at the beginning that you're here for pure enjoyment. You did say you were interested in theory and somehow we've not touched on that again this year. How much do you know?"

"What I know is mainly from osmosis and a little outside teaching. As you know, my mother taught me to read and write music. I don't know much more than that."

I sit straighter on the piano stool and move my fingers across my neck slowly.

"Best not to assume then. You just tell me whether you know something or not as we go along. Let's just start with basics. Can you *write* a treble clef?" Sarah asked.

"Yes, but not for forty years," I reply. Sarah hands me a pencil and paper. I produce a treble clef. As I turn the manuscript page around so that it faces her, Sarah adjusts her rimless glasses with a thin, white forefinger and bony thumb.

"Beautifully formed—and easily, too," she comments with surprise.

I imagine that my mother is still alive. I imagine that, when I shall ring that evening, I shall tell her I have written a perfect treble clef.

FORTY-TWO

THE SUIT

I am looking at myself in the mirror at Robertson's, still the best and now nationwide department store where the selection of overseas designers, all in one place, is widest. I don't have energy to look in more than one place.

I rather wish I were five again, unable to see myself clearly in the mirror until, at six, I was prescribed the ugly pink glasses I loved. Of course, I could take my glasses off but I stare. Surgery, weeks of radiation, and years of drugs make me look older than I am. Once again, I am relieved my mother died before this happened. She would have worried herself to death about me. My father was as comforting and calm as he could be and kept his questions oblique. His voice did tremble sometimes when he spoke about it with me so I downplayed the findings with him; it was tough enough for Andrew to watch me leave daily for the radiation lab before going on to the university and tough enough for Olivia, studying overseas. I insisted she stay where she was—for my sake and for hers.

I have put on weight. The drugs can do that. I ask for the next size up. The Robertson's assistant—no longer wearing black and white or putting on a British accent as she would have when I was young—goes to see if they have a twelve.

I sit on the narrow little bench and wait, surveying the wreck of a body I have become: fatter around the middle; one breast smaller and higher. The surgeon took the lower half. If things had spread further, she would have had to take it off, she said. Half a breast is better than none. I can still wear a swimsuit, even if it is a size larger and I feel fat.

"You're middle-aged anyway," Livi, my best friend since we were both eleven, said on the phone. "We're all fatter."

We talk regularly: she, up north and I, down south. She and her new husband are back in the subtropics after years away, this time with screens and air-conditioning, neither of which we had when we were growing up. She has moved into the old family house with Dougal. Her many siblings, some long married, some divorced, also live in even greater comfort. Their parents' deaths left them each better off than they already were. Livi has stripped the walls, refinished and reupholstered everything, added a pool near the old creek where we used to swim, redesigned the bedrooms for the grandchildren she plans on having, added bathrooms. She and Dougal extended the balcony in the main bedroom where she and I once sat talking to her parents as they sat in bed, holding court with us over early morning tea. I loved staying with Livi for the weekend.

Her daughters went to our school, the school our mothers had attended. My daughter went to a sister school down south. The schools had an exchange scheme for a while. Olivia and Sarah, Livi's younger daughter, stayed in each other's houses. "Mum, you didn't tell me the house was as huge as *that*," Livi said when we picked her up at the airport.

"Yes I did."

"Not *that* big."

"Not as big as that," I said automatically, correcting her grammar just as my mother had corrected mine.

"Big as that. It's *huge!*" Olivia repeated, unfazed by my devotion to grammar.

"Here is twelve," says the assistant. She is slim, blonde, blue-eyed, pretty. Even beautiful. Were my mother still alive, we could discuss the adjective that most accurately describes her. Nan, ruled by beauty and things sartorial, would have thought the girl both beautiful and well dressed and so would have liked her automatically.

I smile at the mirror. My mother and Nan smile back. Small wonder I am here—my organized closet full of good clothes and elegant shoes, looking desperately for something new to wear to Government House. I did try to avoid this. I tried on several outfits I had already but they weren't right. I want to do my father proud when he is honored yet again for his civic work. I shall pick him up at the retirement complex two blocks from our house. He still will be handsome and smart, now in his eighties. I shall be passable in a new outfit, I hope.

I try on the size twelve. It is baggy in the arms. The size ten is tight around the middle. I have already rejected eight suits. Only this one comes close to seeming right. I see Livi's mother and my mother talking, each in navy and white linen and pearls, at one of our Junior School functions. So that's why I like this midnight blue suit. I can finally become, at least in my imagination, Livi's mother. My mother was beautiful but Livi's mother was beautiful *and* striking—at least according to my mother's objective eye. I am neither beautiful nor striking. My mother described me as "lovely" or "attractive" and my hair as "beautiful." I have my grandmother's and mother's need for proportion, color, cut in clothes. My hair has not yet turned white although a few white hairs are emerging near my diamond studs.

"Pierced ears are cheap and nasty," our mothers used to say when I was growing up. I didn't have mine pierced while she was alive.

Olivia arrived home with pierced ears during her summer vacation when she was fifteen. "I did it at the beginning of the holidays, Mum," she explained in her extra patient voice, "because I can take them out and be a perfect schoolgirl by the time I have to go back to boring uniforms and being Form Leader." She had not even told me she was getting it done. "I used Nan and Granddaddy's Christmas money. You and Dad didn't have to pay."

After so many miscarriages, I probably would have let Olivia pierce her ears when she was three if she'd wanted. However, my parents' conservatism and discipline prevailed, and Olivia was a naturally amenable child who seemed to cannily adjust her wishes to what she knew would be our limits. Perhaps she, as I had done, listened through the wall of her bedroom to Andrew and me. Sometimes Andrew and I argued but we always made peace before sleep. His parents loved each other and argued; my parents loved each other and argued. We wanted to love each other and argue if necessary but never let the sun go down upon our wrath. So, if Olivia did listen in, she wouldn't have fallen asleep wondering if we'd both be there when she awoke.

I look in the mirror again. Livi's mother isn't there. Mine is somewhat there. Nan is hovering in my slim nose and the beginning of a double chin. I do not have her perfect skin, unwrinkled and unblemished into her nineties. I tanned religiously. "Wear a hat and take an umbergingum. I always told you to be sure to do that when you and your mother went to the beach. But you had to do what the others did—and look now."

"You *were* right, Nan," I say, unaware I am speaking out loud.

"Sorry?" a voice says. I look in the mirror and glimpse the shoulder of my tall, beautiful assistant on the other side of the curtain.

"I was talking to myself," I say, hearing my mother's phrase come out of my mouth. "I like this suit ... the blue. The cut is lovely.... Do come in, if you want," I say, realizing I have once again floated off into drugland for a few minutes. Another year and I'll be off this drug. I don't know how I lecture—but I have notes, and teaching comes naturally to me as it did to my mother when she taught me grammar and music.

"Grandpapa was a good teacher too," my mother told me, "although he wasn't always patient. He spoke perfect English. Sometimes he would say something unusual. I remember when he was trying to help me with Mental Arithmetic, he'd often say, 'Yes yes yes!' impatiently. Always three times."

Tall Beauty wafts in. "This is big."

"The ten is too small and the twelve is too large in the arms, I'm afraid," I say.

"Alteration woman can fix."

The event with my father is three days away. I have tomorrow free of lectures and student hours. I could drive into town and pick it up if she could alter it quickly.

"Could the alterations woman alter it by tomorrow? I'd need to pick it up then, I'm afraid."

"I call." She smiles an ethereal smile and disappears. My mother would have been able to place her accent exactly. I'm guessing she is Russian.

While I wait, I sit and check my mobile. Four texts, three voicemails. By the time I am tapping out my first text reply, a tall, pale, slim woman arrives. She and Tall Beauty look like each other.

"No problem," she says easily, calmly. She pins the arms with slim, white, short-nailed fingers. "Ready tomorrow," she says. She sticks pins in her mouth and starts pinning until the suit takes a crisper shape. "Skirt also." She takes a wooden stick and pins the hem so it is parallel to the ground. I hadn't noticed it was longer in the back. The woman has a good eye. Like Nan. I am five again and standing while Nan pins.

"My grandmother was an excellent seamstress," I say. "You are like her. You even manage to make me look slim. Well, slimmer!"

The alterations woman smiles, finishes, and leaves. With help from Tall Beauty, I gingerly undo buttons and slip the jacket off, making sure I don't undo any pins. I hand it to her. I am aware of standing there in a lopsided bra with stuffing on the right, my plump middle, and my pinned up skirt. The skirt, except for the length, fits perfectly around the waist. I shall never wear a ten again.

"What time tomorrow?" I ask Tall Beauty as she takes my credit card.

"Ready by eleven," she answers pleasantly.

The next day, I have an appointment with my oncologist, who keeps me waiting, and then meet Andrew for a quick lunch.

"Darling, I *have* to go," I say apologetically. "I know I've only just arrived. A bite of your sandwich is really all I want anyway. I don't think they'll kick me out of the club if I share *one* bite."

"What's the hurry?" Andrew says, deftly cutting a triangle of his sandwich as cleanly as he would distill both sides of a mediation. He puts the triangle on one of the empty plates at our table. "I thought you didn't have lectures today."

"I don't. I have to pick up a new outfit for Dad's thing. Correction: I didn't *have* to get a new outfit. I looked in the closet and couldn't see anything thing I felt good in. It's a woman thing."

"I know. I thought you agonized through that yesterday at Robertson's."

"I did but I agonized myself into something needing alteration. They promised it by eleven. I'll feel guilty if I pick it up much later. It's already twelve-thirty."

"If I didn't think you'd sock me, I'd say you sound just like your mother. The guilt thing. You swore you'd never run around feeling guilty the way she did. There *are* times I wouldn't mind your feeling a *little* guiltier about things that have my self-interest at heart—like making your students wait a few days more for their papers or resting more as the oncologist ordered...."

"I'm *not*. Guilty like her, I mean. She felt guilty about everything, poor darling." I take a small bite. "I wish Nan hadn't waited until she was in her nineties to tell Mamma she wasn't adopted. I was talking with someone in the Psych department about adoption recently—in general, of course. She was saying adoptees often live in guilt and fear the way Mamma did. They're afraid if they do *anything* bad they'll be sent away." I take another small bite. To my surprise, it is beginning to taste quite good. I haven't been hungry since I started taking the drug.

"Of course, Nan didn't know Mamma thought she was adopted. Nan said she was afraid Mamma wouldn't love her if she knew she was born before they got married. Mamma thought Nan sent Grandpapa a photo of her as a toddler and it changed his mind...." I finished the triangle of sandwich. "Andrew, don't mention this to Dad. He'll know I broke my promise."

In a single conversation with Nan, which my mother uncharacteristically insisted on having the year before Nan died, Nan answered my mother's long held question: she told my mother she wasn't adopted. Nan even added, through rare tears, that Grandpapa paid for her lying-in. Until she married him two years later, Nan worked and my mother lived with Aunt Marion.

I privately thought the two-year gap had nothing to do with the photo. My grandfather probably just went north to establish his business and then brought them to live with him. The quiet marriage ensured that Nan and my mother were comfortably off for life. There were bits of the story that would always elude; when Nan had finally answered my mother's desperate question, she was crying, and my mother felt so guilty about upsetting Nan that she couldn't ask why they'd waited to marry.

"I hate to mention it," says Andrew, finishing a Perrier, "but this is not exactly the first time you've told me your grandmother's secret, sweetheart. Nor the second. I've not mentioned it and am not about to. I do have a *little* appreciation of confidentiality. I *am* in the legal field, remember? Mediator? How do you do, Meg, I'm your husband?" He smiles and pats my arm. "You know, nothing changes."

"I'm sorry. I'm repeating myself—again. It's the drug. And I know you're good at buttoning up. I'm sorry.... What do you mean: 'nothing changes'?"

"You've always put your parents, Olivia—me—even your students—ahead of yourself. Stop. You've had a near brush.... Now this bloody awful drug. Stop, Meg. I want you around. Of course, I'm not *always* sure why—after all, I'm the true Scot and you're only a quarter-Scot but you're more thran than *I* am sometimes. Anyway, I want you around—for a long time. Do at least *try* to be stubborn about the *right* things from now on. Starting with your health. End of lecture."

"All I *did* was ask you not to mention it to Dad and tell you I'm picking up a far too expensive suit. So I *am* putting myself first. Proof positive: could I please have another corner of your sandwich?"

"Finish it. Kay brought me biscuits for my morning tea. I ate them without even thinking. I was in the middle of research. I'm not hungry."

"I didn't think I was but now I am. Not very, but more than a corner."

After I leave Andrew, I walk the short distance to Robertson's third-floor designer section.

Tall Beauty sees me and smiles serenely. She says, "One moment," and disappears into the bowels of Robertson's.

I idly wander through the racks I scoured yesterday. I look at the clothes the way I do a term paper I already know will not make a passing grade. I can only hope the suit will look better altered. Nan would be proud of my expenditure; Mamma would wish she could look like me again and be shocked, comparing its cost with the elegant, expensive suits she wore in the thirties. I hope it is worth the effort and outrageous cost.

Tall Beauty arrives with the alterations woman. This surprises me. Normally, I would be given the suit on a hanger in a zipped bag at the counter and thanked cordially. "Changing room, please? Must see," says the woman with surprising authority. "We must be exact." The two of them really do look disconcertingly alike.

Feeling I need to please her—and being glad to assure myself I shall not look dowdy at Government House—I follow them meekly. They hand me the suit, pull the curtain, and wait outside.

I put it on and warily look in the mirror. The suit has been altered superbly, fits perfectly. The alterations woman has even made some kind of slight adjustment in the jacket that makes my lopsidedness less visible. She has altered it as well as Nan might have. I think about Nan's having worked with a dress designer until she and my mother joined my Grandpapa. After her marriage, my grandfather's work ensured she never had to sew again, but she still loved to sew for my mother and me, to paint, to color photographs. Until she couldn't see. Macular degeneration. Would I last long enough to worry about it? I decide not to mention this idle, black question to Andrew. Now I am through the worst, his fears leak at the edges. Yet again, I am glad my mother didn't have to worry about losing me as she had worried about losing Nan and Grandpapa.

"Come in if you like," I say to the curtain. The curtain opens and the two women stand there. Same height, same coloring, same accent.

"Good," the alterations woman declares after making me turn several times. "OK?" She looks questioningly at the younger woman who says, "I think it is good, too, Mamma."

"Mother and daughter?" I ask.

"Of course!" they laugh. "Funny accent! Same hair!"

"I thought you might be related. You don't have a funny accent. You have a pretty accent."

"Russian."

"My mother's father was Russian."

"Russian family here?"

"No. He came by himself. Before the Revolution. They all

stayed in touch but after the Second World War, there was only one letter. Then, nothing...." I am annoyed with myself. I am speaking like them. A childhood spent adjusting myself to align perfectly with my mother still bleeds into unexpected situations.

"Not good, that time, in Russia," says the alterations woman and launches into a sophisticated, mostly grammatical analysis of Russian politics.

"It is interesting to hear these things from you. Your family lived through it all. My grandfather left money for his missing family. But—."

"He made good decision to come."

"My grandmother was Australian. Her parents came from England. She kept my grandfather's photos, map, letters...all the Russian things. My mother kept them too. She let me look sometimes. Now I have them...."

"You like Robertson's? It has always been a very good place but ...I hope you don't think I'm rude but I'm sure you could get a good job."

"English needs to be better. I was physician. Cancer. I see: you had cancer. I cannot be doctor here. My daughter was architect. Now she studies fashion design. We read English better than talk."

"My daughter is an architect, too. She is studying overseas right now."

"We both have smart daughters!" the alterations woman laughs. Tall Beauty looks embarrassed. "The Russian things of your grandfather, they are old."

"Very."

"Your mother and you, you read them, yes?"

"My mother died. No, I don't know anything about any of the

material in Russian. I used to look at the photographs and the money orders with my mother and I know the names of his family. My grandfather didn't teach my mother Russian or the other languages he spoke. During that period in Australia, one was expected to speak English."

"Sad. Now many language radio stations here! You want to know more?"

I thought of the small box of documents, photos, letters. "Yes. But I don't know anyone in the Russian Department at the university where I teach."

"We can help. You want?"

"That would be wonderful! But—please don't be insulted—I must insist on paying you for your help. You are a professional. So is your daughter. You only work at Robertson's because you are a new immigrant—like my grandfather."

"You are different from other Australians. Because of grandfather?" She laughs again.

"I'm almost all English. Some Russian, Scot, and a bit of —."

"Does not matter why. Most people here see us as 'Immigrant.' You see *us*."

Emma and her daughter come to the house the following day. They each have the day off from Robertson's.

I have dug out the Russian files from the garage. My mother put them in one of the fifteen crates she packed when she closed down Nan's house years ago. Later, when she and my father moved to the townhouse in the retirement village, she slowly unpacked each of the crates because there was no longer room for crates in the attached garage. She organized everything. She needed order and liked categories for everything from shoes to books to family history—family about whom she wanted to know but whom she did not wish, particularly, to meet—any more than she sought out anyone. She preferred people at one remove.

She precisely reorganized all the Russian materials Nan had chaotically and lovingly kept after Grandpapa died suddenly. My mother put them neatly into folders, each labeled in her precise writing: *Documents-Russian*; *Documents-English* (my mother's birth certificate, my grandparents' marriage, my grandfather's citizenship, his volunteer work for Australia in both world wars); *Receipts-Money Russia* (sent by my grandfather to his family for decades); *Letters from Russia*; *Exercise book-Russian*; *Diaries (2)-1938* (my grandfather's diaries, written in English describing the family's trip around the world; he was denied entry to Russia); *Letters-English* (an early love letter to Nan when they first met two years before my mother was born; daily letters to Nan thirty years later when he was away on business); *Photographs-Russian*; and *Travel Documents* (including a map of my grandfather's working route to the Black Sea, his ticket to Australia, and his passport from 1938).

She put the piece of mosaic from Samarkand, where Grandpapa had worked to restore a temple en route, in a separate box. While the tiny box of drawers I had loved to open as a child and in which Nan had kept the mosaic and other things—a sea horse skeleton and a fragment of one of my mother's dance costumes—had long gone, its contents were wrapped and in a neat box. My mother, like Nan before her, could throw nothing away; Nan had lost both her mother and her husband too early.

For different reasons, my mother, too, held on to all she could. To throw a thing away or to lend it, even to me, was agonizing for her; she felt as though she were being told to throw away a person—except she cared more about things than people, really.

Nan once said to my mother, long after my grandfather had

died, "There are only two people in the world I love: you and Meg." My mother would have said, "There are only three people I love in the world: you, Michael, and Olivia."

My mother was meticulous in organizing the records. Organizing them was enough for her. To get them translated would have required her to contact someone she didn't know and run the risk of their liking her and wanting to be around her. She was naturally likable, which exhausted her. While she was unfailingly polite, she was content to encounter most people, including Olivia and me, in the abstract. She preferred them on black-and-white film, stage, radio, then colored films, television, video, and DVD. Of course, this made her a good critic all those years, made her articles universally respected, enjoyed: she noticed and noted the subtlest flaws, the subtlest, exquisite touches. She preferred art to life, order to spontaneity. She couldn't bear imperfection in herself or others. After talking with that woman in the Psych Department, I can guess now where my mother's perfectionism began: all those years she thought she was adopted and could be sent away if she was discovered making a mistake. And her fear that she was adopted must have come from Nan's having to put her in Aunt Marion's care until Nan and Mamma joined Grandpapa up north. Poor Nan and her love child. Nan's Great Secret eventually became my mother's.

My father, if forced to choose—which he prefers not to and has to less and less—prefers life, family, and civic activity to the arts. I think it's from his being away at war so long. He is both spontaneous and orderly. I think the war must have taught him those things, too.

I am an odd mix of both. I alternate between my need to lose myself in silence and make a mess when I paint and my need to put my oil paints in order according to color. I move between loving my classes, students, friends, and family, and being desperate for time alone. I did take time alone occasionally when I was having the cancer treatment. All I wanted was to walk on the beach. By myself. Even Andrew was too much, too solicitous at times. I was relieved—for my sake as well as hers—that Olivia was overseas.

I can imagine my mother being horrified that I am inviting Russian strangers to afternoon tea—well, not afternoon tea as my grandmothers or mother would think of afternoon tea, with cloths and napkins and dainty trays of scones and biscuits. I prefer to sit on our low, minimalist chairs on the glass-enclosed verandah overlooking the water and pour good coffee into thin, hand-painted mugs Andrew and I picked up in the south of France years ago. Occasionally, if I have my father for afternoon tea with one of his many friends or invite an older relative for afternoon tea, I break out the delicate china, the tea cloths. It pleases my father to know my mother's and his china is used. I like to have him for dinner frequently but he often is already committed. People seek him out.

Emma and Anna arrive promptly. They are dressed casually, elegantly.

I have the files laid out on the long dining table. We sit on the verandah and smile and talk over coffee. They want nothing to eat. After coffee, they are keen to move to the dining table. Clearly, they have accepted coffee to be polite. They waste no time in getting to work; their original professional selves are showing.

They efficiently review the materials, first setting aside everything written in English—my grandfather's 1938 travel diaries written in his fine hand and elegant English; lists, in my grandmother's artistic handwriting, of clothing sent to Russia to different members of the family; my grandfather's early and late letters to my grandmother; some business records; his will; years of letters from the '50s documenting Nan's fruitless search through her solicitor and the Red Cross to find Grandpapa's surviving family so she could give them their share of his estate. I am glad, now, that my mother organized things as well as she did.

Mother and daughter look at each photograph, turn each over, translate what is on the back. Names fly by: some known, some unknown. They transliterate names from Cyrillic script into English for me. I add new files to my mother's:

Nephews
Nieces
Siblings
Other Relatives
Friends
Unknowns

Into "Unknowns" I put studio photographs given to my grandfather by friends and companions during his time in the Czar's Army and, to judge from the ages of those in the photographs, friends he made en route before he left for Australia. Some have names and inscriptions on the back. Some do not. When a photograph has a name on the back, I put a yellow Post-It and write the English transliteration of the name. I add a second with any translated inscription Anna or Emma briefly give.

On my laptop, I begin a file of names by category. Just as my mother would have. I silently apologize to her for having railed against her need to possess time, things, and events with endless lists.

Mother and daughter move on to the written materials and roughly translate them for me, offer to do so in more detail if I wish at a later date. Single pages from letters. Letters censored with large pieces cut out. Later, I can cross-reference the few letters received and the records of the many money orders sent with my list of names.

My grandfather's family speaks to me across decades.

Then, in a single year, everything stops. It is the same year that my grandfather's support to his family stops.

"Not allowed," Anna comments. "Dangerous."

Anna and Emma's exchange is a mixture of Russian and English. English for my sake. They refuse more coffee. They are deep in concentration and, I begin to realize, captured by a past shaping itself before their eyes, a past they understand from having grown up in the country in which this past evolved.

"Here is diary of your grandfather. Begins 1912 ...." She skims the pages and looks at the end. "Last is 1923."

The ink has faded and the pages are yellowing. The writing, too, is small, and geometric drawings and bookkeeping notations pepper the pages.

"This says Samarkand. He is working. He says he meets a girl. Larisa. They walk in evenings. He does not know what to say.... He writes he goes to family of Larisa to eat dinner one night a week."

I've always thought my grandfather, a handsome man, must have had romances before he finally invited my grandmother to marry him. I have even wondered, at times, if I have informal relatives about whom possibly even my grandfather, moving determinedly onward to buy a ticket to sail to Australia and then to establish himself, never knew. Even when he reached Australia, years passed between his arriving and his courting of my grandmother, and more years passed while they courted, moved north with their child, and finally married.

More pages turn. "He arrives Odessa. Learns English." Anna looks up at me and says with an admiring smile, "Smart. He learns before he leaves." She returns to the diary. "He is working. ... Makes money....Watches ships.... Writes every ruble he earns and spends." She begins to turn the pages more slowly; in the next section, there is more writing and fewer lists and numbers. "He writes *every* ruble! What he eats.... He likes good food but only allows once a week! ... Someone does not pay him for work...."

She rises, stretches her back, and says, "Very charming, this diary. I cannot believe that your family keeps these things such long time." Anna sits down again. She looks tired.

Emma takes the diary and reads in silence for a while. Then she shows her mother and says to me, "Now he is in Australia.... He has work." Silence. "He says no letters from home for long time. No letters from Larisa. He writes often but no reply." She looks at her mother. Anna explains, "Bad time in Russia. War. And Revolution. Bad years after he leaves." Emma goes back to her reading. She passes over pages of lists and then stops at a series of brief entries from later years. "He is getting letters again.... His brother says Larisa has divorce from him." Anna leans forward to look. Emma moves the diary towards her mother and shows her the entry. Anna raises her eyebrows and comments, "Not easy to divorce. Maybe Larisa Jewish. Easier to divorce than Christian."

"My grandfather was *married? Before?*"

"He says brother writes him and says Larisa got no letters for long, long time and no ticket, so divorce. Your grandfather says he sent letters—and ticket—but no letters from her in Australia. Bad time in Russia." She turns the thin pages carefully. "He talks about his business.... Here is practice letter to your grandmother in Russian."

"A draft?" I ask.

"Draft. His Russian much better than mine!"

She turns more pages. The years change. "He writes names of plays he sees and concerts, lists money he sends to brother and family.... This date—entry?"

"Yes. Entry."

"He says on this date he was made Australian citizen.... And this...entry...he says he now has also Australian divorce."

I open the files written in English and compare dates. The date on this entry is a month before my grandparents quietly married when my mother was nearly two.

Anna laughs and says, "I think handsome grandfather has secret from pretty grandmother. Or both grandmother and grandfather know secret but do not tell your mother."

It is dark. We are all exhausted. Anna and Emma offer to return to translate the rest. I accept. They leave. I can hardly wait to tell Andrew, who will be home soon. Olivia will Skype tomorrow.

I wear the suit Anna has altered to the Government House affair with my father. He stands erect as the award is given, walks as crisply as he has walked all his life, another habit of his war years. My midnight blue suit is perfect. I wear my contact lenses. I don't like wearing them much any longer so I only use them for special occasions.

The Governor mingles afterward and greets my father as she has many times before. She greets me cordially as his daughter, not commenting on but smiling at the fact that she and I are wearing the same suit—in different colors.

FORTY-THREE

....

OTTER

I must have been around nine because we were already in the new house. The boxes, which had made a cardboard skyscraper-city of the living room and streets of the polished wood floors had been replaced by pale carpet and gracious furniture made to my parents' specification by the successors to Mehler, who had made my grandparents' furniture. The wicker sides of the armchairs were newly stained and the woven material covering backs and seats was subtly hued. Over the decades that followed, it would slowly, gently fade from the light that flowed across the living room every morning.

We tried closing the blinds and curtains daily when we first moved in but the dimness felt depressing and reminded my mother of my grandparents' houses in mid-summer. The French doors and windows in our living and dining rooms were framed by slim, heavy silk curtains—with small, golden *fleurs-de-lis* woven into the beige silk. No dust had yet gathered on the pleats at the top. The wallpaper was a clean cream with a slight slub. My pale-blue room was the only different-colored room in the house.

After we had moved in and just after the cardboard city disappeared, a date was set for my mother to have surgery. My father walked around looking sad. My mother walked around looking worried. She told me she would be in the hospital for two weeks—and that they had to take out the part where mothers grow babies.

Three weeks before she went into the hospital, she bought me five new cotton dresses to wear to school while she was gone. She washed them, hung them to dry on the Hills Hoist (skillfully avoiding getting caught in an endless conversation with a neighbor), ironed them carefully on the soft ironing blanket and sheet she used on the laminate kitchen table, and hung the dresses on hangers from her wardrobe. Two of the hangers were covered with gathered pink satin (won at the church bazaar); two were crocheted in pea green and yellow yarn (bought reluctantly at the school bazaar); and one was of lacquered wood. I liked it best. It had my Russian grandfather's initials written on it by my grandmother. He had been dead four years now.

The ironed dresses that hung on my wardrobe doors marked the days my mother would to be absent from me. I felt sick looking at them. It was the same feeling I had the day I helped my father clip the grass bordering the garden. As I'd worked on my knees, I clipped something thick and doughy. When I pulled back the tall blades, I saw that I'd cut a grasshopper in half. Its innards were still in place but starting to ooze. I had killed something. A grasshopper. I remember the odd smell. When I occasionally smell something similar, it still wakens in me shame and guilt greater than any I later felt about the pain I would cause my parents by my childhood sins or any I would later cause them by being unable to avoid being me, no matter how hard I tried to pretend I wasn't.

When the day arrived, my mother went into the hospital. Each day she was gone, I would put on one of the outfits she had prepared for me and go to school. She had pinned notes onto each in rounded, blue-ink capitals: Week One, Day 1; Week Two…. Wearing them in order made me feel loyal to her and helped me believe she would be safe as long as I was good.

She had her surgery in a Catholic hospital. Nurses who were nuns ran up and down the wide corridors with large, purposeful smiles. At the entrance to Surgical Wards 2A-4C was a blue and pink statue of a crying Madonna with red eyes. A black wooden Jesus hung on a cross over the door that opened into my mother's corner room. I thought it impressive: in my Protestant church, we didn't have Jesus on our crosses because, I'd been told, He had Risen; besides which, any display of suffering was in bad taste. The Catholics might have had naked Jesuses and crying Madonnas but they also had the best surgical ward in town, so that was where my mother went.

On the first day my father took me to visit her, my mother was wearing an ice-pink, padded satin dressing gown. It had been a gift from Nan. I took my mother the only flowers I could find in our garden—geraniums. I carried them in an empty honey bottle. My mother asked me to please put water in the bottle and to place them in the center of her window, which overlooked the intersection of two main streets.

Some man bellowed in the room across the corridor.

"That's Mr. Levin," my mother whispered. "He's been giving them what-for, especially at night." She dropped her voice further. "He swears at the nurses every time he has to 'go' because they won't give him more pain pills. They keep Godblessing him and he keeps yelling at them not to Godbloodybless him. I think they quite like it.

"He and I talked when we were taking our constitutionals like good children. He recognized my name from the paper and even said he watches for my pieces."

A week later my mother came home. Dr. Ruben told her she could stay up for a few hours and then was to lie down for a few hours. She was to do this for another few weeks.

A few days after my mother arrived home from the hospital, Mrs. Templeton, who lived at the bottom of the street, gave birth to twins. The news prompted me to ask my mother, as I was sitting with her at the kitchen table, how come I was an Only Child. I hadn't wondered why I was an Only until then. However, people were always saying, "Oh, an *Only*," with a sympathetic smile whenever I answered their question about how many brothers or sisters I had. I felt somehow to blame. "Onlies" like me were spoiled, I often heard, so I tried to carelessly drop in examples of how unspoiled I was, such as how I had to dry the dishes *every* night.

After I asked my question about being an "Only," my mother lit a Craven A and looked at the gold watch Nan and Grandpapa had given her for her twenty-first. It was just after four o'clock. My father wouldn't be home for an hour at least.

"Didn't you want more after me?" I asked.

"Daddy did. He'd had years of war and wanted to catch up on—*life*, I suppose, looking back on it. He would have loved a large family." She took a puff on her Craven A, neatly placed the ash in the covered ashtray, and rearranged the German novels beside her so that the edges lined up neatly. "I was content at first with just him, really. We'd been married near the beginning of the war, so we hardly saw each other for years. When he finally came home and I'd *had* him to myself for a couple of years, I thought it'd be time enough for a baby. You were definitely wanted—planned. When I was expecting you, we used to drive along and look at the space between us and imagine what it would be like when you arrived. We called you 'Little One.' "

"What if I'd been a boy?"

"You would have been Michael after Daddy."

The phone rang. It was Nan. She couldn't find the sewing things she had loaned my mother and which my mother promised her she had returned before going into the hospital. After telling her exactly where she had put them, my mother came back to the table. I had helped myself to two Monte Carlos.

"You'll spoil your dinner," she commented with little conviction.

"I promise I won't," I said, wanting to keep her on tack. "I was planned. I wasn't Michael."

"Then—I couldn't decide whether I wanted another. The first time—had been painful and the nurses were unkind. One horror got cross and ordered me to stop ringing the bell—I was cold and she yelled at the woman in the next bed who was screaming. She later said loudly, so all the women having babies could hear, that all the Italian and Greek women screamed, so I gathered one was supposed be quiet.

"At the end, the doctor finally put me to sleep. Remember when you had your tonsils out and they put you to sleep? When I woke up, I was in my room. Daddy was there. We wanted to see you but didn't know whether we were allowed. Finally, Daddy found a nurse and asked what the rules were. She took pity on us and brought you in even though she wasn't supposed to. You were tightly wrapped and crying. I wanted to *see* you! I didn't know if I was allowed but I undid everything and *looked* at you.

You were a solid little thing! We were very happy you were here—but I wasn't keen on repeating the hospital part too quickly.

"Daddy wanted another soon. I was happy with you. When you were three, Daddy suggested I talk to Dr. Ruben about ... things. I did and he promised they could make it easier now. So we decided to have another and soon I was expecting again. One day we had to drive Granddad somewhere. He was just out of the hospital. I did 'The Right Thing.' I picked you up and put you in the car myself. Soon after, I lost the baby."

We were silent at the kitchen table. On the government radio station, Beethoven was playing. The station tuning was slightly off and the bass was crackling. My mother got up, wincing, and adjusted the little white vertical needle that slid across the numbers. The violins stopped shrieking but still didn't sound happy.

"I thought Daddy would be upset if I didn't *offer* to pick you up. I assumed he'd say 'no' and do it. But he was putting something in the boot and didn't see me. Dr. Ruben thought my picking you up wouldn't have made a difference because I lifted you every day. But I wasn't used to putting you in the car. Daddy always did that. All I know is I lost the baby."

"How do you *lose* a baby?"

"It was like a bad tummy ache."

I thought about tummy aches. I didn't like them.

"I didn't want to try again for a long time after that. When I did offer, Daddy was worried I'd change my mind and he didn't want to be disappointed. I did *offer,* so it's not my fault. That's why he still gets sad sometimes, especially when he hears about people like Mrs. Templeton or his cousin's wife. I'm sure he thinks I was selfish. Daddy sees those women as *Giving*—especially his cousin's wife. She's had three and a fourth due any day. However, if one sees it objectively, even she had to go for 'a rest' at one point. That's private, Meg. It's not unusual, though. Quite a few women are sent for 'a rest.' I suppose one would say they've had a nervous breakdown."

"What's 'a nerve us break down'? "

"How did we get on to this? It means a woman might not be able to make decisions or she might cry a lot, be unable to cope. Even *her* doctor said she needed a rest. So having two in two years can't have been *all* beer and skittles. Anyway, because she's given her husband more children, I feel guilty. But I did offer that one last time. It was Daddy who said 'no' so it's not my fault." My mother valued fairness above all.

"You're never selfish, Mamma—and how could it have been your fault? Anyway, I don't miss having a brother or sister. I like being an Only." I hoped I had found the right words.

She brightened. "Don't tell Daddy about this. I don't know how we got on to it in the first place. I feel guilty having told you and it would upset him. Then he'd be upset with me. Talking about it makes me feel funny in the tummy. I think it might help if I just revise a paragraph and practice some scales before I fix dinner. Mrs. Johansen is out. She won't hear and Nan's rung already."

Nan was lonely a lot, ever since Grandpapa had died. My mother talked to her twice a day and we saw her at least twice a week. Women in our town didn't have many friends; they had family. Besides, Nan wasn't keen on people as a whole except for her sisters and brothers and us. Her brothers and sisters were down south.

Nan and her siblings were close. Even though she lived up north and they, down south, they'd lost their mother early and got close, I think. Nan's oldest sister, Marion, had helped Nan's father raise the younger ones. Then Aunt Marion had married a nice Englishman and they'd had a baby. She was happy but the nice Englishman in the sepia photograph on Nan's dressing table—with dark eyes and moustache and thin hand resting on Aunt Marion's taffeta shoulder as she held their firstborn—had had an accident. His back was broken. He died so Aunt Marion raised the baby—Cousin Louisa—alone.

Nan spent several weeks every year with Aunt Marion. Occasionally in winter, Nan would treat Aunt Marion to a visit north. Every summer, Nan would fly south for several weeks with two large, slate blue leather suitcases. She usually wore a silk, hand-tailored suit, gloves, and a hat for the two flights. My parents and I would take her to the airport and, standing by other families waving at people, we would wave at the plane, hoping the gloved hand we could see moving slowly against a little window was hers. Aunt Marion wasn't rich and Nan could have stayed anywhere but Aunt Marion, whose daughter and son-in-law and two grandchildren all lived with her, liked Nan to stay with her. Nan liked to stay with Aunt Marion, too. I don't know what they did all day apart from drink tea but they were close. They didn't talk much, not the way Nan and my mother or my mother and I did, but they were close. They had shared so much, I think, they didn't need to talk.

My mother put away her papers, put the cover on the typewriter, and went to the living room to practice. The piano had been tried in various places in our sitting room and was currently residing on the long wall near the loveseat. I followed her, in my striped blouse and cotton shorts, my legs sprouting hair, and sprawled on the couch. It ran the length of the wall until it met an elegant, wooden cupboard where my mother kept her sheet music. The spine of each book of music had been deliberately cracked by my mother so she could turn the pages quickly; the sheets were well-thumbed and lower corners, often folded. Mr. Levin's packet sat on top.

My mother had tracked down some Dornford Yates novels for herself and *Wind in the Willows* for me at the library. She had read *Wind in the Willows* as an adult and remembered loving it. So I considered it couldn't be too childish for me to read.

I was in the middle of the section on Mr. Toad's iniquities when the phone rang. My mother said "Bugger" and went to answer it.

It was my father. His cousin had telephoned from work to say that the hospital had just phoned him and his fourth child, a boy, had arrived.

My mother came back into the sitting room and sat down at the piano to start on the minor scales. Then she stopped and sighed.

"What?" I asked, looking at her through my toes, which were on the arm of the couch.

"Nothing."

"What?"

"Daddy will be sad tonight now." She sighed another time and went back to playing scales.

It was raining. Again. It was one of the rainiest seasons on record. I was glad to have a good book. I took another sip of soft drink and picked up my third Monte Carlo. My mother pulled out Mr. Levin's music. I carefully separated the top part of my biscuit, with its jam and coconut taste, from the bottom so that the red and white filling that had joined them in holy matrimony was exposed. You could slice it open but that was cheating. It was hard to separate a Monte Carlo without breaking it. It depended, really, on how old and soggy it was.

I had wickedly turned the corner on the last page I had read in *Wind in the Willows*, so I found my place easily. Funny: you were supposed to turn the corners on music but not on books. I started reading as my mother finished the scales. Nan hadn't given her the baby grand yet; she still had the upright with its inlaid, blonde-wood flowers where your legs went. Sometimes I would sit under the piano and listen to the strings being struck. They would vibrate through my body. Sometimes I even took off the front panel beneath the keyboard. I would pluck the strings with my short fingers and chewed nails. The deeper the note, the thicker the string—and the harder to pluck.

I looked outside. Mrs. Johansen was walking against the rain across to the grocery shop. Mrs. Johansen had caught my mother as she was bringing in the washing in the trolley and talked for an hour—an hour my mother had carefully allocated to finishing an article due for a magazine. She had told my mother that she had bad headaches—"hedducks." "Meegrims," she sometimes called them. When they made her ill, she went to bed. Their daughter, Sharon, was younger and there was a rumor that she was adopted. I wasn't interested in whether she was adopted although sometimes I would look at women and wonder if they were Sharon's secret mother. I just thought Sharon was worthy of pity because she was younger. So sometimes I invited her into my cubby to play: I was often short on after-school playmates because we lived far from the local school, which I was to attend for one more year before going to my mother's old girls' school. Sharon had a decent set of paper dolls so we would swap. We also had a Secret Society, whose password and name I have forgotten.

My mother thought Mrs. Johansen got "hedducks" because she was worried that someone might believe the rumor and ask Sharon whether she was adopted. My mother told me that when she, herself, was young, she used to be secretly worried that she was adopted.

Mrs. Johansen came back holding a white parcel. She must have been to the butcher, not the corner grocery store. The rain stopped pounding and settled into a light mist, and a rainbow appeared over the park. My mother opened up the first of Mr. Levin's sheet music and began playing a Ravel piano concerto.

I continued reading Chapter Six of my book while eating Monte Carlos. My mother returned to the beginning of the piece. She couldn't play easily today. She began to break down the piece, playing first the left hand and then the right.

"I'm out of practice," she complained. It only took a couple of days for her to feel out of practice.

"It's new. Try something easier," I said, with a mouthful.

She opened up another of the pieces Mr. Levin had sent. I set the book down, got up, walked over, and looked over her shoulder. Its title was French: "Pavane pour une Infante Défunte." My mother knew that pavane was a slow dance and that infante was a princess. Neither my mother, passable in French, nor I, not yet in love with it, knew what *défunte* meant, so we looked it up later in a tiny French dictionary my mother had kept from when Nan and Grandpapa had taken her around the world. The pavane looked easier than the concerto so she started in on it.

I finished Chapter Six, in which Mr. Toad is sent with dispatch to a dungeon, a gaol, with threats of a murrain if anyone lets him out. I didn't know the word murrain but was not about to interrupt my mother, so I moved on to Chapter Seven, "The Piper at the Gates." In it, Otter's son, Portly, goes missing. Portly is an adventurous type, but this time he's gone too long. Otter goes every night to the weir where he'd taught Portly to swim, and watches. Otter is lonely and "heart-sore" (a word I committed to memory for when I would need it), and "crouched by the ford, watching and waiting, the long night through—'on the chance, you know, on the chance.'" Rat is all for going to sleep, but Mole just can't go to sleep "and do nothing, even though there doesn't seem to be anything to be done."

I took another Monte Carlo and grabbed Chang who was licking up crumbs from the floor and brushing his long tail against the low table legs. My mother was working out phrasing for the pavane bar by bar, marking things in pencil on the music. If I wrote in the book I was reading, I'd get into trouble but people were expected to write on music. I supposed it was because mine was a library book but then again I wasn't supposed to write on my own books unless they were schoolbooks. It wasn't fair.

And so Rat and Mole take off in the boat at night to look for Portly.

I turned on the light; it was getting dark. The rain was down to a light mist. The birds in the bird sanctuary across the road were tuning up for dusk. The music seemed to fit with the book and the weather. Everything was perfect, except for Chang's incessant licking of Monte Carlo jam off his paw.

Rat hears something "so beautiful and strange and new! Since it was to end so soon, I almost wish I had never heard it. For it has roused a longing in me that is pain, and nothing seems worthwhile but just to hear that sound once more and go on listening to it for ever.... Such music I never dreamed of and the call in it is stronger even than the music is sweet. Row on, Mole, row!

For the music and the call must be for us."

The phone rang. My mother banged a discordant set of notes. The phone had to be answered—it might be Nan or Gran or Granddad or someone on one of my father's committees—but I didn't want my mother to stop playing. So I licked the jam off my fingers, shoved Chang to one side, and scrambled off the couch to answer it.

I returned in five minutes. "It was Gran to tell us about the new baby. I said you were lying down. I know you'll feel guilty for not talking, so lie down for five minutes and have a little hedduck so you can tell the truth when Daddy gets home."

"What if someone heard my playing and tells Daddy?"

"Lie down or you will have a headache!"

She walked quickly into their bedroom; they were still sharing a room then. She lay down on her bed, which was the one closer to the window. The hills were rose-gold and mauve from the last light after the storm. A pile of library books was on her side table. She picked up the Remarque novel she was reading and opened it to the last chapter. "I have to finish this anyway. It's due at the library tomorrow."

I ran back to the sitting room, pushed in the piano stool, and turned off her music light. All evidence concealed, I sat down again. Chang hopped up beside me.

Rat seemed to be having an experience that Mole wasn't having. He was "possessed in all his senses by this new divine thing that caught up his helpful soul and swung and dandled it, a powerless but happy infant in a strong sustaining grasp." I had just got to the point where Rat notices that Mole is hearing it, too, when the phone rang again.

"Hello, duckie. How's school?"

"It's alright, thank you, Nan."

"That's good. Is your mother there?"

"She's—. She got a bit wet in the rain bringing washing in so she's having a shower so she won't get a cold."

I was impressed by my quick lie but slightly deflated by the speed with which I had disposed of my grandmother. I wanted to be the heroine who saved my mother. Instead, the speed made it more of a non-event. I went in and told my mother the coast was clear but that now she had to remember that she was lying down for Daddy but having a shower for Nan. "It's better not to tell complicated lies, darling. They're too hard to remember," my mother said. She was on the last page of her book.

"Come in and play again. I'm in the middle of a chapter."

I got her up and to the piano again by gently making her feel guilty because I had lied on the phone. When she started playing again, I went back to where Mole was breathless and transfixed and where, "but for the heavenly music, all was marvellously still."

This was better than Sunday School. No one seemed excited when they sang hymns about the Light and The Way and Heaven when we sang at Sunday School or even when I went to church with my father or grandmother. All my favorite hymns were sung too slowly, too soberly. The water was drained out of their plump words. They were dry by the time they reached my mouth. No one behaved as though things happened to people. People who showed that things actually hurt—like Mr. Levin or the Italian and Greek women having the babies or naked Jesus nailed up there above my mother's hospital room—were treated as suspect.

I read on. The island was there, "reserved, shy, but full of significance, it hid whatever it might hold behind a veil, keeping it till the hour should come and, with the hour, those who were called and chosen."

I wanted to be Called and Chosen. I read and reread what happened to Mole and Rat and I read how Mole "might not refuse, were Death himself waiting to strike him instantly, once he had looked with mortal eye on things rightly kept hidden." But he did look and he looked in the "very eyes of the Friend and Helper."

My mother stopped playing the Ravel and moved on to an old practice piece, "Waltz in C Sharp Minor." She believed that playing it brought my father home. She was convinced that if she started to play really well, someone or something always intervened.

Chang scratched at the front door to be let out. Grumpily, I rose again and opened the door. He walked out onto the grass, green and glistening with rain. The moon had moved from behind a black cloud. The town lights below us were clear in the early evening.

"Come on Chang!" I called. I wanted to get back to the book. Waiting until Chang lifted his leg was not sustaining my mood. He finally lifted a furry, short, dignified leg against a geranium and waddled back in, the fur on his stomach dripping.

"Bugger," I whispered to myself. I got an old towel and dried him off. He wanted to play Catch the Towel but I was in no mood. I needed to find out more about the Presence and what had happened to Portly, the little otter who seemed to have been forgotten in all the majesty of the encounter with the demi-god.

I read the next few paragraphs several times. Slowly it became clear that the "little round, podgy, childish form of the baby otter" was not just "nestling between Pan's very hooves, sleeping soundly in entire peace and contentment." The little otter was dead. I couldn't believe it! He was safe in the arms of Pan on the special island. But he was dead alright. Otter was waiting at the weir. But he would never see his son again. I couldn't bear it. The tears poured down my face as my mother played.

I'd just reached page 156, the bit that read, "As they stared blankly, in dumb misery deepening as they slowly realised all they had seen and all they had lost, a capricious little breeze, dancing up from the surface of the water, tossed the aspens, shook the dewy roses, and blew lightly and caressingly in their faces," when my mother said, "Darling, we have to stop now. Daddy's due home—overdue."

"Just one more page ...." I kept my face turned from her so she wouldn't see my tears.

"You always say, 'Just one more page.' ... Are you crying, sweetheart?"

"Only a little bit."

"Oh darling. I'm sure it will turn out alright."

"You don't remember?"

"I thought it did. I remember it was well written. I just thought you might enjoy it because it's to do with animals. I'm sorry you've reached a sad bit, sweetheart, but it will be alright, I'm sure. I don't remember its ending sadly.

"You know I always let you have one more page but not now. You need to have a bath quickly and put your pajamas on. Daddy will be here soon. He'll be tired and surprised if you aren't ready for bed. Here, let me give you a hug."

She hugged me and handed me her clean, ironed handkerchief, which was a big deal. She worried about germs and never shared her handkerchiefs or her hairbrush with me in case I "had something."

She put a piece of paper that had been sitting on top of the music file into the book where I had stopped reading and picked up the book, my empty glass, and the Monte Carlo plate, now impeccable thanks to Chang. She meant business this time and it never occurred to me to oppose her, only to nag.

I cried in the bath—while the water was running, of course. I imagined how the little otter, dead and now "sleeping" in the arms of Pan, would never feel water around him again. And Otter would watch forever on the banks. I couldn't wait to get back to the book after the light was turned out. I was prepared to read secretly with the little flashlight Nan had brought back from down south for me.

My father arrived home in the middle of my bath. I heard him on the phone, first to Gran and Granddad and then to another cousin who was taking care of the three older children while the father went to the hospital to see his wife and fourth baby.

When I emerged from the bath, fresh, with my glasses clean and pajamas on, my father was reading the mail in the dining room. He had his circles under his eyes. My mother and I exchanged glances as I was setting the table. I took care to be especially bright at dinner as I recounted an eventless day at school in an attempt to make enough noise to sound like more than one child.

I was dawdling over cleaning my teeth when my father called out, "Don't forget to help Mamma with the dishes, Meg. If you had brothers and sisters, you'd be doing that." For the umpteenth time, I stopped myself from pointing out that if I had brothers and sisters, I wouldn't be doing the dishes every night. Instead, I said cheerily, "I was just coming, Dad."

After I finished drying the dishes, I hugged my father good night. My mother waited while I got into bed. I whispered my thanks to her for her telling me her secret and I asked her to please play the piano because I loved going to sleep hearing it, which I did. Then, more loudly, I said the rote prayer my mother and I knew pleased my father: "GodblessMammagod (breath) blessdaddy (breath) godblessNanandGranand (breath) Granddadandbig (breath) Changand (breath) littleChang and (breath) allthepeopleIloveamen."

I silently added to my list the little otter and his father waiting on the weir as I wriggled down beneath the covers. My mother kissed my cheek and left the room with the door half open. The light from the hall walls with their cream wallpaper cut a long, clean, gold line across my deep blue carpet, turning half of it twilight color and the other half, midnight blue.

My parents went into the sitting room and started to talk in low voices. My father was talking with spaces. This told me he was sad. My mother was talking in a tone that told me she felt "picked on" or guilty. After some silence, my mother started to play the new music again, the thing with the dance and death name, but which I now thought of as the little otter music.

I lay looking up at the mosquito net, which flowed like a light, cirrus cloud above me. I decided that praying for little otter wasn't enough. He was already dead in the arms of Pan and would never wake up. I wanted to do something. I would become a veterinarian. My parents had taken me to the veterinarian when we had first got Chang. There were several animals in the office, some in cages. More interesting than our doctor's office. If I became a vet, I could save animals from murrains (a word which by then I'd looked up in the big dictionary in the hall).

I slipped my flashlight quietly from its mooring between my mattress and the wire mesh supporting it and opened the book to where my mother had placed the piece of paper.

I looked at the bottom of the left-hand page of the book and the words were as I remembered: "blew lightly and caressingly in their faces;". There must have been a printing mistake because the sentence finished with a semicolon. We had been doing punctuation and parsing so I was up on these things.

Then my eye fell on the top of the right-hand page. My tears had made spots on the poor-quality paper. When I tried to smooth out the bumps, I noticed: the left-hand page, with the wrong punctuation, was numbered 156; the right-hand page was numbered 165—and was all about a girl pitying Toad's plight. There was a whole bit missing! It wasn't fair! I looked through every page of the rest of the book. There were two other leaves missing later on as well. Either the glue had caved in to the subtropical humidity or someone had torn out the pages. I raced through the rest of the book. There was no mention of little otter or Pan or the island again. There were only two mentions of big Otter but he was clearly being brave and not thinking about what he had Lost because he was going on as though nothing had happened.

I put the book down. My little flashlight was flickering in a way that told me it needed a new battery so I quickly turned it off. My mother had stopped playing. I was furious and frustrated at the unfairness of the library's lending a book that had pages missing but I couldn't help being enthralled by my own future heroism fighting murrains. With that thought in mind, I fell asleep.

In the taxi en route to the city with our library books the next day, I tried to talk to my mother about the story. I couldn't get a word in edgewise. I was competing with the taxi driver's life story. My mother had a way of bringing out strangers' life stories even when she was silent. For someone who didn't like people except in books or on screen, it was a hard destiny. When I finally could get a word in, I told her what was bothering me, ending by adding, "... *and* he never mentions little otter again."

"I didn't remember the sad part, darling." My mother fiddled with her change purse to pay the taxi driver. "I am sorry. It's my fault. I wouldn't have chosen it if I'd remembered it was sad. We should tell the librarian, too, about the missing pages when we return it."

I assured her that her choosing it was fine. Reading it had helped me decide what I would be when I grew up: I was going to be a vet and fight murrains. We scrambled out of the taxi with difficulty, sliding across the cracked leather seat so we could get out on the footpath side. By now, the taxi driver, having lost his audience, was impatient to pull away. My mother was still picking up bags of books and material she was taking to the dressmaker, so her response to my Life Decision was less than satisfactory. I decided I'd corner her later when we were home and get the right response. I knew she would be impressed and moved by my heroism.

When we reached the library, I stood beside my mother and told the librarian with wounded, polite indignation that there were pages missing. The librarian looked at me suspiciously. Then she said, with heavy authority in her voice, that she would have to discuss this with the Head Librarian, that books were never loaned with pages missing. My mother, indignant on my behalf, asked to be put on the waiting list for a new copy when it came in. Over our morning tea, my mother said that it was unfair to have loaned a library book with missing pages and even more unfair of the librarian to look suspicious.

The library didn't call. I thought about asking my mother to buy the book for my birthday but my birthday was a long way off. Finally, I decided that since I already knew what had happened, the missing pages weren't important. Better not to remind my mother, too, how upset I was every time I thought about the otter or the grasshopper or how sometimes I would see, as I was about to sleep, the little otter's father waiting at the weir *"on the chance"*; if she knew I was still thinking about Otter, she would be even more upset that she had shared something she thought was special but had ended up being something I couldn't bear.

So, of course, I didn't tell her that I both loved it and felt sad whenever she played that particular piece of music.

In the decades that followed, I only thought about the otter when I heard the Ravel, which was usually only when I flew up to visit my parents. I never gave the book to my daughter Olivia to read. Once, years later, when I was leaving the Radiation Lab after my daily treatment, I heard the piece being played by the hospital's electronically controlled grand with no pianist.

I did eventually read the rest of the chapter. I came across a battered edition of the book at the back of a shelf in my mother's closet. I was sorting books to go to libraries after she died. It was in the section of volumes purchased secondhand and labeled "Battered Favorites." I sat on the floor and read it all.

I discovered that I had not read that "this is the last best gift the kindly demi-god is careful to bestow on those to whom he has revealed himself in their helping: the gift of forgetfulness. Lest the awful remembrance should remain and grow, and overshadow mirth and pleasure, and the great haunting memory should spoil all the afterlives of little animals helped out of their difficulties, in order that they should be happy and lighthearted as before."

I had not read, as other children had, that the little otter could be adventurous, leave home, go off by himself, be separated from those he loved, even get utterly lost. I had not learned that he could get into trouble, have people look for him, lie down and rest, sleep in the hoofed legs of Pan, and be found; that he could be helped by those who knew the river—who could see things, who could hear the music—and go home.

ACKNOWLEDGMENTS

My immediate and extended family members—two- and four-footed—have lovingly supported this work, offered constructive criticism, been generous and patient beyond imagining, and either kept me quiet company or protected my time alone.

Relaxed affection and humor flowed round us in childhood, both during easy and challenging times; it rarely occurred to us that families might feel or react otherwise. After years as a researcher, I no longer take what we had for granted and I am grateful to those who have shown me that the intricate patterns of each family's pains and delights are as unique as fingerprints.

My parents gave us early exposure to, lifelong curiosity about, and respect for different cultures--and a passion for travel. These gifts, particularly our time in Australia, fed this novel. Dreams, too, have always fed my imagination. Colleagues and distant friends helped with research about the time and place in which this novel is set.

Family, friends, and respected others have encouraged me to let these stories arrive quietly until they eventually wove themselves into a uniquely peopled world unlike any of my own. The book unfolded with authority as a dream does. It surprised me and asked my willing subservience to its creative autonomy. I look at these pages and wonder who wrote them. Such is the mystery of imagination.

CPSIA information can be obtained at www.ICGtesting.com
Printed in the USA
BVOW02s2021211115

428032BV00003B/55/P